Grooms

Do you take this stranger…?

Three passionate novels!

In June 2007 Mills & Boon bring back
two of their classic collections, each
featuring three favourite romances
by our bestselling authors…

BLIND-DATE GROOMS
The Blind-Date Bride by Emma Darcy
Marriage by Deception by Sara Craven
The Blind-Date Proposal
by Jessica Hart

CITY HEAT
The Parisian Playboy by Helen Brooks
City Cinderella by Catherine George
Manhattan Merger
by Rebecca Winters

Blind-Date Grooms

THE BLIND-DATE BRIDE
by
Emma Darcy

MARRIAGE BY DECEPTION
by
Sara Craven

THE BLIND-DATE PROPOSAL
by
Jessica Hart

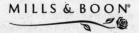

MILLS & BOON®

MILLS & BOON and MILLS & BOON with the Rose Device are registered trademarks of the publisher.
Harlequin Mills & Boon Limited,
Eton House, 18-24 Paradise Road, Richmond, Surrey, TW9 1SR

BLIND-DATE GROOMS
© by Harlequin Enterprises II B.V./S.à.r.l. 2007

The Blind-Date Bride, Marriage by Deception and *The Blind-Date Proposal* were first published in Great Britain by Harlequin Mills & Boon Limited in separate, single volumes.

The Blind-Date Bride © Emma Darcy 2003
Marriage by Deception © Sara Craven 2000
The Blind-Date Proposal © Jessica Hart 2003

ISBN: 978 0 263 85517 3

05-0607

Printed and bound in Spain
by Litografía Rosés S.A., Barcelona

THE BLIND-DATE BRIDE

by

Emma Darcy

Initially a French/English teacher, **Emma Darcy** changed careers to computer programming before the happy demands of marriage and motherhood. Very much a people person, and always interested in relationships, she finds the world of romantic fiction a thrilling one and the challenge of creating her own cast of characters very addictive.

CHAPTER ONE

A BLIND Date…

Zack Freeman rolled his eyes at the idea of putting himself out for a woman he hadn't seen, knew nothing about, and would never meet again, given the work schedule he had lined up.

'She's a stunner,' his old friend, Pete Raynor, assured him.

'Stunners are two a penny in my world. All of them relentlessly ambitious.'

'That might be so in L.A., but this is home time in Australia, remember? Livvy's sister is something else.'

'Like what?'

His derisive tone earned a chiding shake of the head. 'You're jaded, mate. Which is why you're here spending a week with me. A night out with a gorgeous down-to-earth Aussie woman will do you good. Trust me on this.'

Zack winced at the argument, turning his gaze to the soothing view of the sea rolling its waves onto Forresters Beach. They were sitting on the balcony of a house Pete had recently acquired—his getaway from the pressure of being a dealer for an international bank. It was only an hour and a half away from Sydney, the perfect place to relax, he'd told Zack, persuading him into this week together, catching up on old times.

They'd been friends since school days and had always kept in touch, despite their different career paths. Pete was geared to competitive risk-taking while Zack had sought the creative fields opened up by computer technology. He'd built up a company that was now in hot demand for producing special effects for movies.

But he didn't want to think about work yet. Tomorrow he was booked on a Qantas flight to Los Angeles and he'd be getting his mind prepared for a series of important meetings, but today was still about recapturing the carefree days of their youth; eating hamburgers and French fries for lunch after a morning of riding the waves on surfboards and baking their bodies in the sun.

It had been a great week; not having to impress anyone or win anyone over. He and Pete had done all the things they used to do—playing chess, challenging each other to listen to their choice of music, drinking beer, swapping stories…just having fun.

He felt wonderfully lazy and didn't want to give up the feeling. Not until he absolutely had to. Here it was, Saturday afternoon Down Under, midsummer, and the living was easy. He didn't need a blind date. Didn't want one, either. His broad chest rose and fell in a contented sigh. This was more than good enough for him.

'Pete, I don't mind that you've got a date with your girlfriend. Go out and enjoy yourself. You don't have to look after me. I'll be perfectly happy with my own company.'

'It's our last night.'

Pete's unhappy frown pricked Zack's conscience.

'I can't get out of it. It's Livvy's birthday,' he went on, making it clear that Zack's refusal to go along with the plan put him into conflict.

The week had been special.

Was he being a spoilsport, ducking out on sharing this last night?

Livvy Trent, according to Pete, was very special. He'd met her walking her dog on this very beach. She even had a head for finance, holding quite a responsible position in the Treasury Department and living here on the central coast because she worked two days in Sydney and three in Newcastle. This could develop into a serious relationship, which was fine for Pete who was getting close to burn-out and looking for more from life than a tight focus on the world's money markets.

Zack was currently riding a high wave of success with a string of big movies featuring the special effects created by his company. No way was he ready to ease down from that creamy crest. He didn't have the time or the inclination to link up with a woman who wanted any kind of commitment from him. Too demanding. Too distracting. Besides, he was only thirty-three. He wanted what he had achieved. He wanted more of it. Finding *a special woman* could wait.

'I tell you, Zack, if I hadn't got to know Livvy first, I'd probably be chasing after her sister,' Pete ran on, intent on persuasion. 'Catherine is a knock-out.'

'So how come she's available on a Saturday night?' Zack dryly commented.

'Oh, same as you. Taking time out. Spending the weekend with her sister.'

'And I guess Livvy doesn't want to leave her alone, either.'

'No, she doesn't.' Realising he'd been tripped into the truth, Pete screwed his face into a hangdog appeal. 'So help me out here, will you, Zack? Please?'

He really cared for this woman. Zack hoped the feeling was returned and Pete wasn't being seen in terms of a good catch. Which he certainly was, financially. And he wasn't bad in the looks department, either. He was shorter than Zack but his physique was good, no flab on him.

His dark hair was receding at the temples and he'd had one of those ultra-short buzz cuts, defying the signs of encroaching baldness. Definitely a testosterone thing, Zack thought, but it had the advantage of never looking untidy, not like the wild mess of his black curls, although he figured they gave him an *artistic* image which was probably helpful in his business.

Pete had always had a very expressive face, not exactly handsome, but likeable. He had an infectious grin and his green eyes could quickly radiate a mischief that invited fun. Zack knew his own humour was more quirky, challenging to a lot of people, though Pete had always understood it.

Dark, he called it, often adding that Zack had to

have a dark and twisted soul to think up some of the special effects he created for movies. His olive skin tanned darkly, his eyes were dark, his teeth were very white—definitely a vampire in a previous life, Pete joked.

Whatever…on a surface basis, women were more drawn to him than they were to Pete. It was a fact of life outside of his control. He just hoped Livvy Trent would treat his friend right tonight—no roving eye.

'Okay. I'm in,' he conceded. 'As long as you accept that if I find this Catherine a total bore, I'll make an excuse to come home early.'

'Done!' Pete agreed, grinning his head off.

No problem in his mind.

Zack relaxed. Let tonight take care of itself, he thought, having dealt himself a ready bolthole.

A blind date…

Catherine Trent gave her sister a look designed to kill the idea on the spot. Stone dead. This weekend with Livvy was a much needed time out from *men*— one in particular—and even being polite to any male at the moment would be an effort she didn't want to make.

The look didn't work. It spurred Livvy into attack mode, eyes flashing the light of battle. 'You know your problem, Catherine? You've been fixated on Stuart Carstairs for so long, you've developed tunnel vision. Can't even see other men could be more attractive. And a lot better for you, too.'

So find me one, Catherine thought derisively, having done her own looking each time Stuart had strayed, then forgiving him and taking him back because there simply wasn't anyone else she wanted to be with. Compared to Stuart, other men were dull, but this last infidelity went beyond the bounds of acceptability. For him to snatch a bit of sex with a graphic artist in her own office, a woman who worked on the accounts she handled...that was too bitter a blow to her pride.

This had to be the end of their relationship. The final end. All the sexual charisma in the world didn't make up for a long, continuing string of hurts, especially this worst one, right under her nose. It was time to let go, time to move on, but to what?

'I'm not up to a blind date, Livvy,' she said flatly.

'Well, I'm not going to leave you here to mope alone,' came the belligerent retort.

'I won't mope. I'll watch videos.'

'Wallowing in escapism. I'll bet Stuart Carstairs isn't. Good old action man will be unzipping his trousers for...'

'Stop it!'

'No, I won't. He tried it on with me, too, you know. Your own sister.'

Shocked out of her irritation with Livvy's unwelcome nagging, Catherine shot a sharp look at her sister, unsure if she was speaking the truth or wanting to blacken Stuart's character beyond the pale. 'You never told me that before.'

A fierce conviction blazed back at her. 'I'm telling you now. Get rid of him. Get over him, Catherine. He might have the gift of the gab and he might be a great performer in bed, but he only ever thinks of himself. You're an ego trip for him. And every time you take him back you feed his ego more. Holding on to him is sick.'

Catherine frowned over these discomforting assertions. Was it sick to keep wanting a man who couldn't be trusted with other women? Stuart swore she was the only one who really counted in his life, but was that enough to hang on to? Obviously she couldn't count too much when he was hot for someone else, even her own sister.

'I won't hold on this time,' she muttered.

'Then let me see you take some positive action in another direction. Like partnering this other guy tonight,' Livvy strongly argued.

'I'm not in the mood.'

'You never are. Except for Stuart Carstairs who continually does the dirty on you. You've wasted four years on a dyed-in-the-wool philanderer and it's only ever going to be more of the same, him having it off with whomever he fancies, while you...'

'I told you it's over.'

'Until he soft soaps you again.'

'No. I mean it.'

'Fine! So you should be celebrating being free from him, giving yourself the chance to eye off someone else.'

She was just like her dog with a bone. Catherine looked down at the miniature fox terrier sitting by Livvy's feet and was grateful he wasn't yapping at her, too. She did need to be free of Stuart, but in her own mind and heart first. Plunging into dating would only throw up comparisons that would keep him painfully alive in her thoughts.

In fact, Livvy had just spoiled her attempt to forget him for a while. Here they were, seated on the balcony of her sister's apartment, overlooking the Brisbane Water at Gosford, idly watching the boats sailing out from the yacht club, feeling pleasantly replete from a fine lunch at Iguana Joe's, during which Livvy had raved about her wonderful new boyfriend, Peter Raynor. Why couldn't she just be happy with her own personal life instead of attacking Catherine's?

'This guy has been a friend of Pete's since school days. Now that tells you he values the people he likes. He's not a user and a dumper,' Livvy ran on, relentlessly intent on persuasion.

'Friendship between two men has no relevance whatsoever to how either of them view or treat women,' Catherine tersely commented, wanting an end to the argument.

'Right! So now you're cultivating a negative attitude. Not even giving people a chance. And I might add Pete treats me beautifully.'

'Lucky you! But I don't want to be stuck with a guy I don't know and might not like.'

'You like Pete. His friend should be at least an interesting person. The food at The Galley is always good. It's my birthday, and the best birthday present you could give me is to see you enjoying yourself without Stuart Carstairs.'

'I have been. With you. Before you started on this blind date kick,' Catherine snapped in exasperation.

'As for birthday gifts, I thought you liked the bracelet I bought you…'

'I do.'

'…and the lunch at the restaurant of your choice. Wasn't that birthday treat enough for you?'

Livvy's eloquent shrug was apologetic but it didn't stop her from turning the screws. 'I just hate going out and leaving you alone, knowing you're miserable. I won't be able to enjoy the evening with Pete if you don't come with me.'

Emotional blackmail.

But there was caring behind it, Catherine grudgingly conceded, and she didn't want to spoil any part of her younger sister's birthday. Livvy had always been a pet, her naturally happy nature making her a pleasure to be with. Their parents were away on an overseas trip, touring Canada this time, so it was up to Catherine to make up for their not being here, showering love on their younger daughter. She thought she'd done enough but…would it really hurt to make the effort of being pleasant to a stranger tonight?

'It would be such fun, dressing up together,' Livvy pressed.

'I didn't bring dress-up clothes with me,' Catherine remembered, not so much seeking an excuse but simply stating the truth.

'You can try mine on.' The eager offer was rushed out. 'In fact, I've got a little black number that would look fantastic on you. It's a jersey so it doesn't matter you're more curvy than me. It will stretch to fit.'

More curvy and taller. And their taste in clothes

was different. Which was why they'd never swapped or borrowed. But what she wore tonight was not an issue, Catherine decided, as long as she pleased Livvy.

Twenty-nine today. Her little sister…who had her life more in order than Catherine had managed in her thirty-one years. Still, Livvy's career in the public service carried minimal stress and steady promotion, given a reasonable level of performance. The advertising world was far more cut-throat and Catherine spent most of her working days living on the edge.

Different lives, different needs, different natures, different…even in looks.

Livvy's hair had been very blond in her childhood and she'd kept it blond with the help of a good hairdresser. She kept it short, too, its thick waves cleverly cut and styled to ripple attractively to just below her ears. Having inherited their father's Nordic blue eyes and skin that tanned to a lovely golden honey, she always looked sunny and vibrantly alive.

Dark and intense were the words more often attached to Catherine. Her hair was a very deep rich brown, as wavy as Livvy's but worn long. There never seemed to be time in her life for regular hairdresser appointments. Currently it fell to below her shoulder-blades. Luckily she only had to wash it for it to look reasonably good.

Her eyes were more amber than brown, like their mother's, but her eyebrows and lashes were almost black, giving them a dark look. The only feature she'd inherited from their father was height. She was a head taller than Livvy who had his colouring but their mother's more petite figure.

Different to each other but family nonetheless.

Close family.

And Catherine liked to see Livvy happy.

'Okay, I'll go with you. But I'm taking my own car so if Pete's friend is a total disaster I can come home by myself whenever I like.'

Sheer delight lit up Livvy's pretty face.

Yes, it was worth the effort, Catherine thought, and resigned herself to sharing an evening with a man who would probably bore her to death.

A blind date...

She looked down at the little black and white fox terrier, sleeping blissfully at Livvy's feet. He'd been called Luther after Martin Luther King who'd done all he could to integrate the black and white races in America.

Bringing people together.

Catherine smiled at the dog who'd certainly brought her sister and Pete together. Maybe she needed a dog in her life. It was surely a better means of meeting men than Livvy's current plot. Bound to provide more lasting and devoted company, too. A steadfast, uncomplicated love.

Yes.

She'd give up Stuart and buy herself a dog.

A much better solution to her problems than a blind date.

CHAPTER TWO

PETE insisted they set off at a quarter to eight, even though it was barely a ten-minute drive around the coast to the beach town of Terrigal where they were dining in style tonight. Livvy and Catherine were to meet them at the restaurant at eight, which probably meant anything up to an hour later. Zack had little faith in female punctuality, particularly with social evenings. Still, the less time he had to spend with his blind date, the better.

Terrigal was a prettier beach than Forresters with its row of Norfolk Pines lining the foreshore, but it was tame in comparison with none of the wild, dangerous surf that stirred the sense of primitive elements at play. This was a highly civilised beach; calm water, smooth sand, edged by lawns, a large resort hotel and many fashionable boutiques and restaurants. A yuppie place, not a getaway, Zack thought, glad that Pete had chosen to buy a house on an untamed shoreline.

The restaurant they were heading for was called The Galley, built above the sailing club on the other side of town and facing towards the Haven, a sheltered little bay where yachts rode at anchor. The main street traffic was heavy and slow. By the time they got through it and reached the parking area adjacent to The Galley, it was precisely eight o'clock.

Drinks at the bar coming up, Zack anticipated. He watched a zippy red convertible coming down the incline to the car park as Pete was collecting a celebratory bottle of Dom Perignon from the back seat of his beloved BMW. Had to be a Mazda MX-5, Zack decided, and was surprised to see two women occupying the open front seats. It was the kind of car guys would cruise in. Women were always worried about their hairstyles being blown awry.

'Told you they'd be on time,' Pete crowed, nodding to the car Zack was watching. 'That's Catherine driving.'

A long-haired brunette. The blonde in the passenger seat had to be Livvy. 'Is it her car?' he asked, finding himself interested by the unexpected.

'Yes. Livvy calls it Catherine's rebellion.'

'Against what?'

Pete shrugged. 'Being a woman, I guess.'

Zack rolled his eyes at him. 'You mean I'm about to be faced with a raging feminist.'

The answering grin was unrepentant. 'More a *femme fatale*. Just watch your knees. They might buckle any minute now.'

Not a chance, Zack thought.

She parked the convertible right at the end of the row of cars, the furthest point away from the entrance to the restaurant. Ensuring it wouldn't get boxed in, Zack decided, in case she wanted an easy getaway.

Which makes two of us, darling.

He and Pete waited at the BMW for the two women to join them. The black roof of the red convertible lifted from its slot at the back of the car and was locked in at the front. The blonde emerged first, waving excitedly at Pete. She looked very cute, wearing a clingy blue dress with shoestring shoulder straps. A pocket Venus for Pete, Zack thought, smiling at his choice.

Well, Catherine, strut your stuff, he silently challenged as a long rippling mane of very lustrous brown hair rose from the driver's side, the kind of hair that would look good on a pillow, Feel good, too. A tingle of temptation touched his fingertips. He clenched his hands to wipe it away. This was not the time to let a woman get to him. So she had great hair. The workings of the brain under it probably had no appeal at all.

She turned to close the door and lock the car. Zack's attention was galvanised. Pete hadn't lied. He hadn't even exaggerated. Catherine Trent was a stunner. Helen of Troy came to mind. Here was a face that could definitely launch a thousand ships. It seemed to simmer with sexual promise, aided by the erotic positioning of a deep pink flower over her right ear.

The tingle in his fingertips moved to his groin and there was nothing physical he could do to remove it. He tried willing it away. Impossible mission. She moved to the back of the car to join up with her sister and the full view of her was enough to blow any willpower right out of Zack's head. Even his side vision was affected. Livvy Trent blurred. Only Catherine remained in sharp focus.

She had a mesmerising hour-glass figure, mouthwateringly lush femininity encased in a slinky little black dress with a short flirty skirt that barely reached mid-thigh on long shapely legs that Zack thought would feel fantastic wrapped around him. She was tall—tall enough to wear flat black shoes, though they looked like ballet slippers with straps crossed around her ankles. Somehow they were erotic, too, more so than kinky stiletto heels.

His gaze leapt back to her fascinating face as she came nearer. A slight dimple in her chin, a sultry full-lipped mouth, straight nose, angled cheekbones that highlighted the unusual shape of her eyes, more triangular than almond, amber irises, glinting golden between their black frame of thick lashes. Cat's eyes, he thought, but they didn't conjure up the image of some tame domestic cat, more an infinitely dangerous panther, capable of clawing him apart.

And why he should find that idea exciting he didn't know. Didn't think about it. It just was. He felt something dark and primitive stir inside him, wanting to take up the challenge she was beaming at him, wanting her submission to the desires she aroused, wanting to possess every part of her until he'd consumed the power she was exerting over him.

A *Class-A* hunk, Catherine thought when she first saw Pete's friend. Tall, dark and handsome with a body brimful of strong masculinity, his tight black jeans and the short-sleeved, open-necked white shirt showing off his impressive physique. Lots of surface sex appeal, but undoubtedly a bloated male ego to go with it.

'Wow!' Livvy murmured approvingly. 'Pete's friend sure measures up.'

Probably worked out at a gym in front of mirrors. Catherine was determinedly unimpressed, yet as they strolled towards the two men, a flutter started up in the pit of her stomach. It was the way he was looking at her, she argued to herself, assessing her female assets which, unfortunately, were on blatant display in Livvy's dress.

She hadn't cared earlier, even letting Livvy put the silly pink flower in her hair. It matched the spray of pink flowers featured on the black fabric of the dress, spreading diagonally from the left shoulder to the hem of the skirt. Livvy was into flowers in her hair this summer, using them as accessories to her outfits, but it wasn't Catherine's style. Not that it mattered tonight, except…she hoped Pete's friend wasn't seeing it as some flirtatious come-on.

On the other hand, if he wasn't too full of himself, he was certainly attractive enough to flirt with. Though that could be a dangerous play. She wasn't used to partnering a powerfully built man, and as she got closer, this man seemed to emanate power, the kind of big male dominant power that suddenly sent weak little quivers down her thighs.

Stuart was no taller than herself and his physique was on the lean side. His attraction lay more in a quicksilver charm than sheer physical impact. Catherine had always found eye contact and conversation sexier than actual bodies. All the same, she couldn't stop her eyes from feasting on this guy. He had an undeniable animal magnetism that tugged out a wanton wondering about what it might be like to have sex with him.

Different, she decided.

Not quite civilised.

Dark and intense.

Like his eyes…now that he was looking directly into hers.

Catherine sucked in a quick breath as her heart skipped into a wild canter. This guy had *it* in spades. With one searing look he burnt Stuart Carstairs right out of her mind and stamped his own image over the scar. It was a stunning impact. Catherine hadn't even begun to recover from it when she heard Pete Raynor start the introductions.

'Livvy…Catherine…this is my friend, Zack Freeman…'

Another stunning impact.

She *knew* him. Or rather, knew of him. Who didn't in the computer graphics business? Zack Freeman was already reaching legendary status for what he had achieved in special effects. He produced amazing stuff. And he was Pete's friend…her blind date?

Very white teeth flashed a winning smile. 'I'm delighted to meet you both. And I wish you a very happy birthday, Livvy.'

He offered his hand to her first—a perfunctory courtesy as Livvy thanked him—just a quick touch— then to Catherine, who found her hand captured by his for several seconds, making her extremely conscious of the warm flesh-to-flesh contact.

'I appreciate your giving me your company tonight, Catherine,' he said very personally, his voice pitched to a low, deep intimacy.

Her stomach flipped. She'd thought of Zack Freeman as some clever computer nerd with a weird creative genius, occupying some planet of his own. Yet here he was, right in front of her, so dynamically sexy she could scarcely breathe. It was a miracle she found the presence of mind to produce a reply.

'My pleasure.'

His smile was quite dazzling, given the dark tan of his skin. He had a strong nose, strong chin. His eyebrows were straight and low, his eyes deepset, somehow emphasising their penetrating power. His hair was a mass of tight, springy black curls which should have had a softening effect, but perversely added a sense of wound-up aggression.

'Nice car,' he said, nodding to where she'd parked.

'I like it.'

His eyes teased as he asked, 'What does it say about you?'

She already felt under attack from him and instinctively she fended off the probe that was asking her to reveal private feelings. 'Does it have to say anything?'

'Cars always say something about their owners.' He withdrew his hand and gestured to his friend. 'Now take Pete here. His BMW says he's made it. He's solid. He likes proven performance.'

'Right on,' Pete agreed.

'So what car do you own?' Catherine asked Zack, wanting to learn something about him.

He grinned. 'I don't. If I need a car, I hire one.'

'Don't let him fool you, Catherine,' Pete quickly inserted. 'Zack's a bikie from way back. He's got a whole stable of bikes to suit whatever mood he's in and whatever he wants to do.'

'An open road man,' she observed, thinking Zack Freeman had to have the kind of mind that would hate any form of confinement.

'Like you, Catherine,' Livvy popped in, all for encouraging this twosome.

Zack raised one eyebrow. 'True?'

She shrugged. 'I've only ever thought of my car as a somewhat impractical self-indulgence.' She shot a rueful look at her sister. 'Livvy's the one who analyses everything to death.'

'And I love her great sense of logic,' Pete said with relish, beaming pleasure in her sister. He held out the bottle he was carrying. 'Brought the best French bubbly to celebrate your birthday, Livvy.'

'Great!' She grabbed his arm, hugging it as he turned to lead them into the restaurant. 'I just love your sense of occasion, Pete.'

They were so obviously happy with each other, Catherine shook her head over the pressure exerted on her to make up a foursome. She eyed Zack Freeman curiously, aware that he could probably snap his fingers and pick up any woman. So why had he agreed to a blind date?

She remembered Livvy's argument, centred mostly on getting Catherine to rid herself of Stuart and open up to other men. Embarrassment squirmed through her at the thought that Livvy had engaged Pete's help to *fix up* her sister and she was some kind of charity case to Zack Freeman—doing a favour asked of him by his old friend.

A horrible sense of humiliation forced her to blurt out, 'Did Pete coerce you into partnering me tonight?'

He was slow to reply, possibly picking up her inner tension and musing over its cause. 'I had no other plans. Pete wanted me to make up a party of four tonight and I agreed.' His mouth quirked. 'No regrets so far. But if you have a problem with the arrangement…'

'No,' she rushed out on a wave of intense relief. He hadn't been told anything *personal* about her.

His head tilted quizzically. 'You want to cut and run?'

Truth spilled out before she could stop it. 'Livvy would kill me if I did.'

'Ah! So she coerced you.'

Catherine took a deep breath, wanting to get onto some kind of equal footing with him. 'It was more her idea than mine.'

'Does that mean you're anticipating pain with me?'

A nervous gurgle of laughter bubbled out. 'Let me fantasise pleasure for a while.'

'Good idea!' His eyes twinkled wicked mischief. 'I'll do the same.'

He half turned, waving her to fall into step with him to follow Pete and Livvy. He made no attempt to take her arm or hand, for which she was grateful since she was super-conscious of his physicality as it was, and any contact would feel sexual after her blunder in linking pleasure and fantasy.

'Livvy said you and Pete have been friends since school days,' she remarked, trying to dampen the sizzle she'd unwittingly raised.

'Mmm...going on twenty years. We're still the same people to each other. You get to value that as you move through life.'

'I guess you do a lot of role-playing with your work.'

He paused, slanting her a sharp look beneath lowered brows. 'You know what I do?'

Would he have preferred her not to know? To pretend he was just some regular guy for the night? Was he sick of women climbing all over him for what he was?

'It's okay. I won't blab on about it,' she assured him. 'I don't think Livvy knows. I happen to work with graphic artists who are interested in everything you come up with—big discussions—so when Pete introduced you...'

'You're a graphic artist yourself?' he cut in, an angry tension emanating from him.

'No. And I'm not a user, either,' she asserted, resenting the implied assumption that she might angle some benefit out of this meeting with him. 'You're perfectly safe with me, Zack Freeman.'

He gave her a long hard look that bristled with suspicion and she stared right back with fierce pride, finally earning a glint of respect.

'Oh, I wouldn't go that far,' he drawled, his mouth taking on a wry twist. 'You pack quite a punch, Catherine Trent.'

Heat whooshed up her neck and into her cheeks

as sexual electricity crackled from him and zipped into her bloodstream. Catherine was appalled at herself. She never blushed. She might flush in anger, but blushing belonged to adolescence and she was way past that. A sophisticated career woman did not blush.

'You're not exactly harmless yourself,' she retorted defensively, only realising it was an admission of the attraction he exerted after she had spoken. Not that it mattered. He knew anyway. Impossible for him not to be aware of his effect on women, just as she was aware that many men fancied her.

He shrugged. 'Sorry if I gave offence. This is my week off from being *the* Zack Freeman. In fact, it's my last night off. I have to go back to being him tomorrow.'

'You don't like being *him?*' Was being so successful such a burden?

'It has its rewards and I'm not about to give them up,' he stated, determination glinting in his eyes. 'But there's a time and place for everything.'

And it was clear he wouldn't enjoy being with some star-struck woman who raved on about what he'd achieved or tried to ferret out the key to his meteoric rise to fame in his field.

'So what would you like tonight to be?' Catherine asked, somewhat bemused by his wish to set aside the recognition that most men's egos would demand.

He paused to consider. His eyes beamed a speculative challenge as he answered, 'Whatever two strangers want to make of it.'

'Without a tomorrow.'

'Tomorrow I'm gone.'

Well, that was laying it on the line. No future with Zack Freeman. Not that she had had time to even think of one or consider whether it might be desirable.

'Then I'll just take this one night experience with the man behind the name,' she countered, pride insisting that his schedule did not affect her expectations from this blind date, which had been zero before she met him anyway.

Sexual invitation simmered back at her. 'I wonder if you will.'

She hadn't meant a *one-night stand*. Another wretched blush goaded her into being uncharacteristically provocative. 'You win some. You lose some.' It was a warning not to assume anything.

He grinned. 'The game is afoot. And you can't cut and run because your sister is watching and she'll kill you if you do.'

She laughed, trying to lighten the effect of a charge of nervous excitement. 'You think I'm trapped?'

'Why did you come?'

'To please Livvy. It's her birthday.'

'Then you have a giving nature. That's a trap in itself, Catherine.'

'Oh, the giving only goes so far.'

'What would you take, given the chance?'

'That's a big question.'

'And you don't intend to answer it yet.'

'That would spoil the game.'

He laughed, entirely relaxed now and enjoying the

flirtation he'd fired up and was stoking with every look and word. 'I guess we'd better join Livvy and Pete. They're waiting for us on the steps.'

So they were, paused halfway up the flight of steps to the restaurant and viewing her and Zack with an air of smug satisfaction—the successful matchmakers congratulating themselves on getting it right!

Except this blind date wasn't going beyond whatever happened tonight.

Remember that, Catherine sternly told herself as she walked beside the man who had every nerve in her body agitated, her heart thumping, her mind bombarded with tempting fantasies.

There is no tomorrow, she recited, meaning it as a sobering caution to be sensible. Yet somehow it had the perverse effect of inciting a sense of wild recklessness—a desire to *take* what she could of Zack Freeman while she could. To *have* him. All he'd give her. If only for one night.

CHAPTER THREE

SHE had ordered the three scoops of different ice-creams for dessert and was tasting them each in turn, sliding the loaded spoon between her lips, consciously testing the flavour on her tongue. Zack found the action so sensual, his whole body was tightening up. Catherine Trent was one hell of a sexy woman and the urge to race her off into the night and ravage her from head to toe had a powerful grip on him.

He wrenched his gaze away from her mouth and turned it out to sea. Their table was on the open veranda that ran the length of the restaurant and he'd taken refuge in the view several times tonight, needing to cool the desire that kept plaguing him. Was she as hot for him as he was for her? Would she go for it, given the limitation he'd stipulated?

One night…

Problem was, he might end up wanting more and that would mess him up. She was like a fever in his blood and he needed a cool head once he hit Los Angeles. It was the wrong time to meet a woman like Catherine Trent. She appealed to him on too many levels. He liked the way her mind worked, liked talking with her, liked having her across the table from him, watching her face, the expressions in her fascinating eyes, her body language.

She wasn't a stranger anymore, though he'd deliberately refrained from asking about her life, keeping
their dinner conversation to very general topics.
She'd still got to him, more than he recalled any
other woman ever doing.

Better to let her go, he told himself. What had she
said…*win some, lose some?* He'd never liked losing,
but he had a lot at stake right now. Winning what he
planned to win in L.A. was more important than losing out on a night of sex which could get him too
involved with this woman.

'Do you think a full moon really does affect
people?'

There was a full moon tonight, big and white,
hanging in the sky where he had turned his gaze, but
he hadn't been looking at it. Catherine's question
drew an instant reply from Livvy who'd been bubbling with high spirits all evening.

'Course it does. The word, *lunatic* didn't evolve
from nothing.'

'Historically it is associated with madness. And
romance,' Pete chimed in.

'Which could be considered a form of madness,'
Zack observed dryly, looking back at Catherine, hoping she wasn't nursing romantic thoughts about him.

It simply wasn't on.

Yet the pull of her attraction was very strong.

'I was just wondering…' The musing little smile
on her lips had his gut contracting with the desire to
kiss her. '…how connected are we to the physical
world? We get irritated when it's windy. Sunshine
tends to make us smile. The moon regulates the tides,

so when it's at full strength like this, does it tug at things in us, too?'

Was she wanting an explanation for what she felt with him?

An excuse for it?

Something outside herself so she couldn't be blamed for wanting what he wanted, too?

'You mean like amplifying the feelings we have,' Livvy said speculatively. 'Making mad people even madder.'

'Swelling the tides of passion,' Pete rolled out, relishing that idea and proceeding to banter with Livvy about possible lunar effects on human behaviour.

'Don't forget animals,' Zack inserted after a while. 'Why do wolves howl at a full moon?'

'Because they prefer dark nights?' Catherine suggested, looking at him with her head on a tilt as though mentally likening him to a wolf who prowled dark places.

'Or maybe it's part of the mating game,' he couldn't resist saying.

Her thick lashes lowered, veiling the expression in her eyes, though not before he glimpsed a vulnerability to the mating they could share.

Temptation bit into his resolution to let her go.

She wanted him. He wanted her. Where was the harm in a one-night stand? It wasn't as though she was an inexperienced woman. Late twenties, he guessed, and given her face and figure, had probably been fending off or taking on guys since her mid-teens.

Her long throat moved in a convulsive little swallow. Dry-mouthed from the heat coursing through her? The low V-neckline of her dress pointed into the valley between her breasts, shadowed by the soft swell of lush feminine flesh on either side. He wanted to fill his hands with her, wanted to…

'Coffee, anyone?'

The waiter deftly removed the emptied dessert plates as choices were made around the table.

'Short black,' Catherine said,

Strong and dark, Zack thought, which was how he wanted it, too. 'The same for me.'

He didn't hear what the others ordered. The waiter departed. Pete suggested they walk on down the hill to the Crowne Plaza after they'd finished their coffee, disco the rest of the night away. Livvy applauded the idea. Catherine smiled at her sister but said nothing, waiting for Zack's reaction with no persuasion from her either way.

Hours of ear-blasting music and hot, sweaty dancing didn't appeal to Zack. Nor did a long sexual tease with Catherine that promised without delivering. She had burned him enough tonight. If there was to be any action between them, it was now or never, he decided.

Her choice.

'I hope you'll all excuse me—you, particularly, Catherine…' He offered her a rueful smile. 'I wasn't planning on a late night tonight. I have a car calling at seven-thirty in the morning to take me to the airport. I've enjoyed the evening very much but…'

'You don't want to be a total wreck tomorrow,'

she finished for him, smiling her understanding and with more than a hint of relief in her eyes.

Off the hook?

'I won't cut into your plan of action, Pete,' he directed to his old friend. 'I can call a taxi from here and the three of you can...'

'No need for a taxi,' Catherine cut in. 'I can drive you back to Forresters Beach on my way home.'

Excitement zipped through his veins. Opportunity had just been opened up. Was it deliberate, decisive, or merely flirting with a chance she might take? 'Thank you,' he said, anticipation surging into a storm of desire at the thought of being alone with her.

She looked at her sister. 'That's okay with you, isn't it, Livvy? Pete will bring you home after the disco?'

'Absolutely,' Pete agreed, happy to have Livvy to himself.

Her sister heaved a sigh and looked from Catherine to Zack, clearly exasperated by this abrupt end to their foursome. It wasn't what *she'd* planned but the decision had already been taken out of her hands.

Zack smiled at her. 'May I say it's been a delight to meet you, Livvy. You and Pete have yourself a ball tonight.'

'Hey! And wake me for a coffee with you before you leave in the morning, Zack,' Pete demanded.

'Will do.'

'You don't have to go home this early, Catherine,' Livvy pressed, frowning at her sister. 'It will only take ten minutes to drop Zack off at Forresters Beach…'

'I don't want you watching out for me at a disco,' she stated firmly. 'You and Pete should feel free to have fun together. It's your birthday.'

And that might be the straight truth of it, Zack cautioned himself. Being at a disco without a partner, guys on a high trying to pick her up…he could well imagine a fight breaking out over Catherine Trent…and that could be extremely tiresome if she wasn't in the mood to play. With anyone else but him.

Conviction fizzed through his mind. She need not have made the offer to drive him home. She could have waited until he'd left in a taxi, then made the decision not to go to the disco. This was not a safe play. The chance was on.

Catherine beamed her sister a flinty look that said enough was enough and there'd be no forcing her to circulate in a crowded disco where she might or might not hit it off with some guy. Impossible anyway after being with Zack Freeman all evening. Though her impulsive offer to drive him to Pete's place now had her stomach churning.

The move protected her from being thrown at more men, which Livvy had obviously intended once Zack removed himself from the field of play. It also protected her from any argument over her decision to leave since giving her blind date a lift home was a perfectly reasonable and polite thing to do in return for his company tonight. But it did mean she'd be alone with him in her car and when they reached Forresters Beach.

Would she be safe with him?

Did she want to be safe with him?

Livvy's resigned grimace set her free to do whatever she liked and Pete was obviously not troubled by their party being cut in half. He'd done what had been requested of him, supplying Zack for Livvy's sister, and if the two of them went off together, that was fine by him. He had the woman he wanted still at his side.

The coffee arrived.

She hoped its hot bitterness would sober her up. Not from alcohol. She'd only drunk one glass of champagne. It was Zack Freeman's affect on her that needed diluting down to something manageable. He was like a magnet, playing a tug-of-war with every female hormone in her body. Never in her life had she been made to feel so aware of her own sexuality, as well as a chaotic craving to experience his.

He had the most sinfully sexy eyes, teasing, challenging, flirting, knowing and constantly evaluating the response he drew from her. He made her laugh. He made her smile. He made her tingle all over. He was the intoxicant and not even the knowledge that he'd be gone tomorrow lessened the addictive power of his attraction.

'So I get to have a ride in your car.'

She stopped sipping the coffee and looked up to answer him, her heart squeezing tight at the warm pleasure in his eyes. 'A short ride,' she said, reminding herself again of the brevity of this encounter.

One night…which was fast coming to an end.

'An impractical self-indulgence,' he drawled softly.

For a stomach-clenching moment, she thought he was referring to her decision to ride with him, whatever that might lead to between them. Then she realised he was repeating her own words about owning such a car.

'You get wet if it rains before you can stop to get the hood on,' she explained with a shrug.

'But you don't mind the wind in your hair.'

She smiled. 'Nor the sun on my face.'

'You like the feel of nature.'

'Yes.'

He smiled. 'An elemental woman.'

He made it sound intensely sensual, made her feel intensely sensual. She took refuge in sipping coffee again, trying not to wonder just how elemental he was and how he would look as nature had fashioned him.

The open-necked shirt had been tantalising her all throughout dinner, giving her a glimpse of tight black curls arrowing down his chest. His forearms weren't hairy, their darkly tanned skin gleaming like oiled teak. She imagined his whole body would be mainly like that with a sprinkle of black springy curls in the most masculine places. The desire to know, to touch, conflicted terribly with the sensible course of simply wishing him well and waving him goodbye.

He wasn't going to be in her life.

Except for this one night.

Pete paid the restaurant bill, insisting it was his

party treat for Livvy. Everyone had drunk their coffee. It was time to go. Nervous tension gripped Catherine as Zack moved to hold her chair back for an easy rise from the table. She looked at the full moon as she stood up. Was this *lust* for him a madness that she would shake her head over tomorrow?

She didn't understand it.

Was she raw and needful from Stuart's most recent dalliance with another woman? But she wasn't feeling any bitter hurt right now. It was as though all that was in a far distant place. Zack Freeman generated a physical immediacy that completely clouded anything else.

She was super aware of her legs moving in step with his as they followed Pete and Livvy out of the restaurant, aware that the top of her head was level with his chin, aware of the strength of the man and the weak little quivers running down her thighs, aware of her breasts straining against the stretch fabric of Livvy's dress, aware of the flutters in her stomach where the yearning to experience Zack Freeman was strong and deep and beyond any mental control.

Pete decided to drive down to The Crowne Plaza and have his car parked at the hotel for an easy pickup when he and Livvy had had enough of the disco. They said their goodnights at his BMW and Catherine and Zack watched them drive off before moving on to the end of the car park where her red convertible was waiting for them.

'Do you like to dance?' Zack asked as they strolled along.

He wasn't touching her, merely walking beside

her, but Catherine barely found breath enough to answer, 'Yes.'

'I'm sorry if you feel you're missing out.'

She shook her head.

'For me it would have been more of a torture than
a pleasure.'

The wry statement drew her into glancing at him.

His eyes caught hers and delivered their own searing meaning as he elaborated. 'I would have wanted
more than the touching permissable on a public
dance floor, Catherine.'

She wrenched her gaze from his as heat whooshed
through her entire body. The direct acknowledgment
of the desire he was feeling for her left no way of
dismissing it as possible fantasy. It was real. And it
was vibrantly alive, pulsing through her, arousing eager responses that clamoured for expression.

Her mind tried to over-ride them. She didn't *do*
one-night stands. She believed that casual sex diminished what should be really special to a relationship
that shared far more than just sex. Men were different, she'd told herself, having excused Stuart's infi-
delities as meaningless rushes of testosterone. But
she'd never felt so sexually *connected* to a man before, not even with Stuart at his charismatic best.

She fumbled in her evening bag for the car keys.
Just a short ride and this…this raging temptation…would be over. Unlock the car, get in and drive
Zack Freeman to Forresters Beach. He would fly
away tomorrow and she'd come down to earth with
a big thump if she strayed from what she believed in
tonight.

But what if she never felt like this again?

Was she passing up a once-in-a-lifetime experience?

Would she always wonder?

Her fingers found the car key, curled around it, brought it out. Her hand trembled as she pointed the key at her car and pressed the remote control button to unlock the doors. Zack accompanied her to the driver's side, intent on doing the courtesy of seeing her settled on her seat. She waited by the door for him to reach out and open it. He stepped forward, then turned to face her instead.

'Have I embarrassed you?'

His eyes scanned hers with probing intensity, driving her out of her tongue-tied state.

'No.' She tried to smile but her mouth felt as wobbly as the rest of her. 'I think the wolf in you was howling just then.'

'And you didn't want to answer?'

'Wolves tend to keep to their own territory.'

'They have been known to cross boundaries if the call is strong enough.'

He reached up and touched the silk flower in her hair.

'It's not real.' Her voice emerged as a husky whisper.

'No. But this is, Catherine.' His fingers feathered her earlobe before sliding under the fall of her hair to the nape of her neck. 'This is,' he repeated, his voice a low erotic burr as he moved closer and bent his head to hers.

The drumming of her heart filled her ears, blocking out any last second denial her mind might have dictated. A light tug of her hair tilted her face up. She was beyond fighting this moment which shimmered with the promise of answers she craved. His lips brushed hers, stirring a host of electric tingles. Then came the tasting, a feast of sensual pleasure that was more seductive than any kissing Catherine remembered.

Her arms lifted and wound around his neck, her own hands thrusting into his hair, fingers driving through the thick mat of curls, pressing for a continuation, wanting to know and feel more. He scooped her body firmly against his and the hard, heated strength of him was imprinted on her, the muscular wall of his chest, rock-hard thighs, and an erection that instantly set a wave of desire rolling through her, inciting a wild, questing passion for satisfaction when his mouth invaded hers. Long, fierce, ravishing kisses…kisses in her hair, on her throat, shoulders, her breasts yearning to be touched, taken, her stomach revelling in the feel of his urgent wanting.

A burst of laughter jolted them both out of the wild compulsion to pursue more and more sensation. It came from another group of people emerging from the restaurant and heading for their cars. Zack sucked in a deep breath, one hand lifting to cup her cheek, fingers stroking soft reassurance.

'I know a private place. I'll drive us there.'

Her mind was too shattered to think. With quick, purposeful strides, he bundled her around to the passenger side, all his energy focused now on taking her with him. Catherine was still too tremulous to take any positive action herself. He'd already guided her into the car and fastened her seat belt before she remembered...

'The key...' It wasn't in her hand anymore. 'I must have dropped it.'

'I'll find it.'

He bent and kissed her, stoking the need that had been left hanging. She sat dazed by the whole tumultuous eruption of passion. It didn't even occur to her that she hadn't given him permission to take control of her car. He settled behind the driving wheel, flashed her a dazzling grin as he fastened his seat belt, switched on the engine, and they were off.

'Where are we going?' she finally found wits enough to ask.

Another white grin—the grin of a man on a winning streak that couldn't be stopped. 'To a place that was made for us, Catherine Trent...a place that will give us a night to remember.'

CHAPTER FOUR

A NIGHT to remember… The seductive words kept floating through Catherine's mind as Zack drove through Terrigal, crossed the bridge over the lagoon, and headed along Ocean Drive Road—all familiar territory to her, yet nothing felt familiar on this journey with Zack Freeman.

They hadn't put the hood of the convertible down. She was closed in with him and he seemed to dominate the space inside the car, emanating an irresistible power that would pull her along with him wherever he wanted to take her. That was seductive, too, removing from her all responsibility for what happened. Except Catherine knew that wasn't true.

She could still say no, though her gaze was continually drawn to the hands firmly wrapped around the driving wheel, hands in control, sure of what they were doing, and the wanton desire to feel those hands on her clouded any decision. So far he hadn't done anything she hadn't secretly yearned for. Why stop now? Yet wasn't it risky, even dangerous, trusting herself to him like this?

At the Wamberal roundabout he took the road that led towards Forresters Beach. Catherine told herself it would be easy to stop this madness now, insist he drive to Pete's place and say she didn't want to take this night any further. It was the safe thing to do, just open her mouth…and lose out on having Zack Freeman as her lover for one night.

This immensely desirable man…

Even in profile he was strikingly handsome. And his aggressively male physique had a sexual power which stirred basic instincts she could neither ignore nor deny. More than that, every time he looked at her, his eyes seemed to connect to what she was thinking, what she was feeling…dark burning eyes, challenging her to acknowledge that the desire between them was *real*. Not a fantasy. Real and urgent and compelling. Every jangling nerve end in her body was still affirming this reality.

Whether it was right or wrong for her…was such a question relevant at this point?

She was over thirty. *Thirty-one*. And going nowhere with the man who'd monopolised her interest for the past few years. It was time to face the fact that Stuart Carstairs was a footloose philanderer and always would be. Zack Freeman might be one, too, for all she knew, but at least he wasn't pretending to have fallen in love with her and he'd been honest about not holding out more than one night with him. This blind date did not have a blind end to it. She knew precisely what was on offer.

Well, not precisely. Her imagination was running riot, fueled by the feelings Zack had stirred in her. It might be a wild, reckless act to ride this tide until time ran out but she didn't want to go home wondering what it might have been like. She *needed* to know there was something more than Stuart had given her, something she could look for in the future, knowing it was *real*.

The car slowed, turned into Crystal Street, the road to Pete's place. 'We're going to Forresters?' she blurted out, seized by the panicky thought that *he* had changed his mind, deciding she wasn't worth losing sleep over.

'No.' He flashed her a smile that sparkled with anticipation. 'To a little bay just past the headland at Forresters. You'll see. It's the perfect place for us.'

Perfect... He didn't have any doubts. There was no struggle over any sense of right or wrong in his conscience. It was full steam ahead for Zack Freeman. And maybe that was part of his strength, part of his overwhelming attraction. He knew what he wanted and went after it with single-minded purpose.

They turned right at the end of Crystal Street. The car climbed a steep hill—the headland—went over it and down the other side, turning sharp left and coming to a halt in a large dead-end parking circle that was closed in by a nature reserve, a thick belt of trees and bushes cutting off any sight of the ocean.

Shadows from overhanging foliage put them in a pool of darkness. There were no other vehicles here. The sense of being very much alone with Zack Freeman sent a quiver of apprehension down Catherine's spine. Was she mad to do this? Was she?

Then he was opening the passenger door, drawing her out of the car and into an embrace that shot a flood of positive responses through her body, swamping any chilling fears. He planted soft little kisses

around her face, gentle smiling kisses, transmitting a
pleasure in her that Catherine revelled in.

'Do you have a rug in the boot of the car?' he
murmured.

She always kept a picnic rug there. More a rubber-
backed mat than a rug. It could be laid on damp
ground. Or firm, wave-washed sand. She could hear
the ocean now, booming behind the trees, and the
idea of a secluded little beach all to themselves
misted what they'd be using the rug for in a romantic
haze.

'Yes,' she said, and knew it was a *yes* to all that
might ensue, regardless of how reckless it was.

Again he cupped her cheek, subjecting her eyes to
an intense focus from his. 'I didn't come prepared
for this. Tell me now, Catherine, do I need to use…'

'No. There's no risk. Unless…' Did he have sex
indiscriminately, whenever and wherever the urge
took him?

He read her question and shook his head. 'I've
always been careful.' His mouth tilted ruefully.
'You're the only woman who's made me forget…momentarily…what intimacy can lead to.'

The power of his desire for her was exhilarating.
The only woman… And he was the only man who
had ever incited this compelling sense of need in her.
A man of control, she thought giddily, a man she
could trust to look after her.

He collected the picnic rug from the boot of the
car, then took her hand, holding it with warm possessive strength as he led her onto a paved path that
wound through the nature reserve. It stopped where

the beach began. With the shadows of the bushland behind them and the full moon lighting their way, it was easy to see the boards marking sand-filled steps which took them down a long dune to the seashore.

'Sit for a minute,' Zack commanded, pausing to drop the rug on the step behind them. 'I'll take your shoes off.'

The first bit of undressing, Catherine thought, her heart thumping erratically as she sank onto the rug-covered step and Zack descended a couple more before crouching to remove her shoes. She hadn't worn stockings or pantihose. It was a hot night. It felt even hotter as Zack handled her ankles, undoing the criss-cross straps, his fingers sliding along the soles of her feet with each shoe removal, making her toes twitch from the sensitivity aroused by his touch.

'Cramp?' he asked.

'No. Just…'

He massaged her toes anyway, leaving her speech-less and breathless.

It was some slight relief when he handed over her shoes and sat down beside her to take off his own, which were casual slip-ons, no socks.

Rather than stare at his naked feet, she trained her gaze on the big surf which was crashing onto a circle of rocks, sending up spectacular sprays, their froth gleaming white in the moonlight. The rocks enclosed a small bay, reducing the waves rolling past them to small swells, a safe swimming area close to the beach.

'Does this place have a name?' she asked, trying to find some normal level with him.

He grinned at her. 'Spoon Bay.'

Laughter gurgled out, easing her nervous tension about accepting whatever would be between them. 'Made for *spooning* by moonlight?'

His eyes twinkled, happy to have her more relaxed with him. 'I think it refers more to the shape of the area…the way the beach curves into the treeline and the rocks curve around the bay. You can't see it properly from here. Come…'

He stood and pulled her to her feet, grabbed the rug again, tucking it under his far arm so he could still hold her hand as they continued down the sand-and-board steps. Catherine took a deep breath of the salty sea air. Somehow it was as intoxicating as the tingling heat of Zack's fingers, intertwining with hers. All her senses seemed switched onto a much sharper level.

They walked along the beach to the little cove Zack had described, sand squishing underfoot, the surf beating out its own primeval rhythm, the almost eerie light of the full moon lending a mood of ancient timelessness to the scene. They could have been the only man and woman in the universe, making foot-prints where none had been before, surrounded by elements of nature that no human touch had ever controlled.

Would tonight with Zack leaves its imprint on her…a night to remember?

He laid the picnic rug over a stretch of smooth sand in the centre of the cove. The sight of it, ready for them, so *sensible* and *planned,* suddenly put Catherine at odds with its obvious purpose. Her nerves jangled a panicky protest. She tossed her shoes onto it and spun around to face the sea, instinctively seeking a spontaneous rush of something else, more natural, more enticing, more…explosive…like the waves on the rocks, a fierce flow and ebb, driven by mindless forces which were very, very real.

Like what she had felt with Zack before, when he'd kissed her, when…

'Stay right there,' he commanded from behind her, and she heard the rustle and click of his clothes being removed.

She didn't look, couldn't bring herself to look or take any action at all. Her mind filled with a vision of him emerging naked in all his muscular splendour, primal male pulsing with a vitality which he was releasing from all the conventional bonds of their civilised world, and she wanted to be released too, free of all inhibitions. He would come to her…she was waiting…and her heart was drumming louder than the waves now. No turning away from this, no turning…

Her whole body was wire-tight with anticipation when his arms slid around her waist. She almost crumbled at the contact, the need for it was so intense. She leaned back against him, revelling in the sense of being encompassed and protected by his hard, warm strength, wanting to feel a togetherness that could face anything and survive intact. He rubbed his cheek over her hair and she felt his chest rise and fall as he breathed in its scent, mingled now with the smell of the sea.

'You should have been called Eve,' he murmured.

The beginning of time, she thought, elated that he was in tune with her own feelings. 'And you, Adam?'

'The caveman in me has definitely been stirred tonight.'

Was it the cavewoman in her responding? It didn't matter. Having surrendered to whatever it was, she simply wanted to be swept along with it.

His hands slid up to capture her breasts, fingers softly kneading, savouring their fullness. She closed her eyes, inwardly focusing on his touch and the sensations it aroused, the excited tightening of her nipples, the flow of pressures that seemed to make her flesh swell voluptuously and recede in rhythmic waves.

She reached up to pull her hair forward over her shoulders to bare the zipper at the back of her dress, but he didn't do anything about it. He kissed the nape of her neck and glided his hands down over her stomach, her thighs, and gathered up the hem of her dress, lifting the skirt to her waist so the night air shivered over all he'd exposed to it, naked thighs, naked hips, and his palm moved underneath the G-string she still wore, fingers reaching, stroking, building an almost unbearable excitement.

It was unbelievably erotic being caressed like this, without seeing the man who was doing it, only feeling his body behind her, hot flesh pressed to hers while in front of her there was nothing but sand and water and air—elemental nature, swirling, changing, sucking, crashing, wafting—while the fire of desire was being stoked inside her in an echo of the same shifting patterns of movement.

It was wild. And suddenly it was too much for her to keep letting it go on. In a fever of urgency, she dropped her own hands to snatch the flimsy G-string away, pulling it down to step out of it. As she bent over she felt her dress being unzipped, her bra unclipped, and in a few quick seconds, she was completely naked, too, and spun around to face her partner of the night.

He grabbed her hands and stepped back, his eyes feasting on the feminine curves he'd only felt. 'Look at you…'

The awe in his voice filled her own mind as she looked at him, so tall and big and magnificently made in a mould that was utterly perfect manhood.

'…like a siren from the sea, come to lure me away from everything else.'

'Are you a myth?'

'Do I feel like one?'

He lifted her hands to press the palms against his chest, drawing her in to him as he guided them up to his shoulders. The tips of her breasts touched him. Then he released her hands and scooped her into close and intimate contact with all of him.

'Not a myth,' he said gruffly. 'But we can make a legend of tonight, Catherine Trent.'

And he kissed her…. Kissed her as though her mouth held the fountain of life and he thirsted for every drop of it. And she kissed him back with all the pent-up passion from waiting for this, waiting and wanting and needing it to be…just like this.

He swung her off her feet, laid her on the rug, loomed over her, his face ablaze with the fire within, his powerful body dark and taut, rampant male poised to take, primed to take, and a wild elation coursed through Catherine as she positioned herself to possess him.

He came into her with shocking, exhilarating swiftness, the impact of him arching her body in an instinctive and ecstatic urge to hold the deeply penetrating fullness, to have it all, the whole glorious shaft of him imbedded in the warm silky heart of her, surrounding him, enclosing him, drawing him into the ultimate togetherness.

And he paused there to kiss her again, to invade her mouth with the passionate intent to link them in a totality that swam with intense sensation. He was spread on top of her, a pulsing blanket of heated muscle, pressing onto her breasts, their lower bodies locked, her legs wound around his hips, her hands raking his back, her whole body yearning to be utterly joined with his, exulting in feeling everything possible with him.

His arms burrowed under her and she was lifted to straddle his thighs as he sat back on his haunches, his mouth leaving hers to fasten on her breasts, subjecting each one to a wild exquisite suction as he rocked her from side to side, moving the pressure of him inside her to an equally exquisite slide along her inner walls. She threw back her head, instinctively thrusting her breasts forward, loving the hot tug on them, the swirling lash of his tongue on her nipples, and the arc of sweet pleasure that flowed from these ravishing kisses to the tantalising caresses within.

The full moon shone on her face. The sea breeze filtered through her swaying hair. The roar of crashing waves filled her ears. But they were outside things and the vibrant inner life of this union with Zack Freeman swamped her awareness of anything else. It was like an ocean of sensation, whipped by a storm of feeling, tidal waves gathering more and more explosive power.

He surged up and laid her back on the rug, his breath a hot wind on her skin as he hovered over her like a dark mountainous wave about to break. She felt the crest of it, poised within her, holding, holding. Then the pounding began, deep, glorious beats that throbbed through her entire body, convulsing it around him, carrying her into intense turbulence—a turbulence that swept her to an incredible peak of ecstatic excitement, and her body seemed to shatter with the fantastic pleasure of it.

But it wasn't shattered. It floated on rolls of more pleasure, peaking and ebbing, peaking and ebbing, until the driving force of Zack reached its climax on one last brilliant peak and finished in a flood of deep warmth that slowly gentled them both into the sweet peace of utter fulfilment.

They hugged. They kissed. They touched. They revelled in the sensual magic of the night, strolling along the wet sand with the dying froth of waves caressing their feet, swimming in the rock pool, their bodies sliding around each other in the buoyant water, teasing, inviting, savouring the freedom to give and take every pleasure in being together.

To Catherine, he was wonderful. She couldn't have enough of him. And he shared her greed, her lust to have everything possible packed into this one night. Nothing wild was too wild. There was no shame in anything. They loved each other in the water, on the sand, against a rock with the spray of the sea showering over them.

What words were spoken did not relate to any other time or place or circumstance. The past and the future had no bearing on what they shared. There was no breaking of that mutual understanding, no attempt to break it, or change any of the parameters of that one promise…a night to remember.

They didn't sleep.

They left the beach at dawn.

It was time to part.

CHAPTER FIVE

Nine months later...

CATHERINE set the crystal tiara carefully over Livvy's topknot of bright blond curls, watching her sister's reflection in the mirror to position this last piece of wedding finery with perfect precision. 'There!' she said with a satisfied smile, stepping back to fluff out the veil attached to the tiara. 'You look fabulous! A princess bride if ever I saw one.'

Livvy's vivid blue eyes sparkled with happy anticipation. 'I hope Pete thinks so.'

'How could he not?' Catherine's gaze dropped to take in the heavily beaded and embroidered bodice of the wedding dress. It was moulded to every feminine curve like a second skin. Little cap sleeves led into a low heart-shaped neckline, echoed at her tiny waist with a slight dip from which a many-layered tulle skirt frothed to the floor. It was pure romance and typically Livvy. 'You'll take his breath away.'

They shared a sisterhood smile.

'You look fabulous, too, Catherine. That dark red suits you.'

It did. And the simple elegance of the strapless satin sheath was much more her style. Though Livvy had stuck her with a flower in her hair, a dark red rose nestled against the topknot of curls which were more unruly than the bride's but hopefully fastened securely by pins.

All four bridesmaids were wearing their hair up like Livvy's. At the moment, the other three, close friends of her sister, were out of the room, checking out the bouquets which had just been delivered. Livvy seized on the opportunity for a private chat.

'You know what would really make me happy?' she pressed.

'I thought you were over the moon already, marrying the man you love.'

'If you'd just give Kevin a chance. He's Pete's best man. As my chief bridesmaid, you'll be partnered with him and...'

'Please...' Catherine rolled her eyes in exasperation at her sister's persistent matchmaking. '...don't start on that again.'

'But he's really nice. I've met him several times. And he hasn't picked up with anyone since his divorce.'

'You want to land me with a man who has a failed marriage behind him?'

'Now you're being nit-picky. You've got to face it, Catherine. The field of eligible guys narrows down after you're thirty and you've been manless since you finally had the sense to get rid of Stuart Carstairs.'

'And quite contentedly so, thank you. I have my goldfish to keep me company.' She hadn't been allowed to have a dog in her apartment but no one objected to goldfish as pets.

Livvy gritted her teeth. 'Goldfish cannot take the place of a man in your life.'

'You're right. They're something else. Goldfish love you unconditionally. Rhett and Scarlet are always there for me. They're beautiful to look at and they never let me down.'

'Now you're being cynical.'

'Not at all. Just telling it how it is.'

'Rhett and Scarlet,' Livvy scoffed. 'Whoever heard of fish being called after characters from *Gone With the Wind?*'

It seemed apt at the time, since she'd bought them after her night with Zack Freeman...a night that *was* gone with the wind though she'd always remember it.

'At least it shows there's some romance left in your soul,' Livvy reasoned, returning to her pitch. 'Kevin could be good for you.'

Catherine shrugged, not wanting an argument to-day of all days. 'Well, if he is, he is.'

'So you *will* give him a chance.'

'I'll dance with him at your wedding and hope he doesn't tread on my toes.'

Livvy relaxed into a laugh which ended in a rueful grimace. 'A pity Zack Freeman couldn't make it to-day. You made such a striking pair when Pete and I fixed up that blind date for the two of you.'

'Mmm...' It was the most non-committal reply Catherine could come up with.

'You know the last big box-office movie that fea-tured his special effects...it's been nominated for a Golden Globe,' Livvy rattled on. 'In my opinion, it's Zack's work that really makes it so dramatic and memorable. Did you go and see it?'

'Yes. Stunning stuff.' She had sat in the movie theatre, enthralled by the mind that could imagine and create such amazing scenes. It had made the night she'd spent with him all the more extraordinary. Uniquely special.

'He might get an Academy Award for that movie,' Livvy rattled on. 'Pete says…'

The other bridesmaids erupted into the room, carrying the bouquets and exclaiming how beautiful they were, and any further talk about Zack Freeman was abruptly dropped, much to Catherine's relief. She didn't want to discuss him or his work. It was easier to keep him tucked away as a private memory.

Initially he'd been designated as Pete's best man, but commitments on the other side of the world had forced him to regretfully decline the honour. Which was undoubtedly true, yet Catherine couldn't help wondering if that suited him since it neatly avoided meeting her again. Though that was probably too personal a slant on his decision. His long friendship with Pete would surely have taken priority over any sense of awkwardness over partnering her again…for just one night.

A second night…

Her stomach clenched at the need that suddenly clawed through her. Stupid, she fiercely told herself. Magic could never be recaptured. It would be different, a second time around. In fact, it might even spoil the memory she had of him. Better that he was caught up in other things elsewhere.

The only problem was, she couldn't get interested in other men, despite her sister's best efforts to couple her with quite a few reasonably attractive prospects. Livvy thought she'd been too scarred by her long relationship with Stuart Carstairs, but it was actually Zack Freeman who got in the way, making other men seem hopelessly pale in comparison.

She hadn't even been tempted to pick up with Stuart again, despite his abject apologies and begging for another chance. In fact, she'd suddenly seen his charm as totally egocentric, a tool he used in a deliberate play for power over others. Manipulation was his game. She'd been blind to it before, or sucked in by feelings he'd known how to play on.

In the first few months after her night with Zack, Stuart had proceeded to target every woman who was professionally associated with Catherine, focusing all his charismatic energy on them, one by one, until he had them, and then he'd slyly let Catherine know as though that was supposed to make her feel jealous or possessive, firing up a desire to have him back in her bed and her life.

It didn't work.

Stuart couldn't get to her anymore.

An ironic little smile hovered on her lips. Zack Freeman had certainly done her a favour there, but had he wrecked any chance of her connecting to someone else who might very well be good for her…like Kevin?

She wandered over to the window, knowing the vintage cars to transport the wedding party were due to arrive. The cars had been Pete's idea, matching up to the old colonial house Livvy had chosen for the reception. All very romantic. As it should be on their wedding day.

The weather had smiled on them. It was a lovely sunny afternoon. The ceremony at the church was scheduled for four o'clock and it was now three-fifteen. Their parents were already dressed and waiting downstairs for their daughters to appear in their wedding finery. They would all leave together from this family home in Lane Cove where Catherine and Livvy had grown up and gone to school.

A big moment for their mother and father, Catherine thought, their younger daughter getting married. Both she and Livvy had left home years ago, seeking more convenient accommodation to their careers and the freedom to lead their lives without too much critical comment from their parents. The independent set-up had freed their parents, too, removing enough of their sense of responsibility and ties to their children for them to really enjoy the travelling they'd always wanted to do. But different lifestyles hadn't diminished the love and caring they shared as a family and today was a milestone to be cherished.

'The cars are coming up the street now,' she announced, glad they wouldn't cause any hitch in the arrangements.

She wanted everything to be perfect for Livvy.

Her sister's wedding.

It might be the only one her family would have. She couldn't see herself ever getting married. For some women there was only ever one man. Catherine suspected hers had been Zack Freeman.

Zack glanced at his watch as he strode out of the Airport Hilton Hotel. Just past three-thirty. He'd flown into Sydney only an hour ago, no luggage to collect since he'd carried his overnight bag and the suit-holder containing his formal clothes for Pete's wedding onto the aircraft with him. He'd shaved in flight so he'd only had to shower and change here at the hotel. With any luck, he should get to the church on time.

The taxi he'd ordered was waiting for him. He climbed into it and gave the driver the address at Chatswood, adding that he had to be there by four o'clock for a wedding.

'No worries,' the cabbie cheerfully assured him. 'We take the freeway and the harbour tunnel. Being Saturday afternoon, the traffic's not heavy. In any event, the bride is always late.'

Not Livvy, Zack thought, remembering her on-the-dot punctuality in arriving at the Galley restaurant on the night of his blind date with Catherine.

Catherine…

He sighed over the frustrating conflicts she raised in his mind. The memory of her had almost stopped him from coming to this wedding. *Pete's* wedding! As it was, he'd let his old friend down, declining the role of best man because that would have inevitably put him as Catherine's partner in the wedding party.

He shook his head over her lingering and pervasive effect on him. Try as he might, he couldn't set the memory of that one night with her aside and it had proved unsettling too many times over this past year, distracting him from business, insidiously destroying the attraction that other women would have had in the normal course of events. But he should not have let it get in the way of standing up for Pete on his wedding day.

His hands clenched in anger.

Bad decision!

When he'd called from Singapore last night to say he *was* coming, the excitement and pleasure in Pete's voice had shamed him…letting a woman—any woman—put him off sharing in such an important day. Their friendship was worth more than any disturbance Catherine Trent might give him.

'I may be late getting there,' he'd warned.

'Hey! No problem, man. It'll be great to see you. I'll tell Mum to organise a seat for you at the reception. Where would you like to be? With the young bloods?'

He should have been sitting beside Pete. Since he'd given up that place and weddings were really a family affair, he'd answered, 'No. With my mother, if that's possible. Haven't seen her for a while.'

'Done.'

And that had made him feel guilty, too. Pete would oblige him with anything, and he'd...too late to rue it now. Damn Livvy's sister and her power to mess with things that were not related to her. He hoped seeing her again today would put the memory of that one night with her in some reasonable perspective. Get it out of his system.

His mother was always good company. She would claim his attention. Now there was one woman he did genuinely love. She'd always stuck up for him against his father who'd relentlessly put him down, jeering over his interest in computer graphics, saying he was wasting his time and would never amount to anything. Too bad he'd died when Zack was only twenty. Though he'd probably even deride what his son had achieved if he was still alive.

Zack didn't grieve over the loss of his father, though he would have liked the chance to shove his success down the old man's throat. Domineering narrow-minded bastard! Why his mother had stayed in that marriage all those years was beyond his understanding. He'd watched his father crush the joy out

of her countless times, though she'd stubbornly clung
to what she believed in, opposing him when it was
important to her.

Thirteen years she'd been widowed now, and
showed no inclination to look for another husband.
It was probably a relief to be absolutely free to do
as she liked and not have to justify or account to
anyone for what she did. She filled her life with
things she enjoyed; running the arts and crafts gallery
at Dora Creek, playing bridge with Pete's mum twice
a week, still doing her own pottery. She was a lovely
person with a large circle of friends and she'd always
insisted to Zack that she wasn't lonely.

'Follow your star wherever it takes you,' she'd
told him many times. 'Fulfilling what you most want
to do is what gives your life meaning. Go for it,
Zack. Don't let anyone stop you.'

He hadn't.

But his focus on what he was going for had been
knocked slightly awry by Catherine Trent and he intended to correct that today. It was absurd that one
night with her still had the capacity to tie him in
knots. He had to get this…*aberration*…straightened
out. No way was he ready to get tied up with any
woman.

The taxi was emerging from the harbour tunnel.
Zack checked his watch again. Ten minutes left to
get there. He'd probably arrive at the same time as
the bride. Which would mean seeing Catherine as
Livvy's bridesmaid. He felt his nerves tightening and
willed them to relax.

She wouldn't stun him a second time.

He knew what she looked like.

A nod of acknowledgment or a wave as he headed

into the church would get him by. More than likely, he'd find she didn't match up to the memory and this whole *thing* about her would fade into insignificance. They'd shared a great night, but that was all it was…one great night.

He dismissed it from his mind, determined to concentrate on Pete and Livvy. He hoped they'd have a good marriage and the children they both wanted. Maybe that had been part of the problem with his parents, his mother only able to have one child and Zack hadn't been the kind of son his father had wanted…no interest in going into boat-building or taking up a *useful* trade. If there'd been other sons…

Though Pete had been an only son, too, and his father had been happy to let him go his own way. Maybe having two daughters, as well, had softened him. Zack had always liked going to the Raynor home. No-one there had ever criticised his and Pete's absorption in computer games. Pete had loved the challenge of *winning*. Zack had been fascinated by the graphics, wanting to know how they were done and how they could be done better.

They were good times.

'Church coming up,' the cabbie informed him. 'And from the look of the three highly polished vintage cars ahead of us, the bridal party is just arriving.'

Zack smiled at the choice of cars—bound to be Pete's idea. His first car had been an old rattletrap MG which he'd insisted was a classic. Zack had bought his first motorbike—secondhand—at about the same time. Lots of shared memories with Pete, and today would be another one, as it should be.

The vintage cars pulled into a driveway by the side

of the church and came to a processional halt. The chauffeurs were hopping out to open the back doors for their passengers as the taxi passed by and pulled in at the street kerb adjacent to the gate which was the public entrance to the churchyard. Zack quickly paid over the fare, adding a generous tip to thank the cabbie for the timely arrival.

He was out of the taxi and at the gate when a man emerged from the lead car, his age and the flower in the lapel of his black suitcoat marking him as Livvy's father. Movement at the opened door of the second car caught his eye. He deliberately kept heading for the vestibule of the church, trying to crush the urge to look. This was Pete's day. Catherine Trent was a side issue.

'Wait for me to help, Dad.'

The seductive lilt of her voice tempted him.

'Now, Catherine, I'm the father of the bride. Don't do me out of my job.'

She laughed.

That did it.

He stopped and looked.

She'd taken a couple of steps towards the lead car and was swinging towards him, looking at the ground to be covered from the bride's car to the church. Her head jerked in shock at her first sight of him. Disbelief chased across her face.

Now was the time to nod or wave and move right on by, Zack told himself. But his body didn't obey that dictate. She stared at him and he stared at her, both of them totally immobile. It was as if they were caught in a time-warp where only they existed, bonded together by memories that were uniquely theirs.

She was vividly, vibrantly, and undeniably stunning…so beautiful he couldn't tear his gaze away. Her hair was piled on top of her head and he remembered her holding it there like that after they'd been swimming, inadvertantly showing off the long graceful curve of her neck which he'd kissed many times.

She had a flower in her hair again, dark red this time, not pink. The same dark red as the dress she was wearing, a strapless dress that bared her shoulders and arms, the hollow at the base of her neck, and the slight swell of flesh that hinted at the lush fullness of her breasts.

His mouth went dry, remembering the tight texture of her nipples, the salty taste of them in the sea. His hands itched to span her provocatively small waist, to run them over the voluptuous curve of her hips, down the long silky line of her thighs. He could feel himself stirring, the desire she evoked zinging through his bloodstream, pumping up an urgent need to have her again.

'Zack!' The call of his name snapped the dangerous thrall. It came from Livvy, stepping out of her car in a cloud of white. 'You came!' she cried in surprised delight. 'Does Pete know?'

He nodded. He waved a salute to her. It felt as though he was reacting in slow motion. Words finally came. 'See you in the church.'

He didn't risk another look at Catherine. His legs took him where he had to go. A church was supposed to be a safe haven. It felt like a trap but there was no escape from it. He was here for Pete.

Catherine gave herself a mental shake. Zack Freeman *was* here. It hadn't been a hallucination. Livvy had seen him, too. Spoken to him. And he'd answered. He'd come for the wedding, was in the church right now, waiting for it to begin.

The way he'd looked at her…her whole body was still tingling. Despite the most part of a year having passed since their one night together, it had felt as though time had stood still and the intimate connection was just as immediate and powerful as it had been then. No difference at all. And her heart was skittering all over the place at the thought of having another night with him.

But he wasn't her partner tonight.

She had to be with…what was his name? Kevin.

Not *all* the time, she thought fiercely.

Her mind trembled at the enormity of what she was thinking and feeling. He hadn't made any contact with her. He'd come to the wedding out of friendship with Pete. Yet given the chance, she *would* choose to be with Zack Freeman.

All night.

CHAPTER SIX

CATHERINE ached from the tension of waiting for Zack to make some move on her. She couldn't bring herself to accept that he wasn't going to, yet how else could she explain the distance he had kept from her. He was with his mother, she kept telling herself, but surely no mother expected her adult son to give her his exclusive attention.

Besides, it hadn't been entirely exclusive. After the wedding ceremony, there'd been a photo session outside the church. Zack had emerged from the milling guests, headed straight for the just married couple, shook Pete's hand, kissed the bride, a dazzling smile accompanying his congratulations, but the smile hadn't been turned on Catherine. He hadn't even looked at her.

With her heart turning over with disappointment, she'd watched him go to Pete's parents and chat to them, then move to the side of a very stylish middle-aged woman whom she now knew to be his mother, though she didn't look at all like Zack with her flyaway auburn hair, fair skin and green eyes.

Nevertheless, Pete had identified her as such, and Catherine had decided it was fair enough for Zack to put his mother first, particularly since her own role as chief bridesmaid had kept her busy; seeing that Livvy was posed perfectly for the photographs, then helping her into the car with Pete, ensuring the billowing layers of tulle didn't get caught on anything. Zack, she had then argued to herself, was probably waiting until she had some time to herself.

There'd been another much longer session with the photographer in the lovely garden setting at Wisteria House where the reception had been booked. The two-storeyed Colonial home had wonderful verandas, their supporting columns skirted by ornate white lace ironwork. Guests had been invited onto the upper veranda to watch all the formal posing in the garden while they were served cocktails and hors d'oeuvres.

Several times Catherine had felt Zack's gaze burning into her, but when she'd glanced up at the onlooking crowd, his attention was not focused on her at all.

Pete had called him down, insisting he wanted a shot of Zack with himself and Livvy. He'd obliged his old friend but laughingly declined posing for a foursome with Catherine. 'Not my place,' he'd excused. 'Get the best man for that shot.' And he was gone again, leaving Catherine with the feeling he was avoiding any contact with her.

Yet why would that be so?

She hadn't chased him, hadn't made a nuisance of herself. At the end of the night they'd shared, she hadn't tried to cling on or press for some further involvement with him. Did he fear she would now? Make some kind of scene he'd hate? Or…her stomach cramped at the thought…had he met some other woman he wanted to keep? It would explain why he'd refused to be linked to Catherine in a photograph.

The torment of not knowing what he was thinking plagued her all through the reception dinner. Despite his stopping by the bridal table a couple of times to chat to Pete, Zack didn't once switch his attention to her. The only evidence that he hadn't completely forgotten their blind date and its intimate aftermath was the one long sizzling look outside the church, and that certainly wasn't being repeated.

Catherine doggedly ate what was put in front of her, assured Livvy the food was great without knowing whether it was or not, forced adequate responses to the general chat at the bridal table, smiled when a smile was expected.

She sat through the speeches without hearing a word, though her gaze remained fixed on each speaker as though she was listening avidly. But she was dying inside, drowning in a sea of painful confusion and frustration. She could only hope no one noticed. It was her sister's wedding.

Zack gritted his teeth, fighting the surge of violence that urged him to wipe the smirk off the best man's face, tear his arm from Catherine's waist, and break the fingers that were feeling their way up the erotic curve of her spine.

'She's very beautiful.'

His mother's voice filtered through the battle roar in his ears. He wrenched his gaze from the couple on the dance floor and managed a foggy look.

'What?' he asked, not having caught what she was talking about.

An amused smile teased his loss of rapport with her. 'Livvy's sister, Catherine. Don't tell me you haven't noticed how striking she is. You've been fixated on her all evening.'

He frowned, not liking to think his *obsession* with Catherine Trent was obvious. 'She is…very watchable,' he said, trying to brush the issue aside.

'You don't have to stay with me, Zack. I am with friends and they'll look after me. Feel free to pursue your interest in her.'

'I don't have the time for it,' he stated dismissively.

Her eyes gently mocked his assertion. 'Haven't you climbed your mountain? Doesn't it get lonely at the top by yourself?'

He mocked right back. 'Just because Pete's got himself married today doesn't mean I'm ready for it.'

'You make it sound as if it has to be programmed into your schedule.'

'For the best outcome…yes, it does. Nothing works well unless you've planned for it.'

She laughed. 'Do you really think you can plan love, Zack? That you can snap your fingers and…hey presto! The woman you want as your partner for life will roll up and present herself just when you want her to?'

He shrugged. 'I'll put my mind to it when I feel the need.' It certainly wasn't love on his mind right now. More a case of lust raging out of control.

Still looking highly amused, his mother said, 'You can't will it, either. It happens. You can't order the time, the place or the person. It simply…happens.'

'You're talking chemistry, not love,' he answered dryly.

'Am I? Well, let me pose you a question, Zack. Food for thought. How many Catherine Trents have you met?'

Only one. And one was too many, messing with his life.

His mother didn't wait for a reply.

It was his business, his decision.

She pushed back her chair and stood up, offhandedly stating, 'I think I'll find the powder room.'

His gaze instantly targeted the dance floor. Other couples were jigging apart, happily putting their own steps to the beat of the music. Not Catherine and her partner, who was all too conveniently no taller than she was. The guy had her thighs glued to his, and the hand now spread over the lower slope of the pit of her back was definitely applying pressure.

A red haze of fury tinged Zack's thoughts. He knew dancing wasn't on Kevin Macy's mind. More like wet dreams. The guy undoubtedly had an erection. Any minute now he'd be dancing Catherine out the opened French doors, finding a shadowed place on the veranda…

His chair almost tipped over as Zack erupted onto his feet. It had taken iron control not to make any connection with Catherine Trent this time around, but be damned if he was going to let some other guy connect with her right under his nose. He barely stopped himself from charging like a bull, head down, nostrils steaming, horns lowered ready to gore. It was certainly how he felt.

Catherine knew she should stop what Kevin Macy was doing. She'd slid into a careless passive state, too drained of energy to bother forcing a break away from him. Nevertheless, being nice to him did not include allowing him this *frottage* on the dance floor. It was getting downright dirty and he was probably nursing ideas she didn't want to encourage.

He was not the man for her.

He never would be.

And she didn't care if Livvy scolded her for not grabbing what was available. All too available, Catherine thought grimly, screwing up the strength to make a few things clear to Kevin Macy. Just as she was lifting her gaze to his face, she saw a hand clamp over his shoulder, a strong darkly toned hand, its fingers bent like lethal claws, digging into Kevin's suitcoat.

Her heart instantly skipped a beat.

'Hey!' Kevin protested, loosening his grip on her as he half turned to face the threatened assault.

Zack Freeman glowered at him from his intimidating height, the power of his physique a ready deterrant to any argument, though he didn't need it. The aggressive energy he emitted was enough to drop Kevin's jaw and kill any further words Pete's best man might have spoken.

'Excuse me,' Zack grated out, his dark eyes blazing a challenge that would have shrivelled any last scrap of foolhardy courage. 'This dance with Catherine is mine.'

Kevin not only didn't dispute the claim, he didn't even check with Catherine if she wanted to be passed over to Zack. He dropped her like a hot coal and back-tracked off the dance floor, gesturing for Zack to take her over. Which he did, with a speed that almost swept her off her feet. Pressed to another male body—a very different male body—Catherine struggled against the flood of excitement it stirred, a rebellious sense of pride insisting that she shouldn't surrender to it willy-nilly.

'You didn't ask my permission,' she fired at him, her eyes defying his arrogance in assuming he could keep her waiting for hours and still do whatever he wanted with her.

'No, I didn't.' He returned her challenge with blistering mockery. 'You can reject me if you want to.'

She burned. From head to toe she burned with the need to be with him. To deny it would be completely self-defeating. 'I hear you've had a good year,' she said, moving to less contentious ground and being deliberately bland so he wouldn't know her whole body was aquiver from being in contact with his again.

'A very good year,' he answered, his chin tilting belligerently, his eyes blazing with self-determination.

'That must give you a lot of satisfaction,' she ran on, suddenly hating the fact that she'd had no part in it, hadn't been invited to take any part in it.

'Yes,' he acknowledged, but the mockery was

back, deriding this conversation, telling her it had no relevance.

It goaded her into demanding some recognition of her as a person, not just the object of a desire he could pick up and put down as he liked. 'Why don't you ask me about my year?'

'Because I don't want to know.'

Ruthless truth.

He only wanted to *know* her in the biblical sense.

She averted her gaze from the intensely raw penetration of his and writhed through the shame of blushing like a schoolgirl.

'It's trivia, Catherine, and it won't change anything,' he stated harshly.

'Well, my life might be trivia to you but it's not trivia to me,' she flashed back at him, a fierce resentment surging at his dismissive attitude.

His eyes narrowed, weighing the strength of her attack and whether it was worth his while to make any concession to it. 'So what do you want to tell me?' he demanded. 'Give me the important highlights.'

There were none. Her job had provided a few little triumphs—winning accounts against strong competition—but they were hardly huge highlights that would make her shine for him. Her personal life was virtually a void, although she had taken up yoga and done a course in Italian cooking, both activities giving her considerable satisfaction. She wasn't about to admit that her experience with him had put her off other men.

'I bought two goldfish,' she tossed out, not caring

about his definition of trivia. Rhett and Scarlet had become the one daily constant in her private life since he had left it and she loved having them to come home to.

He looked startled, then bemused. 'Two goldfish,' he repeated with mock gravity.

'Yes.' She tilted her chin to a challenging angle. 'And I bought a beautiful bowl for them to swim in.'

His mouth burst into a wide, dazzling grin. Then he threw back his head and laughed, startling her with his wild amusement. He clasped her closer, whirling her around, his thighs driving them both across the dance floor in a flurry of steps that carved a path through the crowd of other dancers, out past the opened French doors and onto the veranda.

The cooler night air did nothing to lessen the heat Zack Freeman generated in her. 'That wasn't meant to be funny,' she protested, feeling intensely vulnerable now that they weren't completely surrounded by people. He had danced her down to the far end of the veranda, away from the other guests who were grouped around the door or leaning against the wrought-iron balustrade nearby.

His dark eyes twinkled amusement as he answered, 'Only you would tell me about goldfish, Catherine.' His chest heaved against her breasts and his slowly expelled breath tingled over her upturned face. 'Only you...' he repeated, his deep voice lowered to a caressing murmur.

Thinking of all the high-flying women he surely met while doing international business in the movie world, Catherine muttered, 'I don't lead your kind of exciting life.'

He shook his head as though she hadn't grasped his meaning. He seemed about to say more, stopped, grimaced, then flatly answered, 'The pace is tough. I'm on a flight back to London in the morning, Catherine. I only came for Pete's wedding.'

Fair warning…like last time…and if she had any sense she would walk away from him right now because it meant—as before—he had no intention of involving himself in an ongoing relationship with her. It was here now, gone tomorrow, no different to their first night together. Yet even knowing this, Catherine could not quash the feelings he aroused.

'It was good of you to make the time. Pete is so pleased you came,' she said in an equally flat tone, her lashes sweeping down to hide the emotional conflict of wanting far more than he was ever likely to give her, yet not wanting to turn away from him.

She stared at his bow tie sitting neatly at the base of his neck and wished she was a vampire, able to sink her teeth into his jugular vein and get into his bloodstream so powerfully he could never shake free of her. Her heart was thumping with the need to hold him to her any way she could. Her hands curled, the urge to claw and dig in sweeping through her in a fierce wave, driving her nails into her palms to stop such primitive and futile action.

'I'm sure your mother is, too,' she forced herself to add, a biting reminder of the hours of torment she had already suffered on his account. Zack Freeman was not going to be swayed from his course. There was no chance of anything more than another brief encounter with him.

He hadn't introduced her to his mother.

Didn't that tell her she was nothing but a bit of fluff on the side to him?

So stop this now.

Stop it and do the walking away herself.

Before she gave her heart and soul to him again.

Though weren't they his already?

'My mother thinks you're very beautiful,' he murmured.

It jolted her into looking up, meeting the simmering warmth in his eyes. 'You talked about me…to her?'

'She's right. You are.' His mouth curved into a sensual little smile. 'Irresistibly so.'

His head dipped towards hers. A kiss was coming. Her heart catapulted around her chest. Her mind screamed that this was the moment to stop him. But her whole body yearned to feel again how it was with him and when his mouth touched hers there was no thought left of pulling back. Any last shred of denial was swamped by a rush of blood to the head, blood that sang for all the sensations she craved.

Yes…it was a lilt of exultation as the desire for passionate possession exploded between them.

Yes…it was a fierce throb of satisfaction as his arms crushed her into an intimate awareness of the power of his need.

Yes…it was a paean of triumph that all the barriers that had separated them were being comprehensively smashed.

They kissed and were united in a deep inner world of their own, feverishly claiming all they could while they could—a savage feast of kissing, of touching, of immersing all their senses in each other. But it was never going to be enough out here on a public veranda in open view of anyone who chanced to look their way. That frustration did eventually break into the headlong rush to recapture all they had spent so many months remembering…or trying to forget.

'I have a room booked at the Airport Hilton Hotel,' Zack breathed in her ear. 'Come with me after the wedding is over.'

A hotel room…

Catherine's emotional recoil was instant.

No!

It would make her feel like a callgirl, visiting a totally impersonal room for sex, and an airport hotel hammered home how fleeting that visit would be. Yet she could not bear not to have him for as long as she could.

'My apartment,' she swiftly countered, pulling back from him to plead her choice. 'It's at Randwick. Not far from Mascot Airport. We could go there. Then I won't feel so bad when you have to leave in the morning.'

He frowned. 'I don't want to make you feel bad, Catherine.'

'I'd hate waking up alone in a hotel room, Zack,' she rushed out, panicking at the thought he might withdraw from any further intimacy. Sharing pleasure was his agenda, not giving pain. 'I'd rather wake up to my goldfish,' she quickly added, hoping that would amuse him again.

The frown cleared as his mouth quirked into a smile. 'I could get jealous of those fish.'

'I don't kiss them.'

'I'm relieved to hear it.'

He kissed her again, a slow sensual promise of what was to come in the hours they would have together. In her home, Catherine thought with dizzy joy. Which would make it all the more real, more intimate, more memorable. Taking him there, having him there, grounded him in surroundings that were hers and hers alone.

'I'll order a car to be waiting for us,' Zack murmured, his voice furred with the desire he had to contain for a little while longer. 'As soon as Pete and Livvy take their leave...'

'Yes,' she agreed, and despite knowing he would be gone in the morning, she could not quell the hope in her heart.

Zack Freeman still wanted her.

He might always want her.

CHAPTER SEVEN

ZACK didn't like the idea of going to Catherine's apartment. He cursed himself for not having thought anything through before taking her from Kevin Macy. Now, finally, they were at the farewell stage of the wedding with Pete and Livvy circling the guests before going off on their honeymoon. The car he'd ordered was waiting at the gates to Wisteria House, and Zack was faced with taking Catherine home, to a place she would have made distinctly her own, and that was getting too close to her.

He was awake to what it meant when a woman invited him to her home ground. It gave her the sense of having some kind of propriety rights over him. As a general rule he avoided the situation, offering a less personal get-together or making some excuse to be elsewhere. The problem was, he'd never wanted a woman as much as he wanted Catherine Trent. He'd given in to her wish with barely a hesitation, driven by the compulsion to have her under any circumstances, not even caring about consequences.

It was stupid.

He'd end up paying dearly for it, too. She'd be etched more deeply in his mind, the memory of her nagging at him when he didn't want to be nagged. Yet even knowing all this, he couldn't bring himself to stop what had been arranged between them. She was standing by her mother, right at the doorway which led to the staircase and out of here. Just a few more minutes…

'Zack, old buddy…' Pete clapped his shoulder and shook his hand vigorously. 'Thanks for coming. Really appreciate it.'

Pete looked drunk with happiness. Getting married to Livvy was certainly sitting well with him. 'You're hooked, man, but I guess the bait was worth taking,' Zack said, grinning at his old friend.

'Right on!' Pete agreed smugly. 'Beat you to it, Zack.'

A typically competitive remark, but there was no race being run here. Not in Zack's mind. Marriage was way down the track for him, though when he looked back at Catherine, his mother's words did beg the question—how often was a guy struck as hard as this by a woman?

He was aching to hold her again.

But that would pass once he'd had his fill of her. Just strong chemistry, he told himself. In fact, going to her apartment might be a good thing, reducing their connection to something ordinary. Not like his memories of their intimacy at the beach. That had been such a fantastic experience it wouldn't be human not to remember it as something special. Tonight would be different. Not that he wanted her any less, but her bedroom was not an evocative setting of sand and sea and moonlight.

'I guess you'll be off as soon as Pete goes,' his mother said.

'Yes.' He tore his gaze from Catherine to pay his

respect to the woman who'd always stood by him through thick and thin. She was literally standing by him now and he gave her a hug and a kiss on the cheek. 'It was good to see you, Mum.'

'Don't stay on your mountain too long, Zack,' she said wistfully. 'There's more of life to live. I'm going to envy Pete's mother her grandchildren.'

He frowned at the sentiment she had never voiced before. It was the wedding, focusing her thoughts on family, he reasoned. Though he was her only child. Had that been a sorrow to her? Did she long for more children through him? Yet she'd always preached he had his own life to live and set him free to do it, as free as any mother could.

He shook his head as his gaze swung back to Catherine. He wasn't ready for marriage and he wasn't ready to father children. Both were serious commitments. He'd give them his best shot when the time came but that wasn't now. There were industry awards coming up that he could capitalise on bigtime. And he would.

This night with Catherine was a brief time-out. He wasn't about to let it become anything more. She knew the score, didn't she? He didn't want to leave her feeling bad.

She was kissing Livvy goodbye. The bride moved on to her parents—the last farewell. Catherine looked at him, her sexy golden-amber eyes gleaming with the same sizzling impatience he felt.

Mutual desire.

No question she wanted what he wanted.

He wasn't doing any wrong by her.

There could be no harm in just one more night.

And the pleasure… Zack sucked in a quick breath…hours of it…with Catherine Trent.

It wasn't a taxi waiting for them. It was a chauffeured Mercedes with plush leather seats. Very comfortable, but Catherine couldn't relax. Since the law demanded they wear seat belts Zack wasn't about to pounce, yet she half wished he would because she was so painfully tense and she needed her doubts and fears obliterated.

Arrow signs to the airport kept flashing at Catherine on their way to Randwick, relentlessly reminding her that Zack would be heading there in just a few more hours…and possibly reminding him of the convenience of his hotel room, raising questions about the wisdom of going with her to her apartment, getting further involved with a woman he'd deliberately shunned for most of the wedding.

What if the impulse to pursue the desire they shared waned before they reached her place? How strong was it on his side? If he stayed with her for the rest of the night…if it was as incredibly wonderful as last time…would he come back for more of what they felt together…again and again and again? Or was that a hopeless pipedream on her part?

He was holding her hand, his thumb moving restlessly over her knuckles, back and forth, back and forth. A fine tension held them both silent. A huge wave of relief washed through Catherine when the car finally diverted from the route to the airport and headed past Centennial Park to where she'd been living since landing her current job five years ago. Almost home now. Her fear that Zack might change his mind about spending the night with her began to ease.

The urge to babble something that might be of interest to him raised feverish streams of thought. The company she worked for, Wavelength Promotions, had its offices at Botany, only a ten-minute drive from her apartment. She could be telling Zack this, relating her own experience with computer graphic designs, the presentations she made to clients. It was the normal thing to do. Yet his hard words—*I don't want to know*—held her tongue-tied. Perhaps he was right and only the feeling between them was important. Just…let it be.

The car arrived at her address. Zack spoke to the chauffeur, making arrangements for a car to pick him up here at 6:00 a.m., giving his mobile phone number for a cross-check with the hire company. Catherine wasn't quick enough to memorise the numbers. Not that it would do any good, she told herself. It was up to Zack to make any future contact. Meanwhile, she now knew precisely how long he would stay with her this time. Six o'clock…sunrise…

She desperately wanted to make a lasting impression on him, something more meaningful than whatever affairs he'd had with other women. Though her mind was helplessly foggy on how to accomplish that, especially when communication between them was overwhelmingly physical. Even as Zack followed her up the central staircase of the apartment block to her door on the first floor, his footsteps behind her made her heart beat faster and her legs feel tremulous.

Lucky that she hid a spare door key in the artificial aspidistra that dressed up a corner of the lobby serving the two apartments on her floor. She'd left her handbag at her parents' home at Lane Cove. Having untaped the key from the back of one of the plastic leaves, she quickly shoved it into the door lock and opened the way for Zack to enter her private space.

'Not the safest place in the world to keep a key,' he dryly commented.

'Green tape,' she explained. 'Unless you know where to look it's not easily found.'

'You let me know.'

'You're flying out, Zack,' she reminded him. 'I don't see you as a danger to me or mine.'

He frowned at her as he stepped past into the small living room. 'Don't be too free with your trust, Catherine. You're at risk…a woman like you living alone in the city.'

Having extracted the key from the lock, she closed the door and pointedly slotted home the safety chain. 'A woman like me takes care of herself,' she lilted, turning to him with a smile. 'But thank you for your concern, Zack.'

It wasn't just sex. He cared about her feelings, cared about her safety. The secret hope she nursed— that he might come to love her—danced a lively quickstep.

Zack thought her self-assurance vastly misplaced. Didn't she realise how sexy and desirable she was?

Any red-blooded man would feel attracted, excited, simply by the sight of her. She had everything that incited lust, a body that curved so provocatively a guy would have to be dead not to want to touch it, a face that fascinated with its feminine mystique, and hair...

That red rose had been teasing him all night. He wanted to pluck it out, rake his fingers through the cluster of curls, scattering the pins that confined them, and wind whole skeins of her long silky hair around his hands, revelling in the feel of it and binding her to him in an inescapable hold.

She pushed away from the door in a skittish rush. 'Let me introduce you to my fish.'

Fish! What she needed was a big brute of a dog—a Doberman pinscher or a German shepherd—trained to go for the jugular of anyone who threatened her peace of mind.

'Why fish?' he demanded. 'Why not a dog? Pete told me your sister's got a dog.'

She'd hurried straight past him. The question made her pause, glance back, and he was struck again by the seductive line of her neck and shoulder...soft, bare, vulnerable, asking to be kissed.

'We're not allowed dogs in this building.'

The body corporate wielding rules and regulations. Zack grimaced at the imposed constraints. Not many freedoms left in city living. But at least they now had the freedom of complete privacy. He moved to close in on Catherine, determined on soothing the nervous agitation which had suddenly seized her once the door to the outside world had been shut.

Her head snapped forward and she gestured to the fishbowl in front of her. 'The gold one is Rhett, and the red-gold one is Scarlet,' she said in a breathless flurry.

He spanned her waist with his hands—intensely satisfying—and smiled at her choice of names. 'Are they destined to have an unhappy end as in *Gone With the Wind?*'

'No. They…'

He licked her earlobe, nibbled on it. She wore an enticing musky perfume that sharply stirred his senses. He tasted her skin…

Catherine scooped in a quick breath. '…they chase each other endlessly around the bowl. I think Rhett and Scarlet did that, even after the book ended.'

'Perhaps they simply feel trapped.' He released her waist and slowly ran his fingertips up her arms, a feather-light touch that gave her the freedom to move if she wanted to. She didn't. She held herself completely still and the tiny little tremors under her skin told him how sensitive she was to his touch.

Another swift intake of breath. 'No. They're happy fish,' she insisted.

'How do you know?'

He trailed his fingers up her neck, over the soft thickness of her pinned-up hair to the dark red rose.

'Because I watch them play. They like their bowl. Its hexagonal shape is good Feng Shui, promoting peace and harmony. They have fun pushing the pebbles around at the bottom and the aquarium plants offer ready food beyond what I feed them. They're *happy* fish.'

He'd tucked the rose in his breast pocket and was pulling out the hairpins. 'Well, I guess they have eight views of the world from their hexagonal bowl, and many of them would be of you, so I'd call them fortunate fish.'

No reply this time. Absolute stillness.

'And very exotic. Like their owner,' he added, feeling her breath-held tension as he loosened the upswept curls and gently massaged her scalp. Her taut submissiveness tempered the fire of need burning through him with a strange flood of tenderness. Instead of hurling the hairpins away and stripping her naked as fast as he could, he tucked them into his pocket behind the rose, then simply enjoyed the spill of her hair, cascading over his hands and arms, brushing her shoulders, tumbling down her back... beautiful, glossy, excitingly sensual...

'You think I'm...exotic?' The husky lilt suggested that Catherine's mind had only just caught on to that word and didn't know how to process it.

'Uh-huh...a rare, exquisite creature with glorious hair and golden eyes.' He stepped around to face her, smiling over the truths he'd just spoken. He lifted her hair up on either side of her face, then let it slide through his fingers to float around her like a living fan. 'Perhaps you don't know how rare you are, Catherine, but I do. I do,' he repeated as desire surged again at the soft, hazy wonderment in her eyes...such a sensuous look, fringed by the long thick lashes that brushed his face when they kissed.

Her lips were slightly parted, lushly inviting, irresistible. He gathered her in...this woman who struck chords that made him almost a stranger to himself…and kissed her with a sense of exploring new territory, wanting to know what it meant, how it was, where it was taking him, and why it was so different to all he had known before.

No need for any haste. He had hours to take her all in, sift through the feelings she aroused, define them, understand them. With understanding came control and Zack *wanted* control over the effect Catherine Trent had on him.

Yet even as he kissed her with a conscious seeking in his mind, he could feel his quest for control melting under the sweet taunting heat of her lips and tongue. The addictive possession of her mouth burned his brain cells. His whole body burned to be inside her, enveloped by the velvet heat he knew was waiting for him. Only the most ingrained discipline drove him to check what had to be checked. It took an act of will to withdraw from the intoxicating fusion of desire long enough to breathe out the necessary words.

'Is it safe, Catherine?'

She didn't reply. Her face remained tilted to his, her lips parted enough for a soft waft of breath to escape, her eyes closed as though all her senses were focused inward, poised to respond to whatever he did. She wasn't listening to anything but the fire raging within, the fire that could so quickly flare into a furnace, consuming them both to the exclusion of everything else.

'Catherine…' he groaned, his whole body screaming against any pause for precaution. 'I didn't bring any condoms with me. I didn't plan…' He was admitting her power to draw him beyond any limits he imposed, but right at this moment he didn't care. 'Is it safe?' he asked raggedly, begging for a *yes,* because any negative now would be intolerable. Impossible to shut down on the blinding urge to take her, have her.

Safe?

Her stomach curled a fierce protest at Zack's caution as her mind reluctantly came to grips with the question. Condoms…contraception…she'd been off the pill for months. No need for it. And Zack hadn't been expected at the wedding. She hadn't anticipated being tempted.

But if she said no….

Panic and rebellion rolled through her. She couldn't let him leave her, not when she was only assured of one night with him. It couldn't stop now. The yearning for some fulfilment of her need screamed at her to lie.

Though it might not be a lie. Where was she in her monthly cycle? She couldn't think. It didn't matter. She could take the morning-after pill tomorrow if there was a risk of pregnancy. She didn't have to lie.

'Yes,' she said on a heady gasp of release from caring about any unwanted consequences. 'Safe.'

Yet it was a lie.

Catherine knew in her heart there was nothing safe about what she was doing with Zack Freeman tonight. She would give him all she had to offer because he drew that from her as no man ever had before, but he might very well take her body, break her heart, and leave her soul empty.

Tomorrow he would be gone again.

Tomorrow she would think about what to risk and what not to risk.

CHAPTER EIGHT

RELIEF curbed the aggression that had gripped Zack, virtually compelling an abandonment of all caution. *Safe* meant there was nothing to fight. *Safe* meant uninhibited pleasure. Safe meant there would be no shadows on his freedom, once this night was over.

He forced himself to relax, determined on regaining control. He didn't want to be swept headlong into the final act of sex within the first few minutes of having Catherine to himself. Much better to savour the excitement of anticipation, take the time to explore every facet of his fascination with her, know all of her so totally there would be no curiosity left to taunt or haunt him in the future.

Softly, slowly, he kissed her closed eyes, feeling the slight flutter of her long lashes brush his chin, a butterfly touch he fancied on other parts of his body. Was she still nervous about her decision to have him? Her tension in the car had been palpable, and using the fish as an almost frantic distraction from his presence here in her apartment were both signs of uncertainty...or apprehension.

She could have said no, Zack argued to himself, and her response to his kiss just now was enough assurance that the desire they shared overrode any doubts or fears, but it suddenly niggled that she might not be fully with him. He could take her. She was willing. But he didn't want any part of her to be withheld from him.

He lifted his hands and gently cupped her face, studying its unique feminine contours, her marble-smooth forehead, the fine arch of her brows with their winged ends, the deeply set lids that gave her eyes their exotic triangular shape, the high slanted cheekbones flanking her neat straight nose, the seductive fullness of her perfectly shaped lips...

She opened her eyes, the dark pupils so large their amber rims looked like rings of gold. Zack felt his heart kick at their luminous concentration on him. They seemed to be scouring his soul, asking questions he had no answers for. Not yet.

Give me time, he thought, but didn't say the words. They would sound like a promise and he instinctively shied from making any promises. He smiled to smooth over any angst she felt and spoke a truth that held no sense of danger to either of them. 'Just looking at you gives me pleasure.'

Her smile rewarded him, warm sparkles in her eyes softening their dark focus. A daring glint emerged as she answered, 'I would like to look at you but you have too many clothes on.'

He laughed, delighted to oblige her wish, swiftly removing his suitcoat and tossing it on a nearby armchair. 'How are you at undoing bow ties?'

She cocked her head in teasing consideration. 'I think I'm up to the challenge.'

Her hands lifted to the base of his throat and Zack sucked in a quick breath as he felt her fingers go to work, his pulse quickening underneath her touch. He concentrated on removing his cufflinks. His own fingers felt thick and clumsy, impatient to be rid of the task, wanting to roam over her again.

Control, he fiercely recited, but by the time he'd dropped the cufflinks on the table holding the fishbowl, the bowtie was gone, half his shirt buttons were undone, and her hands were gliding over his bare flesh, fingers tracing the taut muscles of his neck and shoulders, raising havoc with his determination to move slowly. He found himself tearing at the remaining buttons, almost ripping the shirt in his haste to get it off.

Her hands were stroking his upper arms as he yanked off the long sleeves and even as the frustrating piece of clothing dropped to the floor, she stepped in and pressed her mouth to the hollow between his shoulder-blades, her hot succulent lips firing up his blood, her hands continuing to stroke down his arms, making the fine hair on them crackle with electricity.

He didn't move, didn't dare to move in case he exploded into action. Besides, he'd wanted to register her affect on him, wanted to understand it, and he'd done this to her, hadn't he, while she stood still? He could stand still, too, and let her touch wash through him, building his awareness of how and why she excited him so much.

Her hands were at his waist now. Every muscle in his body flexed as he imagined them moving to unfasten his trousers. But they didn't. They glided up his rib cage, and her mouth trailed hot sensuous kisses over the breadth of his chest, her teeth lightly tugging on the springy curls at the centre of it, her tongue licking, tasting, and Zack's mind was totally jammed by the sensations shooting through him. Thinking of anything else was not an option.

He'd never considered *his* nipples erotic zones but when she latched onto them, the bolt of excitement was so sharp and intense, his hands instinctively took defensive action, burrowing through the thick curtain of her hair, compulsively intent on pulling her head away until... *Her* hand moved down over the flat of his stomach, making his skin crawl with sensitivity, fingers reaching under the waistband of his trousers, distracting him with her touch on other erogenous areas, and he could feel his erection burgeoning. If she took hold of him...

The need for control snapped into action again. He seized her wrists and lifted her arms to his shoulders, automatically raising her head from his chest where she'd heightened his excitement to an almost intolerable level. He kissed her quickly, his head whirling with the urge to be the dominant force, to take and be taken on his terms.

His tongue punished hers with hard invasive strength, overriding the seductive power of her mouth, yet even her submission was insidiously exciting, conjuring up how it would be when he plunged into her, her hot silky flesh giving way, stretching and compressing voluptuously around him.

He had to stop this or it would be over in a flash. 'Clothes,' he muttered, remembering her wish to look at him.

He stepped back, severing all contact, bumping into the chair he'd tossed his suitcoat on. He leaned against it as he whipped off his shoes and socks. *Go slow,* he raged at himself, taking more time over removing his trousers and briefs, wanting at least a little dignity in getting naked in front of her.

She didn't move. He felt her eyes on him, all over him, and when he finally straightened up, he met her gaze with a challenging pride that denied any self-consciousness in being bared to her sight, though every muscle in his body was taut with intensely male aggression, every nerve strung out from the frustration he'd imposed on himself. He was a man and never had he felt his sexuality more keenly.

Yet the instant he saw her expression—the soft look of wonder on her face, the vulnerable awe in her eyes—he was swept by the urge to be gentle with her, which put him strangely at odds with himself. Most of the women he'd met in recent times were ambitious, manipulative. They didn't draw tenderness from him. It was weird feeling the violent pounding of his heart melt into a muted curl of caring, a different form of desire that was intrinsically linked to *this* woman.

'Now your clothes,' he said, his voice gruff with unaccustomed emotion.

'Yes,' she whispered, a soft breathy agreement that tingled in his ears as he moved around behind her, stepping close enough to effect what he wanted without pressing any physical contact.

He parted her long rippling hair and moved it forward, over her shoulders, baring the nape of her neck and the elegant slope of her upper back, no angular bones, just satin-smooth skin leading down to the strapless red dress.

He unhooked the top fastening of the snugly fitted bodice and slowly drew the zipper down to her waist, exposing the highly feminine indentation of her spine. There was no interruption to it. She wore no bra. And Zack was tempted into stroking his fingers down the intriguing little valley, smiling as the caress raised a convulsive little shiver. She was as sensitised to his touch as he was to hers. Which was only right and immensely satisfying.

The dress gaped further open as he lowered the zipper to its full length, revealing the thin strips of a black G-string circling her fantastically small waist and erotically bisecting the luscious twin globes of her bottom. He'd never seen a sexier sight. It trapped the breath in his lungs and shot stabs of urgency to his groin.

Impatient for a full view of her, he quickly peeled the dress from her hips and it fell to her feet, leaving his hands free to trace every delectable curve, to cup the lush roundness that jutted so provocatively, he had to fight the urge to move forward.

Not yet. Not yet.

He hooked his thumbs under the waistline of her G-string and watched it slide over the soft mounds, down the long lissome thighs. The silky crotch of it caught at her knees. He slid his hand between her legs to release it, the flimsy fabric warm and moist from her inner excitement, bringing his arousal to flashpoint again.

Barely controlling himself, he raked the incredibly sexy garment down the taut curves of her calves and lifted her feet, one by one, sliding off her high-heeled sandals at the same time—all black straps trailing over dark red toenails, another exotic touch that stirred the raging heat in his blood.

The blinding need for action had him hooking an arm under her knees and hoisting her up against his chest as he came upright. He whirled her away from the fishbowl table, his gaze darting, seeking the door to her bedroom, finding it, his legs surging towards it with powerful purpose. It stood ajar, only needing a shove to open it wide enough to let them through to the bed—a double bed covered by a leopard-skin rug with the sheen of velvet, gold satin pillows.

The sheer animal sensuality of it tugged deeply at the most primal instincts in Zack. This was the place. This was the time. This was the woman. And he would not leave until he'd had his fill of her. But he wanted more light, needed to see all of her before plunging into the dark jungle of total intimacy where the beat of their bodies would consume his awareness of anything else.

He spotted a switch by the door, turned it on. Two lamps on either side of her bed—black and gold—spread a warm glow around the room. It looked right, felt right. White light was too harsh. It would have been better with a host of flickering candles—fire burning without and within—but this was a fleeting thought, overtaken by the desire to feast his eyes on all the female lushness now pressed so close to his chest.

He stood her on the bed. The lamplight gleamed on the living curtain of her hair swishing softly over the voluptuous fullness of her breasts, rose-red nipples peeking through the seductive veil, hard and pointed, provoking him into closing his mouth around them, lashing them with his tongue, loving the taste of her arousal, wanting more.

She'd wrapped her arms around his head, holding him to her, but he wouldn't be held. Not yet. He pulled back to take in this incredibly beautiful frontal view of her, to glide his hands over every inch of her, the smoothly fleshed midriff, the narrowness over her waist, the wide cradle of her hips.

His gaze locked onto the neatly trimmed arrow of dark hair, pointing to the cleft between her thighs. Her skin quivered underneath his fingertips as he traced it down and stroked around the apex. He stooped, pressing his face to the tight springy curls, breathing in the musky scent of her desire for him.

It wasn't enough. He scooped her legs out on either side of his and lowered her to the bed, dipping his mouth into the soft lips of her sex, tasting her hot wetness, laving the hidden centre of excitement, a sweetly intimate fondling that arched her body in wild and wanton invitation.

She writhed to the rhythm of his stroking, cried out in frantic pleading, snatched at his hair, fingers scrabbling, curling, tugging, and he exulted in her need for him, pushing it to the edge of shattering before he lifted himself over her.

Instantly her legs locked around him, her hips rocking, urging him forward. Her hands grabbed and

plucked at his shoulders, fingernails digging in, dragging. Her hair spilled over the bedcover in a tumultuous tangle and her eyes blazed at him with the
animal ferocity of a leopard about to bring down its
prey and devour it.

The long-suppressed violence of his own desire
burst into action. He seized her hands and slammed
them down above her head, determined on being the
possessor, not the possessed. He surged into the slick
passage to her innermost being and dropped his head
to plunder her mouth in a passionate drive to complete his invasion, to glory in his dominant power to
take as he wished.

Yet she met him with such a feverish fusion of
heat, he lost any sense of separate goals, separate
identities, separate lives with separate needs. They
were immersed in each other, wildly hungering for
every fantastic nuance of being joined. Their mouths
clung, feeding on the explosion of sensations that
savaged any possible denial of togetherness. Her
breasts pressed into his chest, their hardened nipples
rubbing his taut muscles with tantalising sweeps.

He automatically released her hands, craving every
possible touch, uncaring what she did or how she did
it, wanting an absolute twining. They crashed onto
his back, pushing and pulling, egging him into a fast
series of thrusts that she rolled around in an ecstacy
of revelling in the hard heated fullness of him, loving
every powerful stroke, arching herself to receive the
utmost penetration, clamping around him, moaning
with the intense satisfaction of it.

It goaded him into pleasuring her as long as he

could, exulting in her response, feeling like a mountaineer scaling the highest heights and she was drawing him there from peak to peak. His own screaming need demanded a lift in tempo and the last crescendo was his, raising them both to an exquisite cusp of delight before abandoning themselves to the sweet free-fall into blissful peace, wrapped in a togetherness that seeped into his soul and happily resided there.

The rest of the night was spent in a sensual daze of touching, kissing, merging. Zack no longer felt any need for some ascendancy over what they shared. He was awash with all the seductive sensations of intense intimacy, letting it flow as either he or she fancied.

At times he felt his heart swell with the joy of it, his mind float with the wonder of it, and all he ended up identifying was the undeniable fact that Catherine Trent was the source of all these incredible feelings. Whatever made her the woman she was appealed to him on unfathomable levels and he could not have enough of her.

She was his mate on every instinctive level. He knew it to the very marrow of his bones. Yet whether she would mesh with his working life was a question he shied from considering, not wanting this all too brief time with her spoiled by any conflict of interests. It was easier simply to savour the perfection of their deeply mutual desire while it lasted.

In the end, she slipped from the contented languor of satiation into sleep, and still he took immense pleasure in looking at her, stroking her long silky hair, basking in the warmth of her soft breathing, loving the feel of her cuddled close to him. He didn't ask why was it so. It just was. He didn't know if it would always be like this with her. He cared only about now.

There was no place for her in his immediate future which was already mapped out in his mind. When it was time to go he didn't wake her, didn't want to talk, didn't want to say goodbye. Very carefully he slid his body out of contact with hers, watching her settle comfortably without him, though she heaved a sigh that seemed to waft around his heart, silently pleading for him to fill the emptiness again.

For several moments he stood by the bed, torn between the need to go and the desire to stay with her. But there was no choice. He had commitments to fulfil. Catherine knew that. They were here because she hadn't wanted to wake alone in a hotel room—here in the place she called home…with her goldfish.

This last thought brought a smile and eased him out of her bedroom. His clothes were still where he'd left them in the living room. Hers were, too. He nodded to the fish, mentally greeting them—*Hi, Rhett! Hi, Scarlet!*—and grinned as they darted around the bowl to stare at him, their mouths working very energetically as though in a burst of fish chatter that undoubtedly had meaning if only he was a telepath on their wavelength.

Good company, Catherine had said, and he wondered if she made up conversations with them. Happy fish in their Feng Shui bowl. Happiness and harmony…it was what he'd felt with Catherine Trent these past few hours, once his conflict over her power to drive him beyond control had ceased to matter.

As he picked up his clothes and dressed, he pondered the quandary she represented. She did have power over him, an addictive power that made him wary of establishing her in his life. A relationship meant constant ties, limitations to his freedom to be wherever he had to be to fulfil his contractual obligations. Would she drop everything to come with him, be with him?

Unlikely.

It was too much to ask anyway. Women had the right to their own lives, their own careers, and he'd seen what long separations did to relationships in the movie world. Better to leave Catherine to her own work and friends and family.

He finished dressing and looked wryly at Rhett and Scarlet. Catherine couldn't pack goldfish in a suitcase. This was her home and Zack knew he didn't belong here.

He turned to go.

On the floor in front of the armchair lay the dark red rose he'd taken from her hair. He remembered having tucked it into his breast pocket. It must have tipped out when he'd tossed the coat on the chair. He bent and picked it up, meaning to set it on the table by the fishbowl.

It was an artificial rose, perfect, reminding him of many things about Catherine and how he'd felt with her. He twirled it around in his fingers, telling himself it was stupid to keep such a memento. Yet he still held *her* rose as he walked to the door, released the safety chain and let himself out.

He had no idea what he'd do with it.

He just wanted it.

CHAPTER NINE

CATHERINE saw the sparkling excitement in her sister's vivid blue eyes and knew what she was going to say even as Livvy leaned over the table to deliver her news in a confidential whisper.

'I'm pregnant.'

So am I.

The words almost spilled out, the desire to share welling up in a rush. Catherine only just clamped down on them, realising the revelation would totally goggle her sister's happy eyes and switch the focus of this get-together onto her, which would be grossly unfair. This was Livvy's moment in the sun and she certainly didn't deserve to have any uneasy shadows falling over it.

Catherine stretched her treacherous mouth into a delighted grin. 'Congratulations! I'm very happy for you and Pete.'

Livvy sat back, clapping her hands in sheer joy as she crowed, 'And just two months after our wedding!'

They'd be having babies together, Catherine thought in black irony. The difference was Livvy had done everything right—married the man she loved, a man who wanted children with her—while she...

'I thought it might take ages since I've been on the pill for so long,' Livvy rushed on.

105

It took only one night.

Her sister's eyes twinkled wickedly. 'I think Pete must be very potent. Besides which, we've certainly been giving it every chance.'

And she had told Zack it was safe.

'Well, good for you,' Catherine said with as much warmth as she could muster.

'I couldn't wait to tell you,' Livvy bubbled. 'I only found out this morning. So that's why I rang you at work and insisted you meet me for this afternoon tea. You see? It *is* important family business.'

'Very important,' Catherine echoed, and she'd worked through her lunch hour to fit in with Livvy's cavalier command to take time off in order to drive from Botany to Circular Quay and meet her at the Intercontinental Hotel for this private get-together. Her boss wasn't keen on employees skipping out early and Catherine needed her boss to be onside when she was finally forced to confess to single motherhood.

'Pete will be joining us here for drinks after he's finished work. He's just as excited as I am. But I wanted to tell you first.'

'What about Mum and Dad?'

Who were bound to be disappointed in her for getting herself into this situation. Much less stress to stay silent as long as she could.

'We're dropping over to their place tonight, after Pete and I have a celebratory dinner.'

'Better not drink too much then.'

'Only a glass or two of champagne. Ah…' Livvy smiled up at the waiter who had arrived at their table to serve them. 'Our cappuccinos. I ordered for you, Catherine, since you were late arriving.'

And she always had a cappuccino…except she'd gone off coffee, preferring a sweet cup of tea which seemed to settle the queaziness she felt most mornings. Still, at this time of day one cappuccino should be manageable. Unfortunately Livvy had also ordered cream cakes and rich pastries that curdled Catherine's stomach just looking at them. Cucumber sandwiches would have been infinitely preferable.

They did serve elegant afternoon teas here in The Cortile, a huge two-storeyed area that had once been part of the old treasury building, now incorporated in this very classy hotel. The colonnaded walkways running around it gave it a leisurely atmosphere, as did the cane armchairs in which they sat, and the grand piano being played by an excellent pianist, providing pleasant background music. It should have been very relaxing and would have been if Catherine didn't have to guard her tongue.

'No morning sickness yet?' she asked once the waiter had gone.

Livvy laughed and shook her head. 'I guess that's in front of me. I'll have to buy some books and read up on all the dos and don'ts.' She gave Catherine an arch look. 'Now if you were a proper older sister, you'd be able to advise me on all this. Still no man on your horizon?'

Pain stabbed her heart. There'd been no contact from Zack since the night of the wedding. He hadn't even woken her to say goodbye.

Gone with the wind…

She gave her sister a droll look of exasperation to cover up the wretched emptiness in her soul. 'You asked me here to talk happy talk so let's concentrate on you and your baby. Do you fancy a son or a daughter?'

'One of each would be lovely.'

'Twins?'

Livvy laughed. 'I hope not. Just one at a time but in any order. Boy or girl…it doesn't matter.'

Such blissful carefree plans.

A mountainous wave of envy hit Catherine and she struggled to fight through it as her younger sister rattled on about her ideal family. It wasn't Livvy's fault that her own life was in such a mess. She seemed to get herself embroiled in one bad choice after another; holding on to Stuart Carstairs when he wasn't worth holding on to, and now Zack…had she no *sense* of when to let go? Did fantasy have a bigger grip on her than reality?

The morning after Zack had left, she had lain in the bed he had shared, overwhelmingly aware of the empty place beside her, feeling bereft and miserably alone, telling herself she should get up and go to a pharmacy, purchase the pill that would keep her *safe*. It was the sensible thing to do.

Except she'd turned thirty-two this past year, and she couldn't imagine falling in love with another man or accepting second best just to get married and have a family. If she was ever to have a child, she *wanted* Zack Freeman to be the father.

She hadn't actually decided to get pregnant by him, and there'd been no certainty whatsoever about having conceived—women of her age often took months of trying before falling pregnant. She'd simply kept dallying with the idea that it might have happened—could happen—if she did nothing.

None of this had been really *real* to her then. More a romantic fantasy. And the more she'd thought about it, the less inclined she'd been to wilfully take away the possibility that a new life had been created in the heat of her night with Zack—a life she would love and cherish—a part of him she would always have.

She'd left the decision to Fate.

If it was meant to be, it was meant to be.

Not for one moment had she thought the consequences through or considered the practicalities of her situation if she was faced with being a single mother. Reality had only begun to bite when the pregnancy test showed positive. In the past few weeks, more and more frightening realities had been creeping up on her and she didn't know how to handle any of them.

Here was Livvy, chatting on about how she intended to keep working until she was six months into her pregnancy, then put in her resignation because she wanted to be a full-time mother, especially since she and Pete planned to have their babies in reasonably close succession. No worries about ready support for her family dream. Pete was a dependable bread-winner and dying to take on the fatherhood role.

Whereas Zack...

Her stomach cramped. If she dared to contact him

and confess her pregnancy, he'd probably hate her for it, believing she had deliberately deceived him, trapped him into fatherhood. Her mind shied from even considering taking such a step.

Quite clearly Zack had not wanted to risk having a child. She couldn't imagine he'd want a lifelong responsibility loaded onto his shoulders when he hadn't agreed to it. So it was impossible to ask for any child support from him. She had to go it alone.

And she would. Because now that the pregnancy was real, she fiercely wanted this baby, regardless of the difficulties and hardships ahead of her. The need for it was as deeply primitive as the feelings Zack had stirred in her.

More so.

Zack wasn't hers to keep but their child was. If nothing else, she'd have this, and already her love for the life she now carried burned in her heart like a beacon that she knew would shine over any dark days she experienced.

It wasn't the joy Livvy was feeling.

It was a passion.

Maybe that was the difference between their two natures.

Livvy was a straight-line kind of person while she was driven by highs and lows. Her sister was never going to understand any of the choices she'd made, especially those relating to Zack. It was definitely best to keep it all to herself until she couldn't any longer.

'Catherine, you haven't eaten anything and your coffee must be cold by now,' Livvy pointed out.

'It's all too rich for me, Livvy,' she excused. 'I'm sure Pete will help you out with it when he comes.' She quickly picked up her cup... 'Still warm.' ...and sipped before smiling to assure her sister all was well.

'Don't tell me you're dieting.' It was a castigating comment.

'No. But I did have a late lunch,' Catherine lied, hating the necessity to lie, yet needing to excuse her lack of appetite so her sister wouldn't go on and on about it. 'I just don't feel like eating anymore. Sorry...'

Livvy shrugged and helped herself to a second pastry. 'I feel hungry all the time. Must be my hormones getting out of balance or something.'

Again her sister rattled on, leaving Catherine to wonder how many lies she would end up telling. Deceit did not sit comfortably with her. Better to avoid meetings like this until she was ready to confront everyone with the truth.

It was a relief when Pete arrived, lifting the onus of a one-on-one conversation with Livvy. Though again Catherine found herself wracked with envy at the love so openly expressed between her sister and brother-in-law in their greeting and manner to each other.

Worse was their mutual exhilaration in having a baby on the way. Livvy preened as Pete fussed over her, adoring the mother of his child, only too eager to watch over her every comfort and carry out her every pleasure.

So it should be, Catherine savagely told herself,

and if that was not her lot it was because of the choices she'd made and it was now up to her to get used to not having the whole rosy package. Glasses of champagne were ordered and brought to their table. She forced herself to make appropriate toasts, to smile and laugh in all the right places, and was doing fine until Pete brought up Zack's name.

'Hey! Did you hear the news about Zack?' he tossed out, grinning from ear to ear.

She shook her head, not trusting herself to speak in a tone of mild interest.

'He won the BAFTA award for Special Visual Effects in London last night. It was in the newspaper this morning. He's really scooping the pool this year. The film he worked on scored Best Picture Drama in the Golden Globes. Only the Academy Award to go.'

'He's bound to win it,' Livvy chimed in. 'You know, Pete, given the big rush of what's happening for him, it was really good of Zack to drop everything and come to our wedding.'

'Sure was,' he agreed.

Catherine loosened her throat enough to ask, 'Have you heard from him since then?'

'No. Don't expect to until he lands back home,' came the matter-of-fact reply.

'I thought…as old friends…'

'We'll chew over it all when we meet up again.' Pete grinned. 'It's only women who can't wait to share everything over the phone.'

Livvy laughed and playfully punched him on the arm. 'You're not to go ga-ga over the phone bill again.'

'It was only the shock of it, sweetheart. I'll be expecting it next time and won't even blink. Promise.'

'So, are you expecting Zack back in Australia soon?' Catherine pressed, unable to leave the subject alone, craving some personal news of him or a reason to hope…

Pete shrugged. 'The way things are lining up for him, it would only be a flying visit when and if he comes. Like for the wedding. In and out.'

He'd been in and out her life twice. No promises for a third time, yet with Pete now married to her sister, another connection might happen. If it was months from now and he visited Pete, he could well find out his old friend's sister-in-law was pregnant. A year on and he could hear she'd had a child. Would he put two and two together? And then what?

If he ignored the news, then there was no hope of any future with him. Yet if he came to her… Catherine's heart began to quiver at that possibility. His child…would he feel he had to offer financial support? Take up visiting rights? The future was suddenly a minefield that could explode in her face if Zack took a terrible negative attitude towards her for what she'd done.

'Catherine…'

Livvy was eyeing her with concern, a slight frown drawing her brows together. It jolted Catherine into smoothing out her own expression, hiding any stress she might have inadvertantly shown.

'Sorry…wool-gathering. Did I miss something?' she asked brightly.

'No.' Livvy grimaced. 'You just looked a bit lonely and lost. It made me think…'

'Livvy, I'm tired. It was a hard day at work and I think the champagne's gone to my head. If you and Pete don't mind, I'll head off home now and leave you to celebrate together.' She started to rise from her chair.

'No…wait! I need to say this.' Determined purpose in her sister's voice.

Stifling a frustrated sigh, Catherine sank onto the cushioned seat again, hoping not to be held up much longer. Her nerves were frayed from keeping up a happy facade. 'What's so pressing?' she asked, trying for a note of indulgence.

'Maybe I did wrong by you last year,' came the worried reply.

Catherine looked blankly at her, desperately hiding her inner churning. If Livvy brought up the blind date with Zack…

'I truly believed Stuart Carstairs was bad for you, but that was your business and I shouldn't have interfered, telling you stuff you didn't want to hear.'

Catherine held her breath, not knowing where this was leading.

'I guess everyone's different,' Livvy mused. 'Maybe we don't get to pick whom we love. They just complement something in us…' She sighed. 'Anyhow, I just want to say if there's any chance of you getting back with Stuart, don't let my opinion stop you. I had no right to…'

'Stuart?' The name burst from Catherine in almost

hysterical relief. 'There's no way in the world I'd ever want to get back with Stuart Carstairs.'

'No?'

'No!'

'Then why haven't you...? I mean, you've shown no interest in anyone else and I thought... Who am I to judge what suits you best?'

Catherine summoned up a rueful smile. 'Not Stuart, I promise you. Stop worrying about me, Livvy. I'll make my own way.' She pushed onto her feet again, shaking her head fondly at the newly wed couple. 'Be happy for you. I am.'

This time she made good her escape.

She collected her car from the opera house car park and with the evening peak-hour traffic well and truly over, it was a hassle-free drive home to Randwick. It felt good to close her apartment door and shut the rest of the world out.

She walked across the living room to the goldfish bowl and smiled at Rhett and Scarlet who were responding eagerly to her presence. She didn't have to hide anything from them. They gave her pleasure and made no demands...except for food. It cost her very little to supply that.

A baby would cost a great deal more, on many levels. But whatever the price she would pay it...somehow. She would never, never ask Zack for anything. She'd taken the gift of a child from him. He owed her nothing. But the child was not all hers. The big question was...how would he react to it?

The telephone rang, drawing her over to the kitchen counter. Any distraction from her thoughts was welcome. She didn't speculate on who might be calling. She simply picked up the receiver and gave her name. There was a moment of silence then her name was repeated at the other end of the line.

'Catherine…'

The deep timbre of the voice was instantly recognisable, stopping her heart dead and sending prickles down her spine.

'…it's Zack Freeman.'

The confirmation did nothing to loosen her tongue which was stuck to the roof of her mouth. The shock of hearing from him held her utterly frozen.

'I was wondering if you could get a goldfish-sitter?'

The crazy question jolted her into croaking, 'What?'

'Someone to look after Rhett and Scarlet if you flew to L.A. for a week.'

'L.A.?' She knew she was sounding stupid but couldn't snap herself out of the stunned daze.

'I would like very much if you'd partner me to the Academy Awards ceremony.'

Partner him!

'When?' The question tripped off her tongue.

'It would mean flying from Sydney on Thursday, twenty-first of March. I'll book the flight and you can pick up the E-ticket at the Qantas desk. You'll be met at LAX airport by a chauffeur and transported to the Regent Beverley Wiltshire Hotel where I have a suite booked. All you have to do is arrange for time off work and find someone to look after the goldfish.'

The Regent Beverley Wiltshire—it was where they'd made the movie *Pretty Woman*. Was she to be Zack's *pretty woman* for his big Hollywood night?

'Catherine...will you come?'

She should have asked, *why her?* She should have asked dozens of questions. But a wild rush of blood to the head blotted out all of them.

'Yes,' she said.

'Good!' A wealth of satisfaction in his voice. 'Call Qantas tomorrow and they'll give you the details.'

'Zack...'

'Mmm?'

Nothing. She'd just wanted to say his name. 'I'll look forward to seeing you again,' she rushed out.

'I want you with me,' he simply stated.

And that was the end of it.

Or the beginning of something Catherine hadn't dared to count on.

It was the end of February now. Three, four weeks...hopefully she still wouldn't be showing her pregnancy. Whether she would tell him or not depended on...too much for her to even contemplate. She would just go. Whatever happened with Zack Freeman in Los Angeles would make the decision for her.

CHAPTER TEN

SHE was in bed and fast asleep, just as he'd left her three months ago, her glorious hair strewn across the pillows, the seductive curves of her lush body outlined by the sheet that covered her. Catherine…

He didn't say her name out loud but it rolled through his mind, filling it with pleasure, and all the doubts he'd nursed since calling her to come suddenly seemed totally irrelevant. She was here. And so was he. It felt good…right.

He moved swiftly to the bathroom, stripped off, got under the shower to freshen himself up after his flight from New York. It was just past two in the afternoon. The desk clerk had told him Catherine had arrived at seven this morning. She was probably trying to sleep off jetlag. It was a killer trip from Sydney to L.A.

As the water sprayed him in an invigorating burst, he shook his head over the London model who'd accompanied him to the BAFTA awards in the U.K. That woman hadn't known when to stop posing, courting every photographer in sight, puckering up to him as though they were an item, loving all the limelight, thinking she was irresistibly sexy despite her skinny figure and not having half the natural beauty Catherine had. He'd ended up hating her high screechy voice, hating her busy hands, hating her empty name-dropping chatter.

One night with that female egomaniac and the impulse to call the only woman he really wanted had been too strong to deny. The sweet relief of hearing her simple *yes*—no scatty questions, no fluffing around, no irritating drama, just *yes*—had put a smile on his face for days afterwards. He just hoped she hadn't been reading more into this invitation than there was. A week with her was all he could fit in.

But what a week it was going to be!

Catherine...his heart seemed to lift with the lovely rhythm of her name.

He was grinning as he towelled himself dry, the excitement of having her here, waiting for him in the next room, was like a fizzy cocktail running through his blood. He strode back to the bed. She hadn't stirred. The need to touch, to awaken an awareness of him would not wait. He lifted the sheet and slid his body down beside hers, propping himself up on one elbow, wanting to watch for the first flicker of her long eyelashes.

With featherlight fingertips he stroked the wavy hair away from her beautiful face. No make-up, he noticed. She needed none. The fine texture of her skin had no blemishes. Her lips, provocatively pouting in the relaxed state of sleep, were a rosy-brown colour. And he knew her eyes had their own unique attraction that no artifice could improve upon.

He trailed his fingers down the soft curve of her cheek, then slowly traced her full lower lip. Her tongue licked out, instinctively seeking to reduce the sensitivity he'd aroused. A slight crease appeared between her eyes, disturbance at a subconscious level. He was smiling when her lashes lifted, a delicate shift then a sharp flick open, as though consciousness had come in a rush.

'Hi!' he said, happy to greet her into his life again.

'Hi!' she responded with a sigh that spread into a slow sensual smile, and he saw the amber irises warm to gold, welcoming him back into her life.

'Good of you to come.'

'Good of you to ask me.'

He laughed, delighted by her laid-back attitude. 'An act of total selfishness, I'm afraid.'

'Oh, I don't know. Seems to me there's quite a bit of giving in it. The first-class seat on the flight was much appreciated. The limousine made me feel like a VIP. And this suite…' She gave him an anxious look. 'Please tell me it's some kind of perk related to your work.'

Her concern over the cost amused him. Other women he knew would take this for granted. 'Definitely a perk related to my work,' he assured her and it wasn't a complete lie. He was raking in millions from the film that was winning him awards—a percentage deal—and he could well afford this extravagance. Besides, the trappings of success was a power tool in Hollywood. He'd be inviting people here—business under the guise of parties.

'The penthouse suite,' she breathed in awe, rolling her eyes. 'I almost died when I was shown into it.'

'Is that why you're in bed?' he teased.

'I thought it had to be a dream and when I woke

up…' She reached up and touched his face. 'This *is* real, isn't it?'

'It feels real to me.'

He leaned over her, brushing her lips with his, tasting them with light flicks of his tongue. Her arms wound around his neck, inviting more *reality,* and Zack was only too ready to oblige, to reacquaint himself with the whole intensely desirable package of Catherine Trent.

His hands skimmed her beautiful body with possessive eagerness as he deepened the kiss, igniting the passion that flared so quickly between them. Her breasts felt firmer than he'd remembered, her waist less emphatically indented. Probably carrying a bit more weight, he thought, and dismissed the minor physical changes, loving the feel of her anyway, the lush curves, the softness of her flesh, the silky smoothness of her skin.

It was so easy to immerse himself in her. She was instantly receptive, as hot for him as he was for her, shuddering with pleasure as he sank into her creamy depths, locking her legs around him to hold on to the intensely satisfying intimacy, kissing with a hunger that matched his. They fitted in every sense, and he exulted in this perfect union, wallowed in it, drove it to as many heights as he could manage before totally expending himself.

'Now that was better than good,' he said when he'd recovered breath enough to speak.

'Mmm…' she purred against his chest.

'You're not to go back to sleep, Catherine.'

'Just making sure you're real,' she mumbled, gliding a hand towards his groin.

'Believe it.'

He grabbed her seductive hand and pressed it over his heart, which was still thumping at an accelerated rate, very much alive and kicking. However, the practical reality was she needed to get out and do some walking after her long flight or her body clock would never catch up to L.A. time. As much as he was tempted to stay right where he was all afternoon, it wouldn't be good for her. Besides which, he could completely sate himself with her tonight. He had a whole week of nights to do what he wanted.

'Have you been to L.A. before, Catherine?'

'No. First time.'

'And you haven't moved from this suite since you arrived?'

'I was waiting for you.'

'Well, now that I'm here, I'll take you out for some sight-seeing. We'll go to Santa Monica, walk down the mall, pick up something to eat, watch the buskers, look at the stalls. Maybe stroll along the beach.' He grinned as he recalled their first night together at Spoon Bay. She *was* like a siren from the sea, still calling to him. Even her pets were fish. He wound his other hand through her hair and lightly tugged, feeling the tide of desire rising again and knowing he should stave it off. 'Okay with you?'

She levered herself up to smile happy agreement at him. 'Now that you mention it, I am hungry.'

'Want something to eat first?'

'No. I'd rather go out.'

'Then let's get dressed and go.'

She rolled off the bed, picked up a bathrobe and had it on before he could really savour the sight of her naked. But then her arm lifted and hoisted the rippling mass of her hair out from under the collar and he enjoyed watching the long silky tresses float around her shoulders as she headed for the bathroom.

Catherine…. Catherine Trent.

He was fully aroused again. Control was almost a lost cause around her. Cold shower, he dictated, and no looking at her until she presented herself fully dressed. There were three bedrooms and four bathrooms in this suite. He took himself off to the bedroom where he'd directed his luggage be dropped and enforced the necessary discipline, although there was no suppressing the zing of anticipation in his blood.

There was no other woman like her.

Not in his experience.

Maybe spending a week with her would diminish the addictive power she had over him, show him she wasn't so attractive when it came to mixing in other areas of his life. What little time they'd spent together had been hyper-time, intensely sexual. He needed to slow that down, explore more of her, get some all-encompassing perspective that would let him feel free to move on from here.

That was a reasonable plan of action.

But as he forced himself to move out into the living room and plant himself in front of the floor-to-ceiling windows, which gave a magnificent view of the skyline, he could barely bring himself to wait until she appeared.

Catherine was on tenterhooks that Zack might follow her into the bathroom. Her heart was galloping at the prospect, frightened that he would notice the thickening of her waist, which she could do nothing to disguise. He hadn't commented on it in bed, but touch was different to sight and they'd both been caught up in the urgent need for intimate connection.

She beat all speed records under the shower and wrapped herself in the bathrobe again before returning to the bedroom to dress. It was a huge relief to find Zack gone from it, but aware that he was somewhere in the suite and could re-join her at any moment, she wasted no time in choosing what to wear. Walking, he'd said. Her black stretch jeans, matching battle jacket, the red top that skimmed rather than hugged her waist, and Reeboks on her feet—that should take her anywhere with reasonable style and comfort.

Once fully dressed, she relaxed enough to take some time over her hair and a bit of make-up. There was no telling whom they might meet and she wanted Zack to feel proud of her. Fortunately the sleep had done her good. She was no longer feeling like death warmed up, as she had after the long flight, and the queaziness had left her stomach.

But what about tomorrow morning? she asked herself as she brushed the tangles out of her hair. How long could she keep deceiving Zack about her pregnancy? More to the point, did she want to? Apart from subjecting herself to the panic that had just churned through her, she wasn't ever going to feel *right* while she kept this secret from him. She could feel herself tensing up at the thought of the next few hours in his company, pretending she had nothing to worry about.

But if she didn't pretend…this was her first real chance to relate to him on other levels beside the sexual, her first chance to see how much he was drawn to her as *a person,* not just as a *pretty woman* on hand in his penthouse suite. If she blurted out she was pregnant and told him he'd fathered the baby, she was frightened of precipitating a crisis that would shatter any hopeful harmony she might reach with him, given a few days together.

Satisfied with her appearance, Catherine took several deep breaths to calm her jumpy nerves, then walked out to the amazing living room, telling herself not to be overawed by all this spacious luxury. Only Zack's response to her counted, not the glamorous surroundings nor what they signalled about how big a success he was in his world. What lay in his heart…that was what she had to learn while she was here.

The suite was on the top floor of the Beverly Wing with a wrap-around balcony on three sides. Zack stood by one of the floor-to-ceiling windows, gazing out. He had an imperious look about him, the proud cast of his head, the tall, powerful physique, clothed in black jeans and leather jacket. Catherine wondered if he had more worlds to conquer in his mind, or would he feel satisfied with reaching the zenith of this one…an Academy Award…the Hollywood dream?

'Zack…' she called, wanting him to turn to her.

He snapped around, exuding an animal vitality that instantly said he would always have more places to go. There would never be resting on any laurels for Zack Freeman.

'Ready…' he said with relish, his eyes eating her up from head to toe with more than warm approval.

He closed the distance between them with a few quick strides. The magnetic energy targeting her held Catherine breathless and tingling and when Zack hooked her arm around his with purposeful possessiveness, her heart swelled with the wild hope that he wouldn't want to let her go. Not this time.

'I've called for a car. You'll like Santa Monica. It's fun,' he informed her.

And so it proved to be. A whole street was blocked to traffic, an open mall where the most amazingly colourful people strolled along, wearing way-out clothes and incredible hairdos. A jazz band was selling soul at one end of it. At the other was a string quartet offering classical music. There were buskers in between, offering other forms of entertainment, like the balloon blower who created plastic animals for the children. Restaurants with hugely varied cuisines extended out onto the pavements. Street stalls sold a fascinating array of fashion accessories.

A display of wonderful hats tempted Catherine into trying some on. Zack happily encouraged her, offering critical comment on how well or not each one suited her, enjoying the role of arbiter. A soft reversible hat caught her eye. It felt like velvet and it could be worn as mainly black with a turned up tiger-print rim or the other way around.

'Yes, that one!' Zack said emphatically when she modelled it for him.

'Why this one?' She liked it but didn't see it as extra special.

'Because it's you,' he declared without a moment's hesitation.

'Me?'

'Leopard, tiger…a powerful cat. Beautiful, graceful, lethal.'

She was stunned by this description. 'Is that how you see me?'

He cocked his head in teasing consideration. 'Lethal might be overstating it. Definitely dangerous.'

'A cat?' She looked her incredulity. 'Have I ever shown you claws?'

His smile was very wry. 'You keep digging into my mind, Catherine Trent.'

What about your heart?

She returned the smile. 'You do quite a bit of that to me, Zack Freeman.'

'Good! I'd hate to think you had all the power.'

She shook her head, never having thought she had any power, but his admission did indicate there was more than just physical lust on his side. He thought about her. But was it anywhere as much as she thought about him?

'We'll take this hat,' he said, turning to the salesman and whipping out a twenty dollar note while Catherine was still bemused by his responses.

'I'll pay for it,' she protested.

'It's done.' He grinned as he took her arm and led her on. 'You look great in it.'

'Thank you.' It was still on her head. She left it there. 'My goldfish wouldn't like me as a cat,' she dryly observed.

He laughed. 'They don't get to stroke you and hear you purr.'

The simmering look in his eyes sent a wave of heat through Catherine. The desire he stirred flared between them, choking off any further banter.

'Let's choose a place to eat,' Zack said gruffly, steering her towards the closest restaurant.

Neither of them attempted conversation until they were safely seated with a table between them. Catherine found herself fixating on Zack's hands as he perused a menu, thinking of how seductively his long sensual fingers teased and caressed and aroused. She had to tear her gaze off them and concentrate on ordering a meal. She was hungry, desperately hungry for many things beside food.

When Zack stroked her stomach, would their baby feel his touch as she did, deep in her womb? Would he love it if he knew it was there? Would he come to love her? She needed so much from this week with him.

The waiter came to take their orders. Catherine decided on what she hoped was a bland chicken dish, not wanting anything to upset her stomach tonight. Zack ordered steak and a bottle of wine, which she knew she wouldn't share. Maybe a glass of it wouldn't hurt, but she was glad water was served without her even asking for it.

After the waiter had gone, Zack sat back and eyed her with a rueful twinkle. 'I really want to race you back to the hotel. Why do you suppose you have this effect on me?'

It was another chance to probe his feelings and Catherine seized it. 'Livvy says…maybe we don't get to pick whom we love. They just complement something in us.'

'Love…' Zack frowned over the word, a dark rejection of it in his eyes as he tersely asked, 'You've discussed me with your sister?'

'No, I consider what we've had together very private,' she said slowly, the urge to hurt him as he'd just hurt her welling from the cramp in her heart. 'She was trying to explain away my attachment to another man. A guy she doesn't particularly like.'

The frown deepened over a savage glower. 'You're here with me, being unfaithful to some other guy?'

He certainly didn't like that idea but whether it was jealousy or contempt for such behaviour she wasn't quite sure. 'No. That relationship was over before I ever met you, Zack.' She gave him an ironic smile as she delivered the truth. 'In fact, there hasn't been anyone else since I met you. I haven't *wanted* anyone else.'

Her eyes blazed a challenge. She'd laid out his effect on her. Let him speak now. For several long nerve-racking moments he seemed to weigh what she'd said, then to her intense disappointment, the waiter arrived with the bottle of wine, breaking up the intimate flow between them.

After the wine had been poured and they were left alone again, Zack changed the subject, casually asking, 'So how are Pete and Livvy? Still blissful newlyweds?'

'Very blissful,' Catherine almost snapped, then bluntly stated, 'They're expecting a baby.'

His eyebrows rose in surprise. 'Straight off?'

'It's what they both want.'

'Well, good luck to them.' His mouth twitched into a whimsical little smile. 'Pete will make a very proud Dad.'

The highly sensitive question shot out before she could stop it. 'Do you ever think of having children yourself, Zack?'

He shrugged. 'One day.' He picked up his glass of wine and swirled it around, watching the movement of the liquid, not looking at her. *Deliberately* not looking at her?

Tell him, her mind screamed. *Cut through all this and lay it on the line.*

'Pete's father is a good dad,' Zack remarked musingly. 'He always let his children be. Pete will be like that, too.' His gaze snapped to hers, hard and searing. 'My father wanted to order my life as he saw fit. I had to fight against his edicts all through my teenage years. I wouldn't let him own me. No one owns me.'

Her heart sank.

Freedom was like a religion to him, the zeal for it in his eyes telling her he would never be tied down by anyone. Unless he chose it. And he'd been given no choice over her pregnancy.

The scream in her mind dropped to a wail of despair. She said nothing. She picked up her glass of wine and sipped it, barely stopping herself from grimacing over its sour taste.

'He died when I was twenty-one,' Zack went on. 'For me it was a release. For my mother, too, I think. No more conflict.'

If he'd witnessed a difficult marriage all through his childhood, what hope was there of him wanting marriage at all?

'I guess I'm lucky,' she muttered. 'My parents really do love each other and Livvy and I have always felt their warm caring for us. We're a very close-knit family.'

'Yet you live apart from them,' he pointed out.

'I think every adult has a right to their own space. That doesn't mean the connection isn't there to be touched whenever it's wanted or needed.'

'Yes.'

Satisfaction glinted in his eyes and Catherine realised she'd just described what he fancied with her— a connection when the desire for it occurred.

But that wasn't how it was with a baby…a child. She felt sick.

Their food arrived and she picked at it, feeling sicker and sicker. Her womb ached, as though it, too, was being drained of hope. Eventually she had to excuse herself and head for the ladies' room. Something was wrong, too wrong for her to ignore. Her hands were trembling as she locked herself in a

cubicle. A few fumbling moments later she understood what she'd been feeling and her heart was
gripped by a wrenching fear.

She was bleeding.

CHAPTER ELEVEN

ZACK put down his knife and fork, giving up on the half-eaten steak. He'd been forcing himself to eat it, any appetite he'd had completely killed by the guilt he felt at having *used* Catherine to satisfy himself. He hadn't promised her anything, hadn't led her to believe in a continuing relationship, but...telling him there hadn't been any other man...talking of *love*... even *children*.

It was obvious now that she'd come to L.A. hoping for something more from him than a protracted tumble in bed, and he'd just swept that mat out from under her feet with brutal efficiency. Which had hurt her. Hurt badly. The meal on her plate was barely touched. She'd looked sick when she'd left the table and she'd been gone now...what? Five, ten minutes? He hoped she wasn't crying.

His chest tightened at the thought of causing her to shed tears. Damn it! He'd meant to deliver a warning, not completely gut her. She'd been so... *accepting* of the situation on their previous two times together. He'd thought...no harm done. Just pleasure on both sides. But that clearly wasn't the case at all.

Not even for him, he thought with savage self-mockery. No other woman had got to him since Catherine. He'd tried to put her out of his mind, dating women who'd be considered prizes by most men, but they'd all left him cold in the end. He knew exactly what Catherine meant. Nothing else measured up to *their* experience. And the bottom line was, he didn't want to give it up.

So what to do now? Apologise? Explain his position? What if she came back to the table and ended it right here? Walked away from him without so much as a backward glance? How would he feel?

Zack didn't have time to analyse the impact such an action would have on him. Catherine *was* on her way back, a set determination on her face and not the slightest bit of warmth or pleasure in her eyes. She didn't move to sit on her chair. She remained standing by the table, a bleak decision in the eyes that met his with unwavering resolution.

Zack found himself rising to his feet, bracing himself for action, adrenalin shooting through his blood at the instinctive urge to fight. 'What is it?' he rapped out, forcing the issue, wanting to deal with it.

'I need your help, Zack.' A flat, bare statement.

'Whatever I can do,' he promised quickly, not having anticipated an appeal for help.

'I don't know anyone here except you. I don't know where to go or what to do. Please…you must help, no matter how you feel about it.'

Her voice cracked over the entreaty and despair welled into a film over her eyes. Alarmed by her intense distress, Zack automatically reached out and closed his hands reassuringly around her shoulders, which were held too stiffly. 'I'm here for you,' he strongly asserted. 'Tell me how I can help.'

'I'm pregnant. I'm bleeding. I think I'm having a miscarriage.'

Three body blows that took his breath away, blew his mind, and contracted every muscle in his body.

'I have to get to a hospital. I don't even know one in Los Angeles. And I'm frightened of…of passing out.'

He fought off the shock. She looked like death. He had to act and act fast.

'Sit down until I get the information we need,' he commanded, forcibly seating her on the chair she'd vacated. His mind zapped into overdrive as he whipped out his mobile telephone from the pocket of his leather jacket. The hotel would have the contacts. Money would buy the quickest and best treatment. He kept his brain clear to make the necessary moves. Time for questions later.

Once Zack took charge, everything passed in a blur to Catherine. While one part of her mind recognised and was intensely grateful for his efficient participation in getting her to emergency treatment, another part shut him out, focusing entirely on keeping still, keeping calm, willing her baby to hold on.

There were questions to be answered when she arrived at the hospital, distracting forms to be filled out. She hadn't thought to take out medical insurance for this trip. Zack stepped in and cut through the red tape, insisting he would take care of everything. Which didn't feel right but she didn't have the energy to argue. She needed all of it to concentrate on holding the fear at bay and doing whatever she could to keep her baby safe.

A doctor examined her. She hadn't lost the baby yet. It was still there. She was to rest quietly tonight and they'd run a scan on her tomorrow to check the situation. A nurse introduced herself and explained the hospital system, showed the button to press if she required attention, saw to all her immediate needs. Finally she was left alone to sleep the night away.

Except she wasn't alone. Zack was still with her in the private room he had arranged. He'd supervised everything, remaining on hand to facilitate whatever he could. He was sitting on a chair beside her bed, and now there was no more to be done, Catherine could no longer shut his presence out of her mind.

He hadn't asked her any questions.

She didn't want to answer any. No point. He'd made his position clear. Marriage and children were not on his agenda. What had been—a week of pleasure with her—had now lost all viability. To his credit, he had risen to her desperate appeal for help, despite the shock it must have been to him, and it was up to her now to cut him free of an involvement that was totally devoid of pleasure.

'Thank you, Zack,' she said quietly, forcing herself to look at him face to face. He deserved that acknowledgment for all he'd done, though it pained her to see the darkly clouded eyes of the man on whom she'd pinned so many futile hopes. 'Please don't feel you have to stay,' she went on. 'I'll manage on my own now.'

The cloud instantly lifted. The sharply penetrating

look he gave her pierced Catherine's soul. 'It's my child, isn't it,' he stated more than asked. No doubt in his mind.

There was no denying it, no evading it. He'd heard her tell the medical staff she was three months' pregnant. 'Yes,' she said flatly, then gathered breath enough to add, 'I lied to you. It wasn't safe. So it's not your fault, Zack. I'm the only one who's responsible for this child.'

That let him off the hook. He could go with a clear conscience. It hadn't been an accident. There'd been no failure of any contraceptive device. This outcome could be directly attributed to a choice she had made—a choice she'd been prepared to live by. Without him.

She half expected a tirade of accusation but it didn't come. Even so, the long drawn-out silence stretched her nerves.

'Did you *want* to fall pregnant, Catherine?'

His voice was carefully void of any criticism. Yet she read into the question the suggestion she'd planned to trap him into fatherhood and she couldn't bear him to think that of her.

'I just wanted *you* that night, Zack. I'd gone off the pill months previously. No need for it. When I told you it was safe, I meant to get a morning-after pill the next day.' She sighed, doubtful he could understand how she'd thought and felt afterwards.

'But you didn't,' he quietly prompted.

'No. You were gone without a word to me. Call it madness if you like, but I couldn't bring myself to do it.' She managed an ironic little smile. 'If a new life had been conceived by us, I felt it was meant to be. And I guess if I miscarry now, that's meant to be, too.'

Tears welled up. She quickly rolled her head across the pillow, turning her face away from him, swallowing hard to hold in the wave of grief. He would probably be relieved if she lost the baby, relieved to have no permanent tie on his plate. It was only she who wanted the child, loved knowing it was growing inside her, cherished the life she and Zack had made together.

'Please go…please…' she choked out, fiercely telling herself not to weep. It would knot up her muscles and she had to stay relaxed, think of the baby. She'd answered the critical questions, freed him of all responsibility.

She heard the scrape of his chair and the squeeze on her heart grew even tighter. He was leaving. A sense of utter desolation swept through her. A fool's dream…to think he might love her.

Then she felt warm fingers stroking down the hand lying closest to where he'd been sitting, strong fingers spreading hers apart, interlacing, gripping. 'I left you in the past, Catherine. I won't leave you alone tonight,' he said gruffly. 'You just rest now. I'll watch over you. Make sure nothing more goes wrong that I can help.'

She shut her eyes tight, but the tears spilled through her lashes and trickled down her cheeks. If he was angry with her, he wasn't showing it. Caring flowed from the heat of the hand holding hers and she was too weak to reject it. Caring might not be

love but somehow it eased the emptiness that
dragged at her, the fear of what she might be told
tomorrow.

He stroked her hair with his other hand—gentle,
soothing caresses. *Rest now,* he'd said, and his un-
critical acceptance of her situation helped. Even his
silent company helped. She felt no judgment in it, or
her mind was too stressed out to sense any judgment.
It was simply good to be assured she was not alone
in a strange hospital, in a foreign country. Zack was
here, looking after her.

She was fast asleep. The hand Zack still held had
slackened into limp passivity some time ago. He'd
been reluctant to let it go in case she stirred again
and panicked at the sense of being on her own.
Catherine was in L.A.—a huge distance away from
her family and friends—because he'd called her. She
hadn't contacted him about her pregnancy. It was his
call that had brought her here. He felt his responsibility for taking care of her very keenly.

Her breathing was slow and even. Assured she was
unlikely to awake for a while, Zack slowly slid his
hand from hers and stood up, needing to stretch his
stiff muscles, walk around the room a bit. A nurse
had dropped by to check on Catherine and switched
on a night-light when she saw the patient was settled.
Everything was dimly visible. He could walk without
bumping into furniture, and keep an eye on Catherine
for any slight disturbance.

His mind was hopelessly clogged with the idea of
her carrying his child—a tiny life inside her, which

was under threat of ending before it had the chance to grow into what it could be. A son. A daughter. *His* son or daughter. He was stunned at how possessive he was coming to feel about it now that the initial shock had worn off.

Shades of his father?

Wanting himself immortalised by having a child with his genes step into his shoes?

Zack fiercely rejected the reflection. He would never be like his father in that respect. It was wrong. But what he'd done to Catherine was wrong, too…taking all she'd give then leaving her *without a word.* That stark little statement had really stung him. It hadn't been an accusation, just the simple truth.

Like everything else she said.

Simple truths.

She was too direct and honest to try to trap him.

And the one lie she had told—the *safe* lie—the truth was he hadn't wanted that night stopped any more than she did. If she'd told him she had no contraception, would he have left her to buy a packet of condoms? He shook his head, not sure of the answer, recalling how he had pressed her to absolve him of such a necessity.

So he could walk away afterwards without any concern.

Oh, he'd done a truly excellent job of that.

Not a word to her…until two months later when he'd wanted her again.

He suspected his call had thrown her into one hell of a dilemma—whether to tell him or not. He hadn't given her much chance to do so over the telephone. And he certainly hadn't been encouraging down at Santa Monica. But for the threatened miscarriage…would she have told him at all?

Had she told anyone?

He stood at her bedside, scrutinising the face that looked so peaceful and innocent in sleep, hiding her secrets. What did he really know of her? Only that she got to him as no other woman ever had. Was that enough to commit himself to a lifetime partnership?

If this pregnancy ended in a miscarriage…did he want to let Catherine go?

Should the baby be saved…? A primitive possessiveness surged over any reasonable train of thought. No way was he going to walk out of the life of his child. He had to secure his rights as a father. If that meant marriage…well, he wasn't averse to the idea of having Catherine as his wife. At least the sex was great, though sex wasn't everything in a marriage. Adjustments would have to be made. Whatever arrangement they came to, he *would* take care of her…take care of both her and their child, make sure they wanted for nothing.

His course was clear, provided there was no miscarriage.

If the baby was lost…

His mind instinctively shied from even considering that outcome. Tomorrow, after the scan…he would think about it then…if he had to.

CHAPTER TWELVE

'THERE is no heartbeat.'

No heartbeat...

Catherine felt her own heart stop. She closed her eyes. The doctor's words kept on ringing in her mind—a death knell for her baby.

'Are you sure?' Zack demanded harshly. 'Can you check again?'

'I have been trying to find it for some time, Mr. Freeman. There's nothing. I'm sorry, but there's no point in holding out any hope. Given the amount of bleeding, it was highly unlikely that...'

'All right!' Zack snapped.

Silence. Catherine floated in a sea of nothingness. No hope. No baby to love. Her heart had started beating again, sluggishly reluctant to bother with this life. She wanted to die, too.

'Miss Trent...'

The sympathetic tone in the doctor's voice forced her to open her eyelids and acknowledge him. Not his fault that her baby was dead. Fate had decided she couldn't have it after all.

'It's best you have a curette now.'

'Yes,' she agreed. Time to turn over another page. She wasn't pregnant with a new life anymore.

Zack came off his chair, clearly hating this outcome, wanting to fight it, helplessly conflicted be-

cause he couldn't. 'Was it the flight?' he demanded.
'I called Catherine to come here. It's a long flight
from Sydney to L.A. The cabin pressure…'

'No. It should not cause a miscarriage,' the doctor
assured him.

Zack looked wildly distraught. 'We had sex. Just
hours before the bleeding started.'

The doctor sighed. 'Pregnancy does not preclude
sex, Mr. Freeman. If everything was normal…'

'What do you mean…*normal?*'

It occurred to Catherine that Zack felt he had
caused this and was racked with guilt over it.
Through the haze of her own deep inner grief, she
wondered why he cared so much. Had he decided he
wanted their child? He'd stayed with her all night,
all morning. She hadn't asked why, needing the comfort of some familiar presence and he'd provided it,
but if he'd been silently making a claim on their
child…

Gone now.

Beyond claiming.

No claim on Zack, either.

All gone.

'I mean a miscarriage occurs when something is
wrong,' the doctor explained. 'That's not to say Miss
Trent won't carry a pregnancy to full term another
time around, just that this one wasn't right. Nature
has its own way of correcting its mistakes.'

A mistake…

She shouldn't have let it happen, shouldn't have
pinned so much on it…planning a life around a child
she loved, a child she'd stolen from Zack without his

knowledge. That was wrong from the start. Not like Livvy and Pete. They had done it right.

Zack kept on talking, expending a crackling energy that felt wrong, too. Futile. Out of place. It was finished, nothing left to argue over.

'Please…' It was an anguished croak. She looked hard at the doctor, appealing for finality. '…let's get on with it. Do what has to be done.'

Zack didn't know what to do. He couldn't help Catherine through this last grim procedure. It was out of his hands. The medical staff had wheeled her away. But he couldn't bring himself to leave the hospital.

It was Friday. He should be contacting people or letting them contact him. He took out his mobile phone. He'd switched the power off last night. His finger hovered over the button.

No.

Impossible to even think of business when Catherine…no life in her eyes…as dead as the child that might have been.

She'd wanted it.

And God help him, so had he.

Gut-wrenching disappointment that it wasn't to be.

He wandered around the hospital, had coffee in the canteen, found a place to shave and freshen up. They'd already brought Catherine back to her room when he returned to it. She was sleeping. Probably didn't want to wake up. Merciful oblivion. He could do with some of that himself. But he knew what had happened wasn't going to go away. It was a scar on his soul…the lost child.

Zack wasn't used to emotional turmoil. He made a plan and stuck to it, refining it as opportunities presented themselves, though always retaining his vision of where he wanted to go. The end goal.

Where Catherine Trent was concerned, his vision was very muddy. She kept knocking him off his straight-line thinking. The timing for a serious relationship was wrong, yet he had the sinking feeling that if he let her go now, he'd never get her back. And the wanting wasn't even sexual anymore.

He couldn't dismiss it on that basis. There was more to it. Difficult to define. Maybe it was the miscarriage messing him up, but it felt as though she was attached to some integral part of him and without her, there would be a very hollow place in his life that no one else would ever fill.

He picked up her hand, weighing it in his own— a light delicate hand, fine-boned slender fingers, neatly shaped nails. They weren't claws. He doubted she would have scratched him for child maintenance, let alone anything else. It was a soft, giving hand. She'd given him everything he'd wanted from her and made no demands on him. How many women were like that?

A memory from their first night together sprang into his mind—the blind date—Catherine saying she'd agreed to it to please her sister, him saying…

Then you have a giving nature. That's a trap in itself, Catherine.

Her answer— *Oh, the giving only goes so far.*

Him, curious— *What would you take, given the chance?*

That's a big question.

And you don't intend to answer it yet?

That would spoil the game.

He'd laughed, thinking it was a flirtatious game, but none of it had been a game to her. She'd given twice. Unreservedly. And then she'd taken what she'd wanted—the chance of having a child from their union. And now she was left with nothing. Unless he could supply her with something she considered worth having.

Her fingers fluttered, subconsciously protesting their imprisonment. She was waking up. His heart kicked, speeding up his pulse rate, shooting much-needed oxygen to his overworked brain. He had to establish some kind of positive rapport with Catherine. Whatever it was they had together...he didn't want it to end here.

A frown creased her brow. She moaned and turned on her side away from him, drawing her legs up to scrunch herself into a protective ball. She hadn't opened her eyes, wasn't aware of his presence, and Zack suddenly felt like a voyeur to deeply private grief. Yet it might also be physical pain.

'Catherine,' he called urgently. 'Should I get a nurse or doctor?'

Her head whipped around on the pillow. Startled eyes. Puzzlement. 'You're still here?'

'Are you okay?'

She sighed and carefully shifted her body to face

him. 'I'll cope with it, Zack. You don't have to stay and nursemaid me.'

'I brought you to L.A., Catherine.'

'I made the choice. I don't hold you to blame for anything. And you've been more than generous, fixing all this for me. I'm sorry…'

'Don't apologise. I'm the one who should be apologising.'

She looked bewildered. 'What for?'

'Because I…' He gestured an appeal for some stay of judgment as he struggled for words to explain his feelings. 'Because I did this to you,' he finally got out.

'No, Zack. I did this to myself,' she said with firm clarity, then grimaced. 'Though not the miscarriage.'

Her face started to crumple and she fought for composure. Zack stood up and paced around the room, wanting to take her in his arms and comfort her, yet sensing such a move would be unwelcome. Possibly hurtful. He wanted to reach out to her but he didn't know how to. Never in his whole life had he felt so…inadequate, mentally floundering, and deeply frustrated by his inability to resolve what should be done with Catherine.

'I want to go home, Zack.'

The flat statement pulled him up at the end of her bed. He stared at her—this woman who tugged so strongly on him. He didn't see her beauty, her desirability. He saw the distance yawning between them, the determination in her eyes to break away from him.

'I'm to stay here overnight,' she ran on matter-of-factly. 'But after the doctor sees me in the morning…if there's no problem…I'll contact Qantas and…'

'No. It's too soon. You should give yourself more time to recover. I'll take you back to the hotel and look after you, Catherine. At least stay the full week,' he argued forcefully.

Her head rolled in a pained negative. 'You only wanted me with you for the sex, Zack.' Her eyes mocked anything else he might say. 'I can't deliver,' she said flatly. 'And my staying would only make us both miserable, continually reminding us…'

She swallowed hard and closed her eyes.

'I don't want to let you go like this,' he burst out.

'Please…' Her throat moved convulsively. '…it would be…a kindness.'

Kindness… Zack was completely torn by that word. It forced him to examine his behaviour towards her. Everything on his terms. Certainly he'd given her choices but there'd been no consideration for her feelings behind them. No kindness.

You were gone without a word to me.

He couldn't justify that. It was an indictment of how totally selfish he had been. All he'd ever thought about was what he wanted.

It was her right to have the last word now.

'Leave it to me,' he said with grim decisiveness. 'I'll call Qantas and line up a return flight for you. Ensure you'll get a seat.'

She visibly sagged with relief. 'Thank you.' Her gaze dropped from his. Her fingers plucked at the bedcover. 'I'm sorry about…I know the Academy Awards is a big night for you…'

'Don't worry about it. Right now I couldn't care less.' It was the truth.

'I didn't mean to…'

'Catherine, please…'

The anguish in his voice flicked her gaze back to his, a pained wondering in her eyes. 'You've been so good about all this, Zack. I promise I'll pay you back. The hospital costs and…'

'Stop!' He glared at her, fury boiling up at being so pointedly counted out of what should have been shared. 'It was my child, too. I would have paid anything to save it. At least grant me that right, Catherine.'

'I'm sorry.' Tears filmed her eyes. 'I didn't think…didn't know…'

'That I would care?' he cut in savagely.

She nodded, biting her lips.

The anger that had so quickly surged, drowned just as quickly in the swimming vulnerability of her eyes. How could he rail at her judgment of him? He'd given her no reason to believe he would care. He sucked in a deep breath in an attempt to calm himself.

'Responsibility for the medical expenses is all mine,' he growled. 'No argument. And I'll get you on a flight home as soon as it's feasible. Okay?'

'Thank you.' It was a husky little whisper. Her head was bent, lashes lowered, hiding her eyes.

There was no triumph for him in her submission to his will. She looked defeated. He felt defeated. It might be a kindness to let her go, but every muscle in his body ached to fight her decision. The whole room seemed to pulse with the tension of things unsaid on both sides. Which couldn't be good for her after all she'd been through.

'Well, now that's settled, I'll leave you to rest,' he said bruskly. 'Don't worry about anything. I'll let you know what I've organised when it's done. Okay?'

'Yes.' She raised eyes that looked deathly weary. 'I would have told you about our child in the end, Zack. Then it would have been your choice, whether you wanted to be a father or not. It's probably for the best…that you don't have to make that choice now. No ties…' Her attempt at a smile wobbled. 'That's good for you, isn't it?'

It was like a punch to the heart—all the more lethal because it was what he'd told himself countless times since he'd first met Catherine. Ties held you down. Ties prevented you from going after opportunities that closed too quickly if you weren't on the spot, all primed to take them up. Yet faced with that argument from her, he wanted to disown it. Vehemently.

'You can put all this behind you and move on,' she pressed. 'It's easier than…' She took a deep breath and released it in a shuddering sigh. 'You know what I mean. You can have my things sent here from the hotel. I'll get to the airport by myself. There's no need…'

'You *want* me to say goodbye now?'

Her gaze wavered from his. 'You probably should be meeting with other people...'

'Don't make my decisions for me, Catherine. If you'd prefer not to see me anymore, say so. Otherwise I'll be back to visit you tonight. And tomorrow. If you *must* go home, I intend to make sure you're fit enough to fly out before you do and I'll accompany you to the airport and see you into the care of the flight attendants.'

She stared at him, not understanding his motivation. Which was fair enough, because he didn't understand it himself. All he knew—and knew with absolute certainty—was he needed time to sort this inner turmoil through before any final line was drawn. Since she didn't rush to reject his plan, Zack pressed it as a confirmed fact.

'I'll be back,' he stated decisively and left the room before she could make some belated protest.

Catherine stared at the closed door. She had invited Zack to close it, expected him to close it, but he was coming back to open it again. Or so he said.

But why would he?

Her mind jammed with jumbled-up emotions.

They hurt.

Everything hurt.

She curled herself up under the bedcover, buried her face in the pillow and wept for all her lost dreams.

CHAPTER THIRTEEN

THEY sat in the first-class lounge at LAX, waiting for the Qantas flight to Sydney to be called. Catherine glanced at Zack who'd fallen silent, withdrawing into himself, a tense brooding look on his face. She had no idea what he was thinking, or what purpose had been served for him in keeping her company until she left for home. All she knew was the departure time was very close now and the past hour with him had stretched her nerves to breaking point.

It had only ever been sex for him and that was patently over. Ever since she'd made the decision to get out of his life as fast as possible, he'd made no reference to the intimacy they'd shared, gave no indication that he might want it resumed at a later date. No doubt he knew, as she did, it couldn't ever be the same as before. So why had he bothered with the courtesy of treating her like a valued visitor?

Last night and most of today he had been questioning her about her life and her job, whether she considered her work a career worth pursuing or simply the means to a good income, what she liked doing, what she disliked. It was as though he was finally assessing her as a fully rounded person, not just seeing her as a sexually desirable woman—a strange bittersweet experience for Catherine, coming too late

152

to mean he might want a serious relationship with her.

Most likely their conversations had been about keeping her mind—and his—off the pregnancy that had been so traumatically terminated. She had to concede they had helped in that regard, more so when he talked about his work and the kind of things he planned to try in the future—animated films he wanted his own company to produce. That had given her a glimpse of the visions he nursed, what drove him to keep moving on.

Zack Freeman was never going to stand still. It was amazing that he'd actually taken these few days out to be with her, holding her hand through the worst of it. Maybe he had felt some obligation towards her, dragged into it because she'd revealed so much of her own feelings in getting pregnant to him. Guilt…kindness…giving her time he hadn't given before. He was probably champing at the bit now, thinking of what he'd do the moment she was gone.

'Boarding call for Qantas flight QF12 to Sydney, Australia. Will passengers please proceed to gate one-two-two?'

Catherine picked up her bag and rose quickly from the armchair, relieved that the strain of this last togetherness with Zack was over. He was slower to react to the announcement, unfolding himself from his chair rather than springing up. It focused her attention on his height and the powerful physique that made him so *male,* and everything inside her quivered at this last farewell.

This was the man she had chosen to father her child.

This was the man she had recklessly loved.

Forcing herself to face the inevitable end, she thrust out a hand and lifted her gaze to his. 'Goodbye…'

'No!'

The word exploded from him. Her hand was caught in both of his, the doubly possessive grip preventing her from pulling it free. His dark eyes probed hers with searing intensity, making her heart skitter even more painfully at this sudden impasse.

'I don't want you to leave, Catherine.'

Sheer anguish voiced her reply. 'Zack, it won't work…'

'I don't mean the week I'd planned to spend with you,' he rapped out dismissively. 'This is something else.'

'I have to go,' she cried in panic, not believing that anything he suggested could be anything but painful in these circumstances. 'The flight has been called.'

'We could fly to Las Vegas. Get married.'

She stared incredulously at the blazing conviction in his eyes. 'Get…*married?*' Had she heard right?

'Yes. There's nothing to stop us, is there? It won't be the end of the world if you resigned from your job, stayed with me.'

Her job meant nothing.

Staying with him meant everything.

Yet to ask her to marry him now…

All those questions yesterday and today…had he

been considering this proposal all along? Seeing if she would fit the role of his wife? Catherine was utterly dumbfounded by this move. No way had she seen it coming. It was too big a leap from the free-wheeling position he'd stated just two days ago.

'Catherine, we can have other children,' he pressed, as though that was the ultimate persuasion.

She instantly recoiled from it—mentally, emotionally and physically—her stomach cramping over the empty space that had been left by the miscarriage. This wasn't right. His mind was somehow stuck on their lost child. This proposal could be nothing more than an aberrational moment that would be regretted within hours or days.

'No…' She had to choke the word out. Her throat had tightened up. Her chest, too. She shook her head vehemently to get the message across.

'You wanted a baby,' he argued. 'You wanted me to be the father. So let's do it properly. Get married. Set up a home…'

'Stop! Please…stop!' Her mind was spinning. He was offering the biggest temptation of all. Her heart was thumping a wild yes to it, not caring why it was being offered, responding instinctively to the things she'd yearned to hear—married to Zack Freeman, having a family…

He frowned at her resistance. 'I swear I'll look after you. I always live up to my commitments, Catherine.'

Yes, he did, but *commitments* sounded so cold. Where was the passion for her, the love she craved?

'Once I give my word…' he went on.

Like a contract, not the love of a lifetime. He wasn't talking of love. Her need to hear more from him burst into speech.

'Your word is not enough,' she cried, desperate to reach into the heart of the man.

'Why not?' he challenged fiercely. 'What more do you want?'

'I want…' Was she mad to push for more? But how could she bear to be his wife if she was just one of many women he found desirable? It made her too vulnerable. If she plunged into this marriage and then found…no…no…. Words spilled out, begging for the right response from him. 'I want the man I marry to love me.'

'Love…' He shook his head as though it was some irrelevant concept, a vexatious sidetrack to be quickly bypassed. Only the end goal mattered and he had that in his sights. 'Of course you're very special to me,' he declared impatiently. 'Do you think I'd ask *any* woman to marry me?'

'How special, Zack?' she challenged, needing to nail it down. 'So special you don't want to spend your life without me? No other woman will do?'

'Yes. That's it. That's precisely it.'

It sounded too glib, like he was quickly feeding back what she wanted to hear, no pause to express something more deeply personal to him in his own words. And she remembered the sting of neglect, the flame of jealousy. Accusing words tumbled out of the torment of loving a man who could not possibly love her.

'Then how come you had another woman on your

arm at the Golden Globes night, very soon after you'd been with me three months ago? And a different woman again at the BAFTA Awards night, just before you called me to join you for the Academy Awards. I saw shots of you on news programs...'

'Those women were simply...handy,' he said with a grimace, disliking being put on that highly ambivalent spot.

It didn't soothe the hurt of all the silence from him, the hurt that he found other women attractive enough to share important occasions in his life with *them,* not *her.*

And only two days ago had come the warning that this third occasion together was only another one-off—a longer time but to be ended in the same way, no promise of more. It didn't add up to love in Catherine's mind. It didn't even add up to extra special.

The only difference was he knew she'd fallen pregnant to him and she'd lost the child that might have been. His child. Their child. Obviously the whole thing had become very personal to him, linking this proposal to having other children, but it was the wrong time, the wrong place, the wrong sentiment.

It didn't fill her soul with joy.

She needed her love to be returned, not used.

Her baby would have loved her back.

But Zack...the hand of harsh reality squeezed her heart, forcing out the temptation it had nursed. She couldn't accept his proposal. Being married to him would be a hell of uncertainty and fear. That was the truth of it and as much as she might want to overlook it, how could she?

She looked at him with all the emptiness she felt and laid her position on the line. 'I don't want to be a *handy* wife, Zack. I need my husband to think of me as irreplaceable. The *one* woman he wants above all others. I don't believe you can honestly say that, so please…let me go now.'

'Catherine…' His hands gripped more tightly.

'No.' It took every scrap of her will to fight the blazing determination in his eyes. 'You'll think better of this tomorrow. Or the next day. Or the next.' She gave him a savagely ironic smile. 'This, too, will pass.'

A battle light gleamed. 'And if it doesn't?'

That was his problem.

She was sure he'd find some *handy* solution to it.

'I'm going home,' she threw at him, unable to take any more argument with her heart and soul aching so badly. She wrenched her hand from his and held it up to ward off any further attempt to delay her. 'Goodbye, Zack. Thank you for seeing me off.'

She left him without a backward glance, desperately certain in her own mind she was right to go. She was through with making rash decisions where Zack Freeman was concerned. If he'd truly cared for her, he would have shown it by considering *her* feelings, asking her what *she* wanted.

A quickie marriage in Las Vegas.

On his terms.

Where was there any love for her in that?

No family wedding like Livvy's and Pete's.

A shoddy affair, telling her she wasn't worth much time to him. Just a convenience. And a baby machine. She didn't care that he could well afford to look after his wife and family. Not all the money in the world could buy her into that situation.

So she told herself in a rage of pain and pride as she made herself march towards the designated departure gate. Yet every step of the way, her body was begging for Zack to follow her, stop her, convince her she was wrong, heal the hurts and make everything better so she could believe a marriage between them could and would work.

But he didn't come after her.

Didn't stop her.

She joined the line of passengers boarding the aeroplane. She was so tense and tremulous she dropped her ticket when it was her turn to put it through the processing machine. Every second was an agony of waiting for a shout or a hand to clamp on her shoulder.

But nothing stopped her from entering the boarding tunnel. No call came for her to disembark before the flight took off. Once the big Qantas jet started rolling down the tarmac, Catherine sagged into a huge black hole of hopelessness.

It was over.

The baby...

The chance of marrying Zack Freeman...

She'd lost both of them...

Forever.

CHAPTER FOURTEEN

FOR the full week she was supposed to be away, Catherine left her answering machine on, not wanting to speak to anyone. She listened to the messages. Nothing from Zack. Which was only to be expected. It was stupid to feel tense every time the telephone rang. Clearly he had accepted her rejection and was probably grateful for it before she'd even left Los Angeles.

Mostly the calls were from Livvy, increasingly impatient with her sister's absence.

'Where are you?' she demanded on one message.

On her last call came an exasperated, 'Okay, Mum tells me you've gone off on a week's vacation. You could have told me, too. So call me as soon as you're back.'

Livvy…whom she was sure was still happily pregnant. Catherine didn't want to hear baby news. The grief over her own loss could be too easily tapped. But she couldn't block her sister out of her life because Livvy had what she would never have now. That was too mean and miserable. Within a reasonable response time, Catherine steeled herself to chat as normally as she could to her very voluble sister.

'At last!' Livvy greeted with emphatic satisfaction. 'Where have you been?'

'Oh, just up to the Blue Mountains, communing

with nature,' she answered. It wasn't a complete lie. She had driven up there yesterday to get herself out of the apartment and memories that crowded in on her at home. 'Is everything okay with you? Why all the calls?'

'Everything's fine. Wonderful! Did you watch the Academy Awards on TV?' Livvy pressed eagerly.

Catherine's heart turned over. This had to be about Zack. 'No,' she said flatly. The flight home crossed the dateline, losing a day. If Zack had won an award he would have been presented with it while she was still flying over the ocean. Not that she would have watched the ceremony anyway. Why torture herself with might-have-beens?

'Zack won for achievement in visual effects,' Livvy announced as though it was a triumph that she and Pete were still celebrating.

'Well, good for him!' Catherine responded, trying to inject some enthusiasm into her voice.

'And you'll never know what...' Livvy ran on excitedly.

'What?' Catherine obliged.

'He mentioned me and Pete in his acceptance speech.'

'Well, that must have been a nice surprise.' It surprised her, too.

'*And* the fact we're having a baby.'

Catherine's stomach contracted.

'I don't know how he knew. Pete hadn't told him. He must have got the news from his mother who's very friendly with Pete's mother.'

I told him.

'Anyhow, there he was, up on stage receiving an Oscar, and Pete and I were expecting him to rave on about the movie and thank all the people who'd helped to bring his vision to life, which he did, very briefly. Then he said...I know the words off by heart because we videoed it...so listen to this, Catherine.'

'I'm listening,' she said, her nerves in a total mess again.

'I quote... ''I guess it could be said this is a pinnacle of achievement for me. Creative achievement. But the far greater creation is a beautiful new life. I've just heard that my oldest friend in Australia, Pete Raynor, and his lovely wife, Livvy, are expecting a baby. Their first child. I think that's worth more than a thousand Oscars. Congratulations, Pete.'''

Their first child...

Had her miscarriage still been preying on his mind, above and beyond the crowning recognition of his work? Was he finding it much more difficult to set aside than it had been to set *her* aside? Her heart ached unbearably as Livvy rattled on.

'Wasn't that great? Pete was so thrilled. I couldn't believe it, being named like that on an internationally televised show. And the applause was terrific. The camera followed Zack back to his seat in the auditorium. Pete was saying it would give the woman he was with ideas, but the odd thing was, he didn't have anyone with him. The seat beside him was empty.'

Her seat.

Had she been...*irreplaceable?*

An overwhelming sadness clogged her mind. It was like pulling words out through quicksand to make adequate replies to Livvy's happy carry-on. Eventually she managed to end the call, desperately fending off an invitation to view the video, saying she was heavily booked up with activities for the next few weeks. In fact, she was running late for an appointment now.

It was a lie.

She hated telling lies.

But it had been the only defence she could come up with. The hurt was too raw to share with anyone, especially if... Had she been wrong to reject Zack's proposal? Had she misunderstood his motives, mis-interpreted his words and actions? Maybe he would have been faithful to their marriage, cleaving only to her...

Stop it, stop it, stop it! she savagely berated herself.

It was done.

Finished.

Too late to take back.

So he was deeply affected by the loss of their child. It didn't mean he loved her. The empty seat was just an empty seat. It couldn't be concluded that he couldn't bear to be with anyone else. There was no point in tormenting herself with such thoughts. If he'd loved her, everything would have been different.

Catherine kept telling herself this, day after day, week after week. She worked hard at her job, avoided meeting Livvy in person, held endless one-sided conversations with her goldfish who listened sympathetically to her emotional outpourings and her best attempts at logical reasoning. In this regard, Rhett and Scarlet were her perfect companions.

She told herself she was managing okay...until the parcel came. It was a box—a box sent from London—and the sender's name was Zack Freeman.

Zack felt uncharacteristically tense as he belted himself into his seat for take off on the long flight from London to Sydney. He'd failed with Catherine last time—had deserved to fail—and it was impossible to forecast her response to his message. Had enough time gone by? Had he waited too long?

He vividly recalled the bitter irony of her words... *This, too, will pass.* But it hadn't. And it never would. He'd been trying to block Catherine Trent out of his mind for over a year. It had proved impossible. And now...now he couldn't block her out of his heart. Nor did he want to. She was his woman. Somehow he had to undo the damage he'd done so she would accept him back into her life.

Had the rose started that process for him?

It had been a risky gamble, posting it to her. She'd remember him taking it out of her hair the night of Pete's wedding—a prelude to the intimacy they'd shared, after which he'd left her *without a word.* Would it mean anything to her that he'd taken the rose with him? She might think it had represented a crass souvenir of a great night of sex. He couldn't blame her if she did. Yet it wasn't true.

He'd kept the rose because instinctively he'd wanted to keep her. At the time he wouldn't let himself go down that track. Not until he knew about the baby—how much it had meant to her—how much it had suddenly meant to him. Their child. His and Catherine's. It had gradually seeped into his soul— the rightness of their being together. He'd been so blindly stubborn not to recognise it before.

Bad move—his proposal of marriage at LAX. Too quick. Totally inappropriate after the miscarriage. And lacking in credibility in the light of all he'd done and not done.

Her walking away from him had been one hell of a wake-up call, underlining how she had read his behaviour—every action totally self-centred, not even pausing to consider where she had been coming from, nor asking where she wanted to go. It had to be different this time. Very different. He was extremely conscious of the thin line he'd be treading. Any mistake…

The airline steward offered a tray of drinks. He took a glass of orange juice. No champagne for him. Champagne was for celebrating and he had nothing to celebrate on this trip.

'Are we running late?' he asked, impatient to get on his way to Catherine.

'No, sir. We'll be taking off on schedule in ten minutes,' came the confident assurance.

Ten minutes…plus over twenty hours in the air…more time waiting through the stopover in Singapore…it was a long haul to Sydney…and he wasn't even sure Catherine would meet him. Had the note he'd put in the box with the rose said enough to win him another chance with her?

Once again he weighed the words he'd written—

words he'd formulated and reformulated dozens of times during the weeks he'd already waited....

Catherine—

It's long past the next day and the next and the next. No amount of time will wear away the connection I feel with you. Can we meet again?

I'll be in Sydney on the first day of May. There's a rose garden in the botanical gardens, just down from the Macquarie Street entrance. From twelve noon I'll be there waiting for you.

Zack.

If she didn't come...every primitive male instinct pushed to go to her apartment and break down the door if necessary, smash any barrier she put up, take her in his arms, make wild passionate love to her, force her to respond.

But would such action work?

In the end, the choice was hers.

What did Catherine want? That was the critical question. This meeting had to be based on giving, not taking—persuasion, not force.

The steward came and collected his glass.

The jumbo jet started rolling down the runway.

The die was cast.

CHAPTER FIFTEEN

The first day of May…

Catherine stood on the corner of Macquarie Street where the big iron gates to the botanical gardens were wide open, inviting the public to wander in and enjoy the ambience of beautiful trees and flowers. She doubted such pleasantries would even impinge on her consciousness if she entered these grounds.

It was past noon. A steely pride had overriden her usual passion for punctuality. No way would she be found waiting for Zack Freeman. She'd allowed an extra half hour in case he'd run into unavoidable delays, but if his word meant anything, he should be in the rose garden by now.

Still the question hovered in her mind—to meet him or not? It would open everything up again. To what end? More pain? He was in Sydney today. Where tomorrow? Was this meeting with her being fitted into a business trip? What if he just wanted small bites of her life, reconnecting at his convenience? She'd die if that were the case, die of humiliation that she'd turned up to his call.

Yet…the rose he'd kept and sent to her…meeting in a public rose garden in the middle of the day…surely it had to mean more than just sex on his mind. If she didn't go and find out, the torment of wondering what she might have missed would haunt her for the rest of her life.

Her legs felt like jelly. It was a fine sunny day but it didn't warm the chill in her heart. She forced her feet forward, determined now on her course. Signs directed her to the path she had to follow. It wouldn't take long, she told herself, to know the outcome of this meeting.

The sheer physical impact of seeing Zack again caught her completely unprepared. Emotional turmoil had clouded her memory of how it was with him. Her feet came to a dead halt as she took in the shock of his effect on her; the instant quickening of her pulse, the magnetic pull on every muscle of her body, the frightening awareness of her sexuality and her vulnerability to the power of his.

And he wasn't even looking at her!

He was seated on a bench seat under a tree at the other end of the rose garden. His body was hunched forward, head bent, elbows resting on his knees, hands linked, obviously deep in thought. Despite this tightly contained pose, he radiated an intense energy which she knew would engulf her the moment he was alerted to her presence.

A sense of panic jangled her nerves. It was dangerous, letting Zack get close again. She couldn't trust herself not to respond to him. Before she could decide what to do about it, his head jerked up and his dark riveting gaze held her locked into his personal force-field. No retreat possible.

He stood in one swift fluid action, then seemed to come towards her in slow motion, dominating her vision, dominating her mind, dominating her heart. She had no control over any of them, and in her stomach grew the sickening sense that nothing was ever going to change how she felt with Zack Freeman. She was too deeply connected to him.

'What do you want with me?' she blurted out, fighting for a defensive foothold that would guard her against falling into some disastrous decision.

The direct challenge halted him an arm's length away, not far enough for her to feel safe, but at least giving her some space. His eyes scoured hers, undoubtedly looking for chinks of weakness. She stood her ground and stared back unflinchingly, resolved on getting answers before he touched her.

'What do you want with me, Catherine?' he returned quietly, skewering her with her own question.

'You speak first,' she demanded, refusing to take that bait. It would leave her with no pride at all. 'It was you who asked for this meeting, Zack. Not me.'

He nodded. A wisp of a smile curved his lips and his eyes softened with a caressing warmth. 'I'm glad you came.'

'I can go just as easily,' she flashed back, feeling herself start to melt inside and stiffening her spine to counter any crumbling.

'I know.' He gestured to the bench seat. 'Would you like to sit or stroll? A family group is coming down the path and we're blocking it here.'

'I'll sit for a while,' she decided, glad there were other people around. Being alone with Zack was not a good idea.

He turned aside to let her fall into step with him

and made no attempt to take her hand or arm as they walked along to the bench seat he'd vacated. He was dressed in black casual clothes: jeans, T-shirt, leather jacket. Probably travelling clothes. She had defiantly dressed in yellow. At least her sweater was yellow. Her skirt was mostly black with a zigzag pattern of white and yellow. She had wanted to look bright, on top of her world without him.

It was a lie. Amazing how good she was getting at lies when it came to her involvement with Zack Freeman. Desperate, protective lies.

'Have you just arrived in Sydney?' she asked, probing for his current circumstances.

'Yesterday.'

'Is this a business trip?'

'You're my only business here, Catherine.'

'You've come from London just to see me?'

'Yes.'

'No other purpose? No wedding, no award, no deal waiting in the wings that you have to hurry off to?' she tossed out flippantly.

'Not this time,' he answered grimly.

A fierce satisfaction flared through Catherine. At least she wasn't a secondary item on this visit to Australia. There was no other agenda. He'd come for her. Yet that begged the question, 'What if I hadn't turned up, Zack?' She sneaked a quick look at him, wary of taking too much for granted.

He caught her glance and flashed a wry little smile. 'I was considering that situation when you arrived. Should I respect your wishes or should I storm the barricades? I'm relieved not to have to make that decision.'

Storm the barricades... Her heart fluttered at the passion inherent in those words. Could she resist him? Did she want to? They reached the seat and she was careful to keep some distance between them as they sat. There were many questions to be answered and the desire he stirred in her could well be flattened by his replies.

'Okay, here I am. Tell me what this is about for you,' she invited, deliberately evading eye contact with him, fixing her gaze on the nearest rose bed. She could feel his tension vibrating around her, a harnessed aggression that burned under the surface of his control. It increased her own tension and she clung to a calm facade, determinedly hiding her inner turbulence.

She was aware of him leaning forward, resting his elbows on his knees again. 'I'll start at the beginning. Our blind date. I wasn't expecting to meet a woman who'd get under my skin.' His deep voice carried a liberal dash of irony.

'A one-night wonder for you,' she muttered mockingly.

It made him pause, reflect. 'I guess I've given you no reason to think it was any more,' he said ruefully.

'You want me to believe it was?' She shot him a derisive look. 'No contact with me for nine months. And then I was only an incidental on the night of Pete's and Livvy's wedding. You hadn't come for me. You barely acknowledged my presence until you decided you wanted sex with me again.'

He grimaced and shook his head. 'It wasn't like that. I realise it must look that way to you, but it wasn't like that.'

'No?'

'No!' It was a vehement denial, his eyes burning through her scorn, projecting intense conviction.

She wrenched her gaze from his and returned it to the rose garden, frightened of letting his magnetic energy sweep away all reason. 'Then how was it, Zack?' she demanded coldly, not letting the heat from him influence her.

He sucked in a deep breath. She didn't care if she was putting him through some mental wringer. Her need to know the truth of his feelings for her was paramount.

'When I first met you I had a three-year plan,' he stated, obviously deciding to give her the big picture. 'All work,' he said significantly. 'I didn't want to put the effort into building and maintaining a relationship with any woman. It was easy enough to pick up a companion for a social function if needed.'

'With a night of sex thrown in for good measure.' The bitter little comment spilled out. She gritted her teeth against saying any more, hating the fact that he'd put her in the same category as other casual sex partners.

'You were different, Catherine,' he quickly asserted.

Inwardly she bristled. He certainly hadn't treated her any differently to the others who had passed through his life.

'What we shared that night on the beach...I tried

to dismiss it as a sexual fantasy but you remained too real in my mind. I resented the continual intrusion of the memory, tried to downplay it, reason it away, took other women to bed to blot it out. I won't deny that. Won't lie about it, either. Though I did it less and less because it was *you* I wanted and every other woman was a frustration because she wasn't you.'

Was that supposed to be a compliment? It was certainly a backhander if it was—the unforgettable woman he'd do anything to forget. He made her sound like a curse—a blight on his life.

'It messed me up to such an extent I decided not to go to Pete's wedding because *you* would be there, and I didn't want what I thought of as my obsession with you aggravated.'

'Obsession?' It shocked her into looking at him again.

He raised his hands in a kind of exasperated appeal. 'What would you call it? There I was, not even prepared to be Pete's best man because you were sure to be Livvy's chief bridesmaid and if I had to partner you all throughout the wedding…it would get me in deeper with you and mess me around even more.'

'But you did come…' *And avoided me like the plague for most of the wedding.*

'I was angry with myself for letting Pete down. My oldest friend. And I was angry at investing you with so much power over my life. In the end, I had to come, not only for Pete, but to prove to myself that what I felt about you was more fantasy than reality. I wanted you to be…' He hesitated, grimacing over the truth before admitting it. '…something I could finally dismiss.'

It did make sense, Catherine slowly conceded, fitting his thoughts to how he had acted at the wedding.

'But I found myself wanting you so badly…I couldn't stand watching that guy dance with you, touching you…'

The aggression—fiercely possessive aggression. Yes, it did make sense. She frowned, dropping her gaze from his, wondering how much more she hadn't understood…from his viewpoint.

'I had to have you again.'

The throb of passion in his voice echoed through her own heart. She'd felt the same way, despite the lack of any communication from him. The compulsion to take what she could have of Zack Freeman had been overwhelming, even to letting herself get pregnant so she could have his child.

'And still I resented the power you had to do this to me, Catherine. I tried to exercise control over it. Then control didn't seem to matter. Only you mattered. I didn't want to wake you when I had to leave because if I did…' He sighed. 'It was easier to go while you were asleep. I took the rose. I wanted to keep something of you.'

Like she'd wanted to keep part of him.

'I had work commitments and I couldn't see a place for you in the schedule I had planned. But it was worse this time. I couldn't keep you out of my mind. You haunted my nights.'

Days and nights for me, she recalled, especially after learning a baby had been conceived.

'Catherine…look at me!' he commanded.

Her head snapped up. The angst in his eyes begged her belief.

'The women I took to the award ceremonies…they were just window-dressing. I didn't have sex with them. Didn't want to. In fact, it was after barely tolerating the model I was with at the BAFTA Awards that I called you to meet me in L.A. *You* were the one I wanted to be with.'

A wave of sadness rolled through her at the memory of her miscarriage in Los Angeles. It had thrown a black cloud over everything. Though before she'd told him she was pregnant… 'You still didn't see a place in your life for me, Zack. It was just for a week.'

'That was the plan,' he conceded heavily. 'I don't know that it would have stuck, given a whole week together.'

He fell silent.

Catherine knew instinctively he was remembering—mourning—their lost child. As she did.

He heaved another deep sigh. 'I'm sorry I…'

'You did everything you could,' she rushed out, not wanting the grief of that time recalled. When she'd needed his help, he'd given it unstintingly. That was the important thing to remember. And what Zack had been telling her rang true. But what it would mean for her in the future, she still didn't know.

'I was wrong not to make a place for you,

Catherine,' he said gruffly. 'I don't know if you can forgive all I haven't done where you are concerned, but I swear I'll do my best to make it up to you, if you'll give me the chance.'

She understood the vision he had for his work. It was a big part of him. He'd never rest, never feel satisfied, until it had all come alive. The conflict she'd represented in Zack's mind had been real and enduring. There was no longer any basis for the bitterness she'd nursed. It ebbed away.

'Where would I fit, Zack?' she asked, looking at him now with very clear eyes. The murk of the past had been dissipated by his honesty, but the same honesty showed her that any path ahead for them was crowded with other factors that could take their toll on any relationship.

His mouth quirked into an appealing little smile. 'I thought we could create our own fishbowl.'

She shook her head, not comprehending what he meant.

'There'd be a very busy world going on outside it, Catherine, but it needn't touch what we have together. If you're willing to be Scarlet to my Rhett, we could swim around, side by side…'

'All the time?' she asked incredulously, not having dared to hope for so much.

'That's what I'd like.' He searched her eyes for any objections. 'But you must tell me what you want. I'll try to accommodate…'

Her hand lifted, pressing soft, silencing fingers to his mouth. 'I want to be with you wherever you go,' she said, letting him see the truth of her heart shining in her eyes.

He covered her hand with his, pressed a long, lingering kiss of warm promise on her palm. Catherine's heart turned over. Before she dared think it, he said, 'I love you Catherine Trent.' Then... 'Will you be my wife?'

'Yes,' she whispered.

His smile was dazzling—relief, joy, intense pleasure in her. Still holding her left hand, he reached into the pocket of his jacket and drew out a small jeweller's box. Catherine stared in utter amazement as he flicked it open to reveal a huge diamond solitaire ring.

'Diamonds are forever,' he said with relish, and slid it onto the third finger of her left hand.

'We're going to do this right,' he stated, determined purpose pouring from him as he swept on. 'We'll visit your family tonight, announce our engagement, plan a wedding...'

'A wedding?' Catherine repeated dazedly.

'You'd like Livvy to stand by you and I'll ask Pete to be my best man. Tomorrow we'll visit my mother. She'll want to be in the thick of things, too. In fact...'

'Zack...'

'Have I said something wrong?' he asked anxiously.

'No...' She laughed, bubbling over with so many happy emotions she couldn't begin to express them. 'You really were going to storm the barricades,' she finally spluttered out.

He grinned. 'I certainly didn't plan to leave without you this time, Catherine.'

She sobered, remembering the last time he'd proposed marriage. 'I'm thirty-two, Zack. If we're going to have…other children…'

The twinkle left his eyes, too. He gently stroked her cheek. 'No waiting. And when you do fall pregnant again I'll be right beside you all the way, looking after you as best I can.'

Neither of them would forget the one they'd lost, yet perhaps its brief innocent life had bonded them more deeply together.

'I can promise you I won't make the same mistakes with our children that my father made with me,' Zack said with considerable feeling, then made a wry little grimace. 'But I'll probably make others. It'll be your job to correct me, Catherine. And I'll listen. If Dad had ever listened to my mother…' He shook his head. 'My mother's a great person. You'll like her.'

'I hope she likes me.'

'I know she will. You're both great people.'

Zack rose from the bench seat, drawing Catherine to her feet and wrapping her in a tender embrace. 'Let's make this a new start,' he murmured.

'Yes,' she agreed, her heart swelling with the same need to get it right this time. 'I love you, too, Zack. That's a good place to start.'

They kissed.

And the connection between them went soul-deep.

There…in a garden full of roses.

CHAPTER SIXTEEN

SEPTEMBER… The first month of Spring in Australia…and the day was bright and sunny, perfect for the wedding.

'The flowers have arrived!' Livvy yelled from downstairs. 'I'm bringing ours up.'

Catherine stepped into the dress she'd chosen to wear and pulled it up, carefully sliding her arms through the armholes. She was positioning the bodice properly on her shoulders as Livvy sailed into the bedroom. 'I need help with the back fastening,' she appealed to her sister.

'Oh, wow!' Livvy breathed at first sight of *the dress* on Catherine. She quickly laid the flowers on the bed and moved to complete the fitting. When it was done, they both stared at the reflection in the mirror. 'That is fabulous!' Livvy declared in absolute awe.

It wasn't a traditional bridal gown. It was a Collette Dinnigan creation that Catherine had bought—rashly almost emptying her bank account—to wear at the Academy Awards night, desperately wanting Zack to see her as the woman he always wanted at his side. She'd never worn it. The dress was the kind of dress that dreams were made of. It finally felt right to wear it today.

It was made of opalescent sequins, sleeveless, the

front bodice providing graceful movement with a long cowl neckline that dropped to below her waist, also showing quite a tantalising amount of cleavage. The slim-line style flared into a swinging skirt below the knees, allowing room to walk freely, though with a decidedly seductive swish.

'With your hair fluffed out over your shoulders and down your back, plus all those millions of glittering sequins, you kind of look like a mermaid, Catherine,' Livvy remarked assessingly, then laughed as she gestured to her own appearance. 'And I look like a whale.'

'No, you don't. You look absolutely beautiful, Livvy, and I'm sure Pete will tell you so.'

'Just as well you chose midnight-blue for me. It helps to minimise the lump.' She sighed. 'You could have waited another two months until after I'd had the baby. Having a matron of honour this pregnant is not fashionable.'

Catherine shook her head, smiling at the grumble. 'Babies are always fashionable, before and after they're born.'

'I can't see my feet anymore.'

'What's so great about your feet?'

'They're about the only part of me that hasn't swelled up. Which is just as well because I'll have you know I've done a lot of running around, getting this wedding right for you and Zack while you two did your jet-setting thing.'

'I know, Livvy.' Catherine kissed her cheek. 'Thank you so much for everything you've done for us.'

'Well it wasn't just me. Mum and Zack's mother were wild to get in on the act, very eager to get the two of you married. I'm sure Mum thought it was a miracle that you finally found someone.' Livvy raised a wagging finger. 'And she wasn't alone in that sentiment.'

Catherine grinned, recalling all her sister's match-making efforts. 'I didn't find Zack. It was a blind date, remember?'

Livvy rolled her eyes. 'And is Pete going to make capital out of that in his best man speech! He is so wrapped that we're all going to be connected by marriage. And so am I, Catherine.' She gave her a hug. 'It's great!'

'Yes, it is.'

With heartfelt pleasure beaming between them, Catherine couldn't keep the secret to herself any longer. It had to be safe now. The doctor had assured her all was well, and just this past week the scan had actually showed their baby sucking its thumb—so endearing it had brought tears to her eyes. Zack's, as well.

'We'll be sharing more than being in-laws, Livvy. I'm pregnant, too,' she happily announced.

'You're not!' It was a squeal of delight.

Catherine nodded.

Livvy clapped her hands. 'Oh, this is marvellous! How far along?'

'Almost four months.'

Sheer astonishment. 'You can't be! You're not even showing.' Her gaze dropped critically to Catherine's stomach.

'Luckily the long cowl on this dress hides a very definite mound.' She lifted it. 'See?'

Livvy pointedly examined the vital area. 'That's a very small four months. Trust you to keep nice and slim. I had a positive pot belly by then.' She frowned. 'How come you haven't told any of us before this?'

'I am older than you, as you've frequently mentioned,' Catherine answered carefully. 'I wanted to make it through the danger period first before letting anyone know there's a baby on the way.'

Livvy shook her head chidingly. 'You've got a very secretive nature. No doubt about it. We didn't even know you and Zack were an item until you announced your engagement. Honestly, Catherine, you could be a bit more forthcoming.'

'Oh, I don't know.' Her eyes were deliberately teasing. 'You do have a habit of telling me how to live my life, little sister.'

Livvy humphed and planted her hands challengingly on her hips. 'Well, Pete and I got it right putting you and Zack together, didn't we?'

Catherine laughed and hugged her. 'Yes, you did. Beautifully, wonderfully right.'

'The cars are here!' Their father yelled up the stairs. 'Are you girls ready?'

'Yes, Dad,' they chorused.

Livvy quickly pounced on the flowers she'd put on the bed. 'I'm glad I've got a bouquet to hold over my mountainous mound,' she declared. 'Why did you choose to carry just a single red rose, Catherine?'

She smiled, picking it out of the florist's box. 'It has its meaning.'

Livvy arched her eyebrows. 'I suppose that means you're not going to tell me.'

'Remember the red rose I wore in my hair as your bridesmaid?'

'Ah! You and Zack got together at *my* wedding!' Livvy cried triumphantly. 'Oh, I can't wait to tell Pete that!' She sailed off, smugly proud of having *fixed* her older sister's life for her.

Catherine lifted the perfect velvety bloom to smell its glorious scent. Not an artificial rose…a real one…as real as the love she and Zack had for each other.

The wedding guests were milling around the garden at Jonah's, the highly fashionable restaurant/reception centre Catherine and Zack had chosen, mostly because of its site on top of Sydney's northern peninsula, overlooking the ocean.

Everyone was clearly in a festive mood, enjoying the spectacular views as they waited for the bridal party to arrive. Zack and Pete stood closer to the clifftop above Whale Beach, watching the height of the waves rolling in as they'd done together hundreds of times throughout their long friendship.

'Not as good a surf as at Forresters,' Pete commented.

Zack smiled, remembering the night he and Catherine had shared at Spoon Bay. 'If a house comes up for sale close to yours, Pete, let me know.'

'Great idea!'

'Our kids could play together during vacations.'

'Yeah…' A cocked eyebrow. 'You and Catherine thinking of starting a family soon?'

Zack grinned. 'One already on the way.'

Pete punched his arm. 'You sly dog, you. Does your mother know?'

'Only just now. I whispered in her ear and her face lit up like a Christmas tree.'

'I can imagine. She's over the moon about your marrying Catherine.' Pete raised a scoring finger. 'And just you remember, I did tell you right from the start she was a knockout.'

'You did,' Zack happily conceded. 'And punctual.' He checked his watch. 'Five minutes to go. We'd better line up with the celebrant.'

He watched her come to him down the makeshift aisle, sunshine gleaming on her glorious hair, a light sea breeze rippling the long wavy tresses. Far below them the beat of the ocean on the sand echoed the beat of his heart, a rhythm that pounded to the name that swam in his mind.… Catherine… Catherine…

Her dress glittered like brilliant light on water. She seemed to flow towards him like some ethereal primeval goddess who would bestow upon him all the blessings of life. This was his wife to be, the woman who carried his child…the scan had revealed a boy…their son.

She smiled at him, her beautiful eyes glowing golden with love. He smiled back, knowing beyond any shadow of doubt this woman was utterly unique and irreplaceable, the one and only woman he would ever love. He saw she carried a single red rose and knew it represented her love for him—the giving and taking that was not a game, but an essential part of the marriage they both wanted.

He held out his hand to her. She slid hers over his palm and he closed his fingers around it.

Together, he thought.

It had felt right at the very beginning.

He knew it was right now, and would be so for the rest of their lives.

MARRIAGE BY
DECEPTION

by

Sara Craven

Sara Craven was born in South Devon and grew up surrounded by books in a house by the sea. After leaving grammar school she worked as a local journalist, covering everything from flower shows to murders. She started writing Mills & Boon® books in 1975. Apart from writing, her passions include films, music, cooking and eating in good restaurants. She now lives in Somerset.

Sara Craven has appeared as a contestant on the Channel Four game show *Fifteen to One* and is also the latest (and last ever) winner of the 1997 *Mastermind of Great Britain* championship.

Look for Sara Craven's latest novel,
Innocent on Her Wedding Night,
**which will be available in September 2007
from Mills & Boon® Modern™.**

CHAPTER ONE

SHE was late. Ten minutes late.

Sam checked his watch, frowned, and poured some more mineral water into his glass.

Perhaps she'd chickened out altogether. Well, he thought with a mental shrug, he couldn't entirely blame her. A list of the places he'd rather be tonight would run to several pages, plus footnotes.

He'd give her until eight-thirty, he decided abruptly, and if she hadn't shown by then, he'd go home. After all, there were plenty of others on his schedule—and she hadn't even been one of his choices for the short list either.

'Lonely in London', the ad in the *Daily Clarion*'s personal column had read. 'Is there a girl out there who's seriously interested in love and marriage? Could it be you?' And a box number.

As bait, it was well-nigh irresistible, and the replies had flooded in.

He didn't have a name for tonight's lady. Her letter had merely been signed 'Looking for Love'.

She'd been picked because she'd described herself as a beauty executive, and seemed younger than most of the others. And, he suspected, because her envelope bore a Chelsea postmark.

Which was why he was waiting here in the upmarket Marcellino's, rather than some more ordinary trattoria or wine bar.

He glanced restlessly towards the door out of the

restaurant, flinching inwardly as he caught a glimpse of himself in the mirror on the wall opposite. The cheap suit he was wearing was shining enthusiastically under the lights, his dark curling hair had been cut short and flattened on top with gel, so that it stuck out awkwardly at the sides, and gold-rimmed glasses adorned his nose.

I look, he thought, a total nerd—only not as good.

For a moment, the head waiter had hesitated over allowing him in. He'd seen it in the man's eyes. It was something that had never happened to him before, and he would make damned sure it never happened again when all this was over, he vowed grimly. When his life eventually returned to normality.

If it ever did, he amended, his mouth tightening. If he ever managed to escape from this mess of his own creation.

As for his intended companion for the evening—if and when she turned up, she would probably take one look at him and run out screaming.

He drank some more mineral water, repressing a grimace. What he really needed was a large Scotch, or some other form of Dutch courage. But the rules of engagement for tonight were strict. And he needed all his wits about him.

He looked at his watch again. Fifteen more minutes, he thought, and then I'm out of here. And they can't pass quickly enough.

Rosamund Craig sat tensely in the corner of her cab. They seemed to have moved about fifty yards in the past fifteen minutes, and now the traffic ahead was blocked solid yet again.

I should have set off earlier, she thought. Except

that I had no intention of coming at all. There was no need. All I had to do was pick up the phone and it would all have been sorted. End of story.

Now, here I am in a crawling cab with a galloping meter, going to meet a complete stranger. The whole thing is crazy. I'm crazy.

And the dress she was wearing was part of the madness, she thought, furtively adjusting the brief Lycra skirt. Usually she avoided black, and trendy styles. Taupe was good—and beige—and grey in classic lines. Discreet elegance had always been her trademark. Not clinging mini-dresses and scarlet jackets.

And these heels on her strappy sandals were ridiculous too. She'd probably end the evening with a sprained ankle.

Although that could be the least of her problems, she reminded herself without pleasure. And the most sensible thing she could do would be to tell the driver to turn the taxi round and take her back for another blameless evening at home.

She was just leaning forward to speak to him when the cab set off again, with a lurch that sent her sprawling back, her skirt up round her thighs.

Her particular die would seem to be cast, she thought, righting herself hurriedly and pushing her light brown bobbed hair back from her face. And it would soon all be over, anyway. She was going to have a meal in a good restaurant, and at the end of it she would make an excuse and leave, making it tactfully clear that there would be no repeat performance.

Honour on both sides would be satisfied, she told herself as she pushed open the gleaming glass doors and entered the foyer of Marcellino's.

A waiter came to meet her. '*Signora* has a reservation?'

'I'm meeting someone,' she told him. 'A Mr Alexander.'

She could have sworn his jaw dropped, but he recovered quickly, handing her jacket to some lesser soul and conducting her across the black marble floor to the bar.

It was busy and for a moment Ros hesitated as heads turned briefly to appraise her, wondering which of them was her date.

'The table in the corner, *signora*.' The waiter's voice sounded resigned.

Ros moved forward, aware of a chair being pushed back and a man's figure rising to its feet.

Tall, she registered immediately, and dark. But— oh, God—far from handsome. That haircut, she thought numbly. Not to mention that dreadful suit. And those glasses, too. Hell's teeth, what have I let myself in for?

She was strongly tempted to turn on her heel and walk away—except there was something about his stance—something wary, even defensive, as if he was prepared for that very reaction—that touched a sudden chord of sympathy inside her and kept her walking forward, squaring her shoulders and pinning on a smile.

'Good evening,' she said. 'You must be Sam Alexander—"Lonely in London".'

'And you're "Looking for Love"?' He whistled, his firm-lipped mouth relaxing into a faint smile. 'You amaze me.'

Slowly, he picked up the single red rose that lay on

the table beside him and handed it to her. 'My calling card.'

As she took the rose their fingers brushed, and she felt an odd frisson, as if she'd accidentally encountered some static electricity, and found to her own astonishment that she was blushing.

He indicated the chair opposite. 'Won't you sit down, Miss…?'

'Craig,' she said, after a momentary hesitation. 'Janie Craig.'

'Janie,' he repeated thoughtfully, and his smile deepened. 'This is a real pleasure.'

He might look like a geek but there was nothing wrong with his voice, she thought, surprised. It was cool and resonant, with a faint underlying drawl. And he had a surprisingly attractive smile too—charming, lazy and self-deprecating at the same time, and good teeth.

But his eyes, even masked by those goofy glasses, were the most amazing thing about him. They were a vivid blue-green colour—almost like turquoise.

I might have to revise my opinion, she thought. With contact lenses, a good barber and some decent clothes, he'd be very much more than presentable.

'May I get you a drink?' He pointed to his own glass. 'I'm on designer water at the moment, but all that could change.'

She hesitated. She needed to keep a clear head, but a spritzer wouldn't do that much harm. 'Dry white wine with soda, please.'

'A toast,' he said, when her drink arrived, and touched his glass to hers. 'To our better acquaintance.'

She murmured something in response, but it wasn't

in agreement. Sam Alexander wasn't at all what she'd expected, and she found this disturbing.

He said, 'You're not what I'd anticipated,' and she jumped. Was he some kind of mind-reader?

'Really?' she countered lightly. 'Is that a good thing or a bad?'

'All good,' he said promptly, that smile of his curling along her nerve-endings again. 'But I didn't have too many preconceptions to work on. You were fairly cagey about yourself in our brief correspondence.'

She played nervously with the stem of her glass. 'Actually, answering a personal ad is something of a novelty for me.'

'So what attracted you to mine?'

That wasn't fair, Ros thought, nearly spilling her drink. That was much too close to the jugular for this stage in the evening, and she wasn't prepared for it.

'It's not easy to say,' she hedged.

'Try,' he suggested.

She bit her lip. 'You—you sounded as if you wanted a genuine relationship—something long-term with real emotion. Not just…'

'Not just a one-night stand,' he supplied, as she hesitated. 'And you realised you wanted the same thing—commitment?'

'Yes,' she said. 'I—suppose so. Although I'm not sure I analysed it like that. It was more of an impulse.'

'Impulses can be dangerous things.' His mouth twisted slightly. 'I'll have to make sure you don't regret yours.'

He let the words hang in the air between them for a moment, then handed her a menu. 'And the next momentous decision is—what shall we have to eat?'

She felt as if she'd been let off some kind of hook,

Ros realised dizzily, diving behind the leather-bound menu as if it was her personal shield.

There was clearly more to Sam 'Lonely in London' Alexander than met the eye. Which was just as well, recalling her first impression.

However, sitting only a couple of feet away from him, she'd begun to notice a few anomalies. Under that badly made suit he was wearing a shirt that said 'Jermyn Street', and a silk tie. And that was a seriously expensive watch on his wrist, too.

In fact, instinct told her there were all kinds of things about him that didn't quite jell...

Perhaps he was an eccentric millionaire, looking for a latter-day Cinderella—or maybe she was letting her over-active imagination run away with her.

'The seafood's good here,' he commented. 'Do you like lobster?'

'I love it.' Ros's brows lifted slightly when she noted the price.

'Then we'll have it,' he said promptly. 'With a mixed salad and a bottle of Montrachet. And some smoked salmon with pasta to start, perhaps?'

Definitely a millionaire, Ros thought, masking her amusement as she murmured agreement. Well, she was quite prepared to play Cinderella—although she planned to be gone long before midnight.

The bar had been all smoked glass and towering plants, but the dining room was discreetly opulent, the tables with their gleaming white linen and shining silverware screened from each other by tall polished wooden panels which imposed an immediate intimacy on the diners.

At the end of the room was a tiny raised platform,

occupied tonight by a pretty red-haired girl playing popular classics on the harp.

As they were conducted to their table, Ros allowed herself a swift, sideways glance to complete her physical picture of her companion.

Broad-shouldered, she noted, lean-hipped, and long-legged. Attributes that disaster of a suit couldn't hide. He moved confidently, too, like a man at home in his surroundings and his situation. That early diffidence seemed to have dissipated.

She'd come here tonight with the sole intention of letting him down lightly, yet now she seemed to be the one on the defensive, and she didn't understand it.

As they were seated the waiter placed their drinks tenderly on the table, and laid the red rose beside Ros's setting with the merest flick of an eyebrow.

To her annoyance, she realised she was blushing again.

She rushed into speech to cover her embarrassment. 'This is lovely,' she said, looking round her. 'Do you come here often?' She paused, wrinkling her nose in dismay. 'God, I can't believe I just said that.'

'It's a fair question.' His grin was appreciative. 'And the answer is—only on special occasions.'

Ros raised her eyebrows, trying to ignore the glint in the turquoise eyes. 'I imagine you've had a great many of them lately.'

His look was quizzical. 'In what way?'

'Answers to your advertisement, of course.' She carefully examined a fleck on her nail. 'My—friend said you'd get sacks of mail.'

'There's been a fair response,' he said, after a pause. 'But not that many with the elements I'm looking for.'

'So,' she said. 'Why didn't I slip through the net?'

'Your letter intrigued me,' he said softly. He sat back in his chair. 'I've never actually met a "beauty executive" before. What exactly does it involve?'

Ros swallowed. 'I—demonstrate the latest products,' she said. 'And work on stands at beauty shows. And I do cosmetic promotions in stores—offering free make-overs. That kind of thing.'

'It sounds fascinating,' Sam said, after a pause. He reached across the table and took her hand. Startled, she felt the warmth of his breath as he bent his head and inhaled the fragrance on her skin. 'Is this the latest scent?'

'Not—not really.' Hurriedly, she snatched back her hand. 'This one's been out for a while. It's Organza by Givenchy.'

'It's lovely,' he told her quietly. 'And it suits you.' He paused. 'Tell me, do you find your work fulfilling?'

'Of course,' she said. 'Why else would I do it?'

'That's what I'm wondering.' His gaze rested thoughtfully on her face. 'I notice you don't wear a lot of make-up yourself. I was half expecting purple hair and layers of false eyelashes.'

'I look very different when I'm working. I hope you're not disappointed,' she added lightly.

'No,' he said slowly. 'On the contrary…'

There was a silence which lengthened—simmered between them. Ros felt it touch her, like a hand stroking her bare flesh. Enclosing her like a golden web. A dangerous web that needed to be snapped before she was entangled beyond recall. A possibility she recognised for the first time, and which scared her.

She said, rather too brightly, 'Now it's your turn. What do you do to earn a crust?'

He moved one of the knives in his place-setting.

'Nothing nearly as exotic as you,' he said. 'I work with accounts. For a multinational organisation.'

'Oh,' she said.

'You sound surprised.'

'I am.' And oddly disappointed too, she realised.

'Why is that?'

'Because you're not like my—any of the accountants I've ever known,' she corrected herself hastily.

'Perhaps I should take that as a compliment,' he murmured, the turquoise eyes studying her. 'Have you known many?'

The dark-suited high-flier from the city firm to whom she submitted her annual income and expenditure records, she thought. And, of course, Colin, with whom she'd been going out for the past two years. And about whom she didn't want to think too closely just now.

'A couple.' She shrugged. 'In my work, you meet a lot of people.'

'I'm sure you do.' He paused. 'But you've given me a whole new insight into accountancy and its needs. Maybe I should come to you for one of those make-overs.'

'Perhaps you should.' Involuntarily, she glanced at his hair. It was only a momentary thing, but he saw.

He said softly, lifting a hand to smooth the raw edges into submission, 'I did it for a bet.'

'I'm sorry.' Ros stiffened, flushing slightly. 'I didn't mean to be rude. It's really none of my business.'

'If that was true,' he said, 'you'd be at home now, microwaving yesterday's casserole. Instead of tasting this wonderful linguine,' he added as their first course arrived.

Yesterday's casserole would certainly have been the

safer option, she thought ruefully, as she picked up her fork.

'So, what I have to ask myself is—why are you here, Janie? What's the plan?'

She nearly choked on her first mouthful. 'I don't know what you mean. Like the others, I answered your ad…'

'That's precisely what I don't understand. Why someone like you—someone who's attractive and clearly intelligent—should feel she has to resort to a lonely hearts column. It doesn't make a lot of sense.'

'It does if you spend a lot of your time in isolation,' she said.

'But your working day involves you with the public. And men go into department stores all the time.'

A stupid slip, Ros thought, biting her lip. She would have to be more careful.

She shrugged. 'Yes, but generally they come to beauty counters to buy gifts for the women already in their lives,' she returned coolly. 'And when the store closes, like them, I go home.'

'You live alone?'

'No, with my sister—who has her own life.' She put down her fork. 'And I could ask you the same thing. You're employed by a big company, and a lot of people meet their future partners at work, so why "Lonely in London"?' She paused. 'Especially when you seem to have such low expectations of the result.'

'I'm sorry if I gave that impression.' He frowned slightly. 'Actually, I didn't know what to expect. You being a case in point,' he added with deliberation. 'Your letter was—misleading.'

Her heart skipped a beat. She tried a laugh. 'Because I don't have purple hair?'

'That's only part of it. On paper, you sounded confident—even slightly reckless. But in reality I'd say you were quite shy. So how does that equate with being a super saleswoman?'

'That's a persona I leave behind with the make-up,' she said. 'Anyway, selling a product is rather different to selling oneself.'

'You didn't think it was necessary tonight?' Sam forked up some linguine. 'After all, you claimed in your letter to be "Looking for Love", yet I don't get that impression at all. You appear very self-contained.'

Ros kept her eyes fixed on her plate. How did I think I would ever get away with this? she wondered.

She said, 'Perhaps I think it's a little early to throw caution to the winds.'

'So why take the risk in the first place?'

'Maybe I should ask you the same thing. You were the one who placed the ad.'

'I've been working abroad for a while,' he said. 'And when you come back you find the waters have closed over. Former friends have moved on. Your mates are in relationships, and three's very definitely a crowd. Girls you were seeing are married—or planning to be.' His mouth tightened. 'In fact, everything's—changed.'

Ah, Ros thought, with a sudden pang of sympathy. I get it. He's been jilted. So, I did the right thing by coming here tonight.

'I understand,' she said more gently. 'But do you still think a personal ad is the right route to take?'

'I can't answer that yet.' His smile was twisted. 'Let's say the results so far have been mixed.'

'I'm sorry.'

'Don't be.' The turquoise eyes met hers with total

directness, then descended without haste to her parted lips, and lower still to the curve of her breasts under the clinging black fabric. 'Because tonight makes up for a great deal.'

She felt her skin warm, her whole body bloom under his lingering regard. Felt her heart thud, as if in sudden recognition—but of what?

And she heard herself say, in a voice which seemed to belong to someone much younger and infinitely more vulnerable, 'You were right about the linguine. It's terrific.'

In fact, the whole meal was truly memorable, progressing in a leisurely way through the succulent lobster, the crisp salad and cool fragrant wine, to the subtle froth of zabaglione.

Ros was glad to abandon herself to wholehearted enjoyment of the food, with the conversation mainly, and thankfully, restricted to its appreciation.

Much safer than the overly personal turn it had taken earlier, she told herself uneasily.

She'd expected to find tonight's situation relatively simple to deal with. For a few hours she'd planned to be someone else. Only she hadn't put enough effort into learning her part. Because Sam Alexander didn't seem convinced by her performance. He was altogether far too perceptive for his own good—or hers.

And she was looking forward to the time, fast approaching now, when she could thank him nicely for her meal and leave, knowing she would never have to see him again.

And it had nothing to do with his awful hair, or the nerdy glasses, or his frankly contradictory taste in clothes. In fact, it was strange how little all those things, so unacceptable at first, had come to matter as the evening wore on.

And, in spite of them all, she still couldn't figure him for a man who would have to look too hard for a woman. Not when there was a note in his voice and a look in those extraordinary blue-green eyes that made her whole body shiver, half in dread, half in excitement.

But I don't want to be made to feel like that, she thought. Not by a complete stranger, anyway. Someone I'm not even sure I can trust…

'Would you like a brandy with your coffee?' Sam was asking. 'Or a liqueur, maybe?'

'Nothing, thanks.' Ros glanced at her watch. 'I really should be going home.'

'Already?' There was faint mockery in his tone as he checked the time for himself. 'Scared you're going to turn into a pumpkin?'

'No,' she said. 'But it's getting late, and we both have to work tomorrow.'

And, more importantly, something was warning her to get out while the going was good, she realised.

'You're quite right, of course,' he said slowly. His glance was speculative. 'Yet we both have so much more to learn about each other. You don't know my favourite colour. I haven't asked you about your favourite film. All that sort of stuff.'

'Yes,' she said. 'We seemed to skip that part.'

'We could always order some more coffee,' he suggested quietly. 'Fill in some of the gaps.'

She forced a smile. 'I don't think so. I really do have to run.'

'I'm sorry you feel that.' He was silent for a moment. Then, 'So, where are you based at the moment, Janie? Which store?'

She swallowed, as another pit opened unexpectedly in front of her. 'No—particular one,' she said huskily. 'I'm helping launch a new lipstick range—so I'm travelling round quite a bit.' She forced a smile. 'Variety being the spice of life.'

'That's what they say, of course.' He leaned back in his chair, his face in shadow away from the candlelight. His voice was quiet, almost reflective. It engaged her, locking her disturbingly into the unexpected intimacy of the exchange.

'But I'm not sure I agree,' he went on. 'I'd like to think that I could stop—running. Stop searching. That just one person—provided she was the right one— could give my life all the savour it needs.'

There was a tingling silence. Her throat seemed to close, and deep inside she was trembling, her whole body invaded by a languorous weakness. She wasn't used to this blatantly physical reaction, and she didn't like it. Didn't need it.

Let this be a lesson to me never to interfere again in other people's concerns, she thought, swallowing, as she called herself mentally to order. And now let me extricate myself from this entire situation with charming finality. And, hopefully, no hard feelings.

She gave a light laugh. 'Well, I hope you find her soon.' She pushed her chair back and rose, reaching for her bag. 'And thank you for a—a very pleasant evening.'

'I'm the one who's grateful. You've given me a lot to think about,' he returned courteously, as he got to his feet in turn. 'It's all been—most intriguing. Goodnight, Janie.'

'Goodbye.' She smiled determinedly, hoping he'd take the point. Politeness demanded that she offer her hand, too.

The clasp of his fingers round hers was firm and warm. Too firm, she realised, as she tried to release herself, and found instead that she was being drawn forward. And that he was bending towards her, his intention quite obvious.

She gasped, her body stiffening in immediate tension, and felt his mouth brush her parted lips, very slowly and very gently. Not threatening. Not even particularly demanding. Nothing that should cause that strange inner trembling again. But there it was, just the same, turning her limbs to water. Sending a ripple of yearning through her entire being. Just as if she'd never been kissed before. And as though she was being taught in one mind-numbing lesson where a kiss might lead.

When he raised his head, he was smiling faintly.

'No,' he said, half to himself. 'Not what I was expecting at all.'

She said between her teeth, 'Good. I'd hate to be predictable. Now, will you let me go, please?'

'Reluctantly.' His smile widened, but the turquoise gaze, boring into hers, was oddly serious. 'And certainly not without something to remember me by.'

He picked up the dark red rose from the table and tucked it into the square neckline of her dress, sliding the slender, thornless stem down between her breasts.

Then he stepped back, looking at the effect he had created. Seeing how the crimson of the flower gleamed against the cream of her flesh.

And a muscle moved beside his mouth. Swiftly. Uncontrollably.

She felt her nipples swell and harden against the hug of the dress, and had to bite hard on her lower lip to dam back the small, urgent sound rising in her throat.

He said softly, 'Janie—stay, please. You don't have to leave.'

There was the hot, salty taste of blood in her mouth.

She said huskily, 'Yes—yes, I do.' And barely recognised her own voice.

Then she turned and walked quickly away, across the restaurant and into the foyer. Knowing as she did so that he was still standing there, silent and motionless, watching her go. And praying that he would not follow her.

CHAPTER TWO

Ros let herself into her house. Moving like a sleep-walker, she went into the sitting room and collapsed on to the sofa, because, as she recognised, her legs no longer wished to support her.

'My God,' she said, in a half-whisper. 'What on earth did I think I was doing?'

Fortunately there'd been a cab just outside the restaurant, so she'd been able to make an immediate getaway.

Not that Sam Alexander had been anywhere in sight as she'd driven off, and she'd craned her neck until it ached to make certain.

But all the same she hadn't felt safe until her own front door had closed behind her.

And, if she was honest, not even then. Not even now.

I should never have started this, she thought broodingly. I should have left well alone.

Because men like Sam Alexander could seriously damage your health. If you let them.

And it was useless to pretend she hadn't been tempted. Just for a nano-second, perhaps, but no less potent for all that. Which had never been part of the plan.

Oh, God, the plan.

Unwillingly, her mind travelled back ten days, reminding her how it had all begun...

* * *

'Ros, just listen to this.'

As her stepsister hurtled into the room, waving a folded newspaper, Ros stifled a sigh and clicked 'Save' on the computer.

She said, 'Janie, I'm working. Can't it wait?'

'Surely you can spare me five minutes.' Janie operated the wounded look, accompanied by the pout, so familiar to her family. 'After all, my future happiness is at stake here.'

Ros eyed her. 'I thought all your happiness—past, present and future—was tied up in Martin.'

'How can I have a relationship with someone who won't commit?' Janie demanded dramatically, flinging herself into the chintz-covered armchair by the window.

'You've been seeing him for a month,' Ros pointed out. 'Isn't that a little soon for a proposal of marriage?'

'Not when it's the right thing. But he's just scared of involvement. So I've decided to stop being guided by my heart. It's too risky. I'm going to approach my next relationship scientifically.' She held up the newspaper. 'With this.'

Ros frowned. 'With the *Clarion*? I don't follow…'

'It's their ''Personal Touch'' column,' Janie said eagerly. 'A whole page of people looking for love—like me.'

Ros's heart sank like a stone. 'Including a number of sad individuals on the hunt for some very different things,' she said quietly. 'Janie, you cannot be serious.'

'Why not?' Janie demanded defiantly. 'Ros, I can't wait for ever. I don't want to go on living with our parents either. I want my own place—like you,' she added, sweeping her surroundings with an envious glance. 'Do you know how lucky you were, inheriting a house like this from Grandma Blake?'

'Yes,' Ros said quietly. 'But, given the choice, I'd rather have Gran alive, well, and pottering in the garden. We were—close.' She gave Janie a searching look. 'You're surely not planning to marry simply for a different roof over your head?'

'No, of course not.' Janie sounded shocked. 'I really need to be married, Ros. It's the crucial time for me. I wake up in the night, sometimes, and hear my biological clock ticking away.'

In spite of her concern, Ros's face split into a grin as she contemplated her twenty-two-year-old stepsister. The tousled Meg Ryan-style blonde hair, the enormous blue eyes, and the slender figure shown off by a micro-skirt and cropped sweater hardly belonged to someone on the brink of decay.

Sometimes she felt thirty years older than Janie, rather than three.

'Better your biological clock than a time bomb,' she said caustically.

'Well, listen to this.' Janie peered at the paper. '"High-flying, fun-loving executive, GSOH, seeks soulmate". He doesn't sound like a bomb.' She frowned. 'What's a "GSOH"?'

'A good sense of humour,' Ros said. 'And it usually means they haven't one. And "fun-loving" sounds as if he likes throwing bread rolls and slipping whoopee cushions on your chair.'

'Uh.' Janie pulled a face. 'How about this, then? "Lonely in London. Is there a girl out there who's seriously interested in love and marriage? Could it be you?"' Her face was suddenly dreamy. 'He sounds—sweet, don't you think?'

'You don't want to know what I think.' Ros shook her head despairingly. '"Lonely in London"? He's been watching too many re-runs of *Sleepless in Seattle*.'

'Well, you liked it.'

'As a film, but not to be confused with real life.' Ros paused. 'Janie—call Martin. Tell him you don't want to get married this week, this month or even next year. Let him make the running, and build on what you feel for each other. I'm sure things will work out.'

'I'd rather die,' Janie said dramatically. 'I refuse to be humiliated.'

'No, you'd rather run the gauntlet of a series of no-hopers,' Ros said bitterly. 'You could be getting into a real minefield.'

'Don't fuss so. I know how the system works,' Janie said impatiently. 'You don't give your address or telephone number in the preliminary contact, and you arrange to meet in a public place where there are going to be plenty of other people around. Easy-peasy.' She nodded. 'But you could be right about the "fun-loving executive", so I'll go for "Lonely in London".'

'Janie, this is such a bad idea…'

'But lots of people meet through personal columns. That's what they're for. And I think it's an exciting idea—two complete strangers embarking on a voyage of mutual discovery. You're a romantic novelist. Doesn't it turn you on?'

'Not particularly,' Ros said grimly. 'On old maps they used to write "Here be Dragons" on uncharted waters.'

'Well, you're not putting me off.' Janie bounced to her feet again. 'I'm going to reply to this ad right now.

And I bet he gets inundated with letters. Every single woman in London will be writing to him.'

At the door, she paused. 'You know, the trouble with you, Ros, is that you've been seeing that bloody bore Colin for so long that you've become set in concrete—just like him. You should stop writing about romance and go out and find some. Get a life before it's too late.'

And she was gone, banging the door behind her.

Ros, caught in the slipstream of her departure, realised that she was sitting with her mouth open, and closed it quickly.

She rarely, if ever, had the last word with Janie, she thought ruefully, but that had been a blow below the belt.

She knew, of course, that Colin treated Janie with heavy tolerance, which her stepsister repaid with astonished contempt, but Janie had never attacked him openly before.

But then Colin doesn't approve of Janie staying here while Dad and Molly are away, she acknowledged, sighing.

He'd made it clear that their personal life had to be put on hold while she was in occupation.

'I wouldn't feel comfortable knowing that she was sleeping in the room opposite,' he'd said, frowning.

Ros had stared at him. 'Surely we don't make that much noise?'

Colin had flushed slightly. 'It's not that. She's young, and far too impressionable already. We should set her a good example.'

'I'm sure she knows the facts of life,' Ros had said drily. 'She could probably give us some pointers.'

But Colin had not budged. 'We've plenty of time

to think about ourselves,' he'd told her, dropping a kiss on her hair.

And that was how it had remained.

Suddenly restless, Ros got up from her desk and wandered across to the window, looking down at the tiny courtyard garden beneath, which was just beginning to peep into spring flower.

Her grandmother, Venetia Blake, had planted it all, making sure there were crocuses and narcissi to brighten the early months each year. She'd added the magnolia tree, too, and trained a passion flower along one wall. And in the summer there would be roses, and tubs of scented lavender.

Apart from pruning and weeding, there was little for Ros to do, but she enjoyed working there, and, although she was a practical girl, with no belief in ghosts, there were times when she felt that Venetia's presence was near, and was comforted by it.

She wasn't sure why she should need comfort. Her mother had been dead for five years when her father, David Craig, had met Molly, his second wife, herself a widow with a young daughter. Molly was attractive, cheerful and uncomplicated, and the transition had been remarkably painless. And Ros had never begrudged her father his new-found happiness. But inevitably she'd felt herself overshadowed by her new stepsister. Janie was both pretty and demanding, and, like most people who expect to be spoiled, she usually got her own way too.

For a moment Ros looked at her own reflection in the windowpanes, reviewing critically the smooth, light brown hair, and the hazel eyes set in a quiet pale-skinned face. The unremarkable sweater and skirt.

Beige hair, beige clothes, beige life, she thought with sudden impatience. Perhaps Janie was right.

Or perhaps she always felt vaguely unsettled when the younger girl was around.

Janie was only occupying Ros's spare bedroom because their parents were off celebrating David Craig's early retirement with a round-the-world trip of a lifetime.

'You will look after her, won't you, darling?' Molly Craig had begged anxiously. 'Stop her doing anything really silly?'

'I'll do my best,' Ros had promised, but she had an uneasy feeling that Molly would regard responding to lonely hearts ads as rather more silly.

But what could she do? She was a writer, for heaven's sake, not a nanny—or a minder. She needed her own space, and unbroken concentration for her work. Something Janie had never understood.

Ros had studied English at university, and had written her dissertation on aspects of popular fiction. As an exercise, she'd tried writing a romantic novel set at the time of the Norman Conquest, and, urged on by her tutor, had submitted the finished script to a literary agent. No one had been more surprised than herself when her book had sold to Mercury House and she'd found herself contracted to write two more, using her mother's name, Rosamund Blake.

Her original plans for a teaching career had been shelved, and she'd settled down with enormous relish to the life of a successful novelist. She realised with hindsight it was what she'd been born for, and that she'd never have been truly happy doing anything else.

With the exception of marrying and raising a family,

she hastily amended. But, unlike Janie, she was in no particular hurry.

And nor, it seemed, was Colin, although he talked about 'one day' quite a lot.

She'd met him two years ago at a neighbour's drinks party, which he'd followed up with an invitation to dinner.

He was tall and fair, with a handsome, rather ruddy face, and an air of dependability. He lived in a self-contained flat at his parents' house in Fulham, and worked for a large firm of accountants in the city, specialising in corporate taxation. In the summer he played cricket, and when winter came he switched to rugby, with the occasional game of squash.

He led, Ros thought, a very ordered life, and she had become part of that order. Which suited her very well, she told herself.

In any case, love was different for everyone. And she certainly didn't want to be like Janie—swinging deliriously between bliss and despondency with every new man. Nor did she want to emulate one of her heroines and be swept off her feet by a handsome rogue, even if he did have a secret heart of gold. Fiction was one thing and real life quite another, and she had no intention of getting them mixed up.

Life with Colin would be safe and secure, she knew. He'd give her few anxieties, certainly, because he didn't have the imagination for serious mischief...

She stopped dead, appalled at the disloyalty of the thought. Janie's doing, no doubt, she decided grimly.

But, whatever her stepsister thought, she was contented. And not just contented, but happy. Very happy indeed, she told the beige reflection with a fierce nod of her head. After all, she had a perfect house, a perfect garden, and a settled relationship. What else could she possibly need?

She wondered, as she returned to her desk, why she'd needed to be quite so vehement about it all...

Usually she found it easy to lose herself in her work, but for once concentration was proving difficult. Her mind was buzzing, going off at all kinds of tangents, and eventually she switched off her computer and went downstairs to make herself some coffee.

Her study was on the top floor of her tall, narrow house in a terrace just off the Kings Road. The bedrooms and bathroom were on the floor below, with the ground floor occupied by her sitting room and dining area. The kitchen and another bathroom were in the basement.

On the way down, she looked in on Janie, but the room was deserted and there were a number of screwed-up balls of writing paper littering the carpet.

Ros retrieved one and smoothed it out. '"Dear Lonely in London",' she read, with a groan. '"I'm also alone, and waiting to meet the right person to make my life complete. Why don't we get together and—"' A violent dash, heavily scored into the paper, showed that Janie had run out of inspiration and patience at the same time.

Ros sighed as she continued on her way to the basement. She could only hope that 'Lonely in London' would indeed be swamped by replies, so that Janie's would go unnoticed.

In the kitchen she found the debris of Janie's own coffee-making, along with the remains of a hastily made sandwich and a note which read, 'Gone to Pam's'.

Ros's lips tightened as she started clearing up. Pam

was a former school buddy of Janie's, and equally volatile. No wise counsels would be prevailing there.

Well, I can't worry about it any more, she thought. My whole working day has been disrupted as it is.

Nor would she be able to work that evening, because she was going out to dinner with Colin. Which was something to look forward to, she reminded herself swiftly. So why did she suddenly feel so depressed?

'Darling, is something the matter? You've hardly eaten a thing.'

Ros started guiltily, and put down the fork she'd been using to push a piece of meat round her plate.

'I'm fine, really.' She smiled with an effort. 'Just not very hungry.'

'Well, I know it couldn't be the food,' said Colin. 'This must be the only place in London where you can still get decent, honest cooking at realistic prices.'

Ros stifled a sigh. Just for once, she mused, it might be nice to eat something wildly exotic at astronomical prices. But Colin didn't like foreign food, or seafood, to which he was allergic, or garlic. Especially not garlic.

Which was why they came to this restaurant each week and had steak, sauté potatoes, and a green salad without dressing. Not forgetting a bottle of house red.

'I hope you're not dieting,' he went on with mock severity. 'You know I like a girl to have a healthy appetite.'

Whenever he said that, Ros thought, wincing, she had a vision of herself with bulging thighs and cheeks stuffed like a hamster's.

'Colin,' she said suddenly. 'Do you think I'm dull?'

'What on earth are you talking about?' He put down his knife and fork and stared at her. 'I wouldn't be here if I thought that.'

'But if you saw me across a roomful of people would you come to me? Push them all aside to get to me because you couldn't stay away?'

'Well, naturally,' he said uncomfortably. 'You're my angel. My one and only. You know that.'

'Yes, of course.' Ros bit her lip. 'I'm sorry. I just have a lot on my mind at the moment.'

Colin snorted. 'Don't tell me. It's that girl causing problems again, I suppose?'

'She doesn't mean to,' Ros defended. 'She's just a bit thrown at the moment because she's split with Martin and—'

'Well, that's a lucky escape for Martin.' Colin gave a short laugh. 'And I hope a lesson for Janie. Maybe she won't rush headlong into her next relationship.'

'On the contrary,' Ros said, needled. 'She spent the entire afternoon replying to an ad in the *Clarion*'s personal column. "Lonely in London", he calls himself,' she added.

'She's mad,' Colin said. 'Out of her tree. And what are you thinking of to allow it?'

'She's over twenty-one,' Ros reminded him levelly. 'How can I stop her? And it doesn't have to be a disaster,' she went on, Colin's disapproval making her contrary for some reason. 'A lot of people must find happiness through those ads, or there wouldn't be so many of them.'

'Dear God, Ros, pull yourself together. This isn't one of your damned stupid books.'

His words died into a frozen silence. Ros put down her glass, aware that her hand was trembling.

She said quietly, 'So that's what you think of my work. I'd often wondered.'

'Well, it's hardly Booker Prize stuff, angel. You've said so yourself.'

'Yes,' she said. 'But that doesn't necessarily mean I want to hear it from anyone else.'

'Come on, Ros.' He looked like a small boy who'd been slapped—something she'd always found endearing in the past. 'It was just a slip of the tongue. I didn't really mean it. Janie makes me so irritated...'

'Oddly enough, she feels the same about you.' Ros leaned back in her chair, giving him a steady look.

'Indeed?' he said stiffly. 'I fail to see why.'

'Well don't worry about it,' she said. 'From now on I'll keep her vagaries strictly to myself.'

'But I want you to feel you can confide in me,' he protested. 'I'm there for you, Ros. You know that.' He swallowed. 'I'm booked to go with the lads on a rugby tour next week, but I'll cancel it if you want. If I can help with Janie.'

Ros smiled involuntarily. 'I appreciate the sacrifice, but it isn't necessary. I think the two of you are better apart. And the rugby tour will do you good.'

It will do us both good, was the secret, unbidden thought that came to her.

He looked faintly relieved, and handed her the dessert menu. 'I suppose you'll have your usual crème caramel?'

'No,' she said crisply. 'Tonight I'm having the Amaretto soufflé with clotted cream.'

He laughed indulgently. 'Living dangerously, darling?'

'Yes,' Ros said slowly. 'I think maybe I will. From now on.'

'Well, don't change too much.' He lowered his voice intimately. 'Because I happen to think you're perfect just as you are.'

'How strange,' she said. 'Because I bore myself rigid.'

She smiled angelically into his astonished eyes. 'I'd like brandy with my coffee tonight, please. And, Colin, make it a double.'

The days that followed were peaceful enough. Ros saw little of Janie, who was either working or at Pam's house, but nothing more had been said about 'Lonely in London', so she could only hope that the younger girl had thought again.

Colin departed on his rugby tour, still expressing his concern, and promising to phone her each evening.

'There's really no need,' she'd protested, a touch wearily. 'We're not joined at the hip.'

We're not even engaged, the small, annoying voice in her head had added.

'And I think we could both do with some space,' she'd gone on carefully. 'To help us get things into perspective.'

'Good riddance,' was Janie's comment when she heard he'd departed. 'So, while the cat's away, is the mouse going to play?'

'The mouse,' Ros said drily, 'is going to work. I'm behind schedule with the book.'

'You mean you're going to stay cooped up in that office all the time?' Janie was incredulous.

'It's my coop, and I like it,' Ros returned. 'But I am going out later—to get my hair cut.' She laughed at Janie's disgusted look. 'Face it, love. You're the party girl, and I'm the sobering influence.'

Janie gave her a long, slow stare. 'You mean if a genie came out of a bottle and granted you three wishes there's nothing about your life you'd change?' She shook her head. 'That's so sad. You should seize your opportunities—like me.'

'By replying to dodgy newspaper ads, no doubt,' Ros said acidly. 'Have you had a reply yet?'

'No,' Janie said cheerfully. 'But I will.' She glanced at her watch and gasped. 'Crumbs, I'm due in the West End in half an hour. I must fly.' And she was gone, in a waft of expensive perfume.

Ros turned back to her computer screen, but found she was thinking about Janie's three wishes rather than her story.

More disturbingly, she was questioning whether any of the wishes would relate to Colin.

A year ago I'd have had no doubts, she thought sombrely. And Colin is still practical, reliable and kind—all the things I liked when we met. And attractive too, she added, a mite defensively.

He hasn't changed, she thought. It's me. I feel as if there's nothing more about him to learn. That there are no surprises left. And I didn't even know I wanted to be surprised.

It was the same with the house, she realised, shocked. She hadn't needed to do a thing to it. It looked and felt exactly the same as it had when Venetia Blake was alive, apart from some redecoration. But that had been her choice, she reminded herself.

She found herself remembering what the will had said. 'To my beloved granddaughter, Rosamund, my house in Gilshaw Street, and its contents, in the hope that she will use them properly.'

I hope I've done so, she thought. I love the house, and the garden. So why do I feel so unsettled?

And why am I so thankful that Colin's miles away in the north of England?

I'm lucky to have this house, she told herself fiercely. And lucky to have Colin, too. He's a good man—a nice man. And I'm an ungrateful cow.

Janie bounced into the kitchen that evening, triumphantly waving a letter. 'It's "Lonely in London",' she said excitedly. 'He wants to meet me.'

'I didn't know you'd had any mail today.'

'Actually I used Pam's address,' Janie said airily. 'Covering my tracks until I've checked him out. Good idea, eh?'

'Wonderful,' Ros said with heavy irony. 'And here's an even better one—put that letter straight in the bin.'

Janie tossed her head. 'Nonsense. We're getting together at Marcellino's on Thursday evening and he's going to be carrying a red rose. Isn't that adorable?'

'If you like a man who thinks in clichés,' Ros returned coolly. She paused. 'What about Martin?'

Janie shrugged. 'He's called on my mobile a couple of times. He wants us to meet.'

'What did you say?'

'That I was getting my life in place and wanted no distraction.' Janie gave a cat-like smile. 'He was hanging round outside the store tonight, but I dodged him.'

'I just hope you know what you're doing.'

'I know exactly. Now all I have to do is write back to "Lonely in London" telling him I'll see him at eight—and pick out what to wear. I've decided to go on being "Looking for Love" until we've had our date.' She paused for breath, and took a long, surprised look at Ros. 'Hey—what have you done to your hair?'

'I said I was having it cut.' Ros touched it self-consciously. But it hadn't stopped at a trim. There'd been something about the way the stylist had said, 'Your usual, Miss Craig?' that had touched a nerve.

'No,' she'd said. 'I'd like something totally different.' And had emerged, dazed, two hours later, with her hair deftly layered and highlighted.

'It's really cool. I love it.' Janie whistled admiringly. 'There's hope for you yet, Ros.'

She vanished upstairs, and Ros began peeling the vegetables for dinner with a heavy frown.

This is all bad news, she thought. Janie may be using an alias, but Pam's address is real, and in an upmarket area. And I'm ready to bet that old 'Lonely' would prefer to target someone from the more exclusive parts of London.

This is not a game. It could have serious implications. But, apart from locking her in her room next Thursday, how can I stop her?

Janie threw herself headlong into the preparations for her blind date. She spent a lot of time at Pam's, coming back to Gilshaw Street only to deposit large boutique carrier bags. When she was at home she was having long, whispered telephone conversations, punctuated by giggles.

There was another communication from the wretched 'Lonely', which Janie read aloud in triumph over breakfast. It seemed her letter had jumped out from the rest, and convinced him they had a lot in common.

A likely story, thought Ros, sinking her teeth into a slice of toast as if it was his throat.

But when Thursday came Janie's shenanigans were not top of her list of priorities. She'd sent off the first few chapters of her book to her publisher, and had been asked to call at their offices to discuss 'a few points' with her editor.

She returned, stunned.

'Frankly, it lacks spark,' Vivien had told her. 'I want you to rethink the whole thing. I've got some detailed notes for you, and a report from a colleague as well. As you see, she thinks the relationship between the hero and heroine is too low-key—too humdrum, even domesticated. Whereas a Rosamund Blake should have adventure, glamour—total romance.' She had gestured broadly, almost sweeping a pile of paperbacks on to the floor.

'You mean it's—dull?' The word had almost choked Ros.

'Yes, but you can change that. Get rid of the sedate note that's crept in somehow.'

'Maybe because I'm sedate myself. Stuck in a rut of my own making,' Ros had said with sudden bitterness, and the other woman had looked at her meditatively.

'When's the last time you went on a date, Ros? And I don't mean with Colin. When's the last time you took a risk—created your own adventure in reality and not just on the page?'

Ros had forced a smile. 'You sound like my sister. And I doubt if I'd recognise an adventure even if it leapt out at me, waving a flag. But I'll look at the script again and let you have my thoughts.'

She let herself into the house and climbed the stairs to her study, carrying the despised manuscript.

Everything Vivien had said had crystallised her own uneasiness about the pattern of her life.

What the hell had happened to the eager graduate who'd thought the world was her oyster? she wondered despairingly. Has the beige part of me taken over completely?

The first thing she saw was the letter in Janie's impetuous scrawl, propped against her computer screen.

Darling Ros,

It's worked. I knew if I gave Martin the cold shoulder he'd soon come round, and he was waiting outside the house this morning to propose. I'm so HAPPY. We're getting married in September, and we're going down to Dorset so that I can meet his family. I'll E-mail the parents when I get back.

By the way, will you do me a big favour? Please call Marcellino's and tell 'Lonely in London' I won't be there. I've enclosed his last letter, giving his real name. You're a sweetie.

Love...

'"By the way", indeed,' Ros muttered wrathfully. 'She has some nerve. Why can't she do her own dirty work?'

She supposed she should be rejoicing, but in truth she felt Janie had jumped out of the frying pan into the fire. She's too young to be marrying anyone, she thought.

Reluctantly, she unfolded the other sheet of paper and scanned the few lines it contained.

Dear Looking for Love,

I'm very much looking forward to meeting you, and seeing if my image of you fits. I wish you'd trust me with your given name, but perhaps it's best to wait.

'Perhaps' is right, Ros thought. Yet his handwriting was better than she'd anticipated. He used black ink, and broad strokes of the pen, giving a forceful, incisive impression. And he'd signed it 'Sam Alexander'.

She wished he hadn't. She'd had no sympathy for 'Lonely in London', but now he had an identity, and that altered things in some inscrutable way. Because suddenly real feelings, real emotions were involved.

And tonight a real man will be turning up with his red rose, she realised, only to be told by the head waiter that he's been dumped. And he'll have to walk out, perfectly aware that everyone knows what's happened. And that they're probably laughing at him.

Supposing he's genuine, she thought restlessly. He's advertised for sincerity and commitment, and wound up with Janie playing games instead. And maybe— just maybe—he deserves better.

She still wasn't sure when she made the conscious decision to go in Janie's place. But somehow she found herself in her stepsister's room, rooting through her wardrobe, until she found the little black dress and the shoes and thought, Why not?

There were all kinds of reasons 'why not'. And she was still arguing with herself when she walked down the steps and hailed the cab...

Now, sitting on her sofa, the black shoes kicked off, she castigated herself bitterly for her stupidity. She'd prophesied disaster—and it had almost happened. But to herself, not Janie.

She shook her head in disbelief. How could someone who looked like that—who dressed like that—possibly have got under her skin—and in so short a time, too?

Because sexual charisma had nothing to do with surface appearance—that was how.

And Sam Alexander was vibrantly, seductively male. In fact, he was lethal.

He also had good bone structure, and a fine body—lean, hard and muscular.

And she knew how it had felt, touching hers, for that brief and tantalising moment. Recalled the sensuous brush of his mouth on her lips.

For an instant she allowed herself to remember—to wonder... Before, shocked, she dragged herself back from the edge.

She shivered convulsively, wrapping her arms round her body, and felt the sudden pressure of the rose stem against her breast.

She tore it out of her dress and dropped it on the coffee table as if it was contaminated.

'You're not the adventurous type,' she said grimly. 'Back to the real world, Rosamund.'

On her way to the stairs she passed the answer-machine, winking furiously.

'Ros?' Colin's voice sounded querulous. 'Where on earth are you? Pick up the phone if you're there.'

For a second she hesitated then gently pressed the 'Delete' button.

And went on her way upstairs to bed.

CHAPTER THREE

SAM stood watching Janie's slim, black-clad figure retreat. He was aware of an overwhelming impulse to go after her—to say or do something that would stop her vanishing.

But you blew that when you kissed her, you bloody idiot, he told himself savagely as he resumed his seat, signalling to the waiter to bring more coffee.

He still couldn't understand why he'd done it. She wasn't even his type, for God's sake. And he'd broken a major rule, too.

But he'd wanted to do something to crack that cool, lady-like demeanour she'd been showing him all evening, he thought with exasperation, and find out what she was really like. Because he was damned sure the past two hours had told him nothing. That this particular encounter had bombed.

He'd had it too easy up to then, he thought broodingly. The others had been more than ready to tell him everything he wanted to know after just the gentlest of probing.

That was what loneliness did to you, he told himself without satisfaction. It made you vulnerable to even the most cursory interest.

But not Janie Craig, however. She'd simply returned the ball to his feet. And, unlike the others, she hadn't given the impression that the evening mattered. Less still that she hoped it would lead somewhere.

But perhaps there was something he could salvage

from the wreck. Something that would enable him to finish with this assignment and do some real work again.

If he was ever allowed to.

His mouth twisted bitterly. Six weeks ago he'd been lying in the back of a Jeep, covered in stinking blankets and protected by cartons of food and medical supplies, escaping from a Central African republic and the government troops who'd objected to his coverage of their civil war.

He'd come back to London, exhausted and sickened by what he'd had to see and report on, but secure in the knowledge of a job well done, knowing that his dispatches from Mzruba had made front-page news, under his photograph and by-line, day after day in the *Echo*. Expecting his due reward in the shape of the foreign news editorship that he'd been promised before he went.

His editor Alec Norton had taken one look at him and ordered him away on extended leave.

'Somewhere quiet, boy,' he'd rumbled, and tossed a card across the desk. 'This is a place that Mary and I use up in the Yorkshire Dales—the Rowcliffe Inn— soft beds, good food, and peace. I recommend it. Put yourself back together, and then we'll talk.'

Sam had gone up to Rowcliffe, a cluster of grey stone houses around a church, and walked and eaten and slept until the nightmares had begun to recede. The weather had been mixed—all four seasons in one day sometimes—but the cold, clean air had driven the stench of blood, disease and death out of his lungs.

He'd explored the two antique shops that Rowcliffe boasted, eaten home-made curd tart in the small tearooms, and visited the surprisingly up-to-date print works of the local paper, the *Rowcliffe Examiner*. He'd been beginning to wonder how he could ever tear himself away when a message had come for him from a friend on the *Echo* newsdesk via the hotel's fax. 'Houston, we have a problem.'

One telephone call later, his career had lain in ruins about him. Because Alex Norton was in hospital, recovering from a heart attack, and the *Echo* had a new editor—a woman called Cilla Godwin, whom Sam himself had once christened Godzilla.

She was far from unattractive. In her early forties, she had a cloud of mahogany-coloured hair, a full-lipped mouth, and a head-turning figure. Sam's nickname referred to her reputation as an arch-predator, cutting a swathe of destruction through one newspaper office after another, inflicting change where it wasn't needed, and getting rid of those who disagreed with her policies.

He'd no doubt she knew about her nickname, and who'd devised it. When it came to backstabbing, the newsroom at the *Echo* made the Borgias look like amateurs.

But he'd committed a far worse sin than that. During her stint as the *Echo*'s Features Editor she'd made a heavy pass at Sam, after an office party, and he'd turned her down. He'd tried to be gentle—to let her walk away with her pride intact—but she hadn't been fooled, and he'd seen her eyes turn hard and cold, like pebbles, and known he had an enemy.

And now she was the *Echo*'s boss, with the power to hire and fire.

He'd come back to London to find his foreign news job had been given to someone with half his experience, and that he was on 'temporary reassignment' to

Features, which was about the most humiliating de-
motion he could have envisaged. Cilla had told him
herself, relishing every moment of it. She had never
been magnanimous in victory.

It was virtual dismissal, of course. She planned to
make his life such a misery that he'd be glad to resign.
But Sam had no intention of playing her game. He had
company shares, and belonged to the joint profit
scheme, all of which he would forfeit if he simply
walked out.

When he left, he meant to have another job to go
to and a negotiated settlement with the *Echo*. Nothing
less would do.

'Lonely in London' had been all her own idea, of
course. It was to be, she'd told him, her eyes glinting
with malice, 'an in-depth investigation of the women
who replied to the personal columns'.

Sam had looked back blankly at her. 'It's hardly a
new idea,' he'd objected.

'Then it's up to you to make it new,' she said
sharply. 'We want real human interest material—tear-
jerking stuff. You'll have to get close to them—explore their hopes, their dreams, even their fantasies.'

Sam shook his head. 'I don't think so. They've put
themselves on the line already by replying. They
won't want to discuss their reasons with a journalist.'

Cilla sighed. 'You don't get it, do you? As far as
these women are concerned you're the real thing. A
man searching for real love. You'll get them to trust
you—and you'll get them to talk.'

Sam said quietly, 'You have to be joking.'

'On the contrary. Here we are with a new
Millennium, thirty years of women's liberation, and

yet they're still looking to find love with a complete stranger.'

'But I won't be a complete stranger—not if they're *Echo* readers,' Sam reminded her levelly. 'The name Sam Hunter and my picture were plastered all over the front page not so long ago.'

'I'm sure you're not that memorable.' Her smile glittered at him. 'But in case you're right we're going to use your middle name, so you'll be Sam Alexander instead, and we're going to alter your appearance too. Anyway, the women you meet will be eager—hopeful, not suspicious.'

'I think the whole thing stinks,' Sam said tersely.

Cilla regarded her manicured crimson nails. 'Are you refusing the assignment? I'd have thought it was ideally suited to your—peculiar talents.'

No, thought Sam, you know as well as I do that it's sleazy, and probably unethical, and you're waiting for me to say so. The trap's open and waiting. You want me to tell you to go to hell and walk out. Well, tough.

He shrugged. 'I can see problems.'

'There wouldn't be a story without them.' She leaned back in her chair, her gaze sweeping him. 'Just be certain none of them are of your making. It goes without saying that all these meetings take place in public.'

'Cilla,' Sam drawled, 'I wouldn't have it any other way. When do I start?'

He'd thought he was ahead on points—until he'd seen the clothes she'd chosen for him to wear—and the glasses—and also what the barber she'd summoned was doing to his hair.

'Sam isn't short for Samson, I hope,' she'd said gloatingly, as he was sheared. 'I wouldn't want you to lose your strength, darling. All that wonderful male potency I've heard so much about.'

He'd smiled at her in the mirror, his face aching with the effort. 'Keep listening, Cilla. I'll live to fight another day.'

Now, halfway through the assignment, he wasn't sure the battle was worth it. He was ashamed of what he was doing. He'd pick another civil war any day above those anxious, hopeful eyes looking at him across restaurant tables.

Maybe he should have cut his losses and gone, he brooded. Especially as instinct told him that 'Lonely in London' might be a picnic compared with other things Cilla Godwin could be cooking up for him.

He finished his coffee and asked for the bill. At least his expenses would give her a bad few minutes, but he needed to justify them by writing a really good piece on Janie Craig. And he wasn't sure that he could.

Back at his flat, he worked on his laptop for an hour, making notes about his meeting with her, but, as he'd feared, she remained totally elusive. He knew little more than she'd mentioned in her original letter—except that she blushed easily and wore a scent called Organza. And that her lips had trembled when he kissed them.

Not details he would put in his report, he decided sardonically.

Nor could he mention what had surprised him most about the evening—the moment when he'd asked her to stay—and found he meant it.

Sam snorted in self-derision, and switched off the computer.

The traumas of the past few weeks must have softened my brain, he thought, and went to bed.

* * *

Gardening, Ros thought crossly as she attacked the roots of a particularly hostile dandelion, was not having its usual therapeutic effect.

This should have been a really good day for her. After all, she would have the house to herself for the whole weekend, and the problem with Janie had been dealt with and could be put safely behind her.

She wasn't too optimistic about the future of this rushed engagement to Martin, but if it all ended in tears Molly and her father would be back by then, and could cope.

All in all, she should have been as happy as a lark. Instead, she felt thoroughly on edge—as if a storm was brewing somewhere.

The fact that she'd slept badly the previous night hadn't helped, of course. She'd been assailed by vague, tormenting dreams, none of which she'd been able to remember when sleep had finally deserted her altogether just after dawn.

Lying, staring into space held no appeal, so she'd done all the right, practical things. Made herself tea, showered and dressed in leggings and a big sweatshirt, eaten croissants with cherry jam, and started work.

Vivien had been quite right, she'd realised unhappily, as she'd put down the script a couple of hours later. A lot of the book seemed to have been written on auto-pilot. Yet the basic idea of two strangers thrown together in marriage for dynastic reasons was a strong one.

Normally she'd have revelled in every minute of it. Now she could see she'd just been going through the motions. The chemistry—the danger was lacking.

It was more than a question of a few alterations.

Her best bet would be to junk the whole thing and start again.

And she'd made a new beginning. In fact she'd made several. But when the only words she'd wanted to keep had been 'Chapter' and 'One', she'd decided to have a break and do some tidying in the garden.

She knew exactly what was to blame for this cranky restlessness. Last night's ill-judged rendezvous with Sam Alexander, that was what, she thought grimly. And let it be an everlasting lesson to her not to interfere.

Because he seemed to have taken up residence in a corner of her mind, and she couldn't shift him.

And the most disturbing thing of all was that she kept remembering him in ways that made her skin burn, and an odd trembling invade her limbs.

All things considered, she was quite glad she couldn't remember her dreams.

But nothing happened, she thought, irritably shovelling the defeated weeds into a plastic sack. We had dinner—and he kissed me. But that's no big deal. I should have seen it coming and dodged. My mistake. But there's no point in making a federal case out of it.

I'd be better off deciding what to say to Colin when he comes back tomorrow, she told herself, as she stripped off her gardening gloves.

Because she knew now, without doubt, that there was no longer any future in their relationship, and she would have to tell him so.

At first she thought she'd say it when he rang that evening. But that would be the coward's way out. The relationship might be irretrievably stale, but after two years he deserved an explanation face to face.

She wondered how upset he would really be. It had occurred to her some time ago that anyone who seriously wanted to marry Colin would have to get past his mother first. Colin's flat might be self-contained, but he was still where Mrs Hayton wanted him—on the other side of the wall—and she wouldn't let him go without a struggle.

The fact that this didn't bother me unduly should have warned me that things weren't right, Ros told herself. If Colin was really the man for me, I'd have fought for him tooth and nail.

She went indoors and made herself a sandwich lunch. She'd just sat down to eat it when the phone rang, making her jump uneasily. Just as she'd done with every other call that morning.

'Oh, pull yourself together,' she adjured herself impatiently. 'It can't possibly be Sam Alexander. You're being paranoid.'

'Ros?' It was Janie. 'I'll be back on Sunday night—probably quite late.'

'Everything's going well?'

'Ye-es.' Janie hesitated. 'Martin's parents are really nice, but I think I was a surprise to them. And they say it's too soon to be making wedding plans,' she added glumly.

'How does Martin feel?'

'Well, naturally he doesn't want to go against his family,' Janie said defensively. 'But we're trying to talk them round.' There was a pause, then she said in a lower voice, 'Did you contact "Lonely in London" for me?'

Ros swallowed. 'Yes,' she said. 'Yes, I did. I—I think he got the message.'

'You're a star,' Janie said. 'Must dash. We're taking the dogs for a walk.'

I don't feel like a star, Ros thought as she replaced the receiver. More like a black hole.

And why didn't I tell her the truth? I could have made a joke of it. Hey—I checked him out personally, and you had a lucky escape. A haircut from hell, and he buys his clothes from a street market.

She looked at her plate of sandwiches, decided she wasn't as hungry as she'd thought, and went back to her study.

But by mid-afternoon she still hadn't made any real progress on the rewrite of her book.

Maybe if I chose a different background, she thought. A different period—the Wars of the Roses, perhaps. Something that would give me a fresh perspective.

She'd need to do some research, of course, she realised with sudden relish, and a trip to the local library was infinitely more appealing than staring at a blank computer screen. Or allowing herself to become prey to any more ridiculous thoughts...

On her way down she grabbed her jacket and bag from her room, and went out, slamming the front door behind her.

As she went down her steps she looked in her bag, checking that her library card was there, so she only realised that someone was standing by her railings when she cannoned into him.

Startled, she looked up, her lips framing an apology, and stopped dead, gasping as she found herself staring at Sam Alexander.

'What are you doing here?' Her voice sounded husky—strained. 'How did you find me?'

'I went to the address on your last letter.'

'Oh,' she said numbly. 'Of course. And Pam's mother told you…'

'Eventually she did,' he said. 'Although she wasn't too pleased to hear her home had been used as a mailbox.'

'Why did you come here?' She was shaking, nerves stretched tautly. Shock, she told herself. And embarrassment, as she suddenly remembered what she was wearing—gardening gear and no make-up. She wailed inwardly. Because she was rattled, she went on the attack. 'And why aren't you at work anyway?'

'Why aren't you?' he countered.

Ros resisted an impulse to smooth her hair with her fingers. She didn't want to look good for him, for heaven's sake. 'I—I took a day off.'

'And so did I. So that I could find you. Because we didn't make any arrangement to see each other again.' He paused. 'In retrospect, that seemed a bad mistake.'

She lifted her chin. 'Then I'm afraid you've made another one, Mr Alexander.'

'Sam,' he told her quietly.

'Dinner was—nice,' she went on. 'But that's all there was. And it has to stay that way.'

'Why must it? You decided to reply to my ad.'

'A decision I now regret—bitterly.'

'I see,' he said slowly. He looked past her at the house. 'Are you married? Is that the problem?'

'Of course not.' Indignant colour flared in her cheeks.

'You were so cagey about your personal details, it seemed a possibility.' He gave her a meditative look. 'Living with someone, then?'

'I told you,' she said curtly. 'My sister. Now, will you go, please, and let us both get on with our lives?'

'But that's not how I want it,' he said softly. 'You see, I really need to find out about you, Janie. Last night was just a taste, and it made me hungry. And I'm convinced you feel the same, although you're trying to deny it.'

'Oh, spare me the psychobabble, please.' Ros drew a deep breath. 'Everyone's entitled to have second thoughts.'

'A word of advice, then. There's no point in describing yourself as "Looking for Love" if you run for cover each time someone shows an interest in you.' His face was solemn, but the turquoise eyes held a glint that the gold-rimmed glasses couldn't disguise. 'That contravenes the Trades Descriptions Act and involves a serious penalty.'

She'd assumed she was too tense to find anything remotely amusing in the situation, but she was wrong, she realised, as she bit back a swift, reluctant smile.

She said, 'Which is?'

'That you let me see you again.'

'You're seeing me now.'

'That's not what I mean.'

She said, 'Mr Alexander—has it ever occurred to you that it takes two to make a bargain—and that I might not find you attractive?'

'Yes, it's occurred to me,' he said. 'but I've dismissed it.'

'You,' she said, 'have an ego the size of the Millennium Dome.'

'And also a very good memory,' he returned pleasantly. 'I retain this very vivid impression of how you felt in my arms—how you reacted. And it wasn't repulsion, Janie, so don't fool yourself.'

She bit her lip. 'You took me off guard, that's all.'

'Excellent,' he said. 'Because those defences of yours are a big problem for anyone trying to get to know you—to become your friend.'

'Which is naturally what you want.' Her tone was sharply sceptical.

'Yes,' he said. 'But not all I want.'

'What more is there?' It was a dangerous question, but somehow she couldn't resist it.

'Perhaps—to discover everything there is to know.' His voice was soft, almost reflective. 'To explore you—heart, mind—and body.'

A shiver went through her, trembling along her senses, as if they were already naked together. As if his hands—his mouth—were touching her—possessing her. His body moving over hers in total mastery.

From somewhere she found the self-command to smile at him—a cool, even cynical curl of the mouth.

'A little over-ambitious for me, I'm afraid.'

'Fine.' His own grin was wickedly appreciative. 'Then I'll settle for meeting for a drink tonight instead.'

'Perhaps I already have a date this evening.'

'Then we'll fix it for some other time, when you're free. I can wait.'

'You don't give up, do you?'

'That,' he said, 'rather depends on my level of commitment.'

'And if I say—no?'

He shrugged. 'Then I'll just have to hang around here in the street, looking soulful and waiting for your heart to soften. The neighbours will love it,' he added, glancing round. 'We're attracting a fair measure of attention already. Curtains are twitching.'

She saw with annoyance that he was right. She said curtly, 'I could always take action against you for harassment.'

'But you were the one who contacted me in the first place,' he reminded her. 'And you came to meet me looking like a million dollars, as the head waiter at Marcellino's will confirm.'

'Which is more than can be said for you,' she countered waspishly.

But the jibe failed to needle him. Instead, he burst out laughing. 'What can I say? Anyway, no one would blame me for being smitten and trying again. I really don't think your harassment ploy would work—so why don't you give in gracefully?'

His voice deepened to a persuasive drawl. 'Come out with me, Janie, and I'll wear a wig—use contact lenses—start buying my clothes in Bond Street. See how desperate I am to reverse your bad impression of me?'

To her intense irritation she found she wanted to laugh too, and bit down hard on her lip.

She said, 'Mr Alexander…'

'Sam,' he corrected, quite gently. 'Say it for me—please?'

'Sam.' She heard the huskiness in her voice and took a deep, steadying breath. 'If we have this one drink, will you guarantee then to leave me alone?'

'No,' he said. 'But I promise I'll leave the ultimate decision in the matter entirely to you. And that I'll accept your ruling.'

'Very well,' she said. 'There's a wine bar a couple

of streets away called The Forlorn Hope. I'll see you there at eight.'

'Agreed.' His mouth twisted slightly. 'And I'll try not to read too much into your choice of venue. Until eight, then.'

'I'll be counting the moments,' she tossed after him acidly.

Sam swung back. Across the expanse of pavement, their glances met—clashed with the speed of fencing foils.

'No,' he said, quite softly. 'But one day—or night—very soon, you will. And there's another promise.'

She watched him go, aware that her breathing had quickened to danger level.

She thought, I want—I need him out of my life. Permanently. And tonight I must make certain that he goes.

CHAPTER FOUR

IT WAS only when he became aware that people in the Kings Road were giving him curious looks that Sam realised he was walking along wearing a broad grin.

'Get a grip,' he muttered to himself, as he hurriedly rearranged his features, and hailed a cab. You may have got a result, he thought, but it was too close for comfort. Which doesn't leave much to smile about.

More than once he'd lost the prepared script completely. Found himself saying something totally unexpected again. And by doing so he'd pushed the whole situation to the edge.

He'd need to tread more carefully that evening, he thought, removing the hated glasses and thrusting them into his pocket. He couldn't risk startling her into flight before he'd got all the material he needed for the feature.

His lips tightened as he recalled Cilla Godwin contemptuously flicking the piece he'd written back at him over her desk that morning.

'It's a cop-out, Hunter,' she'd declared. 'There's nothing of substance there. You haven't even touched on why she decided to go the lonely hearts route. There's more to this one than meets the eye, and you've missed it. See her again, and this time find out something useful.'

And Sam, reluctantly aware that her criticism was justified for once had gritted his teeth and nodded.

It hadn't really surprised him that tracing Janie

Craig had thrown up a complication. Perhaps all the others had used false addresses too, although he didn't think so.

No, he decided grudgingly, Cilla was right, damn her. Janie Craig was indeed something of an enigma—an irresistible challenge to any journalist.

And tonight, he realised, frowning, would probably be his last chance to solve the puzzle she presented.

He leaned back in his corner of the taxi and reviewed what he'd got so far.

Presumably she'd believed she'd covered her tracks sufficiently well, because she'd clearly been shocked to see him there, literally on her doorstep.

And what a doorstep, he reflected, his frown deepening. An elegant terrace house in a quiet cul de sac, which she shared with her sister. She could hardly support the upkeep of a property like that out of her freelance earnings, so the sister must be the one with the money.

Older? he speculated. Unattractive and sour about it? Jealous of her younger sibling, but reliant on her too? Not wanting her to find a man, perhaps, and make a life for herself, thus forcing Janie to subterfuge?

The possibilities were endless, but he had to establish the truth. And to do that he had to get Janie Craig to trust him. Something she'd not been prepared to do so far, he conceded ruefully.

And which he wouldn't manage by throwing down the gauntlet to her in the open street as he'd just done.

And, what was worse he'd no idea what had prompted him to challenge her in such an overtly sexual way. Any more than he knew why he'd kissed her at their first meeting—or begged her to stay...

And, not for the first time, he found himself wondering what the hell he'd have done if she'd agreed. And unable to produce a satisfactory answer.

One drink, Ros told herself nervously. That was all she was committed to, no matter what Mr Alexander's unbounded self-esteem might hope or believe.

And during the time it took to consume a single glass of wine she would make it abundantly clear that she never wanted to set eyes on him again, and that she would not hesitate to take legal action if he persisted.

And not even he could find her message ambivalent this time.

The whole sorry mess could so easily have been avoided if only—*if only*—she'd stayed quietly at home and minded her own business.

Instead she'd pranced off to meet him, dressed to the nines and sending out all kinds of misleading signals.

That black dress would be going to the nearly-new shop as soon as she'd had it cleaned, she decided grimly, and those shoes with it. She'd tell Janie there'd been some kind of accident, and reimburse her for them.

It was unnerving that Sam Alexander now knew where she lived. And she'd had to apologise abjectly to Pam's mother, who'd left a furious message on the answering machine, when she'd come back from the library.

And to think I complained that I was in a rut, she thought wearily. Welcome back dull normality.

Except that she didn't really mean it. And it was too late, anyway. Because her life had already changed quite incontrovertibly.

And, in some strange, confused way, she knew that even if she had the power to do it she would not change it back.

She was tempted to show up that evening in sweatshirt and leggings again, but eventually swapped them for the conservative choice of a navy pleated skirt topped by a round-necked cream sweater. She looped a silk scarf in shades of crimson, gold and blue round her throat, and slid her feet into simple navy loafers.

She confined her make-up to moisturiser, mascara on her long lashes, and a touch of muted coral on her lips.

Neat and tidy, but definitely not seductive, she thought, taking a last critical look at herself.

She'd seriously considered following Janie's example, and packing a bag and disappearing for the weekend. But she guessed it would be pointless, and that in all probability she'd find him camped on her doorstep when she returned.

No, she would have to be brave and take her medicine.

She would be cool and firm, she told herself, as she set off on the short walk to the wine bar.

It was already crowded, and for a moment she thought he wasn't there, and felt her stomach lurch in what she instantly labelled relief. Because it felt dangerously like disappointment and that wasn't— couldn't be possible…

And then she heard a voice call 'Janie' above the hubbub of voices and laughter, and saw someone on his feet beside a table in the corner.

For a moment she thought she must have been mistaken, and misheard the name, because this man was a stranger.

Then she saw him smile, and realised it was indeed Sam Alexander.

But he's not wearing his glasses, she thought, as she threaded her way towards him through the busy room, her own mouth curving in reluctant response as she reached the table.

Little wonder she'd hardly recognised him, she thought, her brows lifting as she took in the unmistakably Italian cut of his charcoal pants, and the paler grey jacket he was wearing over a black rollneck sweater in what seemed to be cashmere.

She said a little breathlessly as she took her seat, 'You weren't kidding about Bond Street.'

'Their Oxfam branch,' he said promptly. 'Never let me down yet.'

Ros choked on a giggle. 'What happened to your glasses?'

'I left them at home. You made it clear I wouldn't have a menu to read, so I'm relying on you to decipher the wine list for me and stop me falling over the furniture.'

'It's a deal.' She shook her head. 'But you've let me down badly over the wig.'

'I looked like Mel Gibson in one, and George Clooney in the other. It didn't seem fair to expose you to that level of temptation.' He put up a hand and touched his hair. 'And this will grow out, I swear it.'

'But not,' she said, 'during the course of a solitary drink.'

'You never know,' he said. 'There could be a marked improvement by closing time.'

But by then I shall be long gone. She thought the words but did not say them aloud.

A waiter came hurrying up to the table, carrying an

ice bucket which contained, Ros saw, a bottle of Bollinger and two chilled flutes.

Sam said, 'I ordered in advance. I hope you don't mind.'

'Well—no,' Ros said slowly. 'But why champagne? This isn't exactly a celebration.'

He shrugged. 'You said one drink. I wanted it to be—special.'

'It's that all right.' She watched the waiter fill the flutes, and accepted the one she was handed. 'So what do we drink to?' she asked lightly. 'Ships that pass in the night?'

He said quietly, 'Let's start with—friendship.' And touched his glass to hers. 'Although we should really drink to you. You look—terrific.'

She gave a small, constrained laugh. 'That's because you're not wearing your glasses.'

'I can see well enough,' he said. The turquoise eyes travelled slowly over her. 'Terrific—and very different to last night—and this afternoon. How many women are you, Janie Craig?'

Embarrassed, she drank some champagne. It was cold and dry, and the bubbles seemed to burst in her mouth. Colin had never liked it, she found herself remembering. He complained it gave him indigestion. Something that seemed to belong to another lifetime— another age...

'I was going to write down a list of questions for you,' he said. 'So I wouldn't forget anything, or waste the short time we have together.'

'What sort of questions?'

'The kind that it usually takes days—weeks— months to answer. The basic things—do you prefer dogs to cats? Is spring your favourite season, or is it

autumn? What music makes you cry? All the small
details that make up the complete picture.' The turquoise met hers steadily. 'And that people find out
about each other when they have all the time in the
world.'

Ros forced a smile, her fingers playing nervously
with the stem of her flute. 'And things that we don't
need to know—under the circumstances.'

'So, let's cut to the chase instead.' He leaned forward. 'It's clear you're not seriously seeking a relationship, so why did you answer my ad—and why did
you come to meet me?'

Ros hesitated, suddenly aware that she was strongly
tempted to tell him the truth. But if she did, she argued
inwardly, it would only lead to more and more complicated explanations, and recriminations—and what
good could it possibly do anyway, when they were
never going to see each other again?

On the other hand, she didn't want to lie either…

'Replying to the ad was someone else's idea,' she
said, choosing her words with care. 'And once the
meeting had been set up, I felt—obliged to go through
with it.'

He said softly, 'So it was all down to your sense of
duty.' There was an odd note in his voice which she
couldn't quite interpret. It was almost like anger, but
she didn't think it could be that, because he was smiling at her.

'But I suppose it serves me right for asking.' He
paused. 'Are you seeing someone else?'

She hadn't expected that, and was jolted into candour. 'I was—but it's over.'

'And you used me to get rid of him—or was I simply to celebrate your new liberation?'

'Perhaps both—maybe neither,' she said. 'I wasn't thinking that clearly.' She hesitated. 'But I didn't mean to hurt your feelings. In fact that was the last thing I intended…'

'Well, don't worry about it.' His voice was silky. 'I expect I'll recover.' He refilled her glass. 'So, tell me about your sister.'

Ros jumped, spilling some of her wine on to the marble table-top. 'What do you want to know?' she asked defensively, mopping up with a paper napkin.

'She seems to have a fairly profound effect on you,' Sam said, his brows lifting as he watched. 'Is she your only living relative?'

Ros shook her head. 'My parents are abroad at the moment.'

'Ah,' he said. 'And you're house-sitting for them.'

'I'm taking care of things while they're away,' Ros agreed carefully.

Well, that explained the expensive house, thought Sam. It also meant she was still guarding her real address…

He said, amused, 'You're like one of those Russian dolls. Or an onion. Each time I think I've found you, there's another layer.'

Her mouth curved. 'I don't care for the comparison, but I think on the whole I prefer the doll. Onions make you cry.'

'Indeed they do,' he said. He gave her a thoughtful look. 'And I suspect, Miss Janie Craig, that you could break someone's heart quite easily.'

Ros studied the bubbles in her champagne. 'Now you're being absurd,' she said crisply.

'It always happens when I'm hungry.' He pointed to a blackboard advertising the dishes of the day. 'I'm having spaghetti carbonara. Are you going to join me?'

'We agreed—just a drink.' Ros remembered her abortive sandwich lunch, and her stomach clenched in longing.

'I'll let you slurp your spaghetti.' He shrugged. 'Or you can always go back to your lonely microwave. It's your choice.'

'Very well,' she said, adding stiffly, 'But I'm paying for my own meal.'

'That will keep me in my place,' he murmured, signalling to the waiter.

'And another thing,' Ros said, when their order, including herb bread and a bottle of Orvieto Classico, had been given. 'If you aren't wearing your glasses, how did you know that was spaghetti carbonara on the menu?'

Sam shrugged, cursing himself silently. 'In a place like this, it's practically standard,' he countered.

'Yes,' she said slowly. 'I suppose so.'

There were too many contradictions in this man, she thought, and they intrigued her. Or rather they intrigued the writer in her, she corrected herself hastily. And she could put the evening to good use by listening and observing.

'Have you always worn glasses?' she continued brightly.

'No,' he said. 'It happened very recently.'

'I suppose it's working with numbers all day.' Ros sighed. 'I expect using a computer is just as bad. I shall have to be careful.'

'You use a computer to sell beauty products?' Sam stared at her.

'Not exactly.' Ros gave an awkward laugh, aware

that she'd flushed guiltily. That was too much champagne on an empty stomach making her careless, she reproached herself. 'Just for—ordering—and sales reports. That kind of thing,' she improvised swiftly.

'Then I wouldn't worry too much,' he returned drily. 'I think your eyes will be safe for a long time yet.'

She gave a constrained smile, and stared down at her glass.

'But I can't say the same for your nervous system,' Sam went on. He reached across the table and took her hand lightly, his fingers exploring the delicate tracery of veins in her wrist.

'Your pulse is going like a trip-hammer,' he observed, frowningly. 'For someone who spends her life dealing with the public, you're incredibly tense. Are you like this with all the men you meet, or is it just me?'

All the men? she thought. Apart from a couple of totally casual relationships at university, there'd only been Colin...

She withdrew her hand from his grasp, clasping both of them tightly in her lap. 'I told you—I've never done anything like this before.'

'Then let's change the scenario,' he said. 'Let's pretend we did it the conventional way—that I saw you in a department store at one of your promotions, chatted you up, and arranged to meet you later. Would that make you feel more relaxed?'

'I—I don't know,' she said. 'Perhaps...'

'Then that's what happened.' His smile coaxed her. 'Forget everything else. This is just Sam and Janie, meeting for a drink and a meal, and examining the possibilities. No pressure.'

She lifted her head and looked at him, seeing how the laughter lines had deepened beside his firm mouth. She realised with sudden piercing clarity how much she wanted to touch them. How she longed to experience the entire warmth of his skin beneath her fingertips. To learn with slow intimacy the bone and muscle that made him. To know him with completion and delight.

And she felt dismay and exhilaration go to war inside her.

She said, breathlessly, 'Is that what you've said to all the others?'

The turquoise eyes looked directly into hers. His voice was quiet. 'What others?'

A silence seemed to enclose them—a small, precious bubble of quiet holding the moment safe.

A voice inside her whispered, Whatever happens— however long I live—whoever I spend my life with— I shall remember this.

And then the waiter came hurrying up with the platter of bread and the wine, and there was the fuss of cutlery and fresh glasses, and she was able to lean back in her chair and control her breathing, quieten the slam of her heart against her ribcage.

She thought, He said 'let's pretend'—and I will. I'll be Janie, and take the risk. Go where it leads—whatever the cost...

The Orvieto was clean and cold against her dry throat, and she swallowed it gratefully. 'That's so good.'

'Have you ever been to Italy?'

'Yes, I love it. I was there for nearly three months a year or so ago.' She halted abruptly, realising she'd given too much away again.

'Three months?' His brows lifted. 'None of the usual package tours for you, I see.'

'I was there to work,' she said. And it was true. She'd been researching her third novel, set at the time of the Renaissance and featuring an English mercenary who'd sold his sword to the Borgias until he lost his heart to the daughter of one of their enemies. Her trip had taken her all over the Romagna, and to Florence and Siena as well. The book had been fun to write, and had turned out well too, she thought, her lips curving slightly.

'Some of the big foreign cosmetics companies have—training courses for their products,' she added hastily, as she registered his questioning look.

'Do they now?' Sam drank some of his own wine. 'I didn't realise so much was involved.' He frowned slightly. 'You take your career very seriously.'

'Of course,' she said, and meant it. 'Don't you?'

'I certainly used to.' His eyes were meditative. 'But I seem to have reached some kind of crossroads. And I don't know for certain what my next move should be.' He added, 'I suppose you feel the same.'

'What makes you say that?'

He leaned forward. 'Isn't it why we're here together now?' he challenged. 'Because we know that everything's changed and there's no turning back?' He sounded almost angry.

She tried to smile. 'You make it sound—daunting.'

'That's because I'm not sure how I feel.' His voice was blunt. 'And, frankly, I'm not used to it.'

Ros bit her lip. 'Perhaps we should go back to Plan A—where you're "Lonely in London" again,' she suggested.

'No,' he said quietly. 'It's far too late for that, and we both know it.'

Her voice faltered slightly, 'You said—you promised—that you'd let me decide—and that you'd accept my choice.'

'Yes.' The turquoise eyes held a glint. 'Just don't expect me to take no for an answer, that's all.'

Bowls of creamy pasta were set in front of them, giant pepper mills wielded and dishes of grated parmesan offered.

She was glad of the respite, although nervousness had blunted the edge of her hunger by now.

I'm not a risk-taker by nature, she thought. How on earth am I going to get way with this?

'Eat.' Sam waved a fork at her when they'd been left alone again. His smile slanted. 'You need to build your strength up.'

'Please,' she said, her throat constricting. 'Don't say things like that.'

'Why not? Have you looked in the mirror lately? You have cheekbones like wings. A breath of wind would blow you away. And, oddly enough, I don't want that to happen.' He paused. 'As for the rest of it, you can call the shots, Janie. I won't push you into anything you don't want—or aren't ready for.'

'Another promise?' Her smile trembled as she picked up her fork.

'No,' he said, eyes and voice steady. 'A guarantee. Now eat.'

In the end, she finished every scrap of pasta, and followed it with a generous helping of tiramisu.

'That was wonderful,' she admitted, leaning back in her chair as their plates were removed.

'And the best part was when you finally stopped

checking where the door was,' Sam said drily, as he poured the last of the Orvieto into their glasses. 'For the first hour I was waiting for you to do a runner at any moment.'

She blushed. 'Was I that bad?'

'You were never bad,' he said. 'Just strung out.' He paused. 'How's the pulse-rate?'

'Calm, I think,' she said. 'And steady. At the moment.'

'Good,' he said. 'I'd hate to think I wouldn't merit a slight flutter—in the right circumstances.' He paused. 'Shall we have coffee?'

It was, she knew, a loaded question. The obvious response was, why don't I make some back at the house? And that, almost certainly, would be what he was waiting to hear. Hoping to hear. And yet…

The house was her domain—her little fortress. The place where she led her real life—not this pretence she'd been lured into.

To invite him back would be to breach some invisible barricade, and she wasn't sure she was ready for that.

It was all going too far, too fast, she thought, swallowing. One false step and she could be out of her depth—the waters closing over her head.

He said gently, 'Stop struggling, darling. The choice is between filter and cappuccino, nothing else. Though I wish…'

'Yes?' she prompted at his hesitation.

He shrugged. 'It doesn't matter.'

He'd been about to say, I wish you'd trust me, he realised ruefully, and he was in no position to ask any such thing.

It had been good to watch her start to relax—to

laugh and talk with him as if they were together for
all the right reasons, he thought, as they drank their
coffee.

Even so, he was aware that, mentally, she was still
on guard. Emotionally, too, he told himself wryly.
There was an inner kernel to this girl that was strictly
a no-go area. That he suspected she'd fight to protect.

So, he would proceed with caution, and anticipate
the eventual rewards of his forbearance.

There was silence between them, but it was a com-
panionable silence, with neither of them believing they
had to strive for the next remark.

He watched her covertly as she sat, quietly at ease,
looking down at the green-gold of the strega in her
glass. He'd told himself more than once over the past
twenty-four hours that she wasn't his type, but now he
found himself noticing with curious intensity that her
mouth was soft, pink and strangely vulnerable now
that she'd relaxed.

Her lashes, too, were a shadow against that amazing
creamy skin. He imagined what it would be like to see
all of it—to uncover her slowly, enjoying every silky
inch—and found his body hardening in sharp response. Like some bloody adolescent, he mocked himself, dropping his table napkin discreetly into his lap.

But he had to be careful, because she still wasn't
convinced about him, and he knew it. One wrong
move and there was a real danger she'd blow him
away. Which he didn't want, and, as he reluctantly
had to acknowledge, not merely because he still had
no clear understanding of her motivation or needs in
replying to the personal ad.

While they'd been eating he'd tried to probe gently,

but had found himself blocked. She still wouldn't let him get too near. Or at least not yet…

And there had been a time when this would have suited him very well.

While he'd been a foreign correspondent he'd kept well out of emotional entanglements. He'd told himself it wasn't fair to keep a woman hanging around until he returned from yet another assignment, even if they were willing to do so—and, without conceit, he knew that there'd been several who'd been prepared to wait for as long as it took.

Only that hadn't been what he wanted—so he'd taken care to keep his relationships light, uncommitted and strictly physical, making it clear there was nothing more on offer. And inflicting, he hoped, no lasting damage along the way.

But this time it was different, although he had no logical reason for knowing it was so—just a gut reaction.

She glanced up suddenly and found his eyes fixed on her, and he saw the colour flare under her skin, and wondered if there was anything in his face to betray this swift, unlooked-for hunger that she'd aroused.

'More coffee, Janie?' He kept the words and the smile casual.

'No, thanks.' It irked her to hear him call her that, and had done all evening. In fact, she'd been debating with herself whether she should tell him her real name—indeed, whether she should come clean about the whole situation.

But the truth had no part in this game they were playing, she thought, with an odd desolation.

Besides, she wasn't sure how he'd react. He could be angry. Could even get up from the table and walk out of the bar, and out of her life. Which would undoubtedly solve all kinds of problems. Except that she wasn't ready for that.

'Then I'll get the bill and take you home.'

'I was going to pay half,' she remembered.

'We'll argue about that later.' He helped her into her jacket, coolly, politely.

As the fresh air hit her, she felt suddenly giddy—light-headed. Oops, she thought. I've had too much to drink.

Two glasses of wine was usually her limit, yet tonight there'd been all that champagne before the Orvieto had arrived. Had he done it deliberately? Was this part of his grand seduction technique? She asked herself as disappointment settled inside her like a stone.

On the corner, she paused. 'There's really no need for you to come any further. I'll be fine.'

His hand was firm under her elbow. 'I prefer to make sure,' he said. 'One of my little foibles.'

When they reached the house, she found the bulb had failed in her exterior light, and she fumbled trying to get her latchkey in the lock.

'Allow me.' Sam took it from her hand and, to her fury, fitted it first time.

'Thank you,' she said grittily.

'Don't say things you don't mean, Janie.' She could hear the grin in his voice. 'You know you're damning my eyes under your breath. Now, put the hall light on while I check everything's all right.'

'Another of your little foibles, I suppose?' she tossed after him.

'The age of chivalry isn't dead,' he returned, giving the ground-floor rooms and basement area a swift inspection. At the door of the sitting room he paused, as if something on the other side of the room had engaged his attention. When he turned back to her there was a faint smile playing round his mouth, and dancing in his eyes. 'And to prove it,' he went on, 'I'm going to wish you a very good night, and go.'

She felt her lips part in shock. 'But...' she began, before she could stop herself.

'But you thought I was going to close the door and jump on you,' he supplied understandingly. 'And don't think I'm not tempted, but I noticed how carefully you were walking and talking on the way back, and I'd prefer to wait for an occasion when you know exactly what you're doing—and why—so that you can't plead unfair advantage afterwards.'

Ros walked to the front door and jerked it open. 'I'd like you to leave. Now. And don't come back,' she added for good measure.

He smiled outrageously down into her hostile eyes. 'You can't have been listening to me, Janie. I told you—I don't take no for an answer. Now, sleep well, dream of me, and I'll call tomorrow.'

His hand touched her face, stroking featherlight down the angle of her cheek, then curving to caress the long line of her throat before coming to rest, warm and heavy, on her slender shoulder. It was the touch of a lover—deliberately and provocatively sensuous in a way a simple kiss on the lips would never have been. It was both a beckoning and a promise. A demand and an offering.

Ros felt the brush of his fingers burn deep in her bones. The ache of unfulfilled sexual need twisted slowly within her, and she knew that if he didn't take his hand from her shoulder she would reach up and draw him down to her. Take him into her arms, her bed and her body.

And then she was free, and freedom was a desolation.

She heard him say, 'Goodnight,' and the small sound in her throat which was all she could manage in response. And then he had gone, the door closing quietly behind him.

She leaned forward slowly, until her forehead was resting against the cool, painted woodwork.

She thought, What am I doing? What's happening to me?

And Rosamund Craig, the cool, the rational, could find no answer.

CHAPTER FIVE

Ros woke with a start, to find sunlight pouring through her bedroom curtains. She propped herself up on one elbow, pushing her hair back from her face and wondering what had woken her.

A peal on the doorbell, followed by some determined knocking, answered that.

'Who on earth can it be at this hour?' she asked herself crossly as she swung out of bed, reaching for her robe. Then she caught sight of the clock on her bedside table and yelped. It was almost mid-morning. And she'd known nothing about it. She'd still be deeply and dreamlessly asleep but for her morning caller.

'I'm coming,' she shouted, as she launched herself downstairs, kicking the morning mail out of the way and fumbling to unbolt her door.

She was confronted by a mass of colour. Red roses, she registered, stunned. And at least two dozen of them.

'Miss Craig?' The delivery girl wore a pink uniform, to match the small florist's van waiting at the kerb, and a professional smile. 'Enjoy your flowers. There's a message attached.'

Ros, her arms full of roses, shut the door and bent, with difficulty, to retrieve her letters from the mat. She carried the whole shooting match into her sitting room and curled up on the sofa, reaching for the tiny envelope attached to the Cellophane.

Sam's black handwriting filled the card. 'Your first rose looked lonely. I thought it needed friends, and we need each other. I'll pick you up for brunch at eleven on Sunday morning.'

Not so much an invitation as a command, Ros thought with exasperation. And what did he mean about her 'first rose' anyway? It had gone from the coffee table, so it must have been thrown away yesterday morning when the room was cleaned—mustn't it?

But she remembered the way Sam had paused in the doorway last night, and her gaze took the path his had done—straight across the room.

The rose, alive and well, in a narrow crystal vase, now occupied pride of place on her mantelpiece.

'Oh, God,' Ros said wearily. 'Manuela.'

Her Spanish cleaner was round, and smiling, and incurably romantic. To her, a red rose was something to be cherished, particularly if she suspected it came from an admirer.

And now Sam thinks that I kept it, she thought ruefully. Oh, *hell*.

She put the bouquet down on the coffee table while she opened her other post. As well as the usual junk mail there was a letter from her accountants, reminding her of the paperwork they'd need to complete her tax return, and a postcard from Sydney from Molly and her father, who were clearly having the time of their lives. She was still smiling as she opened the final envelope, which bore the logo of her publishers, and her smile widened into a grin of delight as she unfolded the sheet of headed paper and saw what Vivien had written.

As you know, each year *Life Today* magazine offers a series of writing awards, and I heard yesterday that *The Hired Sword* has been named the Popular Novel of the Year. I'm so thrilled for you, Ros, and you richly deserve it. I do hope you'll break your rule about public appearances, and pick up the award yourself at next month's ceremony.

'Try and stop me,' Ros said exultantly. Then paused, as it occurred to her that the resultant publicity would mean that her cover would be blown for ever, and there could be no more Janie...

But there can't be anyway, she reminded herself with a touch of grimness. Because the real Janie comes back tomorrow night. And even if she didn't, all this pretence still has to stop.

Last night had been—exciting, but also dangerous, and she'd taken quite enough risks. Brunch was safe, of course—a popular pastime for Sundays in the city—and there would be no alcohol involved—but when it was over she would tell him she couldn't see him again. And she would produce some good and cogent reason why this had to be—although she couldn't think of one off-hand.

I've got all day, she thought, and frowned a little. But why have I? Why am I not seeing Sam until to-morrow?

Which was not the kind of thing she should be thinking at all, she reminded herself with emphasis.

She picked up the roses and carried them downstairs to put them in water, then filled the coffee pot and set it to percolate while she arranged them properly, her fingers dealing gently with the long stems. They would look good as a centrepiece for her dining table, she told herself. They would not under any circumstances be going upstairs to her study—or her bedroom.

She put them on one side while she poured her coffee. She'd expected to wake with the hangover she deserved, yet in actuality she felt fine—as fit as a flea. And alive and—oddly expectant. As if something wonderful was going to happen.

But it already had happened, she reminded herself sternly. She'd won a prize for her Renaissance novel— a cheque and a silver rose bowl, if the award followed the pattern of previous years.

She didn't need anything else. Certainly nothing that might upset the even tenor of her days. She was a writer, and a successful one, and that was quite enough.

She carried her coffee upstairs, intending to shower and dress, but found instead she was continuing up to the top floor. She sat down at her desk and switched on the computer. The rewritten pages she'd been struggling with lay beside it, and she pushed them away, uncaring when they fell to the floor.

Her fingers moved to the keyboard—hesitated for a moment—then typed in: 'He had eyes the colour of turquoise'.

She looked at the words on the screen, and heard herself laugh out loud in joy and anticipation. Then she began to write.

It was only when the phone rang that she realised she'd been working for nearly two hours without a break.

Normally she'd have let the answering machine pick up the message, but she was sure she knew the identity of the caller, and she was smiling as she lifted the receiver. 'Hello?'

'Rosamund, is that you?' The aggrieved tones of Colin's mother sounded in her ear.

'Why, yes.' Ros was shocked at the depth of her own disappointment. 'How—how are you?' she went on over-brightly.

'Well, naturally I'm very upset, and so is my husband, but the physiotherapist has assured us there will be no lasting damage, so we can only hope.'

'Physiotherapist?' Ros echoed, bewildered. 'I don't follow.'

'You mean no one's told you that poor Colin's had an accident—sprained his ankle really badly? None of his so-called friends?' Mrs Hayton snorted. 'That rugby club. He should never have gone on that tour. Why didn't you use your influence—keep him at home?'

Because if I had done you'd have accused me of curbing his freedom, Ros returned silently.

She said, 'Did it happen in a match?'

'No, afterwards, during some stupid horseplay in the bar. The others were drunk, of course, and my poor boy bore the brunt of it. The physio saw he was hurt, and got him to hospital. Nobody else bothered. His ankle's been plastered to keep it steady, and now he has to rest it. He'll be on crutches for several weeks, I dare say.'

Ros was ashamed of the sense of relief flooding through her. With Colin laid up like this, it gave her the perfect opportunity to ease herself out of the relationship without any major confrontation.

'I'm so sorry,' she said guiltily. 'Please give him my—best wishes.'

'But you'll be coming round to see him, surely?' Mrs Hayton said sharply. 'We've turned our dining room into a temporary bedsit for him, because he can't manage the stairs to his own flat.'

'No, I suppose not. I—I'll try and get over tomorrow some time.' After brunch, she thought, piling up more guilt.

'I think he's expecting to see you this afternoon, Rosamund. I'm sure if the situation were reversed, nothing would keep him from your side.'

Ros groaned inwardly. 'This afternoon it is,' she said, glancing at her watch.

'But not too early,' Mrs Hayton cautioned. 'He's just had lunch, and I want him to have a good rest after it.' And she rang off.

On her way to Fulham, Ros decided that she wouldn't wait. That it would be fairer to tell Colin gently that this would be a good time for them both to stand back and consider their relationship.

She found him very sorry for himself. His thanks for the selection of paperback thrillers she'd brought him were perfunctory, and he was clearly more interested in his own woes.

'Nobody seemed to give a damn,' he declared petulantly. 'The physio looked after me—and brought me back here when I couldn't travel in the coach. I don't know what I'd have done otherwise.'

'How awful,' Ros murmured, wondering how to begin.

'The physio's been excellent,' Mrs Hayton said, coming in with a tray of tea. 'As soon as Colin's ankle has recovered sufficiently he'll be put on a proper exercise regime, with heat treatment.'

'Oh, good,' said Ros, noting with dismay that Mrs Hayton had settled down behind the tea and cakes.

Half an hour later, she was on her way home.

There'd simply been no opportunity for any private conversation. Colin's mother had stayed for the duration, confining the conversation to topics of her choice.

Did she think I was going to take advantage of him while he was helpless? Ros wondered crossly.

She'd tried to lighten the atmosphere by offering to autograph his plaster, only to be told by mother and son in unison that it was no laughing matter.

'I'm considering legal action,' Colin had added, frowning.

Ros had been glad to swallow her cup of weak tea, and the rather dry scone, and go.

Colin hadn't even asked when her next visit would be. He took it for granted that she would simply slot in on some rota of his mother's devising.

And a month ago—even ten days ago—she probably would have done so.

But now, suddenly, she wasn't the same person any longer. All the small dissatisfactions of her life had snowballed into this need for change. A need that had left Colin behind, yet promised nothing for the future.

But I'll always have my work, she rallied herself. And paused as she faced, for the first time, the possibility that it might no longer be enough.

'I don't know what to do,' Sam said.

Alex Norton, his former editor, on the road to recovery in a private clinic, peered at him over his glasses. 'Well, you can't stay on the *Echo*, that's for sure. So far, all Cilla's done is cut your hair. Next time she might go for complete emasculation.' And he chuckled.

'I wish I was dead.' Sam helped himself to some grapes from the bowl on the bedside trolley.

'No, you don't,' Alex corrected him robustly. 'Because I've been close, and I don't recommend it. But you won't rescue your career while Ms Godwin's in control. You made a bad enemy there, so you may as well cut your losses. Find another job and settle for the best severance deal you can get.' He paused. 'How did you like Rowcliffe?'

'I wish I'd never left it,' Sam said bleakly.

Alex nodded. 'I always felt the same. In fact, I had this dream that I'd wind up there, editing that weekly paper of theirs—the *Rowcliffe Examiner*.' He shook his head. 'Some hope, of course. You couldn't prise my Mary out of London, bless her. But it would have been a good life.' He shot Sam a look. 'Does it still exist—the *Examiner*?'

'Absolutely. It was required reading at the hotel,' Sam returned. 'And it still has the local farm prices and auctions on the front page.'

'Ah,' Alex leaned back against his pillows. 'I'm glad some things don't change. And, who knows? With a bit of luck you might find yourself back there—one of these days.'

'Not soon enough,' Sam said bitterly.

He was repeating these words under his breath as he let himself back into his flat that night. He'd had an appointment with one of the final names on his list. She'd provided plenty of good material, but the evening had ended in total disaster. He caught a glimpse of himself in the hall mirror and shuddered. At least he'd never be able to wear this ghastly suit again, so every cloud did have a silver lining.

He went into the bathroom, stripped and showered, letting the water cascade over him until he felt clean again. Then he put on his robe, made some coffee, and went into the living room to work on his laptop.

He'd just started when his door buzzer sounded. Startled, he glanced at his watch, wondering who could be calling so late. It was probably Mrs Ferguson, the elderly widow in the adjoining flat, wanting him to change a lightbulb, or adjust her trip-switch, or some other minor task. She was a sweet soul, and lonely, and it was a pleasure to keep an eye on her. But he wished she'd restrict her requests for help to sociable hours.

However, he was smiling when he opened the door. Until he saw who was standing outside.

'Good evening.' Cilla Godwin was smiling too, her eyes calculating as she looked him over. 'May I come in?'

He said levelly, 'If you wish,' and stood aside to give her access, resisting the impulse to tighten the belt of his robe. She walked ahead of him into the lamplit sitting room.

'Very stylish,' she said, looking round her. 'Do you share with anyone?'

'Not since my last flatmate got married,' he said. 'What can I do for you, Ms Godwin?'

'Don't be formal, Sam, you're not dressed for it.' She looked at the glass standing beside his laptop. 'If that's whiskey, I'll have one too.'

Sam found the bottle of Jameson's and splashed a measure into a cut-glass tumbler. 'Do I take it this is a social call?'

'Oh, I have various reasons for being here.' She accepted the glass from him. 'Cheers.'

'May I know what they are? As you can see, I am trying to work.'

'You were out interviewing tonight? Who was she?'

'A divorcee called Mandy, with a chip on her shoulder and a frank tongue.'

'Sounds ideal. Did it go well?'

'Until the last ten minutes, when she made it clear she expected the evening to end in bed,' Sam said pleasantly. 'When she found out it wasn't going to happen, she started throwing things—the remains of a carafe of red wine and half a pot of cold coffee for starters. We were lucky not to be arrested, and we certainly can't use Albertine's as a venue again. I've written you a memo.

'Oh, and the office suit is a write-off,' he added. 'So unless you want to ask the charity shop for another, I'll be wearing my own clothes from now on.'

'What is this strange power you have over women?' She was smiling again, and Sam's warning antennae were going into overdrive. 'Even when you look like a geek, they're queuing to get laid.'

'I wouldn't use Mandy as a criterion,' Sam said drily. 'I got the impression anyone would have done.'

'You're far too modest.' She took a seat on the sofa, crossing her legs. She was wearing a brief black skirt, topped by a matching camisole, and a white jacket like a man's tuxedo. She had swept her hair up into a loose knot, and her nails and mouth were painted a dark, challenging red.

War paint, thought Sam.

He kept his voice even. 'But then, according to you, I have so much to be modest about.' He retrieved his glass from the table and went to stand by the fireplace.

Not two swords' lengths apart, but the best he could manage.

She laughed. 'Poor Sam—does that still rankle? But I'm having to eat my words. I was notified today that you've been voted Journalist of the Year by *Life Today* magazine for your Mzruba work.' She paused. 'I told the proprietor, and he was well pleased. Asked what you were doing at the moment.' She shrugged. 'I said—a special assignment.'

'The perfect description.' Sam drank some whiskey.

'I thought so.' Cilla leaned back against the cushions, the drag of her camisole revealing that she was bra-less.

She was showing a fair amount of thigh as well, Sam realised bleakly. Surely lightning wasn't going to strike him twice.

'But if you're going to win awards, maybe I should be making better use of you.' Her tone was meditative, her smile cat-like. 'Sam—we don't have to be on bad terms—do we?'

He was instantly wary. 'Of course not.' He added a polite smile. 'It was good of you to come and tell me about the award, Cilla, but I mustn't keep you. It's Saturday night, after all, and I'm sure you have places to go and people to see.'

Like your husband, he added silently. He knew she had one—somewhere—but the basis for their relationship was anyone's guess.

'Mark's out of his depth on the foreign news desk,' she went on, as if he hadn't spoken. 'I'm going to move him, so there'll be a vacancy again. And this time I need to be sure that the right man gets the job.' Her voice deepened, became husky. 'Do you think you're that man, Sam? As we've had our differences in the past, I'd need to assure myself that you'd be—loyal.'

She invested that final word with a whole host of meanings.

Sam leaned a shoulder against the mantelshelf and stared at his whiskey. All he had to do was walk across and sit down beside her and that long-promised promotion would be his—but at a price. It would be a totally cynical encounter—an exercise in sexuality—and not the first to come his way, admittedly. Yet all he could feel was a profound distaste as cold and bitter as gall.

'I promise you the best foreign news coverage anywhere,' he said quietly. 'I hope that's enough, because it's all there is.'

There was a long silence. Her smile, when it came, would have eaten through metal. 'I think, Sam darling, that you've just made a terrible mistake.'

'No,' he said. 'I've just avoided a worse one.'

'Is this your night for turning women down? First the divorcee and now me.' Her hands moved in a brief angry gesture she could not control. The dark enamel on her fingertips looked, he thought, like dried blood.

'But perhaps you have a different agenda altogether,' she went on. 'Maybe you simply prefer other men.'

She was trying to make him angry, he thought. To provoke him into something hasty.

He shrugged. 'Or maybe I'm old-fashioned enough to want to do my own hunting. Have you ever thought of that, Ms Godwin?'

She got quickly and almost clumsily to her feet. 'I shall expect your resignation on my desk on Monday.'

'No,' he said. 'I'm not ready to do that. You'll have to fire me, and at the moment you have no grounds.'

At the door, she gave him a last venomous look. 'Enjoy your little bit of glory over the award,' she said. 'By the time I've finished with you, you'll be a standing joke.'

He said wearily, 'I'm sure you'll try. Goodnight, Cilla.'

It hurt to breathe, he discovered when he was alone, and he felt slightly nauseous.

I never saw that coming, he told himself grimly.

In fact, he could hardly believe it had happened. That it hadn't all been a ghastly hallucination.

Except for the evidence. Picking up the lipstick-stained glass she'd been using between his thumb and forefinger, he took it into the kitchen and dropped it into the wastebin.

Hell hath no fury like a woman scorned—as he'd already found out to his cost that evening. And in Cilla Godwin's case it had happened twice.

He wondered wryly what kind of hell he could expect. Certainly his days on the *Echo* were numbered, but he'd known that already. He'd start looking round for another job on Monday.

The heavy, musky scent she'd been wearing still seemed to hang in the sitting room, he realised, wrinkling his nose. He unlocked the window and opened it wide. The air that flooded it was cold but stale.

I haven't breathed properly since I came back from Rowcliffe, he thought restlessly, as he went back to his laptop.

He read what he'd written, then with an impatient exclamation deleted it all. He'd turned Mandy into a caricature, he thought. The man-hungry blonde. What he'd seen, but hadn't shown, was the pain of her divorce, and her fear of a lonely future.

He'd had compassion enough for the innocents caught up in the Mzruban civil war. Surely he could spare some for Mandy, suffering the after effects of a more personal conflict.

He stared at the empty screen, trying to recreate her image, but the girl's face that swam in his vision was a very different one—pale-skinned and hazel-eyed, with a smile that tugged at some inner heart-cord he hadn't known he possessed.

He swore under his breath. This was a complication he didn't need—particularly when his whole life was at a crossroads.

Janie Craig had started off as a puzzle he'd been determined to solve. But finding the real girl behind the façade had turned into a much more personal quest. Which had somehow been crystallised when he saw she'd kept the rose he'd given her.

But that didn't mean he'd had to surrender to his impulse to deluge her with flowers, he derided himself. She wasn't his type and that wasn't his style.

And it has to stop right here and now, he told himself grimly. Before it really starts running out of control.

Tomorrow would be the last time they saw each other, and he had decided exactly how he would handle it. Locked into her usual environment, she had no reason to lower her guard, he thought, as he switched off the computer. So he would try a different ploy to break down her defences.

A change of surroundings, he mused with satisfaction. A change of approach. Before they walked away from each other.

He hadn't forgotten that she'd told him she'd only kept their first appointment from a sense of obligation. It would be tempting to see if he could induce her to feel just an atom of regret when they parted from each other for ever.

But her smile continued to haunt him, even in sleep, and he woke with a start, realising that he had turned to her, reaching for her in yearning and need, only to encounter the chill emptiness in the bed beside him.

CHAPTER SIX

Ros glanced at the pile of discarded clothing on her bed and groaned.

Look in the mirror, she adjured herself sternly, and say after me—this is only a brunch. It is no big deal.

She'd tried on nearly everything she owned, and rejected it. Now she was back to her original choice, a pair of slim-fitting cream pants and a matching V-neck sweater. Cool and casual, she thought, hooking her favourite amber earrings into her lobes, to complement a day when the sky was almost cloudless and there was real warmth in the spring sun.

It was a long time since she'd been out to a brunch. Not, in fact, since her trip to New York to meet her American publishers, when she'd spent a gloriously relaxed Sunday morning in Greenwich Village.

She wondered if Sam's travels had ever taken him to the States.

There was so much about him she didn't know—and probably never would, she realised with a sudden pang. So she would simply have to invent it. And she had a head start on that already.

She had written until late the previous night, watching the story catch fire, feeling her excitement—her empathy with it—build swiftly and surely.

All it needed was a new hero, she thought, applying a thin layer of pale coral to her mouth. And I found one.

She was humming under her breath as she ran down

the stairs. She'd just reached the hallway when the doorbell sounded. She took a deep, calming breath and opened the door.

'Good morning,' she said. Her voice and expression were sedate, but her eyes were abrim with laughter and delight as she looked up at him.

Sam found he was catching his breath. He said a little hoarsely, 'How do you do that?'

'Do what?' Ros stood back to allow him into the hall, closing the door behind him.

'Make your mouth say one thing and your eyes something completely different.'

She flushed slightly. 'I—I didn't know I could.' He was wearing, she saw, close-fitting denim pants which accentuated his long legs, and a plaid shirt, both garments undoubtedly carrying designer labels. She said, 'You look—good.'

'You've stolen my line,' he said. 'Except that I was going to say—beautiful.'

She managed a small, rather choked laugh. 'I've never been that.'

'Yes, you have,' he said. 'You've never let yourself believe it, that's all. And perhaps you needed the right moment to blossom.'

She said hurriedly, 'Talking of blossoms—thank you for the roses. They're lovely.'

He looked at the vase on the mantelpiece, with its solitary bloom, and smiled. 'I saw that one had survived, and thought it looked lonely.' He added softly. 'I'm glad you kept it.'

Her blush deepened. 'I didn't—I mean—it was my cleaning lady. She's Spanish,' she added with a kind of desperation.

'Ah,' he said. 'Perhaps I should have asked her for a date instead.'

Ros laughed. 'She'd have turned you down. She's a happily married woman.'

'That's not always a guarantee of good behaviour.' He thought of Cilla Godwin's moistly parted lips, and his face hardened slightly.

She saw his expression change. She said quickly, before she could change her mind, 'Are you married, Sam? Or have you ever been?'

'God, no.' His reaction was too spontaneous to be anything but the truth. 'What gave you that idea?'

'I don't know.' She hesitated. 'I just get this—feeling that you're holding out on me in some way. That there are things about you that you don't want me to know.'

'You've forgotten our agreement,' he said, after a pause. 'A whole fresh start. Sam and Janie getting to know each other all over again.'

'It doesn't matter how much we pretend.' Her face was suddenly grave. She was speaking, she realised, to herself. 'We can never escape the people we really are.'

'But we can hide from them occasionally,' he said. 'And I know the perfect hiding place, especially on a day like this.'

'Let me guess.' It had been the right thing to say. Her smile reached out and touched him again. 'Somewhere by the river. Am I warm?'

He shook his head. 'You're not even tepid. And it's a surprise.'

The first part of the surprise was the car, an elegant Audi, parked a few yards down the road.

'I didn't know you drove,' Ros said, tucking herself into the passenger seat. 'I thought we'd be walking.'

'You see—the voyage of discovery has already begun. And I don't use the car a lot.' He paused. 'But at a time like this—a special time—it's convenient.'

She was scared of blushing again, so she frowned instead. 'But don't you need your glasses when you're driving?'

'Actually,' he said, 'I've decided I don't need them at all. Wearing them had simply become a habit. A failed attempt to make me look intellectual. Or something to hide behind,' he added.

She laughed. 'What have you got to hide from?'

'You'd be surprised.' He paused again. 'I thought you'd be glad to see the last of them.'

She gave him a thoughtful glance. 'Well—they never seemed quite right, somehow.'

Ros sat back as he negotiated the traffic on the Kings Road. He drove well, she thought. Positive without being aggressive.

Eventually she broke the silence. 'We seem to be heading out of London.'

'Well spotted.' He slanted a grin at her. 'I should have made you wear a blindfold.'

Her brows lifted. 'You know a brunch place out of town?'

'Not exactly. But I know a good picnic spot. Will you settle for that?'

She'd expected the safety of a busy restaurant. A secluded corner of the English countryside was a very different proposition. And he knew it as well as she did, she thought uneasily.

She swallowed. 'I'm not a great fan of alfresco dining.'

'There's an indoor option as well,' he said, worrying her even more. 'We can decide when we get there.'

'I suppose so.' Her hands, which had been lightly clasped in her lap, now seemed welded together.

'I made an early raid on the local deli,' he went on. 'We've got pâté, French sticks, olives, cold meat and Californian strawberries among other goodies.'

'It sounds—marvellous.' Ros forced a bright smile, then gasped as Sam suddenly pulled the wheel over and brought the car to a standstill at the side of the road.

He said, 'So what's the problem?'

'I don't know what you mean,' Ros defended.

'That's not true.' He shook his head, half reproving, half exasperated. 'In the space of a couple of minutes you've gone from relaxed and smiling to a fair imitation of a coiled spring. God, I can actually feel the tension in you from here. Why?'

There was a fleck on one of her nails. She examined it closely. 'Your change of plan has thrown me a little.' She attempted a laugh that broke in the middle. 'I don't think I'm very good at surprises.'

'Especially when they entail being alone with me? But you took that risk the first time we met.'

'That was a calculated risk,' she said. 'And I didn't intend to repeat it.'

'Yet you did,' he said. 'When I asked you. And here you are again now.'

'Yes,' she said. 'But for the last time—as we both know.'

'Of course.' He was silent for a moment. Then, 'Would it make any difference if I told you there was nothing to fear? That I swear I won't do anything that you don't want. That I won't make a move—lay a finger on you—without your permission—your invitation. Does that reassure you?'

He waited for a moment, then his voice hardened.

'Tell me, Janie, are you most scared of me—or yourself? Be honest.'

She stared ahead of her through the windscreen, seeing nothing. She heard her voice shake a little. 'I don't know. Is that honest enough?'

His tone was quiet. 'I guess it is.' There was another brief silence, then he said with a touch of harshness, 'Look at me. Do it now.'

Ros turned her head reluctantly and met the piercing turquoise gaze. Saw the cold set of the firm mouth.

He said, 'Shall I eliminate the risk factor? Turn the car round and take you back to Chelsea and your safe, comfortable life? Is that what you want?'

She only had to nod in acquiescence and it would be done. She was sure of that.

And equally certain that, for better or worse, it was the last thing she wanted to happen.

She found herself lifting her hand, brushing a finger across that unsmiling mouth, hearing his sharply indrawn breath.

She said huskily, 'I'd like to go on.' Adding, 'Please.'

He captured her hand, held it while his teeth grazed the soft pad of the marauding finger.

'Be careful,' he warned softly, as he released her. 'Because that might be construed in some circles as a definite step on to the wild side.'

Ros let her eyes widen, the lashes veiling them provocatively. 'I was simply thinking of all that food. It would be a crime to waste it.'

'By the time we get there,' Sam said, restarting the car. 'You should have quite an appetite.'

I think, Ros told herself, as she sank back into her seat, that I have one already.

'You might as well have blindfolded me,' she said half an hour later. 'I've no idea where we are.'

'You don't know this part of the world?'

'I don't know many places at all outside London,' she admitted ruefully. 'Except those I visit in connection with my work, of course.'

'Good,' he said. 'I'm glad I'm the first to bring you here.'

'So—where is "here"?' Not even the signposts meant much.

'It's not far now.'

It was turning into a heavenly day. The trees were vivid with new growth, and the lanes they were driving through were lush with cow parsley.

To Ros's pleasure, Sam put Delius's *Brigg Fair* on the car's CD player.

'I love this music,' she sighed. 'It's so incredibly English and romantic. I use it a lot when I'm working.'

'You use Delius to sell cosmetics?'

The astonishment in his voice alerted her to what she'd said, and Ros sat up, guilty blood invading her cheeks at her gaffe.

'Not exactly,' she said swiftly. 'I like to play it when I'm giving beauty treatments. It helps—relax the client.'

'It sounds wonderful.' He slanted a grin at her. 'Makes me wish I was beautiful.'

He would never be that, Ros thought. Not even if he grew his hair to a reasonable length. But those amazing eyes and the crooked smile which lit them to such devastating effect gave him the kind of attraction that transcended classic good looks.

This was a seriously sexy man, she told herself with bewilderment, and the last person in the world who needed to advertise for female companions. It was far more likely he had to beat them off with a stick.

Yet here we are, she thought. And I'm still wondering why. Although there's nowhere I'd rather be...

They drove across a narrow watersplash and into a picture-book village, with an ancient church and charming cottages, their walls washed in light pink, clustering round a central green.

This must be the picnic spot, Ros decided, surprised that he'd chosen somewhere public after all. The occupants of those houses wouldn't miss much.

But Sam was merely slowing for the turn, guiding the car up a narrow lane beside the church. Beside them, she saw a high brick wall, its lines softened by the clematis which was just coming into flower.

Sam turned in between two stone pillars and up a short, curving drive. The house at the end of it was also redbrick, simply and solidly built, and rather square, like a doll's house Ros had once possessed as a child. Above the porch, a wisteria was showing the first heart-stopping traces of blue, and there were climbing roses and honeysuckle trained round the windows.

'It's lovely,' Ros said, puzzled, as Sam parked outside the front door and retrieved a bunch of keys from the glove compartment. 'Is it yours?'

'No,' he said. 'I just know the owners.'

'Oh.' Relief fought with a kind of disappointment. He'd said nothing before about meeting his friends, although it was flattering—in a way—that he should want her to. And rather a nonsense, too, considering this was to be their final encounter.

It also occurred to her that she hadn't expected to share him.

She said breathlessly, 'They're very lucky to live here.'

'They don't,' he said. 'Or not much any more. They spend most of their time in the Dordogne. They bought an old farmhouse there a few years ago, and converted the barns into *gîtes*.' He swung his long legs out of the car and came round to open the passenger door. 'They're down there now, doing pre-season decorating and maintenance,' he said casually. 'So I thought I'd grab the chance to check the place over and sort out the mail.'

Ros managed another feeble 'Oh', swallowing past a sudden constriction in her throat. She paused. 'You're sure they won't mind—that you brought me with you?'

'I promise you,' he said, 'they'd be delighted. Now, wait a second while I deal with the security alarm, then I'll give you the guided tour.'

Ros stayed by the car, looking at the garden. It was worth savouring with its smooth lawns surrounded by wide borders just coming into flower. In the middle of the grass a stone bird bath was supported by a smiling cherub, and the entire expanse was surrounded and sheltered by the high wall.

'It's beautifully kept,' she said when Sam returned. 'Considering it's unoccupied.'

'A couple from the village look after it all,' he told her. 'Mrs Griggs cleans and her husband gardens. It's a perfect arrangement.'

The house itself was cosy and comfortable, with big squashy sofas and well-polished furniture which was a tribute to the efforts of the unseen Mrs Griggs.

The kitchen was mellow with antique pine, and a gleaming range, and there was an open fireplace in the sitting room with kindling and logs laid ready. There was also a baby grand piano, with a selection of music stacked neatly on its lid.

And, Ros saw, in pride of place, a photograph in a silver frame. The face was younger, and the hair longer, but the slanting smile was instantly familiar.

'This is you,' she accused, picking it up. She wheeled round on him. 'And you don't just "know" the owners. They're your parents—aren't they?'

'Guilty as charged,' Sam said ruefully. 'That's my graduation picture. I've never been able to persuade Ma to bury it somewhere.'

'But you said it wasn't your house.'

'Nor is it,' Sam returned promptly. 'It's where I grew up, and I have wonderful memories, but that's its only claim on me. I moved out and moved on a long time ago.'

'But surely...' Ros paused awkwardly. 'I mean it will be yours—in time.'

'No.' He shook his head. 'The parents are planning to move permanently to France, so it will be going on the market—probably this summer.'

'And you don't mind?'

'Not particularly.' His voice was amused. 'It's not a family heirloom. And you have to look forward, not to the past. And one day,' he added matter-of-factly, 'I intend buying a house of my own, so that I can create some good memories for my own children.'

There was a sudden roaring in her ears, and she

could feel the colour draining from her face, leaving only an aching emptiness behind.

From some vast distance, she heard herself say, 'Of course.'

And she turned back to replace the photograph on the piano with great care, terrified in case he noticed that her hands were shaking.

But he was walking past her to the French windows and opening them. 'Why don't you find us a picnic spot while I get the food ready?'

She nodded, and fled out into the open air, standing for a moment to draw great shuddering breaths as she fought for composure.

Because it had hit her with all the savage, overwhelming force of a tidal wave that there was only one woman she could bear to be the mother of Sam's children. And that was herself.

'No,' she whispered, gulping oxygen into her labouring lungs. 'No, this is ridiculous. It's not happening. I won't let it.'

Because she couldn't base a lifetime relationship on the strength of a few hours' dubious acquaintance. Or even casual lust. And that was all it was—however strongly her senses might be telling her otherwise. Even though they might be murmuring insidiously that in reality she had known Sam all her life—had breathed in the fact of his existence through her pores since the moment of her own creation. And had simply been waiting all this time for him to come to her.

Hormonal rubbish, she told herself crushingly. Janie's famous biological clock making itself felt.

Well, she would not allow it to control her perfectly satisfactory life. Particularly when, only a few weeks earlier, she'd been contemplating marrying a very different man with serenity, if not any great enthusiasm.

Hitching herself to the star of someone who advertised for company in a personal column had never been part of her plan.

In fact the whole thing had been a grotesque mistake from beginning to end.

I should never have got involved, she thought, forcing herself to walk along the flagged terrace. And if I'm going to suffer, it's entirely my own fault.

Which was no consolation at all.

And now she had to pull herself together and find somewhere for this picnic, when all she wanted to do was run away so far and so fast that Sam would never find her.

The terrace, she saw, taking her first proper look at her surroundings, had been constructed to overlook a small formal rose garden, and at one end there was a pergola, shaded by a lilac tree and containing a wrought-iron table and two chairs.

The lilac was just coming into bloom, and its faint, enticing scent drifted to her as a soft breeze curled through the branches.

For the rest of her life, she thought, the perfume of lilac would speak to her of love. And loss…

'So you've chosen my favourite place,' Sam said, arriving with a tray which he began to unload on to the table. 'I hoped you would.'

She said lightly, 'I think it chose me.' And felt her heart weep.

She wasn't hungry, but somehow she made herself eat, scared that Sam would notice and query her loss of appetite. And the food he'd provided was certainly worth sampling. As well as everything he'd mentioned, there were tiny spicy sausages, wafer-thin slices of Italian ham, wedges of turkey and cranberry pie, and sweet baby tomatoes, with a tall jug of Buck's Fizz to wash it all down.

Ros praised it lavishly, determined to keep the conversation going at all costs. For the first time in her life she was afraid of silence. Scared of what it might reveal.

And as she laughed and talked, her eyes were feeding a different kind of hunger. Memorising the distinctive bone structure of his face as if she was touching it. Watching his body language—the easy grace of his posture. The movement of his hands—the play of muscle under his shirt.

Each and every precious detail etched irrevocably into her mind to sustain her through the famine ahead of her.

He said at last, smiling at her, 'More strawberries?'

'I couldn't.' She leaned back in her chair, grimacing. 'As it is, I may have to start buying clothes with elasticated waists.'

He lifted an ironic brow, the turquoise gaze frankly appraising her slenderness, then lingering on the swell of her breasts under the creamy sweater.

He said gravely, his eyes dancing, 'I hardly think so. But if you really don't want anything else, I'll shift the debris indoors. I have a feeling the weather's going to change.'

Ros glanced up at the sky, and was startled to see heavy cloud, grey darkening to navy, massing in the west.

She thought, *'The bright day is done…'* And wondered what the dark would bring.

She pushed her chair back. 'Shall I help?'

'I can manage.' He began to load the tray. 'Relax, and enjoy the last remnants of sun while I put some coffee on.'

As he disappeared into the house, Ros got up and walked restlessly down the three shallow stone steps into the rose garden.

Not that there was much to see, except immaculately pruned bushes, but most of the roses were labelled, and she could use her imagination as she strolled down the gravelled path between the beds.

One sheltered corner had been planted with 'old' roses, and she bent down to read the beautiful, evocative names.

Sam said quietly from behind her, 'Rosamund,' and she jumped, whirling to face him, her lips parting in a startled gasp.

'How do you know? How did you find out?'

His brows snapped together in surprise. 'You can't escape knowing about roses if you live with my mother. And that one—Rosa Mundi—Rose of the World—is a favourite of hers. But I'm sorry if I frightened you,' he added with a touch of dryness. 'I thought you'd hear me.'

She bit her lip hard. 'I—I was in another world.' She gestured around her. 'How can she bear to leave all this? Her house, this garden—her roses?'

He said gently, 'She has another house, now, and another garden in the Dordogne, and they're beautiful too. And roses will grow anywhere. She'll simply plant more.' He put out a hand and touched her arm. 'God, you're trembling. I really did give you a shock. And you're like ice too.' His voice was remorseful. 'We'd better go inside.'

She moved away out of range. 'I'm fine.' She kept her voice light. 'Moving to another country is such a big step. What made them decide to do it?'

'My father's hobby has always been playing the stock market, and he made a hell of a lot of money from it back in the eighties.' Sam shrugged. 'They both love France, and nearly all our family holidays were spent there, so they got the idea of buying a house and doing it up. When Dad was offered early retirement it seemed like a golden opportunity to change their lives. So—they went for it.'

She gave a constrained smile. 'And that's where you get your financial skills.'

'Good God, no.' He laughed. 'I can barely add two and two.'

She stared at him. 'But you're an accountant.' She shook her head in amazement. 'An accountant who can't do sums?'

There was an odd silence. Then, 'Fortunately I have a calculator,' Sam said swiftly. 'And most of my work involves compiling reports anyway.'

She thought of her own accountant, and some of the things Colin had told her about his work.

She began, 'But surely....' And got no further. As if some gigantic hand had pulled an invisible plug, the rain came sheeting down with breath-snatching intensity, turning almost instantly to hail.

Sam grabbed her hand. 'Come on. Quickly.'

They ran for the steps, and back along the terrace, the hailstones bouncing around them, piercing their clothing with ice.

Sam thrust her ahead of him through the French windows, and turned to close out the storm.

Ros shook herself, freezing droplets spilling down from her drenched hair on to her face and shoulders.

She said, with a choked laugh, wrapping her arms round her shivering body, 'I'm absolutely soaking. My God—the joys of an English spring.'

She looked at him, expecting him to share her rueful amusement, and saw, instead, that he was watching her, his whole attention arrested, his eyes fixed almost blankly on the rain-darkened clothing clinging revealingly to her skin.

He said quietly, holding her gaze with his as he kicked off his shoes, 'Then maybe we should both get out of these wet clothes.'

And began to unbutton his shirt.

CHAPTER SEVEN

SHE could have stopped it right there, and she knew it. Because he'd promised as much. And he wasn't anywhere near her. He was—dear God—on the other side of the room.

But she didn't speak—or move. Just watched, in total sensual thrill, as he stripped off his shirt and let it fall. She let her eyes roam, hungrily absorbing the width of his shoulders, the brown hair-roughened skin.

The heavy silence in the room was broken only by the faint crackle of the wood he'd kindled in the hearth behind her, and by the harsh throb of her own breath. But maybe she was the only one who could hear it. Maybe—just maybe—his heart was hammering too.

She saw his hands move to the zip of his jeans.

She said swiftly, huskily, 'No—please.'

He paused as if turned to stone, the turquoise eyes sending her a challenge across the infinity of space that divided them.

He said, 'No?'

Hands trembling, she pulled off her sweater, dragging the mass of clammy wool over her head as if she could not wait another minute to be free. A second later her bra joined it on the floor.

She stepped out of her damp shoes and walked to him barefoot.

She said softly, 'Let me…'

She put her hands against his chest, feeling the flat male nipples harden at her touch, then allowed her palms to slide over the powerful ribcage to the flat, muscular stomach, where they lingered tantalisingly, her thumbs teasing the shadowed arrow of dark hair which pointed downwards, forcing a sharp, painful sound from his throat.

She leaned forward, brushing her lips against the wall of his chest, inhaling the potent male scent of him. Then, slowly, she released the single button at his waist and lowered the zip, easing the denim down from his hips.

Sam stepped out of the jeans, kicking them away. The briefs he was wearing did nothing to disguise the fact that he was already strongly and powerfully aroused. Ros stared at him, her eyes dilated, her mouth drying with excitement.

He whispered, 'Now it's your turn.' His hands were shaking as he unfastened her cream trousers and slipped them off.

He pulled her towards him, his hands stroking her naked back, making her gasp in startled pleasure. Instinctively her body arched in reply, and the swollen peaks of her breasts grazed against his chest. For a moment he held her there, moving his body slowly and rhythmically against hers, watching her nipples pucker with delight at the subtle friction.

He said huskily, 'They're like tiny roses. My rose of the world.'

Then he bent his head, and kissed her parted lips, his tongue seeking hers with aching, urgent sensuality. Their mouths clung, their teeth nipping delicately at the soft interior flesh.

The heated hardness of him was like a steel rod pressing against her thighs, and she felt her own fierce flood of moisture in response. A dark, feral scent seemed suddenly to fill her lungs. The scent of mating.

Her breasts were in his hands now, his fingers delicately strumming her nipples, raising their excitement to a new level and sending shafts of an almost unbearable sweetness piercing their way to her loins.

She moaned softly as Sam began to kiss her breasts, drawing each soft mound in turn deep into his hungry mouth, fondling their tautness with his tongue. His hands slid under the lacy briefs, gently moulding her buttocks, before initiating a more intimate exploration, his fingers paying tribute to the dark, wet heat of her surrender.

She was trembling wildly now, tiny golden sparks dancing inside her closed eyelids, as he discovered, then focused on one tiny pinnacle of pleasure, the throb of his caress sending ripples of pure arousal along her nerve-endings—creating the beginnings of a pleasure bordering almost on pain. But, however beguiling, it wasn't the fulfilment she sought. Her body was opening to him. Craving him in entirety.

'You.' Was that small, cracked sound her voice? 'Please—I want you. All of you.'

He said hoarsely, 'Yes.' And, 'Now.'

They sank together to the carpet, the final scraps of clothing hurriedly, clumsily discarded on the way.

For a brief moment she held him, then, with a tiny sob, guided him into her, and clasped him there.

He was still for a few seconds, allowing them both to savour this ultimate union of their bodies, then he began to move, his rhythm slow and powerful, and she echoed it, lifting her hips to meet each thrust, letting him fill her completely.

He whispered, 'Look at me, darling. I want to see your eyes when you come.'

'I—don't.' Her voice was muffled, breathless. 'Not—always.'

'That was then.' His hand slid down between them. 'This is—now.'

Her body imploded into rapture, every interior muscle contracting fiercely, sending liquid fire pulsing through her veins. She cried out, brokenly, ecstatically, and saw Sam rear up above her, his head thrown back, as the convulsions of his own climax tore through him.

They lay, their limbs still entwined, their sweat-dampened bodies joined together, waiting for the world to settle again, and their breathing to return to normal human limits.

His voice was muffled by her hair. 'Are you all right? I didn't hurt you?'

'No.' Her face was buried in his shoulder. She lifted her head and experimentally licked some of the salt from his skin. 'No,' she repeated as a small laugh was torn from her throat. 'You didn't do that.'

'I ask,' he said, his teeth nibbling gently at her earlobe, 'because—for a first time—that was pretty overwhelming.'

'I'd say it was perfect,' Ros corrected with mock hauteur.

'No,' Sam said with more firmness. 'It wasn't that. And never will be. Because "perfect" implies we don't need practice. And I know we do. Hours and hours of it.'

Her lips began to explore the hollow where his neck joined his shoulder.

'In that case,' she murmured, 'let's score it "average".'

' "Could do better"?' he suggested.

'If we live through it.' Ros moved slightly, preparing to detach herself, but his arms tightened round her.

'Keep still. Isn't it nice to lie like this?'

Another laugh shook her. 'It's—nice. But don't you need recovery time?'

'I have amazing powers of recuperation. Besides, it's a fact of nature. After the earthquake comes the aftershock. All we have to do is—wait.'

'That's all?'

'It won't be too dull,' Sam promised lazily. 'We can kiss each other—like this.' He turned her face towards him and caressed her lips softly with his. 'And I can play with your lovely breasts—like this.'

Ros ran her tongue along his lower lip. 'And I...' she whispered, as her hands cupped him intimately. 'I can do—this.'

'Oh, yes,' he said, gasping. 'You certainly can.'

She felt boneless. Boneless and weightless. So much so that without Sam's arm lying across her waist, anchoring her to the bed, she might have easily have floated up to the ceiling.

Sam had fallen asleep beside her, and she couldn't blame him. She was just aching, gently and pleasurably, but he had to be exhausted.

The aftershock had been slow and lingering, his hands and mouth making a feast of her, as if she'd been created simply and solely for his own very personal delight. He had taken her to the brink of rapture and held her there for some endless time, until her body had at last been permitted to splinter into orgasm.

She had come up to his room ostensibly to shower and dress, only to find him joining her in the tiled cubicle, his hands gently massaging shower gel into her shoulders and down the long, vulnerable sweep of her spine to her buttocks and thighs.

She'd stood under the torrent of warm water, hands pressed against the wall to steady herself, her senses tingling into a new and startled arousal as he'd parted her thighs and continued his intoxicating ministrations at a more intimate level.

Then he'd lifted her wet and slippery body into his arms and carried her out of the shower room, heedless of her breathless protests, to his bed.

This, she thought now, can't be happening to me.

Someone new—someone wanton—had crept inside her skin, and transformed her.

Sex with Colin had been conventional, but usually enjoyable, and often satisfying. Certainly she'd never had any real complaints.

But in Sam's arms she'd experienced another dimension. Learned wholly unsuspected truths about her body and the demands it could make. Discovered the delight of using her own hands and lips to give him pleasure.

She'd been sleeping with Colin for two years, but she'd known Sam's body more completely and intimately in a few hours.

She felt him stir drowsily beside her, and turned her head to look at him.

He said softly, 'So you're real. You're here. I was terrified you were still just a dream.' He found her hand and brought it to his mouth, pressing a kiss into her palm.

Faint colour stole under her skin. 'You're saying you've been dreaming about me?'

'Some of the time.' His eyes glinted at her. 'Most of it I couldn't sleep at all. Or work.'

'Nor could I,' said Ros, mentally crossing her fingers as she remembered her turquoise-eyed hero waiting for her in Chelsea.

My God, she thought. Is he in for a shock.

And found herself jumping as a door slammed somewhere downstairs and a woman's voice called out, 'Sam—Sam are you there?'

'Hell, it's Mrs Griggs.' Sam hurled himself off the bed and grabbed a robe. 'She must have come round to check up and seen the car.'

'You can't go down like that,' Ros protested. 'What will she think?'

'Hopefully, that I've been taking a shower.' Sam took a towel from the rail in his bathroom and rubbed his hair vigorously on the way to the door. 'Stay right here, darling.' His smile curled over her like a warm wave. 'I'll be back.'

Sighing, she leaned back against the pillows and waited, listening to the faint murmur of voices from the floor below. But the interruption had left her feeling suddenly restive.

The idyll, she thought, was over. Now it was back to the real world.

She swung her legs to the floor, and stood up. She was aware of all kinds of little aches and tender spots, but they were honourable wounds, she thought, with a small, private smile, and all in all she felt wonderful. On top of the world.

She really ought to get dressed, she thought, eyeing her clothes neatly draped across a radiator. But the lure of looking round Sam's room—the one he'd had since boyhood—was too strong. After all, weren't most of

her misgivings centred around the fact that she knew
so little about him? Well, this was a golden opportunity to find out. To put any lingering doubts to rest.

Not that the room gave much away. The decor was
uncompromisingly masculine, with a stone cord carpet, and bedcover and drapes in olive-green. There
were shelves of books, ranging from childhood favourites to modern novels, and a lot of non-fiction too,
mostly to do with travel, and much of it centred in
Africa, the Middle East and South America.

Presumably he kept the books and professional jour-
nals to do with his job at his London base, she thought,
slightly puzzled.

There were no ornaments, and no pictures apart
from two photographs—one of a good-looking middle-aged couple standing, smiling, with their arms
round each other in front of some crumbling agricul-
tural buildings. Presumably these were Sam's parents,
pictured with the barns in the Dordogne, prior to con-
version.

The other featured a golden retriever dog, who also
seemed to be smiling.

She glanced along the shelves of books, recognising
many titles she'd loved from her own childhood.

She pulled out a shabby copy of *The Wind in the
Willows*, smiling as she recalled Ratty, Mole and Toad,
and their adventures in the Wild Wood.

There was a bookplate in the front, with the name
of a school on it. 'First Prize for English', it read.
'Awarded to S. A. Hunter'.

She stared down at it, frowning. Not Sam's book
after all, she thought with odd disappointment. Then
who…?

'What are you doing?'

She jumped violently in response to Sam's quiet voice from the doorway.

'Snooping.' She felt absurd, standing there naked, peering at books. She pushed *The Wind in the Willows* back on to its shelf. 'I thought these were yours.'

There was a slight hesitation. Then, 'Not all,' he said. 'I suppose, like most spare rooms once the children have moved out, this has become a bit of a dumping ground. Anyway,' he added with mock reproof, 'why aren't you waiting for me in bed, as specifically directed?'

'Because I think it's time we headed back to London, before any other neighbours come calling.' Rose paused. 'Did you manage to pull the wool over her eyes?'

'I was too busy keeping the wool over myself,' Sam said, tightening the belt of his robe as he walked towards her. 'She's a sweetheart, and I didn't want to shock her.'

His eyes were devouring her, already shadowy with desire.

Ros felt shy suddenly, and very undressed. She reached hurriedly for her clothes.

'I see it's stopped raining,' she remarked over-brightly, trying to reduce the situation to a more commonplace level, and aware that she was failing miserably.

'It stopped about two hours ago, but you were too occupied to notice.' Sam came up behind her, wrapping his arms round her and resting his chin on her shoulder. His warm breath caressed her ear.

'Why don't we forget about London and spend the night here?' he whispered. 'We can set off at the crack of dawn tomorrow.'

She could feel herself melting again. 'We can't…'

'Yes, we could.' His voice was husky. 'I want to sleep with you, Janie. To spend the whole night holding you in my arms. Don't you want that too?'

Janie. Whatever she might or might not want flew out of the window as her whole body stiffened.

Oh, God, she thought. Janie—who was coming back from Dorset late this evening. And who would expect to find her at the Chelsea house, alone and untouched.

She moved her head in swift negation. 'I—I have to get back. I have to work tomorrow.'

'Janie.' His voice held sudden urgency. 'Don't push me away again. Not after this.'

'It isn't that.' She turned in his arms, clasped his face between her hands and drew him down for her kiss. 'There are just—things I have to do.'

Like a stepsister to explain to, she added silently. A tissue of lies to unravel. Usual stuff.

'Tomorrow night, then.' The turquoise eyes were urgent—hungry. 'I'll cook you dinner at my flat.'

The wonder of the afternoon was shattering, splintering into tiny shards under the onset of reality.

She freed herself—stepped back—huddling her clothes clumsily in front of her. A gesture that was not lost on him, judging by his swift frown.

'Sam—' She tried to smile. 'This is all going too fast.'

'Janie,' he said, not smiling at all. 'You set the pace. And I didn't take anything you didn't want to give.'

'I don't deny that.' She bent her head. 'But it doesn't change a thing. You had a list. I was a name on it.'

'And now you're another notch on the bedpost. Is that what you're implying?' His tone was harsh.

She spread her hands, her eyes pleading. 'Sam—I don't know. After all, what do either of us really know about the other?'

And that, in spite of everything that had happened between them, was the real crux of the matter.

'I imagined today might have built up the database to some extent.' His smile was sardonic. 'I learned a hell of a lot.'

Her head lifted. She said crisply, 'That was sex.' And the most untrustworthy element in the universe...

'Really?' His brows lifted 'Now I could have sworn we were making love. I apologise for my gross error. It won't happen again.' He saw her flinch at the bite in his voice, but didn't soften. 'Get dressed, Janie, and I'll take you back. Just don't forget you were the one who wanted it this way.'

He stalked to the fitted wardrobe, pulled out jeans, a shirt and jacket, grabbed underwear from a drawer, and left the room, shutting the door hard behind him.

Ros trod over to the bed, and sank down on to the edge of it. She was trembling, and on the edge of tears. But she had to stay in control.

Everything had changed, she thought sombrely. Yet nothing had changed. She and Sam were still as far apart as they'd been when she'd first walked into that restaurant.

In fact, the glorious physical intimacy that they'd shared seemed to have stranded them at an even greater distance from each other. As if fate was tormenting her with a glimpse of what happiness could be like...

She wasn't some naive girl, who thought every bedroom encounter was a declaration of commitment or that being sexually compatible necessarily indicated an equal emotional stability.

But neither was she a risk-taker—someone who lived for the sensation of the moment. She thought she was a realist.

The happy endings she wrote about in her books were compounded from hope rather than experience.

Because sex was the great deceiver. It drew you in, sent you a little crazy, then spat you out.

It made you dream of—long for—impossible things. Plan for a future that only existed in your own imagination. Ignited all kinds of other emotions, like jealousy and suspicion.

She knew all that. Which made her behaviour of the past few hours even more inexplicable.

It had been realism which had tied her to Colin, she thought. The conviction that a relationship needed solid foundations in order to thrive and grow. That liking someone was safer than being head over heels in love.

And yet in less than a week Sam Alexander had blown all her carefully constructed theories to smithereens.

He had shown her more pleasure than she'd ever dreamed of. And opened the door to a pain that could leave her in total devastation.

That was the realisation she now had to live with.

Damn him, she thought, the muscles in her throat working convulsively. And more fool me for allowing it to happen.

And one of the most worrying aspects of the whole situation was that the Sam who'd pushed himself into her life and invaded her dreams no longer bore any resemblance to the wistful personal ad in the *Clarion*.

The emotive words about love and marriage had just been bait. She hadn't trusted them from the first. Yet, in spite of her disbelief, she'd been the one he'd caught in his trap.

How could I have done this? she asked herself bleakly. How could I have allowed it to happen? *Wanted* it to happen?

She stood. Made herself walk to the shower room and wash from head to foot, letting the water cascade over her head and shoulders, and down her trembling body. Then she towelled herself until her skin burned, before wrapping herself, sarong-style, in a dry bath-sheet.

As she walked back into the bedroom, combing her damp hair with her fingers, Sam was standing by the bed.

Ros checked with a faint gasp, and saw his eyes turn to chips of turquoise ice as they scanned her.

He said curtly, 'Spare me the outraged virgin routine, Janie. We both know it's rubbish. Your having second thoughts doesn't suddenly turn me into a monster.'

'What do you want?' she demanded defensively. Anger seemed to surround him like a force field. She could feel its vibrations across the room, and had to resist an impulse to wrap her arms protectively round her body.

'Nothing that your over-heated imagination is suggesting.' His voice jeered at her. He held out her pair of cream suede loafers. 'I found these downstairs, that's all.'

She bit her lip. 'Oh—I'm sorry.'

'I don't think you know the meaning of the word.'

Stung, she threw back her head. 'And, you, of course, are some kind of saint.'

'No,' he said. 'But I'm honest with myself, at least, which is more than you can say, my sweet rose of the world.'

'Honest?' Her voice rose in scornful disbelief. 'Next you'll be telling me that personal ad was for real. So— was it, Sam? Were you genuinely looking for love and marriage? A relationship? For once, tell me the truth— if you can.'

He didn't look away, and she saw his face grow bleak and his mouth harden.

'No,' he said. 'None of it was true.'

'At last,' she said. 'Something I can believe.'

'Oh, cut the self-righteous indignation,' he came back at her grimly. 'Your reply to the *Clarion* ad wasn't exactly a model of candour either. Because you weren't ''Looking for Love'' at all. And you admitted as much.'

'Yes,' she said. 'But I had no ulterior motive. I—I did it for the best of reasons. Can you say the same?' She was shaking inside but she kept her voice steady. 'Which number was I, Sam? How many of the others who fell for your ''Lonely in London'' charade ended up in your bed? Tell me that.'

He tossed her shoes on to the bed. His voice was harsh. 'You're the first, Janie. And the last. However, you can believe what you want.'

He walked to the door. Paused. 'And while we're dealing with honesty, let's be brutal about it.' His glance skimmed her contemptuously. 'Because in spite of everything, I could have you out of that towel and back into bed, my warm and willing partner, for as long as I chose to keep you there. If I wanted to. You know it, and I know it, so come down from the moral high ground, darling. You're not fooling anyone.

'But as you're so hell-bent on getting back to London,' he added curtly, 'oblige me by getting yourself into your clothes and downstairs in ten minutes, or I'll come back and dress you with my own hands.'

His smile flicked her like the edge of a whip.

'Candid enough for you, darling?' he asked. And went.

CHAPTER EIGHT

SHE had no one to blame but herself.

That was the thought that turned her brain into a treadmill during the silent, endless journey back to London.

It rained heavily all the way, and Sam, his face set in stone, drove with an unwavering, almost fierce concentration for which Ros could only be thankful.

She couldn't bear to hear any more, she thought wretchedly. She didn't want to be reminded of what a pathetic fool she'd been.

As they neared Chelsea, she said, 'You can drop me anywhere.'

'I'm taking you home,' he retired curtly, and she subsided, biting her lip.

There was a parking space right outside her house, and he slotted the Audi into it with icy precision.

As she fumbled with the door catch, Sam was out of the driving seat and round to the passenger side to open it for her.

'Thank you,' she said. By now, her lip was bleeding. The bitter, metallic taste filled her mouth. 'And goodbye.'

He ignored his dismissal and followed her up the steps. He held out a hand. 'Let me have your key.'

She began stiffly, 'There's really no need…'

'Another point we differ on. As you already know, I prefer to see you safely into the house.' He paused.

'And I'm not leaving until I've done it, so let's not waste time arguing.'

In seething silence, Ros handed him the key.

She stood defensively in the hall while he briefly checked the ground-floor rooms.

She gave him a small, wintry smile. 'However did I manage before I met you?'

'You didn't have to,' he said briefly. 'The security of the house was your parents' responsibility.' He paused. 'When are they coming back?'

'Two—three weeks.' Of course, she realised, he still thought this was their house.

He nodded, his face resuming the stony expression he'd worn in the car. 'I'll be in touch before then.'

'No.' The word was torn out of her. 'I don't want that. We said—you agreed...' She swallowed painfully. 'It ends here. Now. It must.'

'In spite of today?' His tone was curious—almost meditative.

'Because of today,' she flung at him. 'It should never have happened.'

'I can't disagree about that.' His mouth twisted wryly. 'But I'm afraid it's not that simple.'

'It was a mistake,' she insisted stubbornly. She paused. 'Or have I got it all wrong?' she added scornfully. 'Do I actually have to pay you to go away? Is that what it's all about?'

There was a terrible silence. As the turquoise gaze swept her, Ros felt as if she'd been suddenly encased in ice.

He said softly, 'Believe me, at this moment I'd give every penny I own and more to walk out of here and not look back. That was a cheap crack, Janie.'

She looked down at the carpet. 'I'm sorry,' she mut-

tered. 'But you can leave. We—we don't have to compound the error. Make matters worse.'

He said quietly. 'Nature might do that for us. Unless
you're on the pill, of course?'

Her lips framed another 'no' but no sound emerged.
She stared at him—at this stranger standing in her own
hall—saying the unthinkable. Warning her of the impossible.

She felt the colour draining from her face. Heard
the sudden thud of her heart, panicking against her
ribcage.

He nodded, his mouth set. 'In that case you and I
have had unprotected sex. And that's why I'm staying
in touch, and there's nothing you can say or do to stop
me,' he added, between his teeth. 'Because if there are
consequences, I want to know.'

He walked past her to the front door and paused,
looking back at her.

She wanted to speak his name. Had a crazy yearning
to say or do something that would bring him back to
her. That would close his arms around her, keeping
her safe.

But her mouth felt frozen. Her whole body seemed
suddenly paralysed. She could only stare at him, her
eyes enormous in her white face.

Because there was no safety any more. No security.
And if she'd been capable of sound she would have
howled like a dog.

He looked back at her, his mouth curling in a small,
grim smile.

He said, 'I'll be seeing you.' And walked out, closing the door behind him.

She stood, leaning against the wall, staring unseeingly
at the solid wooden panels of her own front door. The

barricade that was supposed to keep out intruders. To protect her.

Except that of her own free will she'd jettisoned all her defences. Deliberately made herself vulnerable. Surrendered completely.

And now she might have to live with the consequences for the rest of her life.

I never even gave it a thought, she realised with a pang. Yet when I was with Colin, we always took precautions. Or he did.

Wanting Sam had filled her heart and mind to the exclusion of all else—including basic common sense, she thought, wincing. She'd been carried away on a riptide of emotion that had allowed for nothing but the total satiation of her senses.

She stirred restlessly. Being a fool was bad enough. She didn't have to make excuses. Nor did she have to be a victim, either.

It was time she stopped feeling sorry for herself and took control of her own life again, she thought with cold calculation.

So, she would call her doctor in the morning and ask to be prescribed the 'morning after' pill. Endure the lecture he would undoubtedly see fit to give her, and which she so richly deserved. And that would fix everything.

And then she'd be able to tell Sam that there was no need for him to bother any further. That the situation was taken care of. Write 'Finis' at the end of the chapter.

Except that she didn't actually know where to find him, she realised suddenly, and with horror.

Oh, God, she castigated herself. She'd been to bed

with this man—yet she didn't know his address, his telephone number, or even where he worked. The shame of it left her reeling. Not to mention the unmitigated stupidity.

She'd have to keep that from the doctor, she thought feverishly or he'd send her to see a psychiatrist. And who could blame him?

She began to walk towards the stairs, and paused, rigid with a new fear as she heard the sound of stealthy movement on the floor above.

Sam hadn't simply been playing the dominating male when he'd checked the house, she thought, dry-mouthed. There'd been a genuine danger which he'd been aware of but she hadn't. Until now—as all the statistics she'd ever read about women being attacked in their own homes rose up to haunt her.

She backed down the hall, reaching with damp, clumsy fingers for the telephone, only to see a yawning Janie appear on the half-landing.

'Oh God.' Ros drew a deep, shaky breath. 'It's you. You—you startled me.'

'Of course it is. Who else were you expecting?' Janie ran her fingers through her hair, peering down at Ros. 'Where on earth have you been?'

'I went out.' Ros forced herself to smile, to attempt to speak normally. 'I wanted some fresh air. It—it was such a lovely day,' she added lamely.

'Lovely?' Janie echoed incredulously. 'Are you kidding? We've had inches of rain, plus thunder and lightning. I took a couple of paracetamol as soon as I got in, and fell asleep on the bed.' She paused. 'Are you on your own? Because I could have sworn I heard voices. That's what woke me.'

'It was just the answering machine.' Ros took a

deep breath. 'What are you doing back here so early anyway?'

Janie tossed her head. 'I got Martin to bring me home. I couldn't stand any more of his mother clicking her tongue and saying we were in too much of a rush over the wedding. She kept looking me up and down, trying to suss out if I was pregnant, the dirty-minded old bat.'

Ros sighed inwardly. 'I thought you liked his parents.'

'I bent over backwards to like them,' Janie declared moodily. 'But they clearly don't think I'm good enough for their beloved son.'

In spite of her inner turmoil, Ros's lips twitched. 'There's a lot of it about,' she agreed, gravely. 'But I might have reservations too if a child of mine suddenly rolled up with someone I'd never heard them mention before, saying they were engaged.'

'Oh, I might have known you'd take their side.' Janie's tone was pettish.

'I'm not taking sides at all,' Ros assured her wearily. 'I wouldn't dare.' She paused. 'Are there any paracetamol left? Because I'm actually developing quite a headache myself.'

'Really?' Janie sent her a frowning glance. 'To be honest, darling, you do look like hell. As pale as a ghost. Your day out doesn't seem to have done you much good.'

'I was just thinking exactly the same thing,' Ros said with tired irony, and went upstairs to her room.

She wanted to sleep. To close her eyes and sink into blessed oblivion. But she couldn't relax. Her churning brain wouldn't allow it. Nor would her heightened emotions, prodded into turmoil by a host of unwanted memories.

Because Sam was with her—in this house, this room, this bed—and there was no escape from him. She could taste his skin, sense its texture beneath her seeking hands. She could feel the warm weight of his body grazing hers. The silken hardness of him filling her. The joy of him, and the unbelievable, unceasing pleasure.

She pressed a clenched fist against her trembling lips to repress a moan.

She had to do something to rid herself of this torment, she thought desperately. To exorcise this ghost who lay with her and whispered words of passion and desire that she dared not hear.

With sudden resolution, she swung her feet to the floor, reaching for a robe, catching sight of herself in the long wall mirror as she did so.

She paused and was still, observing herself closely and painfully. Searching for visible changes in the body she'd thought she knew so well, and which no longer, in some strange way, seemed to belong to her. Which might, already, be possessed by someone else.

A little quiver ran through her senses. She straightened her back, feeling the faint pull of her aching muscles, the voluptuous tenderness of her breasts.

Impossible, she thought wonderingly, that she should look no different. Yet the slim figure confronting her appeared the same. There were no bruises, she acknowledged wryly. No obvious scars. For a second her hand touched the flatness of her stomach, in a gesture that was pure question, then she realised what she was doing and snatched it away.

It's my heart that's changed, she thought sadly. And my mind. The other—well, that isn't even an option.

She put on her robe and tied the sash tightly, then went barefoot up to her study.

After all, she reasoned, as she switched on the computer, she'd been able to exploit the excitement and sexual tension she'd enjoyed in Sam's company. Now she could use the pain too, if that was all there was left for her.

She was still working two hours later, when Janie put a surprised head round the door.

'I thought you were asleep. I came up to tell you I've put a Spanish omelette together, if you'd like some.'

'Thanks.' Ros smiled at her, flexing weary shoulders. 'That's really thoughtful, love.'

'Oh, well.' Janie gave an off-hand shrug. 'Actually, I need to talk to you, Ros. To ask your advice.'

Ros bit her lip as she got to her feet. 'I'm the last person who should be advising anyone,' she said bleakly. 'My life isn't a conspicuous success at the moment.'

'How can you say that?' Janie led the way downstairs to the kitchen. 'You have your career—this marvellous house. Even a man—of sorts.' She pulled a face. 'Where is Colin, by the way? I thought he'd be back from his rugby tour by now and well ensconced.'

'Actually, no.' Ros tried to sound casual as she sat down. The omelette, which Janie dished up from the pan with a flourish, smelt wonderful, crammed with ham, peppers, tomatoes and cheese. She picked up a fork. 'Colin and I are no longer an item.'

'My God.' Janie's eyes were like saucers. 'Maybe

I should go away more often. You could transform your entire life.'

Ros forked up some omelette. She thought, I'm afraid I already have…

'So what prompted this?' Janie demanded eagerly.

Ros shrugged. 'It just—seemed the thing to do,' she returned evasively.

'Hmm.' Janie gave her a narrow-eyed look as she filled two glasses with Rioja. 'A likely story. My guess is that you've met someone else. And now you're blushing,' she added gleefully. 'Come on—tell me everything.'

Ros said crisply, 'You have a vivid imagination, Janie. There's—no one.'

Janie pouted slightly. 'Well, maybe you have a point. I'm still not sure that Martin's the right man for me. Not if he won't stand up for me against his parents.' She sighed. 'It's all a bit of lottery, isn't it? Perhaps I should have stuck to my plan and met "Lonely in London" after all.'

Ros's fork clattered on to her plate. 'No,' she exclaimed, too quickly.

Janie stared at her. 'How do you know?' Her face was suddenly wistful. 'He could have been the man of my dreams.'

'Possibly,' Ros said coldly. 'And you'd be just another conquest for a serial womaniser. Something for him to brag about with his friends.'

Janie tossed her head. 'Well, there's no need to get so het up about it. After all, I gave him the brush-off, thanks to you. I don't suppose I'd get a second chance, even if I wanted one.'

Ros reached across the table and took her hand. 'Promise me you won't try,' she said urgently.' I'm sure things will work out with Martin in the end—if you want them to—and you're prepared to compromise. But if not you'll meet someone else, Janie. I know you will. But not through some ghastly cheating, lying advertisement,' she added passionately.

There was a pause, then, 'Wow.' Janie gave an uncertain laugh. 'You sound as if you really mean that.'

Ros nodded, her heart as heavy as a stone in her chest. 'Believe it,' she said. And went back to her supper.

One day followed another in bleakness. Ros worked crazy hours, ensuring that when she went to bed she was too tired even to dream.

She went to the doctor, listened to his strictures about prevention being better than cure, obtained her prescription, and then walked, without the slightest hesitation, straight past the pharmacy. When she got home, she locked the slip of paper into a drawer in her desk.

My secret talisman, she mocked herself.

The book, however, began to go well, and by the end of the week she had enough to show Vivien.

She sat tensely, watching the older woman scanning the lines of script, her fingers rapidly turning the pages.

When she'd finished, Vivien said, 'Keep this up and it will be the best thing you've ever done.' She laughed. 'It's a total transformation. What's happened to you?'

Ros thought, I fell in love. And forced herself to smile.

It was raining when she came out of the publishing office. Cursing under her breath, she turned up her collar, tucked her briefcase under her arm and scurried up the road to the intersection to look for a taxi.

She managed to hail one at last, but, to her fury, a man further up the street leapt out of a shop doorway and collared it.

'I hope your tyres burst,' she hurled after it, realising, even before she'd finished speaking, that another vehicle was drawing up at the kerb beside her.

She turned gratefully, and saw it was indeed a black car. But not a black cab.

All the breath in her body seemed to leave in one shocked, painful gasp as she recognised the Audi.

Sam leaned across and opened the passenger door. 'Get in,' he directed curtly.

'No way.' She almost spat the words. 'I'll walk.'

'You'll drown.'

'My exact choice.' Head high, she started off down the street, going in entirely the wrong direction, she realised with chagrin.

She heard the Audi's door slam, and the purr of its engine as it cruised along beside her, making a mockery of her hurrying steps.

Sam spoke to her through the open window. 'Don't make this a problem, Janie. We're starting to hold up the traffic.'

To her annoyance, she saw that, because there were vehicles parked on the opposite side of the road, a van and two other cars were indeed already waiting behind the Audi, with clearly mounting impatience.

As she hesitated, the van driver leaned out of his own window. 'Do us all a favour, girlie, and get in for Gawd's sake.'

The Audi's door opened again, and, face flaming, Ros took the passenger seat.

'This is harassment,' she accused, fumbling with the seat belt. 'Have you been following me?'

'No.' Sam took the metal clip from her and slotted it neatly into place. 'I just happened to be in the neighbourhood.'

'Really?' Her tone was sceptical. 'Doing what, precisely?'

'Visiting a friend in hospital.'

She did not look at him. 'You surprise me.'

'Why? Because I have a friend?' There was an edge to his voice. 'Or because you've given me a compassion rating of zero?'

'Those are both good reasons,' she said. 'But principally because it's an odd time of day to be paying visits. You must have a very lenient boss. That is, of course, if you actually do work at all.'

'Ah, yes,' he said softly. 'At our last meeting you credited me with a career as an extortionist. How could I forget?'

'You obviously have a very poor memory,' she said. 'I also made it plain I didn't want to see you again.'

'And I told you with equal frankness that we were stuck with each other,' he came back at her grimly. 'At least for a while, anyway. So why not graciously accept a ride home?'

Her lips parted incredulously. 'You expect—you want me to be gracious?'

'It wouldn't be my primary option,' Sam returned coolly. 'But beggars can't be choosers. So, I'll settle for what I can get. Even if it's a fit of sulks,' he added, shooting a lightning glance at her defensively hunched shoulder.

'I'm supposed to be pleased that you've—hijacked me in a public street?'

He shrugged. 'No more than I'm glad to have you dripping all over the inside of my car. Let's say they're just—necessary evils.' He paused. 'And as a matter of interest what are you doing in this area? It's hardly the hub of the cosmetics industry.'

'I had a professional appointment,' Ros said coldly. 'If it's any of your concern.'

One moment, they were in an orderly line of traffic. The next, Sam had spotted a gap in the adjoining lane and dived across it and down a quiet side street, where he stopped.

He turned to look at her, the turquoise eyes blazing. He said slowly, 'I can think of circumstances which would make it very much my concern. I've just come from a private clinic. It happens to specialise in cardiac cases, but there are plenty of others round here with very different purposes.'

'Others?' Ros echoed, and then realised. She said, with a little gasp, 'I don't even know if I'm pregnant. Not yet.' She lifted her chin. 'If you got me into this car looking for reassurance you're going to be disappointed.'

She paused. 'But when—if,' she corrected hurriedly, 'I discover it's true, that will be the time for making decisions.'

And tried not to think about the unfilled prescription in the locked drawer.

He said quietly, 'I hope I may be consulted before you finally decide—about anything. Will you promise me that?'

Her throat closed. She said huskily, 'It's my body.'

'But our child.' The reminder was softly spoken, but it struck Ros to the heart.

As he restarted the car, she turned and stared out of

the passenger window at the blur of buildings and traffic.

But whether her view was distorted by the rain or
by the tears she was fighting to control was a question
she could not answer.

CHAPTER NINE

WHEN the car eventually stopped, Ros was still too immersed in her unhappy thoughts to take much note of her surroundings. Accordingly, she was already out of the car and heading across the pavement before she registered that Sam had parked in front of a small block of flats in a street that bore no resemblance to her own Chelsea base.

She swung round to find him locking the car. 'What the hell is this? What's going on? You offered me a lift home.'

'This is home,' he said. 'My home—at least for the time being. I thought you'd like to see it.'

'Then you thought wrong.' She drew a quick, sharp breath. 'Where's the nearest tube station?'

'About a quarter of a mile away.' He pointed out the direction with a casual gesture. 'A brisk and very wet walk. Alternatively, you can stop being bloody-minded, come up with me, and have some coffee or a drink while we wait for the rain to pass. But make your mind up quickly, please. I'm not in the mood for pneumonia.'

She should have turned and gone instantly. Her hesitation had been fatal, and she knew it. She lifted her chin and walked through the double glass doors he was holding open for her.

They rode up in the lift in silence. Ros stood rigidly, her arms folded across her body, looking anywhere but at him. Knowing that he was watching her, and that she didn't want to read the expression in his eyes. Did not dare to.

She waited as Sam unlocked a door on the second floor and stood aside for her to precede him. 'Welcome,' he said with faint mockery.

'If you say so.' One swift appraisal told her plenty. It was a large flat, clean and comfortable, but totally masculine in ambience.

Apart from a couple of photographs, the interior was workmanlike—almost Spartan. There weren't many personal touches at all, but maybe that was deliberate.

In fact, it was more like an office than home. Or a staging post for someone always on the move. It had a strangely transient air, she thought, recalling the travel books at the other house. As if the occupier were simply—passing through.

If any women had stayed there they'd left no traces of their tastes or personalities. Or perhaps they just hadn't been around for long enough...

'Well?' There was still that underlying note of amusement in his voice.

She paused. 'You're very—tidy.'

'Not always,' he said. 'My mother would say I haven't been back here long enough to create any serious mess. Besides, I always make an effort when I'm expecting visitors.'

'You were expecting—me?'

'I was counting on it.'

She lifted her chin. 'So, you were following me after all.'

'No,' he said. 'I told you. I was visiting a friend in the Albermarle Clinic. He's recovering from a mild heart attack and is due to be discharged quite soon, when his wife is going to whisk him off to a quiet village in Yorkshire to recuperate. Now you know it all.'

He paused. 'Anyway, I didn't have to follow. Because I knew I'd find you And I wouldn't even have to go looking.'

Ros shrugged. 'You make it sound important.' Her voice was dismissive.

'And so it is—to me.' He walked into the kitchen, filled the kettle and plugged it in while she watched from the doorway. He sounded almost reflective. 'You see, I've got tired of being dumped outside your door like a bag of trash each time you have second thoughts.'

He smiled at her. 'So I decided, for a change, that you could come here, and we could be together and talk, until we had the inevitable big row, when I could kick you out instead.'

It was not funny, Ros told the silence that followed in outrage. It simply was not. This was the man who'd destroyed her peace of mind and turned her life to turmoil.

So why did she feel laughter welling up inside her, eventually emerging in a small, uncontrollable wail?

She found herself clinging to the doorpost, overwhelmed by a tidal wave of giggles, unable to speak, barely able to breathe, tears running down her face.

Only to realise, suddenly, that she was no longer laughing, but weeping, her giggles replaced by sobs that tore at her throat.

Sam was across the kitchen at her side, his arms enfolding, his voice suddenly, magically soothing. She let her shaking body sink into his embrace, pressing her face convulsively into his shoulder, and felt his hand gently stroking her hair.

At last, her sobs still shuddering through her, she lifted her head and tried to speak. To apologise? To make some plea? She would never be sure.

He shook his head, and touched a finger lightly to her lips, forbidding speech. Then he began to kiss her, swiftly, lightly, his mouth brushing the tears from her lashes and drenched cheeks.

Only it wasn't enough, some drowning part of her recognised. She wanted more. She wanted everything.

Her hands reached up, gripping his shoulders with fierce intent. She stared up at him, her lips parting—trembling...

She heard Sam give a soft, muffled groan, then his mouth covered hers in a demand as deep and unashamed as her own.

She answered it with something that bordered on delirium, savouring the taste of his mouth, the thrust of his tongue, scalding hot and honey-sweet. The kiss clung, broke for the beat of a breath, then raged again, enflaming and engulfing them both.

Ros tipped her head back, letting his lips slide down the line of her throat, feeling the subtle flick of his tongue around the hollow of her ear.

His hands cupped her breasts, moulding them through the ribbed silk of her sweater, and she gasped, arching her body so that the delicate peaks thrust in mute offering against his caressing fingers.

He pushed roughly at her sweater, his fingers freeing the clasp of her bra so that his lips could feed on the untrammelled, scented roundness that he had released.

She encircled his head with her arms, holding him to her, glorying in the bittersweet tug of his mouth on her flesh.

His hands grasped her hips, pulling her body forward so that it ground against his, male and female in the eternal heated conjunction.

Her legs were shaking, her body melting as he lifted her into his arms and carried her away.

As he lowered her she felt the softness of a mattress under her back, and the scent of fresh linen.

Then Sam knelt over her, hands clumsy with haste as he began to rid her of her clothes, and she was aware of nothing else but him. There was no sound in the room now except the rasp of fastenings and the rustle of discarded fabric, combined with the harsh urgency of their breathing.

Naked at last, they came together, his fingers stroking her exquisitely to flame, to prepare her for the first stark thrust of possession. He entered her without hesitation, and her hips lifted eagerly to meet him, her legs locking round him, her hands clinging to his sweat-damp shoulders.

Staring down at her, eyes half closed, the muscles knotted in his throat, Sam drove into her, deeply, rhythmically, and her body rose in response, drawing him further and further into some molten infinity of need.

At the very edge of consciousness, Ros was aware of the first dark stirrings of pleasure unfurling slowly and inexorably within her.

Even as she cried out silently, It's too soon. Not yet… she was overtaken. Overwhelmed. Left spent and shaken, hearing her voice uttering its last moans of voluptuous delight.

Hearing Sam groan in turn, as he reached his own extremity of sensation.

And this time the tears he kissed from her face were tears of joy.

A long time later, she said, 'So this is your bedroom.'

'You don't miss much.' She heard the grin in his voice, and her own mouth curved.

'I didn't get much chance to admire the decor,' she reminded him, dropping a kiss on his shoulder.

He rested his cheek on her hair. 'Now you'll tell me that the ceiling needs painting,' he murmured, and yelped as she bit him softly. 'So—do you approve?'

Without moving from his arms, Ros took a leisurely look round. A plain stone-coloured carpet, she noted, complemented by a classic wardrobe and tallboy in some dark polished wood, navy curtains at the window, and bedding in navy and white percale.

'It looks good,' she said. 'Subdued.'

Sudden laughter shook him. 'What were you expecting—mirrors on the ceiling—black satin sheets—hidden video cameras?'

'I didn't know what to expect,' she said. 'Maybe that's what worries me. Here we are—and yet I know so little about you, Sam. So very little.'

There was a silence, and she felt the chest muscles beneath her cheek tense slightly.

He said, 'That's why I brought you here. So you could see that I have a place to live, and I'm not existing out of a cardboard box on the street. To prove to you that I live alone too.'

He paused. 'And it's not part of some lonely hearts ploy either—before you ask. I've brought no one else here. You're the first.'

She said in a small voice, 'Oh.'

'Is that "Oh, I'm pleased" or "Oh, I'm sorry"?'

'I—I'm not sure.'

He said quietly, 'Do you feel it's all moving too fast for you?'

'I think that's what I ought to feel.'

'But?'

Her fingers strayed across his chest, stroking the flat nipples. She said slowly, 'But it's difficult to believe you haven't always been part of my life.'

He nodded. 'I have something to confess too.' He put his hand under her chin, tipping up her face so that he could look into her eyes. 'I said earlier that I wouldn't have to go looking for you, but it was a lie. I was actually on my way over to your house when I saw you.

'And it wasn't to find out whether or not you're pregnant, either,' he added huskily. 'It was because I couldn't bear to keep away any longer.'

'So it must have been fate,' she said. 'Do you believe in fate?'

'I never did before.'

He kissed her, his mouth moving gently, languorously, on hers.

When her breathing steadied, she said, 'I might not have opened my door to you.'

'I was prepared to take that risk,' he said. 'And I'd have camped on your steps and sung you love songs until you had to let me in. Because I have this really terrible voice.'

A little quiver of laughter ran through her, followed by a deep shudder of anticipation because his hand was moving, slowly but very surely, caressing the tautening swell of her breast, then moving downward to stroke the silken skin of her thigh, before seeking once more the inner heated moisture it protected.

Reducing her in seconds to gasping, molten sensation. A state of exquisite, pulsating chaos where nothing mattered except his lips, his fingers, and the hard strength of his body invading hers—possessing her utterly.

Afterwards, she fell asleep in his arms. But at some point he must have eased himself away from her, because when she woke she was alone in the bed.

Ros propped herself up on an elbow and stared round the empty room. She was just beginning to feel uneasy when the door opened and Sam came in. He was dressed, she saw, casual in jeans and a white cotton shirt, and he was carrying two beakers of coffee.

'I bet the first thing Sleeping Beauty asked for after the prince's kiss was room service,' he remarked, putting the coffee down on the night table.

'Wrong.' Ros pushed her hair back ruefully. 'It was a mirror.'

'We have those too.' His lips touched the top of her head. 'But you look quite beautiful enough, so drink your coffee first.'

Faint colour rose in her face as she sat up, pulling the sheet around her body.

'You're going shy on me again,' Sam lounged on the end of the bed, his eyes disconcertingly intent as they studied her. 'Don't you think that's locking the stable door after the horse has not simply bolted, but vanished over the horizon?'

'I suppose so.' Her colour deepened. 'But this is the way I am. I—I'm sorry.'

'Don't be,' he said. 'I like the way you are.'

She paused. 'I thought you'd be sleeping too. Are you some kind of superman?'

'Far from it,' he said, and paused. 'But I had some heavy-duty thinking to do,' he went on levelly. 'And I think better without a naked and very desirable girl in my arms.'

The coffee scalded her throat, making her gasp. 'Experience has taught you that?'

'No,' he said. 'Some delayed but necessary common sense.'

'Common sense?' Ros echoed, keeping her voice light. 'I don't think I like the sound of that.'

'I felt one of us should try it—however late in the day.' He was silent for a moment. 'I want you to know that when I brought you here I didn't intend—any of this.'

His mouth tightened. 'If I had done, I might have been—better prepared,' he added with rueful emphasis.

She tried a smile. 'What were you just saying about a bolting horse?'

'That's the whole point. We made one serious mistake already.' His own expression was sober—almost grave. 'We didn't have to compound it today. And for that I blame myself totally. We've been playing a kind of sexual Russian Roulette—and it has to stop.'

In spite of the coffee's heat, there was a sudden cold feeling in the pit of Ros's stomach.

She found herself examining the pattern on the beaker rather too carefully. 'There's no question of blame,' she said quietly. 'We both wanted this—didn't we?'

'Yes,' he said. 'But that still doesn't make it right.'

'No,' she said. Fright stirred and shook inside her.
'No, of course not.'

There was another silence, then he said bluntly, 'All
this has happened at a bad time for me, Janie. My
life's a mess. I have to get it sorted.'

And move on. He didn't say it, but she heard the
words in her head. He'd been abroad, he'd come back,
and soon he would be gone again. All the clues to his
life were there, just waiting to be recognised. And
staying around—commitment—was not part of his
agenda.

I noticed, she thought with anguish, but I didn't
build up the pattern. I didn't realise this had 'temporary' written all over it. Not until this moment.

Hurt made her want to hit back. She said, 'I happened at an inconvenient time for you. You happened
at a convenient time for me. I guess we cancel each
other out.'

'Convenient?' His brows drew together sharply.
'What the hell are you talking about?'

'I was having problems with my boyfriend,' she
said. 'I'm sure I told you. Well—since I haven't been
available—he's been coming round again. Phoning
me. Suggesting that we should give ourselves another
chance.'

He was very still. 'And shall you?' he spoke evenly.

'I don't know yet.'

'Of course you don't.' His tone bit. 'A second
chance with another man's child thrown in might be
a little much for him.'

'I—don't think that will happen.'

'How can you be sure?'

Because I'd know if I had your baby inside me,
beginning its life, she wanted to scream at him.

Because I'd feel it there, in every fibre of my being. My body would be a haven—a secure place, warm, dark and hidden—instead of a scared, disintegrating shell…

She shrugged. 'Instinct, I suppose.'

'A very potent thing. And how are his antennae working, I wonder?' He was smiling, but his eyes were blazing. 'Will they pick up that you're not the same person any more? Tell him that you've spent hours in bed with someone you hardly know?'

Ros put the beaker down on the night table. 'I can't believe we're having this conversation.'

'I'm simply trying to make you understand that you don't want him. That you don't need to say these things, because I'm being punished enough already. But you can't involve someone else in our private war. It isn't fair…'

'Don't talk to me about fair.' Her voice shook. 'You haven't been fair with me from the start. Well, have you?'

Deny it, she pleaded inwardly. Oh, please deny it. Say that I'm imagining things. Tell me you want me— that we have a future together some day—and I'll believe you. I swear I will…

He bent his head. His voice seemed to come from the far side of the room. 'No,' he said. 'No, I haven't.'

There was a silence, and pain poured into it. Filled it, so that she could not breath, or think, or speak.

'Janie,' he said. 'Look at me. Accept that I won't offer promises or guarantees that I might not be able to keep.' He took a deep breath. 'You don't know how much I'd like to say ''Live with me and be my love'', but I can't. Not the way things are. And under the circumstances I had no right to bring you here—to make love to you again. Only don't ask me to regret a minute of it. Because I can't, and I never will.'

'Is that supposed to make everything all right?'

'No,' he said. 'That would be asking too much.'

She stared at the stitching on the coverlet. 'Is it another woman? Is that the "mess" you have to sort out?'

'No.' The word exploded from him. 'At least, not in the way that you mean. But don't ask me to explain any more—at least not now.'

'You don't have to explain—or apologise. Not now. Not ever. You didn't force me. My God.' She gave a small, brittle laugh. 'You barely had to seduce me. We're both consenting adults, and there are no broken bones. These things happen.'

'Not,' he said softly, 'in the way that they happened to us.'

She said, 'There is no "us".' And swallowed. 'Could you leave me alone now, please? I'd like to get dressed.'

It was a ludicrous request, when they both knew there wasn't an inch of her that he hadn't explored with his hands and lips. He could probably have sketched her from memory.

She expected at the very least some jeering remark, even if he didn't laugh in her face.

Instead, he nodded silently, and left the room.

Ros huddled into her clothes. She felt numb—empty now. But that wouldn't last. The pain would return, and this time it could destroy her.

In the two years she'd spent with Colin she'd never glimpsed the depth of emotion she felt for Sam after only a matter of days.

How cruel that was, she thought desolately, and

how unjust. Colin had deserved so much better. He'd
always been loyal and decent. She'd been the one
who'd held back, reluctant to commit herself.

And now, like a pathetic idiot, she'd mistaken a few
hours of white-hot passion for love. Chosen a man
who'd only wanted sex without complications, and
was now backing away.

Humiliation clawed at her. She'd meant to be cool
and careful, but she'd let him see too much of her
hopes and needs. She'd opened the door and allowed
him into her heart—into the centre of her being.

Now she had to get out of here with as much self-
respect as she could salvage.

He was speaking on the phone in the living room.
She longed to be able to creep past to the front door
and make her escape while he was still engaged on
his call, but she'd left her bag and briefcase by the
sofa and she couldn't leave without them.

So she lifted her chin and squared her shoulders,
and walked into the room.

Sam was replacing the receiver. He was frowning,
lost in thought, then he looked up and saw her, and
time seemed to stop as they looked at each other. His
expression was set, the turquoise eyes unfathomable.

Ros controlled a shiver.

She said, 'I came for my things.'

She saw a muscle move beside his mouth. 'Yes, of
course.' He paused. 'I'll drive you home.'

'No,' she said. And again, 'No—thank you. I'll get
a cab.'

'As you wish.' His voice chilled her. 'Then I'll find
one for you.'

They rode the lift down in silence, standing on opposite sides of the metal cage.

The rain had stopped, but the air smelt dank and forbidding as they emerged on to the street.

Sam saw a cruising taxi in the distance and hailed it.

As it approached, he said quietly, 'Is there any point in my asking you to be patient—to trust me?'

'None.' Some miracle kept her voice level. 'It's over. Finished.'

She saw sudden colour burn along his cheekbones. He said softly, 'Like hell it is.' And reached for her.

His kiss was hard and angry, plundering her mouth ruthlessly. She felt the burn of it deep in her bones, and, through all the rage and hurt, the tiny coil of response and arousal that she was powerless to forbid.

When he let her go, she stepped back with a gasp, putting a hand mutely to her swollen lips.

'Something to remember me by.' He was breathing rapidly, and his smile glittered at her. 'Until we meet again.'

'All hell,' she said hoarsely, 'will freeze over first.'

Voice shaking, she gave her address to the clearly fascinated driver, and almost threw herself into the back of the cab.

As they drove off, something told her that Sam was still standing there, watching her go.

But she did not turn her head to check. Pride, she told herself, would not allow her to do so.

And besides, she realised with sudden devastation, she could be wrong. And that would be the worst thing of all.

CHAPTER TEN

YOU fool, Sam denounced himself savagely as he watched the cab pull away. You stupid, criminal bastard. Why the hell didn't you tell her the truth—the whole miserable story—from day one?

Because you were scared—that's why. You were afraid to tell her everything in case you lost her. And now you've lost her anyway.

He supposed he'd been hoping wildly that he could emerge from the situation with some kind of honour, but he suspected he'd been praying for the impossible.

He was tempted to sprint after the taxi before it gathered speed, drag Janie out and offer her, on his knees, the complete shambles he'd made of his life.

Anything would be better, he thought wretchedly, then seeing her drive off, hurt and hating him.

And what had possessed him just now—coming on to her like some macho ape? There'd been something about her pale, scornful face that had flicked him on the raw, but that was no excuse. Had he really thought such pitiful 'Me Tarzan, you Jane' tactics would have her melting in his arms?

If so, he knew differently now.

As he watched the taxi round the corner and disappear, he felt the world turn cold. It was as if he'd been suddenly washed up—abandoned on the edge of some wilderness—without food, shelter or hope.

And useless to tell himself that maybe it was for the best, he thought, as he walked slowly back indoors.

That it was hardly the optimum time to be cementing a new relationship when he was likely to find himself jobless at any moment.

The fact that he'd done the correct thing for the right motives was no consolation at all in this new hell of loneliness he'd created for himself.

His thoughts were as bleak as his face as he rode up in the lift. The call he'd just taken had been from Cilla Godwin's secretary, requiring him to present himself in the editor's office tomorrow.

The head of Features had been enthusiastic over the 'Lonely in London' series, but he wasn't expecting any compliments from Cilla. She'd been badgering him for days to have the Janie Craig piece completed and on her desk, and he didn't know what to tell her, what further excuse he could possibly formulate for withholding it.

Certainly not the truth, he thought cynically. That anything he wrote about his meetings with Janie would be tantamount to forcing them both to strip naked in public.

So far, he'd managed to finish one piece about her. He'd written far into the night, driven by some inner compulsion he hardly understood. But when he'd looked at what he'd done the next morning, he'd found himself reading a declaration of love.

That was the moment that had brought him to his senses. That had made him realise what he really felt for her.

And that was why watching her drive away had been like dying inside. Her white strained face would haunt him, he thought, until the end of his days.

Yet now, somehow, he had to drag his thoughts away from her to the problem of Cilla.

He swore softly under his breath. He'd maintained a deliberately low profile since the night she'd come to the flat, but he knew his failure to respond to her overtures would never be forgiven or forgotten. She was, he was convinced, simply awaiting an opportunity to destroy him. And, if it was inevitable, perhaps he should just lie back and let it happen, he thought wearily.

But the fighting spirit which had carried him safely through wars, riots and revolutions was reluctant to concede her so easy a victory.

He went into the bedroom and stood for a moment, looking down at the crumpled bed. He sank down on its edge and picked up the pillow Ros had used, holding it to his face, inhaling the faint fragrance of her skin which still clung there evocatively.

Waking with her in his arms had made so much clear to him. Had made him see exactly what he wanted from life. What he still had to figure was how to achieve it.

'The engagement's off,' Janie announced, marching into the kitchen. 'Ros—did you hear me?' she added sharply to the motionless figure, sitting staring into space at the kitchen table. 'What's the matter with you? Have you gone into a trance?'

Ros looked at her, startled eyes dazed as she struggled for comprehension. 'You've finished with Martin? I—I'm sorry.'

'Don't be. He's being such a pain.' Janie filled the kettle and set it down on the work surface with a thump. 'He won't budge over the wedding.' She snorted. 'I'm glad I realised how completely he's under his parents' control before it was too late.' She paused. 'Do you want some coffee? That stuff in front of you looks stone-cold.'

'It is.' Ros surrendered the mug, and watched her stepsister rinse it out.

'What's wrong?' Janie asked. 'Problems with the book? Publishers giving you the thumbs-down?'

'No,' Ros said. 'It's nothing to do with that.'

'Then what?'

Ros bit her lip. 'Just a few—personal things I need to think through.'

'Oh, God.' Jane turned an apprehensive look on her. 'You're not missing Colin?'

Colin, Ros thought. Colin belonged to another life, another age, another universe. To her shame, she hadn't even given him a thought.

'No,' she said. 'But I'm rather ducking the thought of telling him it's over.'

'Let me,' Janie offered callously. 'It'll be a pleasure.'

In spite of her unhappiness, Ros felt her lips curve in a reluctant smile. 'I thought you'd have had more sympathy—having just been through the same thing yourself.'

'Well, in my case it may not be permanent,' Janie admitted. 'I'm going to let Martin stew for a day or two. He'll come round.'

Ros stared at her, distress closing her throat. 'How can you treat him like that, if you love him?' she protested. 'Can't you imagine what it's like to watch the person you love—your one hope of happiness—just—walk out of your life? What it's like to think that you're not wanted any more? Don't you care that you're making him suffer?'

'Whatever's come over you?' Janie spooned coffee

granules into the mugs. 'Why are you so concerned about Martin? You hardly know him.'

Ros bit her lip. 'I suppose I was thinking of all lovers, and how cruel we can be to each other,' she said, after a pause.

'My word,' Janie said acidly. 'Ditching Colin has had a profound effect. Do you want your coffee black or white?'

There was no point in delaying things any longer, Ros decided. She would go and see Colin and break the news to him that evening. It wasn't a pleasant prospect, but nothing could make her feel more wretched than she already did.

Besides, Janie was going out to a club with two of the girls she was working with, and Ros wasn't looking forward to spending the evening with only her thoughts for company.

Once it's over with, I can draw a line under everything that's happened, she thought, steeling herself against the inevitable shaft of pain. Consign it all to the past and—go on. Somehow.

But go on where? And do what? She had a new life to build—maybe not only her own—and the thought made her feel restless.

Perhaps it was time she made a completely fresh start. She could write anywhere, after all. So she didn't have to stay in London, have to fight her memories every day...

She looked around her in a kind of remote wonder.

My God, she thought. I'm actually contemplating leaving this house. My prized possession. My sanctuary. This cannot be real.

If I sell, I'll be betraying Venetia. Rejecting her legacy.

She wandered out into the garden. It wasn't raining any longer, and a watery sun had struggled through the clouds.

Ros took a quick breath, absorbing the sharp scent of damp earth, And, as if a switch had clicked in her brain, saw Venetia Blake, her old gardening hat crammed on her head, secateurs in hand, moving along the path in front of her, scanning the raised bed for dead flowers.

'Of course, I love it here.' Across the years her voice reached Ros again, bringing a new clarity. 'But a house is only a place. It's the people who live in it that matter—who make it a home. Never forget that, darling.' Her smile was sudden and deeply tender. 'And this house has never meant the same to me since your grandfather died, bless him. He made it special.' She sighed. 'I should have moved, but I'm just too old and too lazy.'

And then, just as suddenly, Ros found herself alone with the chill of the evening breeze. Found, too, she was remembering the wording of her grandmother's will.

'My house…and its contents', she thought, her throat tightening, 'in the hope that she will use them properly'.

And for the first time she realised that Venetia Blake had only ever meant her to use Gilshaw Street as a staging post. And that, when the time was right, she'd expected her to move on.

In spite of her inner misery, Ros felt as if one weight, at least, had been lifted from her shoulders.

And now it was time to remove another, she thought as she went back indoors.

But she'd better let Colin know she was coming, she conceded, and reached for the phone.

It rang a couple of times and then she heard a woman's voice answer. For a second she thought it must be Mrs Hayton, and then she realised it sounded much too young.

She said, 'May I speak to Colin Hayton, please? It's Ros—Rosamund Craig.'

There was a pause, then the voice said, 'Just a minute.'

Ros waited, and was eventually assailed by another voice, which this time really did belong to Colin's mother.

'Good evening, Rosamund. This is quite a surprise.' It was an edged remark. 'Is there something you wanted?'

'Well—yes.' Ros swallowed. 'I was hoping to come over this evening to see Colin—if it's convenient, of course.'

'I fear not,' Mrs Hayton said majestically. 'We have guests.'

The mystery voice, thought Ros. And an honoured guest if she's allowed to pick up the phone. She said, 'Then when could I come?'

'I think it might be better for Colin to contact you,' Mrs Hayton decreed. 'I know he's been planning to do so.'

'I see,' Ros said slowly. 'How—how is his ankle?'

'It's responding very well to treatment.' Mrs Hayton paused. 'Fortunately he does have a few supportive people in his life,' she added with emphasis.

The only silver lining to all these clouds was that

Mrs Hayton was not going to be her mother-in-law, Ros thought, teeth gritted.

She said quietly, 'I need to talk to him urgently, Mrs Hayton. Please give him that message.'

There was a sniff and a clunk as the older woman disconnected.

Her day was not improving, Ros thought grimly, as she replaced her own receiver. And somehow she had to get through the evening.

I'll apply the usual palliatives, she decided, her mouth twisting as she flicked through her phone index. Some mindless violence from the video service, and a Chinese takeaway.

She had some sleeping pills somewhere. She'd take one to ensure she got a night's rest, then she'd be ready to face tomorrow, and all the decisions she had to make. All the heartbreak she had, somehow, to heal.

Nobody said it would be easy, she thought. But I'll survive.

Unbidden, unwanted, the image of Sam forced its way into her mind. She saw the glow in his turquoise eyes, the slant of his smile, and felt her whole body recoil in anguish.

Because she didn't want merely to survive. She wanted to live every moment of her life to the full. And without Sam that was impossible. Because without him she was only half a person.

She wrapped her arms round her body and began to rock slowly, as the first tears scalded her face.

Sam, she whispered silently, desolately. Sam—what have you done to me? To us?

And why do I still have to love you so much?

*   *   *

'Sam. Good of you to spare me the time.' Cilla Godwin's smile held an unpromising glitter as she waved him to a chair.

'I wasn't aware I had a choice,' Sam returned coldly. 'And I won't sit, thanks. I prefer to receive bad news standing.'

'Oh, but all the news is good. As I'm sure he's told you, Phil's delighted with your work on the series—so far, that is. There is still one piece missing, but I'm sure you're dealing with that.'

There was something badly wrong here, Sam realised, all his hackles rising. But what?

'I feel we have to make optimum use of your investigative talents,' she went on. 'And I have a few ideas which I'll discuss with you in due time.

'But first we have to decide how to promote this lonely hearts series—particularly as you've just won this award. A big publicity campaign, I think. National advertising. Billboards and television. ''Award-winning Sam Hunter goes undercover—and how''. Something on those lines. Splashes in the *Echo*, with photographs, naturally.'

Her laugh was like ice cubes falling into an empty tumbler—only not as pleasant.

'I'm going to make you famous, Sam. Or, from another viewpoint, infamous,' she added musingly.

'No,' Sam said, his voice ominously even. 'You can't do that. Phil guaranteed to print the stuff under another name, to protect the interviewees. I've been careful not to identify them too closely, so the chances are they won't recognise themselves even if they read the *Echo*.

'But if you do this, it blows the whole thing out of the water.' He leaned forward across the wide desk, his eyes boring into hers. 'God, Cilla, they're fragile people. If they realise they've been set up, it could do real damage.'

'You're all heart. But the decision's mine. Not Phil's. And certainly not yours.' She picked up a pen from her desk and began to play with it, her fingers moving suggestively over the barrel. 'And you don't have any power to influence things.' Her voice was soft, almost sweet. 'Which was your decision. If you remember.'

'Oh, I remember,' Sam said between his teeth. 'Women aren't immune from accusations of sexual harassment. Maybe you should remember that.'

She shrugged. 'It would be your word against mine. A pathetic attempt at revenge by a disappointed man. Or that's how the tribunal would see it. I'd make quite sure of that.' She smiled again. 'I'm certain that's not the image you want. Besides, your own behaviour doesn't bear close scrutiny,' she added, almost casually. 'We could be looking at breach of contract here, instant dismissal with no comeback.'

'What are you talking about?' Sam felt a sudden chill.

She opened a drawer, produced a folder, and pushed it towards him.

'You've been taking far too long over this Janie Craig interview, and I started wondering why. So I designated someone to keep an eye on you, and yesterday it paid off.'

The photograph spilled out towards him. They were good, some part of him acknowledged. A man and a girl locked together in passion and pain on a London street, their mouths devouring each other. The girl walking away, her eyes like black holes in her strained, tense face. The man watching her go with hunger and regret.

His heart was suddenly like a stone in his chest. He thought, Oh, darling…

'And don't tell me that's not Janie Craig, Sam.' Her glance stabbed him malevolently. 'Because we know that it is. And you had orders not to get personally involved. To look, and talk, but not to touch. I'd say this went much further than touching—wouldn't you? A serious breach of professional conduct,' she added jeeringly. 'Meriting sacking without notice and loss of all financial benefits.'

She paused. 'I'd also make sure you never worked on another national paper. So, if you want to keep your job, and the lifestyle that comes with it, stay in line and do what I tell you. I shall look forward to reading about your exploits with your little beautician. Try not to make them too pornographic.'

She reached for some papers. 'You can go now,' she added casually.

'One more thing.' Sam stood his ground, his gaze and voice level. 'When does this advertising campaign begin?'

'Next week, so that it can peak at the awards ceremony. The highpoint of your career, Sam.' She flicked him with a malicious glance. 'Make the most of it, darling. Things will never be this good again.'

'On the contrary.' Sam walked to the door, and paused. The turquoise eyes were calm, even a little pitying as he looked back at her. His smile was relaxed, and without anger. 'You've made me see that they can only get better.'

*   *   *

Janie, Sam thought, as he ran down to the car park.
He had to see her, tell her the truth about his real
identity before she saw it plastered all over the hoardings.

He'd intended to do it anyway, but now it was a
question of much sooner rather than later.

As he drew up in Gilshaw Street, a dark woman
with a sunny smile was outside, giving the brass a
vigorous polishing.

'Hello, you must be Manuela.' He gave her a coax-
ing grin. 'Is Janie at home?'

She shook her head regretfully. 'She is at work. You
see her there.'

Sam groaned. 'Except I don't know which store
she's at. Have you any idea?'

She looked him up and down with an approving
twinkle. 'She has list of jobs in kitchen. I find out for
you.'

She was back in no time, with a slip of paper bearing the name of a major West End store. 'She is here.
The company name is Beauty Queen.'

'I'll find her.' Sam ran down the steps to the car.
'Manuela, you're a star,' he tossed back over his
shoulder.

Manuela went back to her polishing with a sigh.
Why were the interesting men attracted only to the
little Juanita? she wondered. She was pretty, *sí*, but
the señorita Rosa was a truly lovely girl—so warm—
so kind. When would it be her turn?

But, she thought, shrugging, who would she meet,
shut away as she was at the top of the house, with a
computer, writing another book?

She sighed again, and forgot the whole incident.

The ground floor of the store was crowded with shop-
pers, but there was a large banner advertising the

Beauty Queen promotion and Sam fought his way towards it.

He hadn't worked out how he was going to persuade her to listen to him. She might walk away. She might even slap his face. But he'd deal with it all when it happened.

I just want to see her, he thought, feeling his heart muscles clench.

It would be such a relief to tell her everything at last, with no more pretence and no more secrets.

I thought I had no choice, he told himself. But I was wrong, and I'll admit it on my knees if I have to.

However badly she reacted, he would win her round somehow. Because he needed her as he needed air to breathe.

The fact that she was nowhere to be seen was a total anticlimax.

Perhaps Manuela had got the whole thing wrong, Sam thought with an inward groan.

'May I help you?' A pretty blonde in a strawberry-pink suit smiled at him.

He said, 'Actually, I'm looking for someone—a demonstrator here. Her name's Janie Craig. Do you know her?'

The smile became slightly rigid. 'Is this a joke?'

'No,' he said swiftly. 'No, it's absolutely serious, and pretty urgent. I need to find her now. My name's Sam—Sam Alexander.'

There was an electric silence. The girl's pink mouth formed an 'O' of total astonishment. She took a step backwards, her eyes looking him up and down in frank appraisal. Then she laughed.

'Hi, there,' she said. 'I'm Janie Craig. And you, of course, must be "Lonely in London". So we get to meet after all.'

CHAPTER ELEVEN

IT HADN'T been a productive morning, Ros acknowledged wearily as she came out of her office and started downstairs. But it was hard to give full weight to her heroine's romantic problems when her own were tearing her apart.

She'd have a break, something to eat, even though she wasn't hungry, then try again.

'You are so pale today.' Manuela gave her a concerned look as she entered the kitchen. 'You are ill?'

Sick at heart, Ros thought. If that counts.

She said, 'I'm fine, Manuela. I just didn't sleep very well last night.'

'You should take better care of yourself. Be like Miss Juanita and not worry.'

'Oh, Janie has her problems too,' Ros said wryly. 'She's quarrelled with her boyfriend.'

'No more.' Manuela pursed her lips. 'He came to look for her—to make up—but he didn't know where she was working, so I told him.'

'Martin came here?' Ros's brows lifted. 'You should have let me know,' she commented drily. 'I could have given him some sisterly advice.'

'You were working. He was in big hurry.' Manuela accepted her money, and went off cheerfully.

It looked as if Martin was caving in over the wedding, Ros thought frowningly, as she made herself a sandwich, and she wasn't sure that was a good thing. It would be far healthier for Janie to be thwarted occasionally, and made to see that other people had valid points of view.

She was just about to take a bite of sandwich when the phone rang.

A man's voice said, 'Is that Rosamund Craig?'

She said, 'Speaking,' and stopped dead, her eyes widening as she suddenly recognised her caller's voice. She said, faltering slightly, 'Sam—it's you...'

And heard the phone go down, cutting her off with a kind of awful finality.

When her mind cleared, she found she was kneeling on the floor, whispering, 'Oh, God,' over and over again.

He's found out, she thought desperately. He knows who I really am—and that I've been lying to him all this time. Pretending to be Janie. But how?

Shakily, she remembered Manuela's beaming account of their morning visitor. The man she'd assumed was Martin—and sent off to find the real Janie...

That had to be the answer.

I should have told him myself, she berated herself. Confessed that first night. Because after that it never seemed to be the right time. And now it's too late.

It's all—too late.

She threw away the uneaten sandwich, and went upstairs to her room. Her mouth curled with distaste as she surveyed the tearstained, bedraggled figure in her mirror.

She couldn't face the world looking like this. And she'd no doubt she'd have to face it—principally in the shape of Janie, who'd be erupting through the front door, demanding an explanation, in just a couple of hours.

But I've no explanation to offer, she thought wretchedly. Not one that makes sense, anyway. I can hardly say I was just following her advice—going out to meet life head-on.

Yet how can I tell her the truth? That I met a stranger, and fell in love with him almost before I knew it. That's ridiculous too. Because I don't do things like that. Or the person I used to be never did. The girl I am now is capable of anything. She could even be expecting a baby by a man who doesn't want to know.

And she's brought it all—*all* on herself.

There was a taste of tears in her throat, and she swallowed them back. There was no point in crying any more. Now she had to pull herself together, and sort out what was left of her life.

She'd have a bath, she thought, and shampoo her hair. If she looked better, she might feel marginally better too.

She'd just finished drying her hair when she heard the doorbell. The dryer slipped from her hand and fell to the carpet unheeded.

She whispered, 'Sam,' and flew downstairs, tightening the sash on her towelling robe as she went. As she reached the hall, the bell sounded again.

He was certainly impatient, Ros thought as she fumbled with the chain, fingers made clumsy by haste. He was undoubtedly very angry. But at least he was here, and prepared to talk. So there was hope. Of a kind. Wasn't there?

She flung open the door and stood for moment, feeling her jaw drop with surprise and disappointment.

'So you are at home,' said Colin, his tone cool.

'You said you wanted to see me. Aren't you going to ask me in?'

She said, dry-mouthed, 'Yes—yes, of course,' and stood aside as he limped into the hall, leaning on a walking stick.

'But there was no need for you to come all this way,' she said, following him into the sitting room. 'Put yourself to all this trouble. I was prepared to go to you. I said so to your mother.'

'We decided it would be better this way,' he said. 'Less awkward. And my ankle's much improved. I've been having brilliant physiotherapy.'

'Oh,' she said. 'Well—that's good.'

He nodded. 'It's time we met up, Ros. We haven't seen each other for quite some time. And there are certain things—things about the future—that we need to discuss.'

She swallowed. 'Colin—I...'

'Hear me out, please.' He lifted a hand. 'There's no easy way to say this to you—not after all the time we've been together, the plans we've made. But the fact is I—I've met someone else. And we're going to be married.'

For a moment she stared at him incredulously, then she threw back her head and started to laugh uncontrollably.

'Oh, God,' Colin muttered. 'You're hysterical. I was afraid of this. I wanted to break it to you more gently, but Mother said there was no point in beating about the bush, and Valerie agreed with her.'

'No.' Ros wiped her streaming eyes. 'No, I'm fine, I promise you. Look—totally straight face. Totally normal human being.' She took a deep breath. 'I gather Valerie's your new fiancée. How on earth did you meet her when you couldn't walk?'

'She's the physiotherapist,' he said eagerly. 'The one who brought me home after I did the initial damage. She started driving down to give me treatment each day.' He looked slightly shamefaced. 'And then she stopped driving back.' He paused. 'Ros, I'm so sorry. I feel such a heel…'

'No,' she said gently. 'No, you mustn't. It wasn't working for us—not any more. And we both sensed it. But you did something about it. And I'm happy for you.'

'Really? You mean it?'

I bet his mother told him I'd be clinging to his knees, begging him not to go, thought Ros.

She said, 'Absolutely. It's terrific news.'

On his way to the door, something occurred to him. 'Is that what you wanted to say to me?'

'More or less,' she agreed levelly.

'Oh,' he said. 'That's all right, then.' He hesitated. 'Valerie drove me over, and she's parked a few doors away. Would—would you like to meet her?'

'I'm hardly dressed for guests,' she pointed out, grimacing at the old robe. 'Another time, perhaps.'

'Yes,' he said. 'Another time.'

They smiled at each other with slight awkwardness, both knowing that there would be no other time.

On the doorstep, he deposited a clumsy peck on her cheek, then hobbled gingerly down the steps. Ros breathed a silent sigh of relief when he reached the bottom in safety, knowing that if he'd fallen his mother would have sworn she'd pushed him.

She was just about to turn away and shut the door

when an odd prickle of awareness alerted her to the fact that she was being watched in turn.

The unknown Valerie, she wondered, riding shotgun on her man?

She glanced casually up the street and saw Sam, leaning against his car and staring at her.

She gripped the metal rail, feeling it bite into her hand, waiting as he walked slowly towards her and up the steps.

'Who was that?' His voice was terse.

'Colin,' she said. 'The man I used to see.'

His mouth twisted bitterly. 'You didn't waste any time.'

'No,' she said. 'It's not what you think...'

'But then what is?' His smile grazed her. The look in his eyes made her shiver. 'Well—are you going to ask me in, my Fair Rosamund—my Rose of the World—or are we going to stay here and give the locals another field-day?'

She led the way into the sitting room. 'You saw Janie.' It was a statement not a question.

'Yes,' he said. 'She was most informative about her sister the bestselling novelist, who was also fortunate enough to be left a house worth at least four hundred grand.' He whistled. '*Very* impressive. So what were you doing with me, darling? Slumming? Did you fancy a bit of rough?'

She winced, scared by the anger in his voice. 'Sam—don't. It wasn't like that.'

'No,' he said. 'I forgot. You told me. It was duty. Sometimes above and beyond the call—' his eyes stripped the robe away '—but I'm not complaining.'

'Say what you want,' she said quietly. 'I suppose I deserve it.'

'I knew from the start there was something wrong,' he said. 'Something that didn't quite ring true. That was what intrigued me. But I never guessed the extent of your little charade. Never realised that the girl I'd fallen in love with didn't exist. That you were simply playing a game that went a little too far.'

'You fell in love with me?' Her voice shook. 'That's the first time you've said that.'

'Well, don't let it bother you.' His tone was scornful. 'I shan't let it trouble me.'

'And it wasn't a game. You must believe me.'

'Now you're asking the impossible. So, what was it, then, my sweet? A plot for you latest novel?'

She remembered her hero with the turquoise eyes, and betraying colour warmed her face.

He noticed, of course. 'My God,' he said slowly. 'I was right. You were using me as copy. What a joke. And what an amazing coincidence.'

'I don't know what you mean.'

'I meant the ad in the *Clarion* was a put-up job— placed there by the Features department of the *Daily Echo*.' He watched her absorb that and nodded grimly. 'I was assigned to investigate the lonely hearts scene—from the inside. Meet Sam Alexander Hunter, ace reporter.' He sketched a mocking bow.

'So,' he went on, 'while you were using me, I was using you too. Both biters well and truly bitten. There's a certain poignant justice in the situation— don't you think?'

She said again, 'Sam,' her voice a whisper.

'I felt so guilty about you,' he continued, as if he hadn't heard her. 'I couldn't write a word of the piece about you. And I've been tearing myself to pieces over deceiving you. Because you were wonderful—my per-

fect, unique girl.' He laughed harshly. 'And now I find
I've been blaming myself for nothing. Because you're
no better than I am.'

Ros flung back her head. 'I'm sorry if I didn't fit
your pedestal. But I didn't ask to be measured for it.
I never meant any of this to happen. Janie was going
to stand you up, and I decided to take her place. For
one evening, that was all. Because I didn't want you
to be disappointed. But once it had started there
seemed no way back.'

'There's always a way back,' he said. 'I came to
find you today to warn you that the *Echo* are launching
a major campaign to publicise the series and blowing
my cover in the process. I was going to tell you everything, and ask you to forgive me. To give me another chance. How many kinds of fool does that make
me?' he asked savagely.

'Can't we—forgive each other?' She was trembling.

'There's no need,' he said. 'We're back at square
one. I've now met Janie, and she tells me she's still
"Looking for Love". It's all worked out neatly.'

Her mouth felt numb. 'You—and Janie?'

'You have some objection?' He paused. 'She's a
little—stunned by everything that's happened, so she's
decided to stay away for a few days. I'm sure you
understand. If you'll put some things in a bag for her,
I'll see she gets them.'

She lifted her chin. 'Of course. Will she—be staying
with you?'

He smiled. 'I don't think that's any of your business. Do you?'

She had to behave with dignity, she told herself as
she packed Janie's weekend case with toiletries, un-

derwear and a change of clothes. Because dignity seemed all she had left.

She felt as if she'd been wounded and left to die on some battlefield. Her world was reeling. She was sick, and frightened, and in terrible pain.

And presently she was going to have to watch Sam walk out of her life for ever—and go to Janie.

She thought, I can't bear it. But I must—somehow.

He was waiting in the hall. She handed him the case.

'I hope I haven't forgotten anything.'

'I can get her anything else she wants.'

She said huskily, 'You do realise she's engaged?'

'I gather it's in abeyance at the moment.' He shrugged.

'And that makes it all right?'

'It's a bit late to occupy the moral high ground, Ros,' he said harshly. 'So just leave it out.'

He walked to the door. 'It's been an instructive interlude, for both of us. I'm not sure I can wish you well, but I hope your book sells as many copies as my newspaper. Because that's what it's all about in the end. And we both have our lives to pay for.'

'Will you go, please?' Her voice shook.

'One last thing,' he said. He put the case down and walked back to her. She tried to step away, but his hands descended on her shoulders, anchoring her. His voice slowed to a drawl. 'Do satisfy my curiosity, darling. Are you wearing anything under that robe?' He reached down and untied the sash, then drew the edges apart. 'No, I thought not. No wonder the boyfriend needed a walking stick.'

She said unevenly, 'You bastard.'

'I try.' His hand stroked the length of her body, and

she had to grit her teeth to avoid crying her need, her yearning aloud. But she wouldn't give him that satisfaction.

He bent, and she felt his mouth fasten fiercely on to her breast.

As he raised his head, the crooked smile he sent her pierced her heart.

'My brand,' he said softly, touching the small red mark with his fingertip. 'But don't worry, my love. It will fade. Everything does—in time. Or so they tell me. We'll just have to wait and see.'

She stood. Eyes closed, so that she did not have to see any more. Hands pressed over her ears, so that she would not hear the door closing or his car drive away.

But she could not silence the clamour of her flesh, or the black, empty loneliness which had invaded her soul.

She thought, He's gone. And now I have nothing left. Nothing.

And she began to cry like a child raging against a world it does not understand.

CHAPTER TWELVE

'BUT of course you're going to the award ceremony,' Vivien said severely. 'I accepted on your behalf.'

Ros sighed. 'I know. But that was then. This is now. And I don't feel like dressing up and going out. Especially if people are going to look at me and I have to make a speech.'

'Then that's exactly the time you should dress up and go out,' said Vivien. 'It will do you good. You've been looking washed out for weeks.' She paused, giving Ros a shrewd look. 'You are all right? I mean, there's nothing the matter—nothing that you should see a doctor about?'

'No.' A small, sad pain twisted inside her. 'There's—nothing wrong.' *Not even that. Not even Sam's baby.*

'Then treat yourself to some blusher,' said Vivien briskly. 'And you don't have to make a speech. You just thank them nicely for the rose bowl. It's not the Oscars,' she added. 'You don't have to mention everyone you've ever known. Oh, and thank them for the cheque as well. Although heaven knows you don't need the money after what you've been offered for your house.' She paused. 'Have you decided where you're going to live yet?'

'No. I might wander around for a while. See all the parts of Britain I've never visited before I decide.'

'But after you've finished your book, I hope?' There was a touch of anxiety in her editor's voice.

'Yes.' Ros tried a reassuring smile. 'The Cuthberts don't want to move in immediately, so I'll have plenty of time to do that. And then I'll probably rent somewhere while I write the next book.'

'Any idea what it's going to be about?'

Ros shook her head. 'Not yet.'

She usually had several ideas jockeying for position, but not this time. She couldn't think that far ahead. She was managing—just—to live one day at a time.

She could write the current book because it seemed to bring her closer to Sam. Because she could fabricate the happy ending for her heroine that she'd been denied. And that, she found, was strangely comforting.

There wasn't a great deal else to be happy about.

Janie had eventually returned, but had been unusually reticent, volunteering no information about where she'd been or what she'd been doing.

But then, Ros thought unhappily, maybe she would rather not know at that...

On the first evening she'd said, 'Janie—you must be wondering...'

'I did at first.' Janie shrugged. 'But not any more. And you don't need to explain. It happened, and it's all finished, anyway, so you don't have to beat yourself with it.'

Ros bit her lip. 'Perhaps I need to.'

'No.' Janie shook her head. 'Everyone makes a complete idiot of themselves somewhere along the line. It just took you longer than most people, but you got there in the end. And that's all there is to it. *Finito.*'

It seemed that her relationship with Martin was equally *finito*. When Ros ventured to ask if they were still seeing each other, she got a flat, 'No.'

'I'm sorry,' Ros said quietly.

'Don't be. I realise now I was never really in love with him. I was just hung up on the marriage and babies scene. But none of that has to be a priority. There are other things in life.'

And she relapsed into silence, leaving Ros to draw her own unhappy conclusions.

It was the nearest to a confidence that they approached, because things were not the same between them. Every time Janie left the house, Ros found herself wondering if she was going to see Sam, but dared not ask. And, which was worse, Janie seemed to be silently challenging her to do so. When the phone rang Ros avoided answering it, using the machine as a shield.

Therefore it was almost a relief when Janie abruptly announced that she and Pam had booked a last-minute holiday in Minorca and were flying out the following week.

By the time she returned their parents would be back from their trip, and that would ease the pressure too, or so Ros hoped.

What she couldn't avoid was seeing Sam's picture plastered over hoardings and bus shelters, with banner headlines promising lurid revelations about the singles scene.

She could not, she knew, hope to escape unscathed. But wondering how much he was going to reveal about their relationship was driving her slowly mad.

At last, despising herself, she took a taxi round to his flat. But although she rang the bell and knocked until her knuckles felt bruised, there was no answer.

'Did you want Mr Hunter?' An elderly woman

emerged from the opposite flat. 'I'm afraid you won't find him. He's gone away and the flat's to let.'

'Oh,' Ros said numbly. 'I—I didn't know.'

The other nodded. 'It was a shock for me too. He was always so kind. An ideal neighbour.' She sighed. 'Ah, well. Nothing lasts for ever.' She smiled at Ros, and turned away.

No, Ros thought. Nothing lasts.

On her way back to Chelsea she called in at an estate agents and put her house on the market. And forty-eight hours later it was sold.

She bought a new dress for the awards ceremony, simple and stylish in black silk, cut on the bias, with a skirt that fluttered around her knees as she walked. The sleeveless bodice was held up by thin straps and the neckline dipped deeply towards her breasts. The matching cape was lined in silver.

As she walked into the Palais Royal on Park Lane, she wondered vaguely who her fellow winners were. Vivien, she thought, had mentioned that the journalism award had gone to someone who'd covered the Mzruban civil war and just escaped with his life. But that was as much as she knew.

The first thing she saw in the foyer were two giant blown-up photographs of herself and Sam side by side. The shock of it stopped her in her tracks.

What was this? she asked herself frantically. Was someone playing some monstrous joke?

Vivien came through the groups of chattering people. 'What is it?' she demanded. 'You look as if you've seen a ghost.'

'That's how I feel.' Ros pointed at Sam's photograph. 'What's that doing here?'

'He's the journalist I told you about,' Vivien said patiently. 'The extremely un-civil war. Remember?'

Ros swallowed. 'He's not actually here tonight, is he?'

'I've no idea,' Vivien retorted. 'He's not my responsibility, thank God. Getting you up to the mark was problem enough.' She paused. 'Anyway, what's wrong with Sam Hunter? Very sexy guy, they tell me, and unattached, although there have been rumours recently that he's seeing someone.'

Ros bit her lip. 'Actually,' she said, 'I think I've mistaken him for someone else.'

Before the awards dinner there were drinks for the winners in a private room, hosted by *Life Today* magazine.

Ros was handed a glass of champagne, and chatted to the magazine's editor, Henry Garland, a genial, bearded man with a booming laugh. Ros tried to smile appreciatively at his jokes, and respond to his remarks, but her concentration was shot to pieces. She'd scanned the room as she entered, but, to her relief, there was no sign of Sam. Now she was sneaking constant glances at the door, expecting it to open and admit him at any moment.

She was thankful when Henry Garland moved on to greet someone else.

'That's Cilla Godwin over there,' Vivien hissed in her ear. 'She's the new editor of the *Echo*. I wonder what she's done with her golden boy.'

Ros gave a casual glance in the direction indicated and encountered a look of such dislike that she almost took a step backwards.

'I wonder what she's done with common civility,'

she muttered back. 'And isn't she a little old for that dress?'

Vivien patted her approvingly. 'Well done. You're coming back to life. Funnily enough, she was asking about you earlier.'

Ros stiffened. 'She was?'

'Yes, she cornered me in the powder room and said wasn't your real name Janie, and hadn't you once worked as a make-up girl? I said she was confusing you with your stepsister, and I thought she was going to have a heart attack. I've never seen anyone so angry.'

'How—very odd,' Ros said faintly. 'I hope she doesn't—corner me.'

'Don't worry,' said Vivien. 'Our table's at the opposite end of the room from the *Echo*. Oh, good, they're calling us in to dinner. And mind you eat properly and put back some of the weight you've lost,' she added.

'Yes, Mother,' said Ros, her mouth curving reluctantly in her first real smile of the evening.

She dutifully swallowed her portion of the vegetable terrine, and the chicken in wine sauce that followed. She even managed some of the chocolate roulade, but was thankful when coffee was served.

The *Echo*'s table might be at the other end of the room, but the empty chair next to Cilla Godwin's was clearly visible, even when she didn't crane her neck.

She glanced restively at her watch, calculating how long it would take to receive her award, make polite noises, and escape.

She waited while the non-fiction award was made to a travel writer, and the prize for children's writing was also handed over. Then it was her turn.

She stood, holding the rose bowl and the cheque, while Henry Garland congratulated her on the popularity of her novels and their worldwide sales success. As he finished, she moved to the microphone and began her few planned words of appreciation. She was aware of a stir in the audience, and glanced up instinctively.

Sam had appeared in the doorway at the back of the room. He was lounging against a doorpost, seemingly relaxed, but as their eyes met Ros felt as if she'd encountered an electrical urge.

The words died on her lips. She tried to recapture her thread, failed, and said, 'Thank you all so much,' in a small, nervous voice, and dashed off the stage.

'Now you know why I don't do public appearances,' she told Vivien as she slid into her chair.

'They're applauding, not throwing things. You did fine.' Vivien was warmly consoling. 'Shy is this year's flavour. Unlike the ''in your face—I'll break your legs'' attitude of Ms Godwin.' She nudged Ros. 'I see her foreign ace has finally arrived.'

'Yes,' Ros said, dry-mouthed. She paused. 'Would anyone notice if I slipped away?'

'The whole room, I should think.' Vivien was firm. 'It won't take much longer. There's television writing next, and then it's Sam Hunter—who, may I say, is much dishier than his photograph.'

She had a point, Ros admitted. Sam was wearing dinner jacket and black tie, like all the other men present, but on his tall figure the formal dress had an added distinction. His dark hair had grown back to its normal length, too, and looked attractively tousled.

As if, she thought, he'd just got out of bed...

She sat staring at her cooling coffee as he mounted

the platform to receive his award, amid enthusiastic applause.

When the room quietened, he began to speak, his voice cool and slightly sardonic.

'I'm grateful to *Life Today* for giving me this award,' he said. 'Because it will always remind me that I was once a half-decent writer. Something I almost lost sight of.

'I was proud of my civil war coverage. But I'm certainly not proud of my most recent assignment, which many of you will have seen advertised.

'I'd like to take this opportunity to apologise to all the decent women who were fooled into giving me their time and attention. I found the whole episode shameful, but there has been an up-side. It helped clarify once and for all what I want from life, and how I want to live it. And I know this isn't the *Echo*, in spite of all the financial advantages. They mattered once, but not any more. They can chain someone else to their treadmill. I prefer my freedom.

'The "Lonely in London" feature also, and most unexpectedly, introduced me to the woman I hope to marry. So who says personal columns don't work?'

There was a concerted gasp, and then a ripple of applause. At the *Echo* table, Cilla Godwin appeared to have turned to granite.

'This award is particularly precious because it's the last one I'll ever get,' he went on. 'I'm quitting national journalism altogether, to join a weekly paper in the Yorkshire Dales. Nominally, I'm editor, but I suspect I shall also be making the coffee and accepting small ads. It's that kind of set-up, and I can hardly wait. At the moment there's no personal column, but that's my first planned change.'

He held up the rose bowl. 'Roses are my favourite flower—particularly Rosa Mundi—the Rose of the World. I look forward to seeing this filled with them.

'And the cheque will pay the deposit on a house I've seen—if my bride-to-be approves. So—a heartfelt thank-you to you all.'

The whole room was on its feet applauding as he left the platform, apart from those at the *Echo* table, who stayed in their seats, transfixed by a look from Godzilla.

Ros said in an undertone, 'I must go.' She sped out into the reception area, where staff were doing some desultory clearing up, and pressed the bell for the lift, fretting as she waited for it to descend from the top floor.

A hand closed on her shoulder, and Sam said softly, 'Nice try, darling. Now we're going to talk.'

He steered her across to the room where the drinks party had been held.

'Excuse me, sir, that's a private room,' called a voice.

'Excellent,' Sam said affably, and closed the door behind them, fastening the small brass bolt as he did so. 'And that's real privacy.'

Her heart was beating so hard she felt suffocated. She confronted him, head high. 'Will you let me go, please?'

'Yes,' he said. 'Eventually. If that's what you really want. But first you're going to listen.'

'Say what you want.' Ros said curtly. She sat down on a small gilt chair. 'What difference does it make?'

'All the difference in the world, I hope.' He shook his head. 'We're both supposed to be professional communicators, but when we're together it all goes wrong.'

'Then maybe we should cut our losses.'

'No,' he said. 'We should try again. We've made a mess of being together in the past, but when we're apart the world becomes a living hell of loneliness and cold. You're the other half of me, Ros, and I can't let you go.

'I know I've nothing much to offer. You're a high income lady, with a beautiful house, and I can't match that. The salary's a fraction of what I was earning on the *Echo*, and the house is made of grey stone, with a garden and a view. I know you'd be making a terrible sacrifice.'

His voice deepened, became passionate. 'But it's a real place to live, with real people, and it's offering me a life with some quality—some integrity. But even that won't mean anything if you're not there to share it with me.'

She said huskily, 'Why did you say none of this before?'

'Because I didn't know about the job then—just that I had to leave the *Echo*. Get out before I was destroyed. And I couldn't ask you to marry me if I was going to be out of work.

'I'm not a New Man, Ros. I want to be able to support my woman—and my children. And I want our baby to be born with my name, and my ring on your finger, however old-fashioned that is.

'And I needed my pride back—and my sense of humour—before I could come to you.'

He went down on one knee in front of her, his eyes urgently searching her face. 'Let's face it, darling. If tonight's prizes were for admirable behaviour, neither of us would qualify. But we don't have to let past mistakes poison the future.'

She looked down at her clasped hands. 'What about Janie?' she said in a low voice. 'You were—seeing her.'

'Yes,' he said. 'To collect material for my lonely hearts piece. But she was staying with her friend Pam, not me.'

'Was that her choice?'

'I don't think I gave her the option,' he said carefully. 'Your stepsister is very pretty, but she's not irresistible, and I think she found that a shock. She's clearly been riding roughshod over some poor bastard. Maybe the next man along will find her easier to deal with.'

Ros looked at him open-mouthed. 'You turned her down.'

'Of course.' His tongue was matter-of-fact. 'I belong to you, and no one else will do for me. And I shall maintain that stance until you prove to me I haven't a hope—and probably long afterwards.'

'But you let me think that you wanted her.'

'I'd just found you next door to naked with another man,' he retorted. 'I was jealous and hurting, and I wanted to hit back. I'm not proud of it.'

He took her hands in his, and she let a soft ripple of excitement tremble through her body.

She said hurriedly, 'How—how did you hear about the job?'

'From Alec Norton, who used to run the *Echo*.' His thumbs were stroking her palms. 'He's up there convalescing, and he called to say that the editor was retiring and they were looking for someone to take his place.' He smiled. 'Locally, it's regarded as a job for life. They like stability. So I went up for an interview and they offered me the job.'

'You left your flat...' Her voice died into silence as Sam lifted her hands to his lips.

'A colleague on the *Echo* is taking over the tenancy. When I've not been in Yorkshire, I've been staying at my parents' house.'

He shook his head. 'And that's been a total nightmare. Everywhere I looked there were all these memories of you, and it was driving me crazy, especially at night.

'I told myself you'd probably never want to see me again—but I had to try.' He put his cheek against her black-stockinged knee. 'Have mercy on me, Ros. Tell me that "Lonely in London" hasn't ruined everything for us both. At least it brought us together.'

He looked up at her, the turquoise eyes pleading. 'Is it too much to ask? Does your life in Chelsea mean too much to you?'

She slid off the chair and knelt beside him, her arms going round his neck. She said, 'I've sold my house. I was going away somewhere—anywhere—because I couldn't bear being without you. And I'd love a house in Yorkshire, with children—and a view. As long as you're there.'

For a moment he held her closely. He whispered, '"Live with me and be my love",' then he began to kiss her, his warm, questing mouth banishing the chill of loneliness for ever. And Ros surrendered gladly, her body aglow with a happiness she had not dreamed was possible.

When she could speak, she said, 'But there isn't going to be a baby, Sam. Not yet. I know that definitely now.'

He lifted her to her feet. He said softly, 'Then let's go home and practise.' And kissed her again.

Ros removed the final page from the printer and put it neatly with the rest of the manuscript. She moved her shoulders, putting a testing hand to the small of her back.

She was glad that she'd finished the new book before the baby came, although she suspected it was going to be a closer finish than she'd realised.

Vivien, she thought happily, had better start packing her godmother's outfit.

She went over to the window and looked out. The small first-floor room she'd commandeered as a study at the back of the house overlooked the vegetable patch where Sam was digging, vigorously assisted by their golden retriever puppy.

As if he sensed her presence at the window, Sam looked up, shading his eyes, and blew her a kiss.

Ros smiled, resting her fingertips lightly against the glass, feeling her love for him open like a flower within her.

Her case was packed and waiting in the freshly decorated nursery next door. But she wouldn't tell Sam about the slight contractions she was having. Not quite yet. In case he panicked and started phoning their respective parents, and insisting she go into hospital immediately.

Because she'd rather spend her waiting time here, quietly, with him, in this home they'd made together.

In the end they'd combined their cheques from *Life Today* to provide the deposit, while, at Sam's suggestion, the money from the Chelsea house had been set aside as a trust fund for their children.

She'd go downstairs, she thought, and make some coffee, and they would sit on their verandah and drink it, and look at their view with a contentment that went too deep for words.

Sam was walking up the path towards the house, his spade on his shoulder, the dog leaping excitedly beside him.

My family, she thought, placing an exultant hand on her abdomen. My life.

Then, moving slowly, with the dignity befitting a heavily pregnant lady, Rosamund Hunter went down to join her husband.

THE BLIND-DATE
PROPOSAL

by

Jessica Hart

Jessica Hart was born in West Africa and has suffered from itchy feet ever since, travelling and working around the world in a wide variety of interesting but very lowly jobs, all of which have provided inspiration on which to draw when it comes to the settings and plots of her stories. Now she lives a rather more settled existence in York, where she has been able to pursue her interest in history, although she still yearns sometimes for wider horizons. If you'd like to know more about Jessica, visit her website, www.jessicahart.co.uk.

Don't miss Jessica Hart's exciting new novel
Outback Boss, City Bride
out in September 2007 from
Mills & Boon® Romance.

CHAPTER ONE

'WHAT time do you call this?'

Finn looked up, scowling, as Kate knocked on his door with some trepidation.

She looked at her watch. 'It's…er…nearly quarter to ten.'

'And you're supposed to start at what time?'

'Nine o'clock.'

Kate was horribly aware of her pink face. She was hot and flustered, having run up the escalator from the tube and all the way to the office, where she had panted past the surprised receptionist to fall into the lift. Somewhere along the line she had laddered her tights, and a tentative glance in the mirror was enough to confirm that her hair, a mass of wild brown curls hard to control at best of times, was tangled and windblown.

Not a good start to the day.

She was at a distinct disadvantage compared to Finn, too. In his grey suit and his pristine shirt, her new boss had always seemed to Kate buttoned up in more ways than one. He had a severe face, steely grey eyes and strong dark brows which were usually pulled together in a frown and whenever he looked at Kate, like now, his mouth was clamped together in a disapproving line.

'I know I'm late, and I'm *really* sorry,' she said breathlessly and, oblivious to Finn's discouraging expression, she launched into a long and convoluted explanation of how she had befriended an elderly lady confused by the underground system and intimidated by the rudeness of officials.

'I couldn't just leave her there,' she finished at last, 'so

5

I took her to Paddington and showed her where to find her train.'

'Paddington not being on your way here?'

'Not *exactly*...'

'One might even say that it was in completely the opposite direction,' Finn went on in the same snide tone.

'Not quite *opposite*,' said Kate, mentally consulting her tube map.

'So you got halfway here and then turned and headed off in a completely different direction, even though you must have known that there was no way you'd be able to get to work on time?'

'I had to,' Kate protested. 'She was so upset. There was no reason for everyone to be so rude to her,' she remembered indignantly. 'Her English wasn't that good, and she couldn't be expected to know where she was going and how to get there. How would that ticket collector like it if he had to find his way around...oh, I don't know...the Amazon, say...where he didn't know the language and nobody could be bothered to help him?'

Finn looked at her wearily. 'You're mistaking me for someone who cares,' he said. 'The only thing I care about right now is keeping this company going, and it's not that easy with a PA who turns up whenever she feels like it! Alison makes a point of arriving ten minutes before nine every day,' he added pointedly. 'She's always reliable.'

Not so reliable that she didn't break her leg on a skiing holiday, Kate thought, but didn't say out loud. She was sick of hearing about Alison, Finn's perfect PA who was discreet and efficient and immaculately dressed and who reputedly typed at the speed of light. She could probably read Finn's mind too, Kate had decided sourly after he had shouted at her for not being able to find a file that he himself had dumped onto her desk. Alison's desk, of course, was always tidy.

The only marvel was that Alison had been careless enough to break her leg, leaving Finn to get through eight weeks without her.

He wasn't finding it easy. Already two temps had left in tears, unable to cope with the impossible standards Alison had set. Kate was just surprised that she had hung in as long as she had. This was her third week and, judging by Finn's expression, it might well be her last.

She wasn't surprised the others had given up. Finn McBride gave a whole new dimension to the notion of grumpiness and he had an unpleasantly sarcastic edge to his tongue. If she hadn't been desperate for a job, she would have been tempted to walk out on him as well.

'I said I was sorry,' she said a little sullenly. 'Not that I should have to apologise for community spirit,' she went on, still too fired up by her encounter that morning to be able to summon up the correct degree of subservience that no doubt came naturally to Alison.

Finn was unimpressed. His cold grey eyes raked her from head to foot, taking in every detail of her tangled hair and dishevelled clothes and stopping with exasperation on her laddered tights.

'I encourage my staff to do what I pay them to do,' he said frigidly, 'and that's what they do. You, on the other hand, appear to think that I should pay you to breeze in and distract everyone else in the office all day.'

Kate gaped at the unfairness of it. She had made efforts to get to know the rest of the staff, but without any great success. They didn't seem to be great ones for gossiping and, on the few occasions she had managed to strike up a conversation, Finn had been safely shut in his office. He must have X-ray eyes if he had noticed her talking to anyone!

'I don't distract anyone,' she protested.

'It sounds that way to me,' said Finn. 'You're always out in the corridor or in the other offices chatting.'

'It's called social interaction,' said Kate, provoked. 'It's what humans do, not that you'd know that of course. It's like working with robots in this office,' she went on, forgetting for a moment how much she needed this job. 'I'm lucky if I get a good morning from you, and even that I have to translate from a grunt!'

The dark brows twitched together into a terrifying glare. 'Alison never complains.'

'Maybe Alison likes being treated like just another piece of office equipment,' she said tartly. 'It wouldn't kill you to show a little interest occasionally.'

Finn glowered at her, and Kate wondered whether he was so unused to anyone daring to argue with him that he was taken aback.

If so, he soon recovered. 'I haven't time to waste the day bolstering your ego,' he snapped.

'It doesn't take long to be pleasant.' Kate refused to be cowed now. 'You could always start with something easy like ''how are you?'', or ''have a nice weekend'',' she suggested. 'And then, when you'd got the hang of that, you could work up to trickier phrases like ''thank you for all your help today''.'

'I can't see me having much need of that one while you're around,' said Finn nastily. 'And frankly, even if I did, I don't see why I should change my habits for you. In case you haven't noticed, I'm the boss here, so if you can't cope without constant attention, you'd better say so now and I'll get Personnel to find me another temp for Monday!'

That was enough to pull Kate up short. She really couldn't afford to lose this job. The agency had been reluctant enough to send her as it was and, if she messed this up, she'd be lucky if they didn't drop her from their books.

'I can cope,' she said quickly. 'I just don't like it.'

'You don't have to like it,' said Finn tersely. 'You just have to get on with it. Now, can we get on? We've wasted quite enough time this morning.'

He barely allowed Kate time to take off her coat before she had to endure a long and exhausting session being dictated to at top speed without so much as a suggestion that she might like a cup of coffee before she started. What with befriending old ladies and diversions to Paddington, she hadn't had time to grab her usual cappuccino from the Italian coffee bar by the tube station, and the craving for caffeine did nothing to improve her temper.

She simmered as her pen raced over the page—at this rate she would get repetitive strain injury—and could barely restrain a sigh of relief when the phone rang. A breather at last!

Holding her aching wrist with exaggerated care, so that Finn might take the hint and slow down—although there was fat chance of that!—Kate studied him surreptitiously under her lashes. He was listening to the person on the other end of the phone, grunting the occasional acknowledgement, and absently drawing heavy black boxes on a piece of paper on the desk in front of him.

Doodling was supposed to be highly revealing about your personality. What did black boxes mean? Kate wondered. Probably indicative of someone deeply repressed. That would fit with his closed expression and that reserved uptight air of his.

Although not with that air of fierce energy.

Or his mouth, come to think of it.

Kate jerked her eyes quickly away. She looked instead at the framed photograph that stood on his desk, the only personal touch in the otherwise austerely efficient office. From where she sat, she could only see the stand, but she knew it showed an absolutely beautiful woman with dark hair and enormous dark blue eyes, holding the most gorgeous baby, and both smiling at the camera.

Finn's wife, Kate had assumed, marvelling that he had had enough social skills to ask anyone to marry him, let alone a beauty like that. It was hard to imagine him smiling or kissing or even holding a baby, let alone making love.

Bizarre thought. An odd feeling snaked down Kate's spine and she shook herself slightly, only to find herself looking straight into Finn's glacial grey eyes. He had finished his phone call while she was distracted and was watching her with an expression of exasperated resignation.

'Are you awake?'

'Yes.' Faint colour tinged Kate's cheeks as she sat up straighter and picked up her notebook once more.

'Read back that last bit.'

Please, Kate wanted to mutter, but decided on reflection that this might not be the day to try and teach Finn some manners. His brusqueness left her feeling crotchety and, when he finally let her go, she took out her bad temper on her keyboard, bashing away furiously until the phone rang.

'Yes?' she snapped, too cross to bother with the usual introductory spiel.

'It's Phoebe.'

'Oh, Phoebe…hi.'

'What's up? You sound very grumpy.'

'It's just my boss here,' Kate grumbled. 'He's so rude and unpleasant. I know you thought working for Celia was bad, but honestly, he gives a whole new dimension to the idea of the boss from hell.'

'As long as he's not a creep like your last boss,' said Phoebe bracingly.

Kate wrinkled her nose remembering her ignominious departure from her last job, where her boss hadn't even made a pretence of listening to her side of the story once

Seb had got in first. Seb, of course, was an executive, and she was just a secretary and by implication dispensable.

'No, I don't think you could call him a *creep,*' she said judiciously, 'but that doesn't make him any easier to deal with.'

'Attractive?' asked Phoebe.

'Quite,' Kate admitted grudgingly. 'In a stern sort of way, I suppose. If you like the dour, my-work-is-my-life type—which I happen to know that you don't!'

'I don't think anyone could call Gib dour, no,' said Phoebe.

They both laughed, and Kate felt a lot better. It was wonderful to hear Phoebe so happy. The transformation in her friend since she had married Gib a few months ago had been remarkable, and it made up for her own dismal love life since Seb had dumped her so unceremoniously. She didn't even get wolf-whistles in the street any more, Kate thought glumly.

'I was just ringing to remind you about supper tonight,' Phoebe was saying. 'You are coming, aren't you?'

'Of course,' said Kate, but Phoebe pounced on her momentary hesitation.

'What?'

'Well, it's just that Bella hinted that you might be setting me up on a blind date tonight.'

'She shouldn't have told you!' Phoebe sounded really cross. 'I only told her because I invited her and Josh as well so it would seem more casual, but she's met some new man who's taking her to some swanky club tonight instead. Josh is coming, though,' she added reassuringly, 'so it won't be too much of a set-up.'

'Why didn't you tell me?'

'Because I wanted you both to be natural, and I knew you wouldn't be if you were nervous about whether he liked you or not.'

'Hhmmnn.' Kate wasn't entirely convinced. 'What have you told him about me?'

'That you're a high-powered PA—which you could easily be if you put your mind to it!' said Phoebe. 'He's got his own consultancy or something, so I wasn't sure if he'd be that impressed by you temping, but apart from that we told him the truth, the whole truth and nothing but the truth,' she finished virtuously.

'Oh, the *truth*!' said Kate, her voice heavy with irony. 'And what's that, exactly?'

'That you're warm and funny and attractive and basically completely wonderful,' Phoebe said firmly.

Perhaps she should ask Phoebe to put in some PR for her with Finn McBride, Kate thought, and then frowned slightly as she realised that she had been unconsciously doodling in her turn as she listened to Phoebe.

At least she didn't go in for severe black boxes. She had done her favourite, a tropical sunset complete with leaning palm tree and a couple of wiggly lines to indicate the lagoon rippling gently against the shore. What did that indicate about her?

Probably that she was a hopeless fantasist, in which case she could save herself the cost of a professional analysis. She already knew that she was far too romantic for her own good. People had been telling her for years that she needed to shape up, get real, wake up and smell the coffee, and do all the other things that simply didn't come naturally to her.

Suppressing a sigh, Kate carefully added a bunch of coconuts to the palm tree. 'So won't he wonder why if I'm that perfect I'm reduced to being set up on blind dates by friends? Why aren't men falling at my feet wherever I go?'

'I don't know. Why aren't they?'

That was one of the things Kate liked about Phoebe. She really believed in her friends.

Kate put down her pen and forced herself to concentrate.

Perhaps all this was a sign to stop dreaming about Seb miraculously turning into a different person and to start making an effort to meet someone new. To wake up and smell the coffee, in fact.

'So what's he like, this guy?'

'I've never met him,' Phoebe had to admit. 'He's an old friend of Gib's.'

'How old, exactly?'

'In his early forties, I think.'

'Just coming up for his mid-life crisis then,' said Kate with an uncharacteristic touch of cynicism.

'He's already had more than enough crises,' said Phoebe soberly. 'He's a widower. His wife died when their daughter was just a toddler, and he's been struggling to bring her up on his own ever since.'

'Oh, how awful,' said Kate, her ready sympathy roused and feeling instantly guilty for her flip comment. 'It must have been terrible for him.'

'Well, yes, I gather it was. Gib says he absolutely adored his wife, but it's six years ago now, and he's thinking that his little girl is getting to the stage when she really needs a woman around. He's out of the way of dating, though, and since you were complaining about not meeting any men, Gib suggested a casual supper to introduce you. It's no big deal, but he thought you might get on.'

'I don't know that I'm really stepmother material,' said Kate doubtfully. 'I don't know anything about children.'

'Nonsense!' Phoebe wasn't having any of that. 'Look how good you are with animals, and children are just the same. They need someone to take them under her wing, and you know what a soft heart you've got for lame ducks.'

'Yes, but I don't want to go out with a lame duck,' Kate protested. 'I want someone sexy and exciting and glamorous.'

Like Seb.

The same thought was clearly in Phoebe's mind. 'No you don't,' she said firmly. 'You want someone kind.'

Kate sighed. 'Why can't I have someone who's kind *and* sexy and exciting and glamorous?'

'Because I married him,' said Phoebe smugly. 'Now listen, this guy's had a hard time, so be nice to him.'

'Oh, all right,' grumbled Kate. 'What's his name, anyway—' She broke off as Finn's door opened. 'Uh-oh, here comes Mr Grumpy! I'd better go—I'm not supposed to use the phone for personal calls. See you later.' She put the phone down hastily.

Finn looked at her with a suspicious frown. 'Who was that?'

Well, she wasn't going to tell him the truth and, although she could have made up something innocuous, Kate had an irrepressibly inventive streak and as a matter of principle resisted the simple option when she could complicate matters. She embarked instead on a long, involved and utterly untrue story, inventing an accountant who had met Alison skiing but who had subsequently been on a business trip to Singapore and had only just heard about the accident and, remembering that Alison had told him where she worked, now wanted to know where to send a card.

'I said it would be all right if he sent it here and we would forward it,' she finished, having embroidered the story with so many details that she almost believed it herself.

Finn's expression was glazed with irritation by the time she got to the end. 'I wish I'd never asked,' he sighed. 'You've just wasted a quarter of an hour of my life!'

'It's not as if we do brain surgery here,' said Kate, a trifle sullenly. 'I don't see what difference fifteen minutes here or there makes.'

'In that case, you won't mind staying late tonight to make up for the hour you missed this morning,' Finn said

with an unpleasant look. 'We've got an extremely important project coming up and I need to get this done to fax
to the States before tomorrow morning.'

'I can't, I'm afraid,' she said, not sounding at all regret-
ful. 'I'm going out.'

Finn frowned. 'Can't you ring and say you'll be a bit
late?'

For anyone else, Kate would have offered to do just that,
but something about Finn McBride rubbed her up the
wrong way. It wasn't as if he had made the slightest effort
to be pleasant to her.

'Oh, I don't think my boyfriend would like that very
much,' she said instead, trying for the unconscious smug-
ness that so often seemed to accompany the words 'my
boyfriend'.

'You've got a boyfriend?' Finn was unflatteringly surprised, and Kate bridled. It was bad enough putting up with
his rudeness without knowing that he thought her incapable
of attracting a man as well!

'Oh, yes,' she said, determined to convince him that
while she might not be a perfect PA, *somebody* wanted her.
'In fact,' she went on, leaning forward confidentially, 'he's
taking me somewhere really special tonight. I think he
might be going to pop the question!'

'Really?' Finn raised a contemptuous eyebrow, not even
bothering to try and hide his disbelief.

How rude, thought Kate indignantly. He clearly didn't
think she was the kind of girl who would get a man at all,
let alone one who wanted to marry her.

Her brown eyes narrowed. 'Oh, yes,' she said on her
mettle. 'Didn't you know? That's why I'm temping. Ever
since I met—'

She searched wildly for a name before remembering
Bella's current and very glamorous man. Your best friend's

boyfriend was normally out of bounds, but she didn't think Bella would mind her borrowing him mentally.

'—Will,' she carried on after the tiniest beat, 'we've both known that we were meant for each other. He's a financial analyst,' she went on breezily, deciding that she might as well take Will's career as well, 'so I didn't want to commit to a permanent job when he might be posted to New York or Tokyo at any minute. Of course, he keeps saying to me, "Darling, there's no need for you to go out to work every day," but I feel it's important to keep some financial independence, don't you?'

'I wouldn't have thought your earnings as a temp would make much difference if you're living with a financial analyst,' said Finn with something not a million miles from a sneer.

'It's a matter of principle,' said Kate airily, quite enjoying the thought of herself destined for a life of expatriate luxury.

Finn turned back to his office. 'Perhaps you could make it a matter of principle to turn up on time tomorrow,' he said nastily. 'That would make a nice change.'

It was a pity she wasn't as good at real life as she was at inventing it, Kate reflected glumly as the bus inched through the rush hour traffic, vibrating noisily. Wouldn't it be nice to be going home to a real adoring man with pots of money and to be told that she never had to go and work for the likes of Finn McBride ever again?

Kate sighed and rubbed the condensation from the window with her sleeve and peered down at the crowds hurrying along Piccadilly in the rain. They all seemed to know exactly where they were going. Why was she the only one who drifted along from one muddle to the next?

Look at her. Thirty-two and what did she have to show for it? No career, no home of her own, no relationship. The only thing she had gained over the last few years was twenty pounds. Even the misery diet hadn't worked for her. When their hearts got broken the weight fell off her friends, but comfort eating had been the only way Kate could deal with losing Seb and her job together before Christmas. A double whammy.

Fortified by Bella and Phoebe and a good deal of champagne, Kate had resolved that things would change in the New Year. She was going to sharpen up her act. She would get another, better job and another, better man, she vowed. She would lose weight and start going to the gym and get her life under control.

It was just that all those things seemed a lot easier to achieve after a bottle or two of champagne. It was February already, and her New Year resolutions were still at the talking stage.

She ought at least to have found herself a proper job by now, but nothing was being advertised—no doubt everyone was staying put while they paid off their Christmas credit card bills—and even temping hadn't proved to be the guaranteed fall-back position she had assumed. Nobody seemed to be getting flu this year, and Kate had been about to sign on as a waitress at the local wine bar when Alison had broken her leg.

Tomorrow, Kate told herself. She would buy a paper and check out the appointments page, go to the gym on her way home and cook herself something healthy and non-fattening for supper.

Tomorrow would see the start of the new Kate.

Bella was eating toast in the kitchen with her hair in rollers when Kate let herself into the house. Since Phoebe had married and moved in with Gib, the two of them and Kate's surly cat had had the Tooting house to themselves.

The cat was waiting, a brooding presence by the fridge, and Kate knew better than to try and sit down until he had

been fed. He was more than capable of shredding her ankles, so she fished out a packet of the over-priced cat food
that was all he would accept and forked it into his bowl
before she had even taken off her coat.

'I thought you were going out?' she said to Bella, eyeing
the toast enviously.

Bella could eat whatever she liked and still not put on
weight. 'Metabolism,' she said cheerfully whenever she
was challenged by her less fortunate friends. She was ridiculously pretty, a blue-eyed blonde with legs that went
on forever and a sunny disposition. The worst thing about
Bella, Kate and Phoebe had often agreed, was that it was
impossible to hate her.

'I am, but Will's taking me to some incredibly cool restaurant where the portions are bound to be tiny. I thought
I'd have something to eat now so I don't pig out when I
get there. Anyway, I'm hungry,' Bella added simply.

Lucky Bella, going out with the gorgeous Will while she
got some poor old widower who needed someone to be
nice to him. Kate sighed to herself. Typical.

Without thinking she dropped a slice of bread into the
toaster.

Bella pointed her piece of toast at her. 'You'll regret
that,' she warned through a mouthful. 'Gib always cooks
enough for an army. Anyway, I thought you were on a
diet?'

'There's not much point in starting a diet when I'm going
out to dinner,' said Kate, taking off her coat at last. 'And
we've got to eat up all the fattening food before we can
restock with the healthy stuff.'

It was a good enough excuse to slather butter on her toast
as she told Bella about borrowing Will mentally. 'I wasn't
going to tell Finn McBride that I was just going on a blind
date with a sad widower.'

'A widower?'

Kate told her the little she had learnt from Phoebe. 'It doesn't sound like it's going to be a bundle of laughs, does it?'

'Come on, he might be gorgeous,' said Bella.

'Not with my luck,' grumbled Kate, but she did her best to talk herself into a more positive frame of mind as she got ready to go out. Perhaps Bella was right. Perhaps a fabulous hunk of manhood was going to walk into her life tonight and sweep her off her feet. It had to be her turn sometime soon, surely?

Just in case, she dressed carefully in a flounced dress whose plunging neckline showed off her best assets. At least there were some advantages to having a figure like hers. It was just a shame that a curvaceous bust came with equally curvy hips and thighs and tummy.

Wriggling her feet into high heels, she felt instantly taller and therefore better. Kate had often thought that life would be so much easier if only she had slightly longer legs. An extra couple of inches wouldn't have been asking too much now, would it? And a couple less around her hips, which would have balanced her out nicely.

She studied her reflection in the mirror. Amazing what a bit of make-up could do. In a dim light she might even pass for exotic. The warm red in her dress gave her a vaguely gipsyish look that went quite well with her tumbling brown curls and vibrant lipstick. Would the widower be into gipsies? Somehow Kate felt not. Perhaps she should have gone for a rather more demure look?

Could she carry off demure? Kate wondered, unaware that she had lost track of time. It was only when Will arrived to pick up Bella that she thought to look at her watch, and gave a yelp of fright. How could it be eight o'clock already?

It was little comfort to know that Bella wasn't ready either. Will was reading the paper resignedly in the kitchen, and he raised a laconic hand in greeting as Kate teetered down in her heels to ring for a minicab.

'It'll be another twenty minutes,' said the bored voice at the other end of the phone.

Oh, God, now she would be *really* late. Punctuality was another of Kate's New Year resolutions that didn't seem to be working out as planned.

'Sorry, sorry, sorry,' Kate gabbled when she finally arrived at almost quarter to nine, practically falling in the door when Phoebe opened it. 'I know I'm late, but I really didn't mean to be. Please don't be cross with me! It's just been one of those days.'

'It's always one of those days with you, Kate,' said Phoebe, trying to sound severe as she gave her friend an affectionate hug.

Kate hung her head. 'I know, I know, but I am trying to get better.' She lowered her voice conspiratorially. 'Is he here? What's he like?'

'A bit stiff—no, reserved would be a better word,' Phoebe corrected herself. 'But he's very nice when you get to know him, and he's got a lovely smile. I think he's quite attractive, too.'

'Really?' A hot widower after all! Kate perked up. Things were sounding promising. 'No beard?'

'No.'

'Beer belly? Wet lips?'

'No!' Phoebe was laughing now. 'Come and see for yourself.'

Maybe her luck had changed. Smoothing down her top, Kate took a deep breath and followed Phoebe into the sitting room.

'Here's Kate,' she heard her say, but Kate had already stopped dead as she saw who was standing by the mantelpiece with Gib and Josh. He had turned at Phoebe's words, and she had a nasty feeling that his expression of horror only mirrored her own.

It was Finn McBride.

Then he was blocked from her view temporarily as Gib came towards her, grinning. 'Kate!' he cried, sweeping her up into a warm hug. 'Late as usual!'

'I've already grovelled to Phoebe,' Kate said returning his hug and hoping against hope that she had been mistaken and that when Gib moved she would see that the stranger wasn't Finn at all, but just someone who looked like him and either didn't care for the gipsy look or disapproved of unpunctuality. Or both.

But no. Gib was turning with his arm still around her to face the others and there was no doubt about it. There stood Finn, looking as if he had been turned to stone to match the granite of his expression.

Clearly *not* enjoying discovering that he had been set up on a blind date with his own secretary.

Mortified beyond belief, Kate considered her options. Wishing that she had never been born came top of her list, closely followed by that old cliché, a bit tired but effective nonetheless, of wanting the ground to open up and swallow her.

Could she get away with pretending to faint? Probably not, she decided regretfully. She wasn't the fainting type.

Which just left brazening it out.

CHAPTER TWO

'HELLO.' Plastering on an artificially bright smile, she stared Finn straight in the eyes, daring him to acknowledge her. Finn looked back at her with a glacial grey gaze.

'Kate, this is Finn McBride,' said Gib. 'We've been telling him *all* about you.'

Great, thought Kate. Now Finn would know just how sad her life was.

She stuck out her hand and Finn didn't have much choice but to take it. 'Kate Savage,' she introduced herself in a brittle voice, trying not to notice the feel of his fingers closed around hers. In spite of his obvious reluctance, his clasp was firm and warm, much warmer than she had expected, and she snatched her hand away, oddly unsettled.

'You're being very formal, Kate,' said Gib amused. 'At least I don't need to bother introducing you to Josh.' He turned to Finn. 'Josh practically lives with Kate.'

'Oh?' said Finn coldly.

'Kate shares a house with a very good friend of mine,' Josh explained, and the quick smile he gave Kate was sympathetic. He had obviously been told that he was there to make it less obvious that this was a blind date, although his presence wasn't fooling Finn one little bit. 'How are you, Kate? I haven't seen you for a while.'

'I'm fine.' Apart from wanting to die of embarrassment, that was.

Phoebe handed Kate a glass of wine. 'Finn's just been telling us about his disastrous experiences with temps in his office,' she said cheerfully. 'We thought you could give him a few tips on how to handle them.'

22

Oh, yes, Gib and Phoebe had built her up into a top-flight PA, hadn't they? As if her humiliation wasn't complete enough!

'Really?' Kate produced an acidic smile. 'It does seem to be difficult getting good secretarial staff these days! What's wrong with the temp you've got?'

'She doesn't seem to have any idea of time-keeping for a start,' said Finn with a sardonic glance at the clock on the mantelpiece. No doubt he had been here on the stroke of eight, long before Phoebe and Gib would have been ready for him. 'She's completely unreliable.'

Unreliable, was she? Kate took a defiant gulp of her wine. 'It doesn't sound as if she has much motivation to work for you. Why would that be, do you think?'

Finn shrugged. 'Sheer laziness?' he suggested. 'She seems to have a very vivid fantasy life too,' he went on and Kate coloured in spite of herself, remembering how she was supposed to be sitting here being proposed to right now by a financial analyst called Will.

No doubt Gib and Phoebe had already filled him in on her disastrous relationship with Seb, and even if they hadn't he would still know that story wasn't true either. After all, if she had a financial analyst to go home to, she wouldn't be the kind of sad person who needed to be set up on blind dates by friends.

Kate suppressed a sigh. Could things get any worse?

'It can be just as bad on the other side of fence,' Phoebe was saying loyally. 'Tell them about your horrible boss, Kate. He sounds ghastly.'

Ah. They *could* get worse.

'Oh?' said Finn, thin-lipped. 'Why's that?'

Oh, well. In for a penny, in for a pound. She might as well take the opportunity to tell him what she thought, and it wasn't as if he had spared *her* feelings!

'He's just generally rude and unpleasant,' she told him.

'He doesn't seem to have even the most basic social skills. He can hardly be bothered to say ''good morning'' and as for ''please'' and ''thank you''…well, I might as well ask him to talk Polish!'

A muscle had begun to beat in Finn's jaw. 'Perhaps he's busy.'

'Being busy isn't an excuse for not having any manners,' said Kate, meeting his gaze levelly.

'He's absolute death on personal calls in the office as well,' Phoebe put in, apparently unaware of the antagonism simmering between Finn and Kate. 'Kate's always having to put down the phone in the middle of a conversation when his door opens, and we can be in the middle of a really good chat when she suddenly starts putting on an official voice and telling us she'll get back to us on that as soon as possible. That's our cue to call back later when he's gone! It's very frustrating.'

She turned politely to Finn. 'You let people in your office use the phone, don't you?'

'I don't encourage it, no,' he said with a nasty look at Kate, who was almost beyond caring by now.

She was obviously never going to be able to use the office phone again—not that Kate could imagine going into work again after this. On the scale of embarrassment, being blatantly fixed up with your boss must rank pretty high, she thought. It was certainly one of the most excruciating situations Kate had ever found herself in and, let's face it, she had plenty to compare it to. Sometimes she seemed to spend her life lurching from one mortifying episode to another.

'Access to phones and email for personal business is good for staff morale,' she pointed out. 'If you treated your staff like human beings who have a life outside work, I think you'd see productivity shoot up.'

'There's nothing wrong with our productivity,' snapped

Finn, and this time his irritability did catch the others' attention. They looked at him a little curiously and he controlled his temper with an effort.

'There's a difference between dealing with a crisis, in which case of course staff can use the phones, and spending hours gossiping on my time,' he said in a more reasonable voice.

'Doesn't your temp get the job done?' Kate asked sweetly.

'In a fashion,' he admitted grudgingly.

'Perhaps you should go and work for Finn,' said Gib in such a blatant attempt to push them together that he might as well have shown them to the spare room and tucked them in to bed together. 'You might get on better with him than with the boss you've got at the moment.'

'Now, there's an idea!' said Kate as if much struck by the thought. 'Have you got any jobs going at the moment?'

'It's very possible that there might be a vacancy for a temp in my office coming up,' Finn said with something of a snap, 'but that wouldn't interest you, of course, you being such a high-flyer! Gib and Phoebe here were telling me that you practically run the company where you are at the moment. I'm not sure I could offer you anything that challenging.'

A hint of colour touched Kate's cheekbones at his sarcasm. 'No, well, I'm thinking of changing career anyway,' she told him loftily.

'Really?' the other three all said together.

'Yes,' she said, thinking that it wouldn't be such a bad idea, come to that. It didn't look as if she had much future in the secretarial world, anyway. 'I'm sick of being treated like a lower life form, so I've been thinking that I might…what's the word?…downscale.'

'Downscale?' Josh echoed doubtfully, clearly wondering how it was possible for her to downscale from her current position. Being a temp was hardly the giddy heights of a career, was it?

'Or do I mean diversify?' said Kate. 'Do something different anyway. Think out of the box. Use my talents.'

'What exactly are your talents?' Finn asked, the sardonic lift of his brows belying the apparent interest in his voice.

Yes, what *were* her talents? Kate's normally fertile imagination went inconveniently blank at the very moment she needed it most.

'She's a great cook,' Phoebe prompted, evidently still under the impression that Kate might make a suitable wife for Finn.

For some reason it was only at this point that Kate made the connection and remembered that his presence here meant that Finn was a widower. She had been so shocked to see him that she hadn't thought beyond the awkwardness and antagonism, and now she felt suddenly contrite. That beautiful, glowing girl in that photo on his desk was dead. No wonder he seemed so grim.

Kate was conscious of a twinge of guilt about all the times she had thought Finn abrupt and rude, but then, how was she to know that his brusqueness hid a broken heart?

The others were still madly promoting her. 'Kate's a communicator,' she heard Gib say. It was the kind of thing that made you realise just how long he'd spent in the States. 'She's got wonderful people skills.'

'Not just people,' said Josh dryly. 'She's pretty good when it comes to animals too. Remember that dog in the pub, Phoebe?'

'God, yes.' Phoebe gave an exaggerated shudder, and Josh grinned.

'I still wake up in a cold sweat sometimes thinking about it,' he told Finn. 'Kate confronted a skinhead with huge hands and no neck. He was covered in tattoos and snarling and swearing at his dog. Kate told him he wasn't fit to own an animal and took the dog away from him while the rest of us were dancing around in the background being mealy-mouthed and saying I'm not sure this is a good idea, Kate, why don't you let the RSPCA deal with it? Meanwhile Kate was about half the size of this guy, and giving him a piece of her mind, and the rest of the pub was squaring up for a good fight.'

There was a flicker of interest in Finn's eyes. 'What happened to the dog?'

'Oh, Kate got it,' said Josh. 'We knew she would. It was a savage Alsatian cross, and I wouldn't have wanted to go near it myself, but Kate had it eating out of her hand in no time.' He turned to Kate. 'What *did* happen to that dog?'

'I took him down to my parents,' she said, uncomfortable with all this blatant promotion. 'He's spoiled to death now, of course, and getting much too fat.'

Finn glanced at Kate. 'Do you think the dog really cared one way or another?'

'I don't know,' she said, meeting his eyes defiantly. Why did people like Finn always have to make you feel so stupid and sentimental when it came to animals? 'But someone had to.'

There was a tiny silence.

'A word of warning,' Gib confided to Finn. 'Kate might look sweet and cuddly, but don't ever try mistreating an animal when she's around, or you'll find yourself in big trouble! She's got a hell of a temper when roused.'

Finn's cold grey gaze flicked to Kate, whose cheeks were burning by this stage, and then away. 'I'll remember,' he said.

'What Kate really needs,' said Phoebe as she ushered them all through to the dining room, 'is a house in the country where she can make chutney and keep chickens and dogs and all the other stray people and animals that cross her path.'

'No, I don't,' objected Kate. A big house in the country sounded perfect, but also a bit too much like she was hanging out to get married. She wasn't having Finn thinking that she was desperate for a husband, certainly not desperate enough to consider him!

'I'm a metropolitan chick, really,' she said loftily. 'I don't think I'm ready to make jam yet. I was thinking more along the lines of PR—' She broke off as Phoebe, Gib and Josh burst out laughing, and even Finn managed a sardonic smile. 'What's so funny?' she demanded, offended.

'Kate, darling, you're not nearly tough enough for PR! You'd always side with the underdog regardless of what your client wanted. You might as well decide to be a brain surgeon!'

With that they were off, vying with each other to think up more unlikely careers that Kate could try. Josh's suggestion—pest controller—was voted the best.

'Kate would take all the rats home and make up little beds for them!'

Kate gritted her teeth. She could feel Finn watching her with a curling lip. He was probably one of those people who thought that a soft heart equalled a soft head.

She wouldn't have minded so much if the other three hadn't been so determined to push her as a homemaker. Couldn't they *see* that Finn wasn't the least bit impressed? Things got even worse over dinner when Phoebe manoeuvred the conversation, none too subtly, round to Finn and his daughter.

'What's her name?'

'Alex,' said Finn almost reluctantly.

Kate didn't blame him. He could obviously see the subtext—how much he needed to get married again to provide his daughter with a stepmother—as clearly as she could, and she was conscious of a treacherous twinge of fellow feeling. He couldn't be enjoying this any more than she was.

'She's nine,' he added, evidently recognising that the information was going to be dragged out of him somehow, so he might as well get it over and done with.

'It must have been very hard, bringing her up on your own,' said Phoebe.

Finn shrugged. 'Alex was only two when Isabel died, so I had various nannies to help. She never really took to any of them, though, and since she's been at school full time we've managed with a housekeeper who comes in every day. She picks Alex up from school and cooks an evening meal, and she'll stay with her if I'm late back from work.'

His voice was emotionless, as if his small daughter was just another logistical problem he had had to solve. It was Alex Kate felt sorry for, poor motherless child. Kate had never taken a phone call from her, or seen her at the office, so she clearly wasn't encouraged to disturb Finn there. Having grown up with four brothers, Kate thought Alex's life sounded very lonely. It couldn't be much fun growing up with just a housekeeper and Finn for company.

Certainly not if Finn was always as boring as he was tonight. He was driving, so he drank very little, and although Kate couldn't object to that, she did feel that he could at least *look* as if was enjoying himself.

He was obviously terrified that she was going to throw herself at him and force him to marry her. It was understandable, Kate supposed, after the way the others had built her up as a domestic goddess, but he needn't worry. Getting together with him was the last thing on her mind. She wasn't *that* desperate for a relationship!

Finn sat beside her at dinner, radiating disapproval as Kate laughed and drank rather too much wine and talked about clubbing and parties and generally made it clear that she was absolutely not in the market for uptight widowers, no matter how sorry she felt for his poor daughter. Of course, the more poker-faced and buttoned up he was, the more she she had to compensate for Phoebe and Gib's sake. They had gone to so much effort, she felt that the least she could do was try and make it a successful evening.

Defiantly ignoring the way Finn was looking down his nose, Kate held out her glass for more wine. Anyone with a sense of occasion would relax and have a drink as well. They would agree to call a taxi and come and pick up the car in the morning, but the Finns of this world evidently didn't do relaxing or having fun.

Of course, it was a bit tricky trying to impress her complete lack of concern on Finn and ignore him at the same time, especially when she was so aware of his austere presence beside her. It wasn't that he didn't contribute to the conversation, but he made it very clear that he thought Kate was too silly for words, which just made her nervous, and nervousness made her drink more until she was trapped in a vicious circle. As the evening wore on, she could hear herself getting louder and more outrageous, and had reached the owlish stage when Finn, obviously unable to bear any more, looked at his watch.

'I must go,' he said, pushing back his chair to forestall any objections.

'I think you should go too,' said Gib to Kate with a grin, 'or you'll never get to work tomorrow.'

Kate didn't want to think about going into work. 'Don't talk about it,' she groaned, closing her eyes, but that was a mistake. The room started to spin and she opened them again hastily, clutching her tousled curls instead.

'I don't suppose you could give her a lift home, could you?' Gib asked Finn. 'She can't be trusted to get home alone in this state!'

'I'm absolutely fine,' Kate protested instantly, lifting her head and trying not to sway at the sudden movement. 'I'm great!'

'You're fab,' agreed Phoebe soothingly, helping her to her feet, 'but it's time to go. Finn's going to take you home.'

'Why can't Josh take me?'

'Because I haven't got my car with me and I live in completely the opposite direction,' said Josh ungallantly.

'I'm very happy to give you a lift,' said Finn with a certain grittiness, clearly feeling far from happy but unable to think of a good excuse.

Outside, it was raining and making a determined effort to sleet, if not actually to snow. Finn watched, resigned, as Gib and Phoebe helped Kate into her coat like a little girl for the short walk to the car, buttoning her up and kissing her goodnight before consigning her into his charge.

Kate thanked them both graciously for supper, although she had a sinking feeling that the words might have come out a bit slurred, and set off down the path, very much on her dignity. Unfortunately, the effect was spoilt by stumbling on her heels, and only Finn's hand which shot out and gripped her arm stopped her landing smack on her bottom.

'Careful!' he said sharply.

'Sorry, the path's a bit slippy…slippery,' Kate managed, wincing at the iron grip of his fingers. She tried to pull her arm away, but Finn kept a good hold of her as he marched her along to his car.

'You're the one that's a bit slippy,' he said acidly and opened the door with what Kate felt was unnecessarily ironic courtesy.

Tired of being treated like a child, she got in sulkily, and he shut it after her with an exasperated click.

The car was immaculate. There were no sweetie wrappers, no empty cans, no forgotten toys or scuffed seats. It was impossible to believe that a child had ever been in it, thought Kate, wondering where poor little Alex fitted into Finn's efficiently streamlined life.

Still buoyed up by a combination of alcohol and nerves, and anticipating an uncomfortable journey, she leant forward and switched on the radio. Classical, of course. Pressing random buttons, she searched for Capital Radio, until Finn got in to the driver's seat and switched it off with a frown.

'Stop fiddling and do up your seatbelt.'

'Yes, sir!' muttered Kate.

Finn lay his arm along the back of her seat and swivelled so that that he could see to reverse the car along the narrow street to the turning place at the bottom. Kate was acutely aware of how close his hand was to her hair and she made a big deal of rummaging in her bag at her feet in case he thought that she was leaning invitingly towards him.

It was a relief when they reached the turning place and Finn took his arm away to put the car into gear. At least she could sit back.

Only it wasn't that much easier then. Finn was a fierce, formidable presence, overwhelming in the dark confines of the car while the rain and the sleet splattered against the windscreen and made the space shrink even further. The light from the dashboard lit his face with a green glow, glancing along his cheekbones and highlighting the severe mouth.

He was concentrating on driving, and Kate watched him under her lashes, daunted more than she wanted to admit by his air of contained competence. It was evident in the calm, decisive way he drove, and when her eyes followed his left hand from the steering wheel to the gear stick, something stirred inside her and she looked quickly away.

Her wine-induced high had shrivelled, leaving her tongue-tied and agonisingly aware of him. It was ridiculous, Kate scolded herself. He was still Finn. He was a disagreeable, if thankfully temporary, boss and an ungracious guest. She didn't like him at all, so why was she suddenly noticing the line of his mouth and the set of his jaw and the strength of his hands?

'Where am I going?'

His brusque question broke the silence and startled her. 'What?'

'Gib asked me to take you home. Presumably he knows where that is, but I'm not a mind-reader.'

'Oh…yes.' Kate huddled in her seat, too appalled by this new awareness of him to rise to his sarcasm the way she would normally have done.

She directed him through the dark streets while the windscreen wipers thwacked rhythmically at the sleety rain and the silence in the car deepened until Kate could bear it no longer.

'Why didn't you tell Gib and Phoebe that you recognised me?'

Finn glanced at her. 'Probably for the same reason that you didn't,' he said curtly. 'I thought it would make the situation even more awkward than it already was.'

His tone was so uninviting, that Kate subsided back into silence. Anyone else giving her a lift home would have made some attempt at conversation, even if only to talk about the evening or the food or even, if things were desperate, the weather, but Finn was evidently in no mood for idle chit-chat. His face was set in grim lines and when he glanced in the rear-view mirror, Kate could see that he was frowning.

'It's just along here.' She pointed out her street in relief. 'There's never anywhere to stop, so if you could drop me here, that would be fine, thanks.'

Finn ignored her, turning down the street she had indicated. 'How far down are you?'

'About halfway,' admitted Kate, surrendering to *force majeure*. She pointed. 'Just past that streetlight.'

As usual, the street was lined with cars bumper to bumper, so Finn had no choice but to stop in the middle of the road. Kate fumbled for the doorhandle as he put on the handbrake.

'Thank you for the lift,' she muttered. 'I hope I haven't brought you too much out of your way.'

A gust of sleet hit her full in the face as she opened the door, and instinctively she recoiled. 'Yuck, what a horrible night!'

'Wait there.' Cursing under his breath, Finn reached behind him for an umbrella and got out of the car. He'd managed to get the umbrella up by the time he made it round to the passenger door. 'I'll see you to your door.'

'Honestly, I'll be fine. You don't need to—'

'Just hurry up and get out!' said Finn through his teeth. It was hard to tell whether they were gritted with temper or with cold. 'The sooner you do, the sooner I can get home!'

Reluctantly Kate scrambled out of the car and into the shelter of the umbrella. The wind was bitter and the rain ran down her neck, but she was still able to notice how intimate it felt to be standing so close to Finn. He was tall and solid and she had a bizarre impulse to put her arms round him and lean into him, to feel how hard and strong he was.

'Right, let's move it before we both freeze to death out here!' said Finn, fortunately unable to read her mind. Or possibly telepathic and quick to take avoiding action. 'Which house is it?'

He set off towards the pavement with Kate teetering on her heels in an effort to keep up with his long stride. 'Why on earth don't you wear something more sensible on your feet?' he demanded, holding the umbrella impatiently above her.

'If I'd known I'd be going on a polar expedition, I might have done!' said Kate, her teeth chattering so loudly that she could hardly speak, but obscurely grateful to the vile weather for disguising the shakiness that might otherwise be obvious in her legs and her voice. She couldn't *believe* what she had been tempted to do just then!

Finn would have had a fit if she had thrown herself at him like that. Or might he, just possibly, have pulled her towards him and kissed her under the umbrella? What would *that* have been like? Kate swallowed, torn between relief and disappointment that she would never know.

Still blissfully unaware of her wayward thoughts, Finn protected her with the umbrella while she fumbled for her key. Her hands were shaking in time with her teeth by that stage, and she was shivering so much that she couldn't get the key in the lock.

Unable to bear it any longer, Finn put out his hand for the key, but his fingers brushing hers were enough to make Kate jerk back in alarm, dropping it into a puddle.

Mortified, she crouched down to retrieve it. Finn was holding out his hand with barely restrained impatience and meekly she dropped the wet and dirty key into his outstretched palm.

Without a word, Finn unlocked the door and pushed it open for her. 'Thank you,' said Kate awkwardly. 'And thanks again for the lift.'

That was Finn's cue to say that it had been a pleasure, an opening he pointedly missed.

'I'll see you tomorrow,' he said gruffly instead.

Fine, if that's the way he wanted to be, she wouldn't invite him in! Kate hugged her coat around her. 'Are you sure you still want me to come into work?'

'That's generally the idea behind paying you,' said Finn with one of his sardonic looks.

'But I thought I was a disaster?'

'You're not exactly a resounding success as a secretary,' he agreed, 'but you're the best I've got at the moment. We've got a big contract coming up, as you would know if you'd been paying attention, and I can't afford to spend the time explaining everything to yet another secretary. I'm better off sticking with you.'

'Well, thanks for that warm vote of confidence!'

'You didn't make many bones about how much you dislike working for me,' Finn pointed out, 'so I don't see why I should dance around saving your feelings! The fact is that you can't afford to lose this job just yet, and I can't afford the time to replace you.'

'You're saying we're stuck with each other?' said Kate, lifting her chin.

'Precisely, so we might as well make the best of it.' He looked down into her face from under his umbrella. 'I suggest you drink a litre of water before you go to bed,' he said dispassionately as he turned to go. 'We've got a lot to do tomorrow, so please don't be late!'

Groping blearily for the alarm clock, Kate forced open one eye to squint at the time, only to jerk upright with what should have been a cry but which came out more as a groan. The sudden movement was like a cleaver slicing through her aching head and she put up a shaky hand to check that it was still intact.

Unfortunately, yes. Right then death seemed preferable to the pounding in her head and the horrible taste in her mouth.

Not to mention what Finn would say if she was late again.

Kate grimaced as she looked at the clock. If she skipped

the shower and was lucky with the trains, she might *just* make it…

Somehow she got herself out of bed and along to the tube station, but regretted it deeply when she had to stand squashed in with thousands of other commuters, all wet and steaming from the rain above ground. Kate clung to the rail with one hand, swaying nauseously as the train lurched and rattled its way along the tunnels, and tried to ignore the queasy feeling in her stomach.

To make matters worse, her memory of the night before was coming back in fragments of intense clarity separated by the blurry recollection of having generally made a complete fool of herself.

The things she did remember were bad enough. The appalled look on Finn's face when the terrible truth dawned that his date for the evening was none other than his much-despised temporary secretary. The windscreen wipers thwacking in time to the beat of her heart as she fixated inexplicably on his mouth and his hands. Huddling under the umbrella, wondering what it would be like to touch him.

She must have been completely blotto.

God, what if she'd made a pass at Finn? Kate thought in panic. Surely she would remember *that*?

If she had, she would have been firmly repulsed. That was one thing she did remember. Her much loved top and favourite shoes had gone down like a lead balloon with Finn. Kate had always been told that she looked really hot in that top, but he had just looked down his nose and averted his eyes from her cleavage. If any pass had been made, it certainly wouldn't have come from him!

She got to the office with less than a minute to spare. Finn was already at his desk, of course. He looked up over his glasses as Kate held on to the doorway for support.

'You look terrible,' he said.

'I feel worse,' she croaked. 'I've got the most monumental hangover.'

Finn grunted. 'I hope you're not expecting any sympathy from me!'

'No, I don't think I could cope with any miracles today,' said Kate tartly before remembering a little too late that her job was very much on the line. Finn was obviously thinking much the same thing because his eyes narrowed slightly behind his reading glasses.

'You'd better be in a fit state to work,' he warned her. 'We've got a lot to do today.'

'I'll just have some coffee and then I'll be fine,' Kate promised, holding her head.

'You can have five minutes,' said Finn and picked up the report he had been reading once more, effectively dismissing her.

Kate groped her way along to the coffee machine and ordered a double espresso, trying not to wince at the sound of ringing telephones and clattering keyboards. There was a tiny manic blacksmith at work inside her skull, banging and hammering on her nerve endings.

Perhaps Alison would have some paracetamol, she thought, sinking gratefully down at her desk. That might help.

Any normal girl would keep hangover cures handy in her top right-hand drawer, but not Alison. Having rummaged through the desk, Kate was forced to accept that Alison didn't have hangovers. Alison probably didn't even know what a hangover *was*. She probably never got nervous or drank too much or showed off in front of Finn.

The coffee was only making her feel worse. Groaning, Kate collapsed onto the desk and buried her head in her arms. That was it. She was giving up. She was just going to have to die here in Finn's office. He would just have to decide what to do with her body although, knowing him, he'd get the next temp to deal with it. Just dispose of that corpse, he would say, and then come in and take notes at the speed of light.

'You didn't drink any water before you went to bed, did you?' Finn's voice spoke above Kate's prostrate form.

'No,' she mumbled, mainly because it was easier than shaking her head.

'You're dehydrated.' Somewhere to the right of her ear, she could hear the sound of a mug being set on the desk. 'Here. I've brought you some sweet tea, and a couple of aspirin.'

The promise of aspirin was enough to make Kate lift her head very cautiously. 'Thanks,' she muttered.

She took the pills and screwed up her face at the taste of the tea, but her mouth was so dry that she sipped it anyway. After a few minutes, she even began to feel as if she might live after all.

Finn was leaning against the edge of her desk, frowning down at the file in his hands. He always seemed to be frowning, Kate thought muzzily. Was he like this with everyone, or was it just her? The thought that it might be her was oddly depressing. Granted, turning up for work late or massively hungover probably wasn't the best way to go about getting him to smile, but still, you'd have thought there'd have been *something* about her he could like.

CHAPTER THREE

As if aware of her gaze, Finn glanced up. 'Feeling any better?' he asked, although not with any noticeable degree of sympathy.

'A bit,' croaked Kate.

'Good.' Closing the file, he dropped it onto her desk with a loud slap that made her wince, and he sighed. 'Why on earth do you drink so much if you feel this bad the next day?'

'I don't usually,' she said a little sullenly. 'Last night I was trying to have a good time, since *you* obviously weren't going to! Why did you come if you weren't going to make an effort?'

'I went because Gib asked me,' said Finn curtly. 'He said Phoebe had a friend he thought I might like to meet. I was expecting someone gentle and motherly, not a goer with a plunging cleavage, ridiculous shoes and a determination to drink everyone else under the table!'

Aha, so he *had* noticed her cleavage, Kate noted with a perverse sense of satisfaction.

'They've obviously got no idea,' she agreed sweetly, but with an acid undertone. 'They told *me* that you were really nice. How wrong can you be? I don't think I'll be letting them fix up any more blind dates for me!'

A muscle worked in Finn's jaw. 'I couldn't agree with you more.'

'Well, there's a first!' Kate muttered.

Finn got to his feet. 'If you're well enough to argue, you're well enough to do some work,' he said callously. 'I think we can both agree that last night was extremely awk-

ward for both of us. Frankly, I'd rather not know about
your personal life, and I don't believe in mixing mine with
business. However, as I said last night—although of course
you won't remember this!—I can't afford the time to explain everything to someone new at this stage, so I suggest
that we pretend that last night never happened and carry
on as before. Although it would help if you would turn up
on time and in a fit state to work occasionally,' he added
nastily. 'That could be different!'

Kate held her aching head with her hand. She just wished
she was in a position to tell Finn exactly what he could do
with his job. She had a hazy recollection of telling everyone
last night that she was planning a major career change,
which had seemed like a good idea at the time, and still
did, frankly.

One of these days she would have to do something about
it but, in the meantime, she had to live, and this crummy
job was her best hope of paying her bills for the next few
weeks. She had never been big on saving, and she had
bailed Seb out too many times to have anything left to fall
back on. It looked as if she was going to have to stick with
Finn for now.

'Alison should be back in a few weeks,' he said as if
reassuring himself.

'Meaning you won't have to put up with me for too
long?' In spite of her own reluctance, Kate was obscurely
hurt to realise that Finn couldn't wait to get rid of her.

'I was under the impression that the feeling was mutual,'
he said coldly.

'It is.'

'Are you trying to tell me you want to leave now?'

'No,' said Kate, forced into a corner. 'No, I want to stay.
I haven't got any choice.'

'Then we're both in the same boat,' said Finn. He turned
for his office. 'And if you do want to carry on working

here, I suggest you go and freshen up, and come back ready to start work!'

Three hours later, Kate was reeling after a barrage of complicated instructions and tasks which Finn rapped out, making no allowances for her hangover, before going out to an expensive lunch with a client.

'Have that draft report on my desk by the time I get back,' was his parting shot.

Kate pulled a face at his receding back and dumped the armful of files and papers onto her desk. Did she really want to hang onto this job that badly?

Finn's expression had been as grimly unreadable as ever, but she could have sworn that beneath it all he was enjoying the sight of her struggling to cope with a hangover and an avalanche of work. She was prepared to bet that a lot of this stuff could easily have waited and that he had only pulled it out to punish her. It was hard to believe that for a peculiar moment or two last night she had actually found him attractive!

Running her fingers wearily through her hair, Kate sighed as she contemplated the scattered piles of paper on her desk. She needed another coffee before she could tackle that lot!

In spite of everything Finn had to say about his staff not going in for gossip, Kate had noticed that the coffee machine was a favoured meeting place. Of course it was possible that the two older women from the finance department were talking about work, but somehow she doubted it. They stopped as she approached and moved aside politely to let her through to the machine.

'Thanks,' said Kate with a smile. 'I'm desperate!'

'Feeling rough?'

'Awful,' she admitted, searching her memory for their names. 'I am never, ever, going to drink again!'

Elaine and Sue, that was it. They had been polite if rather

cool with Kate in her few brief dealings with them, but she noticed they thawed slightly at her frank admission of a hangover.

'So, how are you getting on?' the older one—Sue?—asked.

'I don't think I'm ever going to live up to Alison's standards,' Kate sighed as the machine spat out coffee into her cup. 'What's she like? Is she as perfect as Finn makes out?'

Sue and Elaine considered. 'She's certainly very efficient,' said Elaine, but she didn't sound overly enthusiastic. 'Finn relies on her a lot.'

Kate sipped her coffee, still disgruntled by the amount of work Finn had thrown at her. 'She must be an absolute saint to put up with him!'

Wrong thing to say! The two women bridled at the implied criticism of Finn. 'He's lovely when you get to know him,' Elaine insisted, and Sue nodded.

'He's the best boss I've ever had. You want to count how many people have been here years and years. We don't get the same kind of turnover as in other companies. That's because everyone here feels involved. Finn expects you to work hard, but he always notices and comments on what you've been doing, and that makes all the difference.'

'He treats you like a human being,' Elaine added her bit.

It was news to Kate, thinking about that morning.

'Of course, Alison's absolutely devoted to Finn,' Sue said. She lowered her voice confidentially. 'Between you and me, I think she might be hoping to become more than a PA one day.'

'Oh?' Kate was conscious of a sudden tightening of her muscles. 'Do you think that's likely?'

'No.' Elaine shook her head definitely. 'He's never got over losing his wife, and I don't think he ever will.'

'Isabel was a lovely person,' Sue agreed. 'She used to come in to the office sometimes, and we all loved her. She was so beautiful and sweet and interested in what everyone did. There was just something about her. She made you feel special somehow, didn't she, Elaine?'

Elaine nodded sadly. 'Finn was different then. He absolutely adored her, and she was the same. She used to light up whenever he came into the room. Oh, it was such a tragedy when she died!'

'What happened?' asked Kate, hoping she didn't sound too ghoulish.

'Someone got into a car having had too much to drink, and poor Isabel was coming the other way…' They shook their heads at the memory of it. 'She never came out of the coma. Finn had to make the decision to switch off her life-support machine.'

Sue sighed. 'You can only imagine what it was like for him. He had Alex to worry about too. She was in the car as well, so she was in hospital too, although not so seriously hurt.'

'She wasn't much more than a baby,' Elaine added. 'Just old enough to cry for her mummy.'

Kate's hand had crept to her mouth as she listened to their story. 'That's…terrible,' she said, feeling hopelessly inadequate.

'Terrible,' Elaine agreed. 'Finn's never been the same since. He closed in on himself after Isabel died. Alex is his life now, and he won't let anyone else close. He kept the company going, but I've always felt that was more for all the staff here than for his own sake.'

'We all hope he'll remarry one day,' Sue said. 'He deserves to be happy again and Alex needs a mum. Maybe he'll miss Alison while she's away,' she added hopefully. 'I know she can be a bit cool, but that's just her manner, and she's very attractive, isn't she?' she demanded of Elaine, who nodded a bit reluctantly.

'She's always beautifully groomed.'

'And she must know him pretty well after working for him for so long. I think she'd be a good wife for him.'

It didn't sound to Kate as if Alison was at all the right kind of wife for Finn. He was quite cool and efficient enough by himself. What he needed was warmth and tenderness and laughter, not practicality and good grooming.

Not that it was anything to do with her, of course.

Still, she couldn't get Finn's tragic story out of her mind all afternoon. She kept imagining him by his wife's side, with the life-support machines beeping in the background, willing her to open her eyes, or trying to explain to his baby daughter why her mother couldn't come.

'No wonder he didn't approve of me drinking last night,' she said to Bella that evening, having told her about the disaster of her blind date and what she had learnt from Elaine and Sue. 'I feel terrible now. I've been so nasty about him, and all the time he's had to cope with all of that.'

'Don't do it,' said Bella, handing Kate a drink.

'Don't do what?'

'Don't get involved.'

'I'm not involved,' said Kate a little defensively. 'I just feel desperately sorry for him.'

Bella sighed as she contemplated her friend. 'You know what you're like, Kate,' she warned. 'One tiny tug at your heartstrings, and you're turning your world upside down to try and make things better, and sometimes you just can't. You were desperately sorry for Seb, too, and look where that got you!'

'This is entirely different,' Kate protested. 'Finn's not trying to get anything from me. He hasn't even told me about Isabel himself. I'm not sure he'd even want me to know.'

'I just don't want you jumping from feeling sorry for him to wanting to help him to falling in love with him,' said Bella with a warning look. 'You've got to admit it's a bit of a pattern with you, and this time you really could get hurt. It would be much worse than Seb. You'd never be able to live up to a perfect wife like that, Kate. You'd only ever be second-best.'

'Honestly, Bella!' said Kate crossly. 'Anyone would think I was planning to marry him! All I'm saying is that maybe I should be more understanding when he's grumpy with me.'

'Hhmmnn, well, just be careful. You didn't like him when you thought he was happily married, and he's exactly the same man. Being a widower isn't really an excuse for being unpleasant to you, is it? You said it's six years since his wife died, that's long enough for him to be coming to terms with it. Don't let him take advantage of your soft heart, that's all.'

Kate didn't say any more—*ER* was on, and there were more important things to do—but afterwards she thought about what Bella had said. Her friend might seem the quintessential feather-headed blonde at times, but she could be very pragmatic when it came to relationships.

Of course, it was nonsense to suggest that there was any chance of her falling in love with Finn. She had no intention of doing anything of the kind. What she *would* do from now on was make allowances for his brusque temper instead of getting cross about it.

It would be part of her new, professional image, Kate decided. She would be cool, courteous and discreetly efficient. If all she could do to help him was to create a calm atmosphere in which he could work, then that's what she would do.

That was nothing like falling in love with him, was it?

Changing the atmosphere in the office was all very well in theory, but in practice it was less easy.

Kate really tried. Sick of hearing about the immaculately

groomed Alison, she had made more of an effort to dress smartly. She was never going to look completely at home in a suit and her hair just didn't do neat, but at least she was showing willing. When Finn snapped at her, she bit her tongue and didn't answer back. She just got on with her work and waited for him to notice how much easier his life had become. She even practised an understanding speech for when he told her how grateful he was.

That was a waste of time! Far from being grateful, Finn seemed deeply suspicious of her new, improved attitude.

'What's the matter with you?' he demanded.

'Nothing,' said Kate, a bit taken aback.

'You're too polite,' he grumbled. 'It makes me nervous. And why are you dressed like that?' His expression sharpened. 'Have you got an interview for another job?'

Chance would be a fine thing. 'No,' she said. 'I'm just trying to look professional. I thought you would approve,' she was unable to resist adding.

Finn looked at her. Her attempt to tie back her hair had failed miserably, most of the soft brown curls escaping their confines to tumble around her face once more. Her one and only suit was a rather dull grey affair and the white shirt was creased. It was hard to believe they came from the same wardrobe as the vibrant dress with its swirling skirt and its daring neckline that she had worn to dinner at Phoebe and Gib's.

'I'm not sure you can carry off the professional look,' he said dryly.

There was no pleasing some people, thought Kate with an inward sigh.

Faced with a comprehensive lack of encouragement on Finn's part, she found herself slipping back into her old ways, especially after an interesting little chat with Phoebe one evening. Kate had braced herself to confess that she had known exactly who Finn was, and was a little peeved to discover that Finn had told Gib himself the very next day when he had rung to thank them for supper.

'Did he say anything about me?' Kate heard herself ask when Phoebe had finished telling her how amused they were by the whole situation.

'I think he was a bit thrown by seeing you dressed like that,' said Phoebe, carefully avoiding a direct answer. 'Presumably you don't usually wear quite such revealing tops in the office?'

'Of course not,' said Kate, miffed for no obvious reason. 'What was he expecting? Me to turn up to dinner in a suit?'

'I gather Finn told Gib that I wasn't his type,' she said when she reported the conversation to Bella.

She was cross that she hadn't spoken to Phoebe earlier so that she could have passed a message onto Finn that he wasn't Kate's type either.

'I don't think I'll bother being nice to him any longer,' she grumbled. 'He obviously doesn't appreciate it anyway.'

Still, that was no reason to give up her new cool image. Kate was determined to show Finn that Alison wasn't the only one who could be professional. Every morning she tried to be at her desk before he arrived, calmly going through the post. It meant getting up at the crack of dawn, of course, but it was worth it to see the disconcerted look on his face when he came in, and it wasn't as if she would have to do it for ever. She fully intended to go back to her slovenly ways the moment Alison returned.

She was nearly a week into her newly punctual mode when she emerged from the underground one day, turning up her collar against the cold. It was a dreary morning, with a sleety drizzle giving the pavements a slippery sheen, and Kate paused to put up her umbrella. Normally she wouldn't have bothered, but the rain made her hair even more uncontrollable than ever, and she was determined to achieve a style that would stay halfway neat for the morning at least.

She glanced at her watch. Just time to get a cappuccino from the Italian café on the way to the office.

Kate stood in line with all those others unable to face another revolting coffee from the machine at work. Accepting a perfunctory 'Bella, bella!' from the Italian as he handed her the beaker to take away, she cradled it close to her chest for warmth. She would really enjoy this when she was sitting calmly at her desk, waiting for Finn to appear.

Putting up the umbrella with one hand turned out to be a tussle of wills, but after some wrestling, Kate won. It was raining more heavily now, and the wind was coming in gusts, so she had to hold the umbrella almost in front of her face to stop it blowing inside out. It made it tricky to see where she was going, but she set off, telling herself that there was only a block to the office. She might as well try and stay dry.

The next moment there was a yelp and she was sprawling full length, her fall partly cushioned by a pile of rubbish bags waiting to be collected.

'Are you all right?' someone stopped to ask reluctantly.

'I'm fine…I think,' said Kate, struggling to her feet and looking down at herself as she brushed the rubbish off her jacket in dismay. The cappuccino had ended up all the way down her skirt. Her hands were filthy, her tights torn, and as for her hair…well, she might as well forget it for today.

Relieved at not being roped into a scene, her reluctant Samaritan had hurried on. Kate bent stiffly to retrieve her umbrella, remembering the yelp and wondering what had caused it. She could see now that some of the pile of black bags had been torn open, so that rubbish spilt out onto the pavement, and in the middle of them, cowered a little dog with bony ribs and fearful eyes.

Her bruises forgotten, Kate crouched down among the bin bags and held out her hand. 'You poor sweetheart, did I tread on you?' she asked gently, holding out her hand, until the dog crawled closer to lick it. It was wet and shivering, and when Kate looked closer she could see that it had no collar.

'You're not much more than a puppy, are you?' she said, letting it smell that she was unthreatening before she stroked it behind its ears, one of which was cocked and the other flapping disreputably.

It was not perhaps the most beautiful dog she had ever seen. A dispassionate observer might even have thought it was ugly with its legs disproportionately short in relation to its long shaggy body, its pointed, whiskery nose and big ears, but Kate saw only the thinness of its ribs and the untreated sores, and her blood boiled.

There was no point in looking round for an owner. This was a business district, the streets lined with office blocks and no one would be walking a dog around here. This little dog wasn't lost, it had been abandoned, if indeed it had ever had a home in the first place. But something in the way its tail wagged feebly in response to her gentle pats made Kate's heart crack.

'Come on, darling, you're coming with me,' she told it firmly. She couldn't leave it here to starve if it didn't get run over first.

Very gently, she pulled the little dog towards her. It whimpered but didn't struggle when she lifted it up. When she examined it, it didn't seem to be badly hurt. 'I think you're just cold and hungry,' she decided.

There was a mini-market back by the tube station. Tucking the now useless umbrella under one arm and the dog under the other, Kate retraced her steps and bought some bread and milk, and a couple of newspapers in case of accidents. She would have to worry about a lead and collar later. This wasn't the kind of area you found a pet shop, even if she had time to track one down. By this stage she was almost as dirty and bedraggled as the little dog, and it was nearly half past nine.

So much for being early.

Well, it couldn't be helped. Ignoring the receptionist's appalled expression, Kate walked towards the lift with the precious burden under her arm. She could feel its little heart battering and her own didn't feel that steady at the prospect of facing Finn, but she was still too angry at the cruelty of anyone who could abandon a defenceless animal to care what she looked like.

The door of her office was open. Kate took a deep breath and walked inside, only to stop dead when she saw that there was someone sitting at her computer. For a heart-stopping moment she thought that she had been replaced, but a second look showed her that the occupier of her desk had quite a bit of schooling left before she had to think about getting a job.

The little girl stopped typing when Kate came in and stared at her with unfriendly eyes. She had thick glasses and a thin, guarded face, together with an air of self-possession quite intimidating in one so young.

'Who are you?'

'I'm Kate. Who are you?' countered Kate, although she had already recognised that steely expression. Like father, like daughter.

'Alex,' she admitted. 'My dad's angry with you,' she went on.

'Oh, dear, I was afraid he might be.' Kate put the little dog down and stroked it soothingly.

'He said a rude word.'

That sounded like Finn. 'Where is he now?'

'He's gone to find someone to look after me and to fill

in for you until you deign to turn up,' said Alex, obviously quoting verbatim. 'What does ''deign'' mean?'

'I think your father thought I was late on purpose,' said Kate, sighing. She took off her jacket and hung it up while she wondered what to do next. She really ought to find Finn and explain, but the little dog was still shivering with a combination of nerves and cold.

She knew how it felt.

Alex had been studying her critically. 'Why are you so dirty?'

'I fell into a load of rubbish.'

'Yuck.' Alex wrinkled her nose. 'You do smell a bit,' she informed Kate, who lifted an arm and sniffed the unmistakable odour of rotting rubbish. Eau de bin bag.

Great. That was all she needed.

Alex had come round the front of the desk and was regarding the quivering dog with some wariness. 'Is that your dog?'

'He is now,' said Kate.

'What's his name?'

'I don't know…what do you think I should call him?'

'Is it a boy or a girl?'

Good question. Kate lifted the dog gently. 'A boy.'

Alex came a little closer. She seemed cautious but fascinated by the dog, who was sniffing the floor with equal uncertainty. Kate waited for her to suggest Scruffy or Patch or Rover.

'What about Derek?'

'*Derek*?' Kate started to laugh, and Alex looked offended.

'Don't you think it's a good name?'

'It's a great name,' Kate recovered herself quickly. 'Derek the dog. I love it. Derek!' she called to the dog, snapping her fingers for his attention.

He pricked up his ears and sat down clumsily, which

made Alex smile for the first time. Her smile transformed her rather serious little face, and Kate wondered if a smile would have a similar effect on Finn's expression.

Not that she was likely to see him smile just for the moment.

Alex squatted beside her. 'Hello, Derek,' she said.

'Let him smell your fingers before you pat him,' said Kate, and smiled when Derek wagged his tail and licked Alex's hand.

'He's cute,' said Alex.

'I'm not sure your father will think so.'

The words were barely out of her mouth before Finn came striding into the room, scowling ferociously. 'Oh, there you are!' he said as he spied Kate. 'Nice of you to join us!'

Kate got to her feet, acutely conscious of her bedraggled state. 'I'm sorry I'm late,' she began but Finn interrupted her as he got a proper look at her.

'For God's sake, Kate, look at the state of you! What on earth have you been doing?'

'Please don't shout!' she said, but it was too late. Cowering at the sound of Finn's raised voice, the little dog had squatted and made a puddle on the carpet.

'Now look what you've done!' Kate accused Finn as she pulled one of the newspapers apart and spread a couple of sheets over the puddle to mop up the worst of it. 'It's all right, sweetheart,' she said, caressing the still trembling dog. 'I won't let the nasty man shout at you any more.'

She glanced up at Finn from where she was crouched. 'You're upsetting Derek.'

'Upsetting…?' Finn shook his head in baffled frustration. 'Who?'

'It's his name, Dad,' Alex told him.

'*Derek*?'

'Alex thought of the name,' said Kate quickly, before he

could say anything to upset his daughter. 'It suits him, don't you think?'

Finn ignored that. He looked as if he was counting to ten in an effort to keep his temper. 'Kate,' he said at last in a voice of careful restraint, 'what is that dog doing here?'

'I found him on my way to work.'

'Well, you'd better lose him pretty damn quickly! An office is a totally inappropriate place for a dog.'

'It's not that appropriate for a child either.'

His mouth thinned. 'That's a completely different thing,' he snapped. 'My housekeeper has been called away unexpectedly to look after her sick mother, and the school is having a training day. I didn't have any choice but to bring Alex in today. I couldn't leave her in the house on her own.'

'I couldn't leave Derek in the street on his own,' countered Kate. 'He would have been run over.'

Finn ground his teeth in frustration. 'Kate, this is an office, not Battersea Dogs Home! I thought you were trying to be more professional?'

'Some things are more important than being professional,' she said, and bent to pick up the dog.

'Where are you going?' he snarled. 'I haven't finished with you!'

'I'm going to dry him and give him something to drink,' Kate answered patiently, 'and when I've done that, I'll come back and you can be as cross with me as you like.'

'Can I come and help you?' Alex asked while her father was still spluttering in outrage.

'Sure,' said Kate. 'You can hold Derek while I dry him.'

'Now just a minute—' Finn began, unable to believe that he had lost control of the situation so easily.

Alex rolled her eyes in an impressively adolescent fashion. 'Dad, I'll be fine,' she said wearily, and followed Kate out of the room before he could assert his authority.

In the Ladies, they found some paper towels and wiped the worst of the dirt and wet off Derek, and then off Kate, who was in nearly as bad a state.

She pulled a face at her reflection as she washed her hands. 'I don't think I'm going to win any awards for glamour today,' she sighed.

Alex was cuddling the little dog, murmuring to reassure it about finding itself in yet more strange surroundings. 'You're not like Alison,' she commented.

Kate sighed and lifted her hopelessly tangled hair in despair. 'So your father is always telling me.'

'I don't like Alison,' Alex confided. 'She talks to me in a stupid voice like I'm a baby! She's soppy about Dad, too.'

'Is your dad soppy about her?' Kate couldn't help asking, although she knew that she shouldn't. She hoped she didn't sound too interested.

Alex shrugged. 'I don't know. I hope not. I don't want a stepmother. Rosa fusses, but I'd rather have her as a housekeeper than Alison.'

Poor old Alison, thought Kate. There was a very stubborn set to Alex's chin, inherited from her father no doubt, and she wouldn't like to bet on Alison's chances of winning her round.

Feeling more cheerful for some reason, she sent Alex in search of a couple of bowls while she made a bed of newspapers for Derek behind her desk where he would feel secure. He seemed quite happy to curl up there, but when Alex reappeared with a bowl of water and a saucer, he got up to investigate, and the offer of some bread soaked in milk got his tail wagging eagerly.

'He's so sweet!' said Alex, watching him adoringly. 'I wish I could keep him! Do you think Dad would let me?'

Kate thought the answer would be definitely not, but Finn could presumably deal with his own daughter. 'You'd have to ask him. I'd wait until he's in a better mood though,' she cautioned.

This looked like good advice when Finn emerged glowering from his office. 'Alex, you can go and sit with the girls at the reception desk for a while if you want. You know you like doing that sometimes.'

'Only when Alison is here,' muttered Alex. 'Anyway, I'm going to look after Derek. Kate says I can.'

'Yes, well, I want a word with Kate,' said Finn ominously.

'I won't disturb her,' Alex reassured him, misunderstanding. 'It'll make it easier for her to work because she won't have to check on Derek the whole time. You don't mind, do you, Kate?'

'It's fine by me.'

'It's not a question of what Kate minds,' Finn bit out, goaded beyond endurance. 'Come into my office,' he ordered Kate. 'If you've quite finished turning my office into a branch of Animal Rescue, that is,' he added sarcastically, standing back with mock courtesy so that she could go ahead of him.

'Would you like to explain what the hell is going on?' he said furiously as he sat behind his desk.

Kate wondered if she was supposed to stand in front of him with her hands behind her back, like being brought before the headmaster. She opted to sit anyway. Finn was so angry that one more thing wasn't going to make any difference. He certainly couldn't look any crosser.

'Nothing's going on,' she told him. 'I didn't mean to be late, but I couldn't just walk past that dog. You saw the state of him. Someone's just got bored of him and thrown him out. I don't know how people can be so cruel.' Her voice shook with emotion.

'They should bring back public flogging,' added Kate, who rescued spiders and stepped carefully round snails and loathed all forms of violence. 'That might teach them what cruelty feels like! I once saw—'

Finn cut her off. 'Kate, I'm not interested,' he said curtly. 'I've got a business to run here. It's distracting enough having to cope with Alex in the office, and now we've wasted half the morning on that dog.'

'Alex is quite happy looking after him, so I'd say that's solved your problem. In fact, it's all worked out very well,' said Kate, unrepentant. She waved her notebook at him and smiled brightly. 'I'm ready to start work whenever you are.'

CHAPTER FOUR

'DAD?' Alex waited until Finn had finished giving Kate a long list of orders which she was scribbling into her notebook.

Finn peered round the desk to where his daughter sat in the corner, Derek's head on her lap. 'Are you OK down there?'

She nodded vigorously. 'You know you said that I could have whatever I wanted for lunch if I was good this morning?'

'Yes,' he said with a certain wariness.

'I don't really want any lunch,' she told him. 'Can we go to a pet shop and buy Derek a lead and collar instead?'

'Alex, I don't want you getting too attached to that dog!'

'No, I won't,' she promised fervently. 'But please, Dad! You did promise.'

'I was thinking more of going out for a pizza.' Finn glared at Kate as if it was all her fault. 'Perhaps we should let Kate take responsibility for the dog. She rescued it, after all.'

'Kate hasn't got time to go out to lunch,' said Alex before Kate had a chance to speak.

How true, thought Kate, looking at her list. She had just been thinking that she would need to improvise a lead and collar. 'I'm sure I'll be able to find some string or something,' she said, opting for the martyr approach which she was fairly sure would annoy Finn. 'You go out and enjoy your lunch. Don't worry about me.'

Finn scowled. 'Oh, yes, that's going to do wonders for

our professional image, isn't it? My PA leaving the office with a dog on a piece of string!'

'I can wait until everyone else has gone,' Kate offered innocently.

'Oh, Dad, please say we can go to a pet shop,' Alex interrupted. 'I've been good—haven't I, Kate? And you did say just the other day that everyone should keep their promises.'

Kate suppressed a smile as Finn champed in frustration. Alex clearly needed no advice in managing her father.

'I don't know where we're going to find a pet shop in the middle of London,' he grumbled, but he had obviously given in on the point of principle.

'Most of the big department stores should have a pet department,' said Kate helpfully.

Not that Finn looked very grateful.

When Alex had gone off with her father, the dog crept closer to Kate, wriggling ingratiatingly. Really he wasn't very beautiful, but his liquid brown eyes were so trusting that her heart melted.

She knew that she shouldn't let herself get too attached to him either. She couldn't keep him and would have to find him a good home somewhere else but, still, she lifted him up, unable to resist the appeal of that tail. He was small enough to sit on her lap, where he licked her hands and curled up comfortably.

To hell with professionalism, Kate decided. It wasn't as if he was stopping her working. She could still type and email and make phone calls.

It was nearly half past two by the time Finn and Alex returned, laden with basket, toys, bowls, a pooper scooper, and dog food, as well as the lead and collar that had been the ostensible purpose of the exercise. Kate quickly put Derek on the floor before Finn spotted him.

He—Finn, not the dog—wore a resigned expression as

Alex proudly showed Kate what she had persuaded her father to buy.

'Here's his collar,' she said, producing it with a flourish.

Kate couldn't help laughing when she saw it. It was made of red velvet and studded with mock diamonds, the kind of nonsense that cost a fortune.

'Don't tell me!' she said. 'Your dad chose this!'

The irony went over Alex's head, but Kate saw the corner of Finn's mouth twitch, and felt as if she had conquered Everest. OK, it wasn't exactly a smile, but it was a response.

She forced her attention back to Alex, who was assuring her that it was a present. 'I used my own money,' she said proudly.

'That's very nice of you,' said Kate, looking doubtfully at the pile of goodies for Derek. Alex must have a very generous allowance.

'Dad paid for the rest,' Alex admitted, almost as if she had read her mind.

Kate glanced at Finn. That tantalising glimpse of humour had vanished, leaving him aloof and austere once more. 'I'll write you a cheque,' she promised.

'Please don't,' he said. 'I'd rather forget the whole business as soon as possible. I can think of better ways to spend a lunch hour than trailing around the pet department being subjected to emotional blackmail by a nine-year-old!'

'Well, thank you anyway,' said Kate, deciding to make it up to him somehow later. She stooped to fasten the collar around Derek, who shook himself at the unfamiliar feel of it. 'Look how smart you are now!' she told him, and smiled at Alex. 'It *was* kind of you to give up your lunch for him.'

'I had a pizza as well,' Alex had to admit.

Kate laughed, even as her own stomach rumbled with hunger. 'I didn't think your dad would let you go hungry.'

'Look, we brought you a sandwich,' said Alex to her

surprise, taking a bag from her father. 'Dad said you needed some lunch.'

Kate peered into the bag to find half a baguette temptingly stuffed with chicken and bacon and avocado. All of her favourite things in fact. How on earth had he known?

She lifted her eyes to meet Finn's, and something shifted in the air between them. 'Thank you,' she said, ridiculously breathless.

'I can't afford to have you passing out from hunger,' he said gruffly. 'We've still got a lot to do this afternoon.'

Still, he had thought of her. A little thrill went through Kate at the knowledge, at least until she managed to suppress it. Letting herself feel little thrills like that about Finn would be bad, bad, bad, and Bella's voice seemed to echo in her ears. *Don't do it, Kate.*

She moistened her lips and handed him a folder of letters for him to sign. 'I've made those appointments you wanted, and the final draft of the tender is being copied right now.'

'And the arrangements for next Thursday?'

'Yes, they're done.'

'You've been busy,' he grunted, and in spite of everything Kate felt herself warm at his grudging approval.

Oh, dear, careful, Kate, she warned herself.

She was busy all afternoon, and in the end Finn arranged for one of the girls from reception to go with Alex when she wanted to take Derek for a little walk. The rest of the time the little girl was quite happy to play with him and the two of them spent hours chasing balls up and down the corridor, but by five o'clock they were both flagging.

Kate knocked on Finn's door. 'I think Alex needs to go home,' she said, bracing herself for him to tell her to mind her own business. 'I'll stay and finish up here if you want to go.'

Finn looked at his watch and frowned. 'I didn't realise

the time. Yes, I'd better take her home.' He glanced at Kate. 'Are you sure?'

'Yes. I owe you extra time anyway after I was late this morning. Then we can call it quits,' she suggested. 'I don't mind staying, honestly. I don't want to take the dog home in the rush hour, and anyway, there's not that much more to do.'

'Well...thanks,' said Finn roughly as he got to his feet and shrugged on his jacket. He sounded deeply uncomfortable and Kate guessed that he didn't like having to be grateful to anyone for anything.

'It's nothing,' she said, brushing it aside. 'I'm sorry for all the hassle I've caused.'

Finn was patting his pockets for his keys. 'What are you going to do about that dog?' he asked abruptly as Kate turned for the door.

'My parents live in the country. They love animals and they've got lots of space, so I'm sure they'd take him, but they're away on holiday at the moment, and won't be back for a few weeks. I'll keep him with me in the meantime.'

She chewed her lip as she considered what it would mean. 'It would mean leaving him all day, but I could walk him as soon as I got home—unless I could bring him to the office with me?' She looked at Finn hopefully. 'He wouldn't be any trouble. You've seen how quiet he is.'

Right on cue came the sound of excited barking and Alex's laugh. Finn looked at Kate.

'Normally,' she added.

Finn sighed. 'I think Alex is going to be more of a problem than the dog. She won't want to be separated from it now.'

He was right. Alex was adamant that Derek should go home with her. 'He's just got used to me,' she protested. 'He'll be confused if I leave him now.'

'You trust me to look after him, don't you?' said Kate,

trying to defuse the imminent stand-off between Finn and his daughter.

'It's not that.' Alex's bottom lip stuck out mutinously. 'If I can't take him home, I won't see him again, and I want to keep him,' she wailed. 'Please, Dad! You know I've always wanted a dog.'

Finn raked his fingers through his hair in frustration. 'Alex, you know it's not possible for you to look after a dog. You're at school all day.'

'Rosa wouldn't mind looking after him during the day.'

'I'm not so sure about that, and anyway, Rosa's not there, so we can't ask her at the moment.'

The bottom lip wobbled. 'But what's going to happen to him?'

Patiently, Finn explained that Kate would look after the dog until she could take it down to her parents.

'Well, couldn't I keep him until then?' pleaded Alex desperately.

'He'll still need a walk during the day, Alex.'

Alex pounced on the flaw in her father's argument. 'How is Kate going to walk him then? She's at work longer than I'm at school.'

Finn gritted his teeth at the realisation that he had been boxed into a corner. He was going to have to give in to one of them. 'Kate's going to bring him into the office,' he said, succumbing to the inevitable.

'Then why couldn't you bring him in, Dad?' Alex persisted. 'You've got a car, so it wouldn't make any difference to you. I'd walk him in the morning and in the evening when you bring him home, and he could spend the day with you.'

Finn cast a meaningful look at Kate. It was crystal clear that he thought that it was her dog and her responsibility to knock the idea on its head once and for all. Kate met his eyes with a bland smile. She was rather enjoying seeing Finn comprehensively out-argued by a nine-year-old.

'I think that's a good idea,' she said, wilfully ignoring her cue and Finn's baleful glare. 'I could walk him at lunch time so your dad doesn't have to be bothered with him,' she offered to Alex, whose face brightened instantly.

'Oh, yes, *please!*'

'And what happens when Alison comes back?' demanded Finn, annoyed at being outmanoeuvred. 'She might not feel like walking a dog in her lunch break!'

Alex barely missed a beat. 'Rosa's mother might be better then and she can come back. I bet she wouldn't mind Derek.'

Kate suppressed a smile at Finn's expression. 'You've done a wonderful job of bringing Alex up,' she told him with mock seriousness. 'Not many girls of nine could argue so well! You must be very proud of her.'

'I don't think I'd choose proud to describe the way I'm feeling right now,' said Finn, exasperated, but it was obvious that he had decided that he was fighting a losing battle.

'Very well,' he said, turning back to his daughter. 'But—'

He was interrupted by Alex throwing herself into his arms with a shriek of delight. 'Oh, thank you, thank you, thank you!' she cried, almost drowned out by Derek who went into a frenzy of shrill barking as he picked up on the excitement.

For a moment, there was chaos, and Kate couldn't help laughing. At the same time she couldn't help being touched by the way Finn hugged his daughter back. He might hide behind a gruff exterior but it was obvious that they adored each other.

Kate even felt a little bit excluded, which of course was ridiculous. *She* didn't want to be gathered up and hugged and included in their little family unit with the dog. She was supposed to be a hip metropolitan chick, not yearning for security and love, right?

Right.

'*But*—' Finn managed to raise his voice above the commotion at last. 'On one condition. You're not to get too attached to this dog, Alex. You're at school, I'm at work, and it's not part of Rosa's job to walk a dog. You can take him home with you now, but only as long as Kate is working here, or until she can take him to her parents. That's the deal. OK?'

Alex looked up at him speculatively. Kate could practically hear her thinking that this was the best offer she was going to get for now, so she might as well accept and find another plan for when the first one came to an end.

'OK,' she said, and looking at the tilt of her chin, so like her father's, Kate thought that Finn was probably going to end up having a dog whether he wanted it or not.

Kate herself thought it had worked out pretty well. Her parents would take Derek, of course, but she didn't really want to ask them again, having landed them with so many other waifs and strays in the past. She wished she could keep Derek, but it was hopeless when you were temping and, anyway, she could already see the bond that existed between the dog and the little girl. Derek would be happier with Alex.

'I hope Alison never comes back,' Alex whispered when Finn went to get his coat, and Kate was disconcerted to realise that she didn't want Alison to come back either.

The next morning it was Finn's turn to be late. He came into the office with Derek prancing and chewing on his lead, to find Kate sitting behind her desk and looking innocently at her watch.

'Don't say anything!' he warned her, unamused.

Kate grinned. 'I wasn't going to.'

'I suppose you realise that you and this dog between you have completely disrupted my life?' grumbled Finn, letting Derek go as he recognised his saviour of the day before and went into frenzy of excitement.

Released, he dashed over to Kate, who picked him up, still wriggling ecstatically, but then had to turn her head away from his attempts to lick her cheek and chin, her face lit with laughter.

The suit had had to go to the cleaners after yesterday's encounter with a pile of rubbish, so she was back to wearing a long skirt in some vaguely ethnic pattern with a top that clung to her curves and was, in spite of its long sleeves and high neck, somehow much more disturbing than the more revealing one she had worn to dinner at Phoebe and Gib's.

She had given up on her hair as well, and it fell in soft brown curls to her shoulders. To Finn she looked vaguely scruffy but startlingly warm and vivid as she stood there with the squirming dog in her arms against the background of sterile office equipment.

'That dog is completely out of control,' he said, his voice very dry as if his throat was tight.

'Oh, but he's so sweet! How could he possibly be any trouble?'

'Have you ever tried taking him for a walk? He's got no idea how to walk on a lead and if you let him off he goes round in manic circles or runs off and won't come back. It's hard enough getting Alex to school on time as it is without coping with a miniature whirlwind on four legs. *And* he's chewed my best shoes!'

'Well, he's just a puppy,' said Kate. 'That's what puppies do. You'll have to be careful to keep things out of his reach.'

'That's not a puppy, that's a fully grown dog and uncontrollable with it!'

'Nonsense,' she said briskly, and Derek squirmed with pleasure as she kissed the top of his head. 'You just need a bit of training, don't you? We'll have you sitting and staying in no time.'

Finn snorted. 'You take him, then, and while you're at it, train him to do something useful like make breakfast or tidy the kitchen.' He sighed as he took off his coat. 'God, what a morning! It's bad enough Alison being away without losing Rosa as well.'

'When is she coming back?' asked Kate, putting the dog back on the ground and trying not to feel hurt at the knowledge that he was missing Alison.

'Not soon enough!' Finn picked up the letters Kate had opened for him and began to flick through them. 'I'm not the most domesticated of men, and there's only so much take-away food that you can stomach. But Rosa's mother is still in hospital and she doesn't know how long she's going to be away.'

'Couldn't you get someone to help temporarily?'

'It's a bit difficult not knowing how long it would be for. Besides, Alex hates change. She doesn't like having a housekeeper at all and would rather it was just the two of us. She tolerates Rosa, but that's about as far as it goes.'

'I can see it's difficult,' said Kate, and Finn frowned as if recollecting too late that he was confiding his personal concerns.

'Yes, well, I'd better get on,' he said abruptly. 'Any messages?'

'Mr Osborne's PA rang. Could you call him back?'

'What does he want?'

Kate consulted her notebook. 'I gather he wants you to go and see him this afternoon. There are some points he wants to clarify before they make their final decision. What's the problem?' she asked as Finn cursed under his breath.

'I'll have to go. We can't afford to lose that contract, but I promised Alex I'd pick her up from school today as it's Friday. She wants everyone to see the dog.'

He stuck his hands in his pockets and frowned worriedly at the floor. 'She's always been a very solitary child—inevitable I suppose—but I hoped she'd make more friends at this new school. This morning's the first time she's shown any interest in what the other children thought,' he went on reluctantly. 'I'm afraid that if she's told everyone about the dog and he doesn't appear they'll think she's been making it up.'

'Why don't I go and meet her with Derek?' Kate offered, and his head jerked up to stare at her.

'You'd do that?'

Kate couldn't quite meet his eyes. She wasn't quite sure what had prompted her impulsive offer herself. It couldn't be wanting to ease the lines of strain around his mouth or the worry from his voice...could it?

'I wouldn't mind,' she said. 'It's partly my fault anyway. If I hadn't landed you with a dog, you wouldn't be in this situation.'

Finn hesitated. 'I might not get back until after seven if Osborne's in a nit-picking mood.'

'That's all right.' She busied herself sorting the papers on her desk into neat piles. 'I'll stay with Alex until you get home.'

'Are you sure? It's Friday night. Haven't you got anything planned?'

'Nothing special,' said Kate, 'and anyway, I can always go out later.'

'No heavy date with a financial analyst then?'

'What? Oh.' Colour crept into her cheeks as she remembered the elaborate story she had made up to impress him. 'No, that's the advantage of a fantasy man,' she said, putting up her chin. 'He fits in with all your other arrangements. He's the perfect man, really.'

'I see.' A disconcerting gleam lit Finn's grey eyes. 'Well, if you're sure you don't mind, I'd really appreciate it if you could go and meet Alex. I'll give you a note for the school and arrange for a car to take you there and then on home.'

Why was she doing this? Kate wondered as she sat with Derek in the back of the limousine Finn had booked. She had been so determined to stay cool and professional, too. Bella would say that she was getting involved, but she wasn't really. She was just helping out in a crisis. She'd do the same for anyone.

It was nothing whatsoever to do with the warm glow inside her when she remembered the almost-smile in Finn's eyes and the approval in his voice.

Because that wouldn't be at all professional, would it?

Standing at the school gates with all the other mothers and nannies was an odd experience. Kate could feel their curious sidelong glances at the impostor. She was sure they were all wondering what on earth she was doing there. What would it be like to be one of them, a bona fide mother instead of a pretend one? To be waiting for your own children, to take them home to the warmth and security of a loving home?

Kate had never allowed herself to think about having children too much. Even in the depths of her obsession with Seb she had known that he would be aghast at the very idea of children. Seb needed the world to revolve around him, and he wouldn't want to share the attention with anyone else, least of all a baby who wouldn't blend in with his décor. He was much too fickle and unreliable to make a good father anyway, unlike Finn.

Just for instance.

When the children started pouring out into the playground, Kate wrenched her mind away from the thought of

Finn as a father and craned her neck to find Alex. She spotted her at last, searching the crowd in her turn for her father. Kate saw the moment when it dawned on her that he wasn't there, and sullenness masked the bitterness of her disappointment.

Pushing forward through the press of mothers and push-chairs with Derek, she waved to get her attention. 'Alex!' she called.

The terrible withdrawn look was wiped from Alex's face as she caught sight of Kate with the dog. It lit up instead and she rushed towards them.

'Dad's really sorry he couldn't come,' said Kate quickly, 'but he sent Derek instead. You don't mind, do you?'

'Not if Derek's here,' said Alex, crouching down so that the little dog could put his paws on her knees and greet her properly.

There was soon a circle of curious children staring at Derek. 'He's my dog,' said Alex nonchalantly, and Kate approved the careless way she dealt with the attention, as if it didn't matter to her whether anyone envied her or not.

Derek played his part brilliantly, greeting every child with enthusiasm and generally behaving in such an en-dearing way that none of them could resist asking Alex if they could pet him. He was clearly winning her lots of kudos in the playground, and her cheeks were pink with satisfaction when she finally left, holding tightly onto Derek's lead and waving a casual farewell.

The office was so modern and streamlined that Kate had somehow expected Finn to live somewhere similar, but it turned out to be a substantial Victorian house close to Wimbledon Common, with a large, safe garden. Ideal for a dog, in fact.

Inside, the house had evidently been decorated profes-sionally, but it had a sterile, unlived-in air that Kate thought was rather sad. It was a house and not a home, and she wondered whether it had been that way since Isabel had died.

Alex led the way to a big kitchen with French windows opening onto the garden. 'I wanted Derek to sleep in my room, but Dad said he had to stay here,' she told Kate, pointing out the basket and bowls set out in the corner.

'He's probably better off in the kitchen,' said Kate tactfully. That must have been another battle of wills. No wonder Finn had looked harassed this morning!

She looked around the kitchen while Alex had a drink and then, remembering what he had said about being sick of take-away food, suggested that they walk Derek along to the shops and buy something to cook for supper.

'You can cook?' Alex looked at her strangely.

'Well, nothing very impressive, but I can knock up the basics. What do you like to eat?'

Alex was fascinated by the fact that Kate knew how to make her favourite meal, macaroni cheese. 'Rosa doesn't make it, I don't think they have it where she comes from,' she said. 'Can you make puddings too?'

'Yes, some. Why, do you want a pudding as well?'

'Dad likes puddings, but Rosa's not very good at them either.'

Kate liked the idea of Finn having a weakness, even if it was only a sweet tooth. 'Do you think he'd like a chocolate pudding?' she asked Alex.

'Oh, yes, he loves chocolate.'

Better and better.

'Well, let's see what we can do.'

When Finn came home, he found his daughter, his temporary secretary and the dog in the kitchen. Unnoticed by any of them, he hesitated in the doorway, taking in the scene. Normally Alex retreated to her room, but today she was sitting happily at the kitchen table, the dog panting at her feet, helping Kate cook. There was flour everywhere and the sink was piled with dirty bowls and cooking implements. Alex's face was smudged with chocolate, and Kate's was not much better.

It struck Finn that he had never seen the kitchen look messier or more welcoming.

Kate was wearing Rosa's apron. She looked warm and dishevelled, her cheeks pink and her brown curls tumbled. As Finn watched, she lifted a hand to push her hair back from her face, leaving a streak of flour on her forehead.

'Not much of a guard dog, is he?' Finn's sarcasm disguised the sudden dryness in his throat.

At the sound of his voice, Kate started and Derek leapt belatedly to his feet, barking and wagging his tail so furiously that it would have taken a much harder heart than Finn's not to feel gratified at the warmth of his welcome.

'He's pleased to see you,' Alex told him as he bent to kiss his daughter.

Kate bent her head over the bowl into which she was sifting flour and tried to get her breathing back to normal. The sudden sight of Finn in the doorway had sent her heart lurching into her throat, where it lodged, jerking madly.

Shock at seeing him so unexpectedly, Kate told herself, in which case she wished her heart would just calm down. There was nothing to get excited about. It was just Finn, Finn with his cool eyes and his stern mouth and dark, austere presence. Nothing to make her senses fizz, or the breath evaporate from her lungs. And absolutely no reason to suddenly feel so ridiculously, embarrassingly shy.

'Hello,' she croaked in return to his greeting and carried on sifting with a kind of desperation.

Under her lashes, she could see Finn taking off his jacket and wrenching at his tie to loosen it. 'Something smells good,' he said.

'Kate's made macaroni cheese.' Alex tugged at his sleeve excitedly. 'And I have to have some salad, but then there's a chocolate pudding. We made it especially for you.'

Finn glanced at Kate, who blushed hotly and made a big deal of banging the sieve against the edge of the bowl. 'Alex said you liked chocolate.'

'I do.'

'I hope you don't mind me taking over your kitchen like this,' said Kate awkwardly. 'I thought I might as well make supper for you since I was here.'

'Mind?' echoed Finn. 'I'm very grateful!'

He seemed less dour and formidable than usual, as if the rigidity had gone from his jaw and his spine. It was only natural, Kate thought. He was at home, so it wasn't surprising if he was more relaxed than at the office.

But it was more disturbing, too. She wasn't sure how to deal with Finn when he was being approachable like this, and it made her nervous in a way that his brusqueness didn't any more.

'I won't be long,' she said, uncertain as to what she ought to do now, 'and I'll tidy up before I go.'

'But you'll stay and eat with us, won't you?' said Finn, and Alex added her voice as well.

'Oh, yes, you must stay!'

He might be just being polite. Kate twisted the sieve between her hands. Part of her longed to stay, and the other part was apprehensive. She felt very odd, all jittery and jumpy and it was something to do with the way Finn was standing there, looking at her.

Don't do it. Wasn't that what Bella had said?

'Well, I—'

'You said you didn't have anything special on tonight,' Finn reminded her.

'No, but—'

'I'll get a taxi to take you home later,' he promised. And

then, almost as if the words were forced out of him, 'Please stay.'

What could she say? 'All right,' said Kate. 'Thanks.'

At which point Finn really threw her by smiling. A real smile. At her. 'I'm the one who should be thanking you,' he said.

Kate's hands were shaking as he went to change. She had imagined what he would look like when he smiled often enough, but she was still unprepared for how it transformed his face, illuminating those piercing grey eyes and softening the hard mouth. It had only been a brief smile, enough to glimpse the whiteness of his teeth and the way it creased his cheek and the edges of his eyes, but hardly enough to justify the sudden weakness at her knees or the bump and thump of her heart which had already been working overtime ever since he walked into the kitchen.

Guiltily, Kate faced the fact. She was doing exactly what Bella had warned her against. She had felt sorry for Finn since learning his tragic story, and now she was fancying herself attracted to him.

Which was just silly. She had had enough of falling for unobtainable men, and they didn't come more unobtainable than Finn. Not only was he utterly committed to the memory of his dead wife, but he was her boss. Getting involved when she had to see him every day at the office was a bad idea.

A *very* bad idea given that Alison would be coming back soon, and then where would she be? She was supposed to be out there meeting someone with whom she could have some fun, Kate reminded herself, not stuck in a Wimbledon kitchen with an apron on, all twitchy and flustered because Finn had smiled at her.

She was just going to have to pull herself together. She

had helped him out today, but that was as far as it was going to go. She would have supper, Kate decided, and then she would leave and she wouldn't even *think* about getting any closer.

CHAPTER FIVE

'THIS is a nice room.'

Alex had gone to bed and Finn had suggested to Kate that they had coffee in the sitting room. He had pulled the heavy red curtains across the window to shut out the cold, dark night, and had put on a lamp in the corner. Now he bent to switch on the fire. It was gas, but the appearance of real flames was very effective.

A bit *too* effective, Kate thought. The flickering light made the room dark and intimate, and now she was even more nervous about being alone with him. It hadn't been too bad while Alex was there, but now there was only Derek as chaperon and, in spite of all her efforts to keep up a flow of bright conversation, a tension was seeping back into the atmosphere.

It was Finn's fault, she had decided. He looked different tonight. It was the first time she had seen him out of a suit. He'd changed before supper and, in casual trousers and a warm shirt, he seemed younger, less austere, and Kate was disturbingly aware of him.

She tried not to look at him as he straightened from the fire and sat down at the other end of the sofa, which was when she was forced to make her inane comment about the room instead.

Finn glanced round as if he had never seen it before. 'I don't use this room very much,' he said. 'It's too big. I rattle around in it when I'm on my own. I usually sit in my study.'

Kate thought of this beautiful room sitting empty while Finn retreated to his study every night. 'It must get lonely sometimes,' she said, and felt Finn's eyes flicker to her face and then away.

'I'm used to it now,' he said.

Kate swirled the wine around the bottom of her glass. 'Do you miss her all the time?' she asked, emboldened by the darkness and the firelight.

'Isabel?' Finn sighed and stared into the flames. 'It was hell at first, but now…it comes and goes. Sometimes I think I've accepted that she's gone and others I miss her so much it's like a physical pain. I look at Alex and I get angry that she didn't get the chance to see her daughter growing up.'

'I'm sorry,' said Kate quietly, not knowing what else she could say.

Finn looked across at her again, his face unreadable in the dim light. 'You know what happened?'

'Someone at work told me it was a car accident.'

He nodded. 'She was in a coma for a week. I couldn't do anything, I could only sit there and hold her hand and tell her how much I loved her.' He turned back to the fire. 'The doctors said she couldn't hear me.'

Kate's throat ached for him. 'Maybe she could feel you.'

'That's what I told myself. I promised her that I would look after Alex, that I'd do on my own, for both of us, but I'm beginning to wonder if I can keep that promise.'

Draining the last of his wine, Finn leant forward to put the glass on the coffee-table in front of them. 'It's hard being a single parent. The worst bit is not having anyone to share your worries with. Alex can be difficult sometimes, and that's when I miss Isabel most. She was so calm and gentle. She would know how to handle her.'

'But Alex seems very happy,' said Kate, thinking of the way the little girl had chattered through supper.

'Thanks to you.'

Kate's jaw dropped. 'To me?'

'She's happier now than I've seen her for a very long

time, and it's because of that mutt you gave us.' He stirred Derek with his foot where he lay under the coffee-table, and ecstatic at the least bit of attention, the dog rolled over onto his back with a sigh of contentment.

'Alex doesn't make friends easily,' Finn went on. 'She's very reserved for a child. I worry that she's too possessive of me, too.'

'I suppose that's inevitable when it's just the two of you,' said Kate.

'Perhaps.' He leant forward, resting his elbows on his knees, and the firelight cast flickering shadows across his face, highlighting then concealing the lines of strain. 'She resents the fact that we have to have a housekeeper, and doesn't understand why it can't just be the two of us.

'I've thought about selling the company and staying at home,' he admitted, 'but what would happen to everyone who's worked for me so loyally, and what would I do with myself? Alex is at school all day. There's only so much cooking and cleaning I can do, and I'd still have to make a living somehow.'

Finn hunched his shoulders. He had obviously been over his options again and again. 'The other alternative, of course, is to marry again,' he said. 'Alex is growing up. She's going to need a woman around even more, but it doesn't seem fair to ask someone to marry me just to be a stepmother…'

He trailed off with a hopeless gesture. He sounded so tired that Kate had a terrifying impulse to put her arms around him, to draw his head down onto her breast and tell him that everything would be all right, that she was there.

Not the best way to go about not getting involved.

Swallowing hard, she stared at the fire instead. 'Is that why you came to dinner with Gib and Phoebe? Looking for a suitable stepmother?'

'Partly,' said Finn. 'I'd talked myself into making an

effort to go out and meet more people. I thought maybe if I actually met someone, things might change somehow, but…'

'But you just met me,' Kate finished for him.

'Yes,' said Finn after a moment. 'I met you.'

There was a silence. To Kate it seemed to last for ever, fraught with unspoken implications. That she wasn't the kind of stepmother he was looking for, that she hadn't changed anything for him. Or that she might have done if she hadn't turned out to be working for him?

Or if she hadn't been determined not to get involved, of course.

It was Finn who broke the silence. 'What were *you* doing there?'

'Phoebe's one of my best friends.'

'Did you know I was going to be there?'

'Yes. I didn't know it was *you* of course,' Kate added hurriedly, 'but I knew that they'd invited someone for me to meet.'

Finn looked at her curiously. 'I don't understand it.'

'What do you mean?'

'You're a pretty girl,' he said. 'You must know that. You're lively, intelligent—when you want to be, anyway—and you've obviously got lots of friends. I'd have thought men would be queuing up to take you out. Why would a girl like you need her friends to fix her up on a blind date?'

Kate shrugged. 'It's not as easy as you think, especially when you get past thirty. All the nice men are settled in relationships, usually with your friends, and you end up making a fool of yourself over the ones that are available.' A tinge of bitterness crept into her voice. 'That's what seems to happen to me, anyway.'

'Not Will the financial analyst?'

'No.' Kate half smiled. She might as well admit it. 'Will exists all right, but he's Bella's boyfriend, not mine. I just borrowed him for my little fantasy to try and impress you. Not that it worked.'

'I don't know,' said Finn. 'You had me convinced for a while.'

Without thinking, Kate had made herself more comfortable, putting her feet up onto the coffee-table and leaning back into the cushions so that she could rest her head against the back of the sofa. Finn's eyes rested on her face.

'So if it wasn't Will, who was it?'

'His name's Seb.' Kate looked up at the ceiling, remembering. 'I was mad about him. He was one of the junior executives where I used to work, and I used to fantasise about him from afar. He was so good-looking and charming and he had a terrible reputation—but of course, that was part of his appeal,' she said ironically. 'When he noticed me amongst all the other girls there, I couldn't believe my luck.'

She sighed a little. 'Phoebe and Bella never liked him, but I was in thrall to him. It's hard to explain now. He had this kind of sexual charisma. I couldn't think properly when I was with him.

'I told them they didn't understand him the way I did. I persuaded myself that his selfishness was a result of the way he'd been brought up and that there was a little lost boy inside him. I thought that all he needed was the love of a good woman, and that I'd be the one to change him, you know the sort of thing.' She laughed but there was an undercurrent of bitterness to it. 'I was such a fool.'

'We all make mistakes,' said Finn neutrally.

'Most people learn from theirs. I didn't.' Kate leant forward to pick up her coffee. 'We had what magazines call a "destructive relationship". I humiliated myself for months. I'd go out of my way just to bump into him, and wait desperately for him to call. I got obsessed with checking the phone and my email, and Seb knew it. He'd say that he would contact me, then he'd ignore my existence, until I'd just given up hope.

'He always timed it perfectly. He'd ring or drop round out of the blue, and I'd be so pleased to see him that I didn't realise until too late that he was only there because he wanted something. He wanted to borrow some money or get his washing done.'

Kate caught Finn's look. 'Oh, yes,' she said with a rueful smile. 'I'd wash and iron and cook and clean for him. I cringe when I think about it now, but at the time it seemed the only way I could keep him.'

She must sound completely pathetic. Finn would probably despise such spineless behaviour, but it was hard to tell from his expression what he was thinking.

'What made you change your mind about him?' was all he asked.

'I went up to his office one evening,' Kate told him. 'I'd found an excuse to work late as usual, knowing that he'd be there, and I found him shouting at one of the cleaners. I don't even know what she was supposed to have done, but the poor woman was terrified. English obviously wasn't her first language, and I just hoped that she couldn't understand half the things he was calling her.

'It was horrible,' she said with a shudder at the memory. 'I couldn't believe how unpleasant he was! When I told him he couldn't talk to people like, he turned on me, and we had a huge argument. I ended up saying that I was going to report him for verbal abuse.'

'And what did Seb say to that?'

'He told me not to bother, because *he* was going to report *me* for harassment.'

'And who do you think they're going to believe?' Seb had sneered. 'A not very efficient secretary or a rising executive?'

'That's exactly what he did,' Kate finished. 'And I lost my job.'

Finn was looking grim. 'Couldn't you fight it?'

'The trouble was that everyone knew I was mad about him, and the way I'd made excuses to see him made it easy for him to make everyone believe that I was practically stalking him. Of course he didn't tell anyone about the times he showed up on *my* doorstep.'

'Is that why you had to leave your job?' Finn sounded even grimmer now.

'Yes. Oh, I wasn't sacked. Nothing as crude as that. It was merely suggested that I might be happier elsewhere, and that if I stayed my position might become ''untenable''.' Kate hooked her fingers in the air to add extra emphasis to the pomposity of the phrases they had used.

Seb had been promoted. She didn't tell Finn that.

'You should have appealed,' he said, frowning.

She shrugged. 'By that stage I didn't want to work there any longer anyway. It was ironic, really. After all those months desperate to catch a glimpse of Seb, the moment I didn't want to see him any more, he seemed to be around the whole time. I was glad to leave.

'The only trouble was that they gave me a really grudging reference, which meant I couldn't get another job,' she went on. 'Joining the temp agency was my only option in the end, and working for you is my first job with them.' No harm in reassuring Finn that she hadn't forgotten that their relationship was strictly professional.

She smiled brightly at him. 'That's why I have to try and make a good impression and stick with you until Alison gets back.'

It was true. If Finn gave her a rotten report, she might find herself off the agency's list, but Kate didn't think there was any need to labour the point.

'Is that what you're doing now?' he said, putting his coffee-mug very deliberately back onto the coffee table.

'Now?' she echoed blankly.

'Picking Alex up from school, making supper, all of this.' There was a harsh note in his voice, almost as if he was disappointed.

'No,' said Kate. 'I didn't even think about it. Besides, the ability to make macaroni cheese isn't the kind of thing employers look for in a reference. I was just hoping you'd notice that I was being more punctual and efficient.'

'I see,' was all Finn said, but he sounded less hard.

'It's all part of my new attitude,' Kate went on to make sure he understood that she was in absolutely no danger of misinterpreting that they were alone in the dark and fire-light.

'I've decided to sharpen up my act all round. Seb taught me a valuable lesson—two, in fact. From now on I'm going to keep my personal life quite separate from work, and I'm not going to get too serious about anyone. I'm going to take any opportunity to meet new people, even if it means going on a blind date. So when Phoebe rang and said they had invited someone to meet me, I thought "why not"? I wasn't interested in finding a deep and meaningful relationship,' she told him. 'I just wanted some fun.'

'But you just met me,' Finn quoted Kate's words back to her.

Something in his voice made Kate turn her head. He was watching her from the other end of the sofa, his expression unreadable, but his eyes trapped hers without warning, stopping the breath in her throat and holding her mouse-still, skewered by the directness of his gaze. Kate wasn't sure how long they sat there with the air evaporating around them, and the silence stretching unbearably, broken only by the faint hiss and splutter of the gas fire and the booming roar of her pulse in her ear, but when Finn looked away it was like being released from a pinion-hold.

Now all she had to do was remember what they had been talking about before she turned her head.

Ah, yes. Impressing on him that she was just out to have a good time and not in the market for marriage or anything remotely serious. So he needn't panic.

'Yes, it was a bit of a shock.' She forced a smile. 'It's not much fun to find yourself on a blind date with your boss.'

'No,' said Finn, looking into the fire. 'I imagine not.'

It was all very well convincing Finn that she just wanted to have a good time, but Kate found it harder to live up to in practice. There was no problem about going out. Bella was relentlessly social, and Kate could always tag along with her. But somehow going out wasn't quite as much fun as it had used to be.

Kate was exasperated to find herself in the middle of a party, fretting about how Finn and Alex were managing with the housekeeper still away. It wasn't her problem, she reminded herself endlessly. She was supposed to be having fun and being cool, and worrying about grieving widowers and motherless children wasn't part of the plan.

Sitting in a bar with a City type baying at her about his bonuses and his flash car, or pretending to study the menu in a crowded restaurant, Kate would find her mind wandering to the house in Wimbledon. She thought about Alex and the little dog, but mostly she thought about Finn, sitting at the other end of the sofa in the firelight. She thought about the way his smile illuminated the severe face, about the line of that stern mouth and, whenever she did, which was too often for comfort, something twisted and churned inside her.

It was even worse in the office, though. She was jittery

and on edge in the same room as Finn, and if he came anywhere near her she would suddenly become clumsy, spilling her coffee or dropping papers, and colouring painfully when he looked at her in surprise.

Only three weeks until Alison was due back. Kate wasn't sure whether she longed for an end to the daily embarrassment of making a complete fool of herself, or dreaded it. Sometimes she tried to imagine working for someone else, in a different office, but she just couldn't do it. No dog to walk every lunch time. No willing her nerves not to jump whenever Finn walked into the room.

No Finn.

Ever since that evening when she had picked Alex up from school the atmosphere between them had been one of careful constraint. Finn was gruff but polite, and Kate found herself wishing more than once that he would go back to shouting at her and being grumpy and generally disagreeable. Things had been easier then.

Somehow Kate struggled through to the Friday, but by that afternoon she was in no fit state to deal with the long and complicated list of instructions Finn decided to give her. Sitting across the desk from him, she was supposed to be taking notes, but she kept getting diverted by the sight of his hands as he moved papers around, or letting her eyes rest on his mouth while he searched for a particular bit of information, and then when he looked up again, his eyes would be so piercing that she instantly lost track of what she was supposed to be doing.

'Are you all right?' Finn asked at last, after she had had to ask him to repeat himself for the sixth time.

'I'm fine,' stammered Kate, colour rushing into her cheeks. Honestly, it was getting to the point where she couldn't talk to him without blushing like an idiot.

'It's just that you seem even vaguer than usual today.'

'No, I'm a bit tired that's all,' she said. 'I had a late

night.' That was true enough, she had been out with Bella. 'We went out to a club, and you know what it's like when you're having good time,' she went on, spotting another opportunity to persuade Finn that, while she might be behaving like a love-struck schoolgirl, it was nothing whatsoever to do with him.

'You forget to look at your watch,' she told him, all ditzy brunette, the kind of girl who danced till the small hours and whose only aim in life was to have fun. The last kind of girl to waste her time even *thinking* about a man preoccupied with domestic problems.

'I'll take your word for it,' said Finn dryly.

He paused, shuffling papers unnecessarily. 'I told Alex that you had a very social life,' he said unexpectedly, 'but I promised her that I'd ask you anyway.'

'Ask me what?' said Kate, surprised into normality.

'She seems to regard you as an authority on dogs. God knows, you've got to know more than we do anyway! Anyway, she wanted to know if you'd come over and show her how to train Derek one afternoon this weekend. Apparently you told her that you would give her a few tips,' he went on almost accusingly, as if the invitation was her fault somehow.

She *had* promised Alex that she would show her how to train Derek, Kate remembered. That wasn't the problem. The problem was how much she wanted to go.

'I told her you'd be busy,' Finn said as she hesitated.

'No…no…I'm not busy,' said Kate, who had opened her mouth to take the let-out clause he offered and found herself saying something completely different instead.

'I mean, an afternoon would be fine,' she stumbled on, her mouth still operating contrary to strict orders from her brain which was telling her to do the sensible thing and not get any more involved than she was already. 'Perhaps we could go for a walk on one of the parks?'

'That's kind of you,' Finn said in such a stilted voice that Kate wondered if he had wanted her to refuse. 'Alex will be pleased.'

What about you? she wanted to ask him. Will you be pleased?

'Would Sunday afternoon suit you?' he was saying, still repressively polite.

'Sunday would be fine.'

'We'll come and pick you up in the car. About two o'clock?'

In spite of giving herself a good talking to on the way home, and reminding herself of all the reasons why she didn't want to get involved with Finn or his daughter or his dog, Kate was appalled at how much she looked forward to Sunday afternoon. Saturday night, another wild session orchestrated by Bella, was just an endurance test, and she left as early as she decently could, hoping that Bella wouldn't notice her lack of enthusiasm.

No such luck. 'What is up with you at the moment?' Bella accused her when she finally emerged, yawning and tousled, on Sunday morning.

'Nothing,' said Kate brightly.

'I lined up Will's friend specially for you, and you blew him off. I thought Toby would be just your type.'

'He was OK.' Kate fidgeted around the kitchen, putting jars and packets away, and wiping down the work surface with a cloth.

Bella looked at her in deep suspicion. 'And why are you tidying the kitchen suddenly?'

'No reason,' said Kate. 'It's just a mess.'

'It's always a mess and it never bothered you before. Who's coming round?'

'Finn and his daughter might come later.' Kate tried to sound casual, but she should have known better than to try and fool Bella.

'Finn as in the boss you hated and then felt sorry for? The one you had no intention of getting involved with?'

'Yes,' she had to admit.

'Explain to me how having him round to your house on a Sunday afternoon is not being involved?'

'If you must know, it's a date with his daughter. We're going to take the dog for a walk, and Finn's just going to drive us from A to B.'

'Right,' said Bella, obviously not believing a word.

'It's true. I'm only going because I feel a bit responsible for the dog.'

Bella filled the kettle at the sink. 'So what will I tell Toby if he rings and wants to see you again?'

'Absolutely,' said Kate firmly. 'I'm into fun, fun, fun.'

'That'll be why you're getting ready for a *walk* about four hours early! What are you going to wear?'

Oh, God, good point. What *was* she going to wear? Back in her bedroom, Kate rummaged through her clothes. She really must hang some of those skirts up some time.

It was all too difficult. She didn't want to look a mess, but she didn't want to look as if she was trying too hard either. Her jeans were a bit tight, but she squeezed into them and pulled on a red jumper which was one of her favourites. Not that Finn was likely to see it under her jacket, of course.

Unless she offered them some tea? And scones might be nice after a cold walk.

Kate galloped back down to the kitchen and began burrowing through the cupboards for flour and cream of tartar. 'Do you know if we've got any bicarb of soda?'

Bella looked up from the gossip pages in the Sunday paper. 'What do you want that for?'

'I thought I might make some scones,' said Kate carelessly.

'Scones?' Bella shook her head. 'You have got it bad!'

and then when Kate swung round to protest, 'try the cupboard above the toaster.'

Kate fidgeted around the kitchen for the rest of the morning, driving Bella mad by trying to tidy up around her.

'I wish this Finn would just come and put you out of your misery,' Bella grumbled as she gathered up the paper and her coffee and retreated to the sitting room.

By the time the doorbell rang, Kate had worked herself up to a pitch of nerves she couldn't remember since her very first date. Pulling down her jumper, she ran her fingers through her curls and took a deep breath before opening the door.

Finn was standing behind Alex, and Kate's heart gave a great lurch when she saw him. She looked quickly away at Alex, who greeted her with an unselfconscious hug. In similar circumstances Kate would think nothing of kissing a visitor like Finn on the cheek, but the thought of touching him, however briefly, seemed fraught with difficulty, and in the end she contented herself with smiling stiffly.

'Hello.'

Alex sat in the back seat with an over-excited Derek. She was in a chatty mood, so all Kate had to do was nod and smile and put in the occasional comment, which was just as well as she was having trouble concentrating with Finn's hand moving competently on the gears so close to her knee.

It was a relief to get out of the car and concentrate on Alex and the dog. She showed her how to offer little treats when Derek did as he was told, and before long he was sitting and waiting until he was called before he came lolloping towards her.

Alex was delighted. 'He's clever, isn't he, Dad?'

'Clever enough to know what it takes to get some food,' said Finn, who had been watching them with a resigned expression.

Afterwards they walked around the park. It was a cold, blustery day and the wind blew Kate's hair around her face. Alex ran ahead with Derek, while Kate tried not to be too conscious of Finn striding beside her, his head down, his hands thrust into the pockets of his jacket, his dark hair ruffled by the breeze.

Every now and then Alex would come galloping back, her cheeks pink and her eyes shining behind her glasses. 'I wish we could do this every weekend!'

'You never liked walking before,' said Finn.

'It's different if you've got a dog. I'm so glad you came to work for Dad,' she told Kate fervently. 'Aren't you, Dad?'

Finn glanced at Kate, who was trying unsuccessfully to hold her hair back from her face. Her brown eyes were bright in the sharp light and the exercise had brought colour to her cheeks.

'She's certainly changed my life,' he said, and Kate smiled uncertainly, not sure how to take that. Was changing his life a good thing or a bad thing, or was he just joking?

In the end, she decided it would be safer just to ignore it. She asked about the housekeeper instead. 'Will Rosa be coming back soon?'

'We don't know. She's been very good about keeping in touch and she's obviously anxious not to lose the job, but her mother's still very ill and she just can't tell when she'll be able to leave her. In the meantime, Alex and I are managing as best we can.'

'It's great,' said Alex. 'It's much better without a housekeeper at all.'

'You won't think so when your Aunt Stella arrives,' Finn said. 'She'll be horrified that there's no one to look after you properly.'

'You look after me,' Alex said loyally, tucking her hand into his, and Kate saw the rueful twist of his smile.

'Stella will tell me I'm not enough, and she'll be right.'

'Who's Stella?' she asked.

'She's Dad's sister. She's so bossy!'

'She lives in Canada,' Finn said, more measured. 'She comes over here every year to make sure Alex and I are all right.'

He hesitated. 'She's got a good heart, but she can be a bit…domineering.'

'Bossy,' said Alex.

'Overbearing,' Finn overruled her and turned back to Kate, ignoring the way his daughter muttered an insistent 'Bossy!' under her breath. 'Stella decided a couple of years ago that Alex needed a stepmother, and now whenever she's over she lines up a string of what she thinks are suitable women for me to meet.'

'They're always awful too,' Alex put in. 'Aren't they, Dad?'

'Let's just say that Stella has different ideas from us about the kind of stepmother Alex needs,' said Finn. 'I'm fond of her, and I know she means well, but I wish she'd just let me organise my life my own way.'

Kate was intrigued. 'I can't imagine you being bossed about by anybody,' she confessed.

'You don't know my sister! It's a pity, because now Alex and I dread her visits.'

'You know what we should do, Dad?' said Alex, skipping along beside them.

'What?'

'We should pretend that you've already got a girlfriend, then Aunt Stella wouldn't be able to say anything.'

'I don't think Stella is that easy to fool,' said Finn wryly. 'She'd insist on meeting any girlfriend, and we'd look a bit stupid if we couldn't produce one, wouldn't we?'

'Maybe we could ask Kate to pretend,' suggested Alex.

'Pretend what?'

'Pretend to be your girlfriend.' Alex bounced up and down as she realised the full potential of her idea. 'You could say that you were going to get married. That would shut Aunt Stella up!'

There was an uncomfortable silence. Kate's heart had lurched oddly at Alex's suggestion, but she knew that she had to treat it as a joke, so she forced a laugh to show that she wouldn't even *think* of taking the suggestion seriously.

'I don't think that's a very good idea,' said Finn after a moment.

'Why not? Kate wouldn't mind, would you, Kate?'

Kate made a noncommittal noise, which seemed the only option.

'It would be fun,' Alex went on. 'Imagine Aunt Stella's face when she comes in all ready to bully you into getting married and you told her that you'd found someone without her interfering! I think it would be great.'

'That's enough, Alex,' her father said sharply.

'But why not?' Alex insisted. 'We could have a nice time instead of spending our whole time trying to avoid those women Aunt Stella insists on inviting round.'

'I *said*, that's enough!'

Alex subsided, muttering sullenly, before working off her bad mood by throwing sticks for Derek.

'I'm sorry about that,' said Finn when she had run off. 'She gets a bit carried away.'

'That's all right.' There was another awkward pause. 'Is your sister really that bad?' Kate asked after a moment.

'Worse,' he sighed. 'I know it's just because she worries about Alex, and I know she's right, but she's a very...forceful personality.

'Really?' Kate was unable to resist murmuring. 'Fancy you being related!'

Finn shot her a sharp look but evidently decided to ignore her ironic interruption. 'She and Alex have clashed ever since Alex realised what Stella was trying to do. The thing about Stella is that she hasn't got a lot of tact and she thinks she can bully people into doing what she thinks is the right thing. She's always been the same.'

Kate tried to imagine a female version of Finn, and quailed at the thought. Stella sounded very scary.

'Can't you just tell her that you and Alex are happy with the way things are?'

'Believe me, I've tried,' said Finn. 'The thing is, I owe her a lot. It was Stella who kept things together when Isabel died. I don't know what I'd have done without her. She's a good person to have around in a crisis. She lives in Canada and has her own family, but she came straight over and looked after Alex—and me—until I could cope.

'I've told her that I can see that she's got a point, and I'll think about getting married again, but Stella thinks that unless she nags and bullies and introduces endless divorcees I'll never get round to it. And the truth is that it's hard to face up to trying to meet women when Alex is so against the idea, so in a way she's right. I just wish she wouldn't go on about it so much.'

CHAPTER SIX

'IT'S hard when people care about you,' said Kate. Her collar was turned up against the wind, and her hands were deep in her pockets to stop them wandering over towards Finn of their own accord.

'When I was going out with Seb, Bella and Phoebe used to go on and on about how bad he was for me. Deep down, I knew they were right, but it didn't make it any easier somehow. I couldn't be cross with them because I knew it was only because they loved me and wanted me to be happy, but sometimes,' she admitted, 'I wished they would just shut up and leave me alone.'

Their pace had slowed without either of them realising it, and now Finn stopped and looked down at Kate, a curious expression in his flinty grey eyes. 'Yes, that's just what I feel about Stella,' he said.

Clouds were scudding across the sky in the wind, and for a moment the sun broke through the greyness like a biblical picture. To Kate it was as if the two of them were standing alone in an intense beam of light that held them motionless, breathless, isolated from everyone else in the park. She was intensely aware of her heart beating, and the blood pulsing through her veins, of the flecking of silvery light in Finn's cool grey eyes and the dark ring around his pupils.

Then the clouds shut out the sun again, like someone switching off a light, and Alex was running back, calling to Derek, and Finn looked away. Kate felt oddly shaken and disorientated. Her heart was beating in her throat and there was a constricted feeling in her chest, so that she had to concentrate to breathe.

Finn cleared his throat and made a big deal of looking at his watch. 'Maybe we should think about going back.'

Kate was very glad of Alex's chatter as they drove back to Tooting. She felt very strange. Her body was thumping and there was a disturbing quiver deep inside her that made her excruciatingly aware of Finn, of his hand shifting gear, of his eyes flicking to the mirror, of the turn of his head.

She really *must* pull herself together! All he had done was meet her eyes for a few seconds, and for all she knew he was thinking about something else entirely. Anyone would think he had pulled her down on the grass and made mad, passionate love the way she was carrying on!

What had made her think of *that*? The image was so clear that Kate caught her breath and she had to stare desperately out of the side window, trying to force the picture of what it might be like if Finn did pull her towards him, did kiss her, did let his hands slide over her body, out of her mind. But it was as if the thought was lodged there now, so real and so vivid that Kate was terrified it was emblazoned across her face.

Finn found a parking space right in front of the house, and switched off the engine. 'Would you like to come in and have some tea?' Kate heard herself asking into the sudden silence. Her voice came out all funny, thin and high, as if she was really nervous or something. 'I've got some scones.'

'Proper tea!' said Alex approvingly. 'Can Derek come?'

'Of course.'

In fact, Derek got an extremely frosty reception from Kate's cat, who had been curled up comfortably on the sofa and was outraged to find himself nudged by a cold, wet nose attached to a tail wagged in tentative greeting. Arching his back, he puffed out his fur and hissed, adding a swipe of his paw to reinforce the message.

'What's his name?' asked Alex as Derek squealed and backed off hastily.

'We just call him Cat,' said Kate. 'He was a stray like Derek, but he was practically wild when I brought him back. He used to bite our ankles and scratch and Phoebe refused to let me give him a name because she said I'd want to keep him then. But I could never find a home for him, so we just got used to calling him Cat.'

'He wouldn't have gone anyway,' said Bella who had been lying in one of the chairs painting her nails when they came in. 'Say what you like about that cat, he's not stupid and he knows he'd never find a sucker like Kate anywhere else!'

She smiled at Finn and Alex. 'If you want to be spoiled to death and never do anything in return, Kate's your gal! I'm sure all the stray animals in London have passed the word around about what a pushover she is, because they're always turning up on the doorstep, holding up a paw and looking needy.'

'Bella, I'm sure they don't want to hear all those stories,' said Kate with a meaningful glare at her friend. Once Bella got started, there was no stopping her.

'Yes we do!' Alex piped up, and Bella grinned.

'Of course they do,' she said with an unrepentant wink at her friend, and proceeded to regale Alex and Finn with her repertoire of stories, each one more exaggerated than the last and all illustrating Kate's ridiculously soft heart and/or capacity to get herself into an unholy muddle.

Bella was outrageous, but knew how to lay on the charm, and she could be very funny. Alex was giggling and even Finn's mouth twitched occasionally.

Mortified, Kate fumbled around making tea and heating up the scones. She could feel Finn's eyes on her every now and then. Probably wondering how such an idiot could ever have been taken on by the temp agency, she thought gloomily.

'I hope you realise she's making most of these stories up,' she said as she carried the tray over to the comfortable chairs where they were sitting.

'I am not!' Bella protested.

'Grossly exaggerating, then. I notice you never tell any stories which show me as intelligent and sophisticated!'

'There aren't any of those, Kate!'

'Very funny,' said Kate mirthlessly, but at least Bella was diverted by the scones.

'I could tell loads of stories about what a good cook you are,' she offered.

'We already know that,' said Finn, glancing at Kate, who immediately started blushing and stammering that she wasn't really, honestly, she just muddled her way through recipes like everyone else…

A story that showed her as sophisticated? Dream on, Kate, she thought, listening to herself with a sinking heart.

Bella looked from Finn to Kate, blue eyes suddenly speculative. Kate could practically see her deciding to unleash the full force of her considerable charm on Finn, and just hoped he was ready for it. Bella on top form was hard to resist, and Kate wondered if Finn guessed quite how thoroughly he was being interrogated. Judging by his responses, which were civil but not exactly revealing, she guessed that he had a good suspicion of it anyway, and she didn't know whether to be glad or sorry that he was apparently impervious to her friend.

'This is a nice kitchen,' Alex said when Finn started to make a move. 'I wish ours was more like this, Dad.'

Kate could see Finn looking around the clutter, the empty bottles waiting to be recycled, the magazines strewn everywhere, Bella's nail polishes, the lingerie drying haphazardly on the airer. He didn't actually wince, but he might as well have done.

'It takes a lot of work to keep a room as messy as this,' she told Alex solemnly. 'I'm not sure your father's up to it.'

She felt quite giddy when Finn laughed. He actually laughed at something she'd said! 'You've obviously had years of experience,' he said, oblivious to the way her heart was somersaulting around her chest at the whiteness of his teeth and the deep crease in his cheeks and the humour crinkling the edges of his eyes.

'I like to practise at the office, too,' she said a little breathlessly, and then he smiled again.

'I can tell,' he said.

Bella was finishing off the last scone when Kate came back from seeing them all to the car, her elation evaporated by the mundane nature of Finn's farewell. She had hugged Alex and patted Derek, but Finn made sure that things were firmly back on a neutral footing.

'See you tomorrow,' was all he had said.

Well, what had she expected? That he would be flinging his arms round her or drawing her close for a passionate kiss? It would take more than a laugh for Finn to forget that they had to go back to work.

Back to reality.

'Yes, see you tomorrow,' Kate echoed flatly.

'Not very forthcoming, is he?' mumbled Bella through a mouthful of scone.

Kate didn't pretend not to know who she meant. Drearily, she began gathering up the tea things. 'He's... private,' she said.

'He's that all right. I've never met anyone that hard to read.'

Kate was conscious of a twist of disappointment. More

than a twist, if she was honest. A pang would describe it better. Or a knife turning in her gut.

She didn't want Bella to find Finn unreadable. Her friend was so much more perceptive than she was. She wanted her to confide that she had seen Finn watching Kate, perhaps, or that having talked to him it was obvious that he was in love with her. If there had been the slightest hint of anything like that, Bella would have spotted it.

But there hadn't been.

'It doesn't bother me,' she said, even managing a creditable shrug. 'As far as I'm concerned, he's just my boss, and only temporarily at that. I don't particularly want to know every last detail about his private life.'

The trouble was that Bella was just as perceptive about her as she was about everybody else. 'Sure,' she said, then she got up and put an arm round Kate's shoulders. 'Never mind,' she consoled her. 'There's always chocolate!'

'Finn McBride's office,' Kate answered the phone the following Tuesday.

'This is Alison, Finn's PA,' a cool voice told her.

'Oh…hello. How's your leg?'

'Much better, thank you. How have you been getting on?' There was a slight but distinct note of condescension in Alison's voice that made Kate bristle.

'Fine, I think,' she said, striving for equal coolness. 'Would you like to speak to Finn?'

'Please.' Alison sounded as if she disapproved of Kate calling him Finn instead of Mr McBride. Perhaps you were supposed to be his PA for five years before you were allowed to use his Christian name.

'I'll put you through,' said Kate evenly.

Finn came out of his office a few minutes later. 'That was Alison,' he said unnecessarily.

'Oh,' said Kate, convinced that Alison's call would have

reminded him of how efficient and reliable she was. Unlike her temporary replacement.

'The doctor has said that she can come back to work next Monday.'

'Next Monday?' Kate was unable to keep the dismay from her voice. She had been expecting to stay at least another couple of weeks. Monday's too soon, she wanted to shout.

Finn cleared his throat. 'I told her there was no need to come back before she was ready, but she says she's keen to get back to things.'

'I see.' What else could she say?

'I thought…you might be staying a bit longer,' he said.

There was an awkward pause, as if neither of them knew what to say next.

'Well,' said Kate eventually with an attempt at heartiness, 'that's good news.'

'Yes,' said Finn, not sounding entirely convinced.

'You'll have a bit more organisation in the office again.' She glanced at Derek who had trotted in beside Finn and now flung himself panting at her feet. 'No stray dogs, anyway.'

'No.'

'I'd better tidy my desk,' said Kate after another agonising pause. She looked at the piles of papers and files without enthusiasm. Three days wasn't long to sort some order out of the chaos.

She forced a bright smile. 'Shall I get Personnel to ring the agency and let them know?'

'What agency?' asked Finn, who was standing by the window with his hands in his pockets, staring down at the street.

'The temp agency. They might be able to find me another job for Monday.'

'Oh.' He turned. 'Right. Yes.' He looked at Kate, and

then away, as if he wanted to say something but had thought better of it. 'Yes, you'd better do that.'

So that was it then. Just as well she hadn't got involved, thought Kate as she sat miserably on the bus that night. And she *wasn't* involved, whatever Bella might say. She had always known that there was no point in falling for Finn. She didn't want to spend her entire life being second-best to the beautiful, perfect, irreplaceable Isabel. That had been decided after intensive chocolate therapy on Sunday evening.

She wanted fun, fun, fun instead.

Somehow that had been easier to believe after the stiff vodka and tonic prescribed by Bella than it did now when she had to face up to the fact that after Friday she would never see Finn again.

The last three days were agony. Finn was taciturn and any conversation they did have was stilted in the extreme. By the time Friday came round, Kate almost began to be glad that she was leaving. At least she wouldn't have to endure this awful, constrained atmosphere any longer.

When Finn called her into his room, she braced herself for him to say something about her leaving. She had already decided how she was going to be: friendly but professional. He had to say something, surely, if only to sort out what to do about Derek, who had now become a familiar part of the office routine. Kate tripped over him at least six times a day.

She could hardly believe it when Finn merely asked her to tidy up a few matters before Alison came back. 'We want to try and leave things as clear for her as possible,' he said.

Right, they didn't want his precious Alison to have to do too much when she came back, did they? Kate was furious. OK, she might not be Alison, but she had been here six weeks, and she had worked really hard, not to mention walking his dog for him every lunchtime. It wouldn't kill him to say thank you.

'Is that it?' she asked him coldly as she got to her feet.

'There is just one thing,' said Finn almost reluctantly. His eyes rested on Kate, who was clutching her notebook to her chest and looking cross and ruffled. 'Sit down,' he added.

Kate sank resentfully back onto the edge of her chair and opened her notebook once more with martyred sigh. Pen poised, she looked at him. 'Yes?' she prompted him.

'You don't need to take notes,' he said with an edge of his old irritation. 'I was only going to ask if you'd got a job lined up for Monday.'

'Oh.' Kate lowered her pen. She had been trying not to think about Monday. 'No, not yet.'

'How would you feel about a change of career?' asked Finn carefully.

She stared at him. 'What?'

'You mentioned when we were at dinner with Gib and Phoebe that you were thinking about changing career. I wondered if you were serious or not.'

'I suppose that rather depends on what I'd be changing *to*,' said Kate. 'Did you have something in mind?'

'Housekeeper,' he said.

Kate laughed. 'You're not serious!'

'Why wouldn't I be?'

'You know how messy I am,' she said, still smiling. 'And you saw the state of our kitchen on Sunday. I'd have thought I'd be the last person you'd want as a house-keeper!'

'Tidiness isn't important. The fact that Alex likes you is.' Finn got up abruptly and began pacing around the of-fice. 'She doesn't like many people. What I really need is someone who can meet her from school and keep an eye on her until I get home. You can cook, too, which is a bonus.'

Narrowly avoiding stepping on Derek who was stretched out in the middle of the floor, Finn muttered something under his breath and turned back to Kate. 'You could also look after that dog,' he pointed out crossly. 'I think we might as well forget the fiction that Alex is ever going to let you take him to your parents, so it looks as if I'm stuck with him, and I don't think Alison is going to be that keen on a dog in the office.'

'What about Rosa?' Kate asked. 'Isn't she coming back?'

'She rang last night. Her mother is going to need her full time for the foreseeable future. I told her I would make temporary arrangements, so that if she was in a position to come back in a couple of months, she could if she wanted to, but I don't think she will.'

'So you're not thinking about a permanent post?'

Finn shook his head. 'No. Alex isn't keen on anyone else living with us, so I might see if we can manage without a housekeeper—although it's going to be a lot more difficult now there's a dog to consider,' he added.

'Then why are you asking me?' Kate asked, ignoring that little sideswipe.

He stopped pacing and shoved his hands in his pockets. 'Because my sister's coming in a couple of weeks.'

Ah, yes, the scary Stella, Kate remembered.

'She'll just make a fuss if we haven't got anyone to help,' Finn went on, unaware of her mental interruption. 'It would just be for while she's here, so we're not talking about you staying for ever. That's why I thought if you didn't have anything else organised you might consider it. I'd pay you, of course,' he added. 'It would be more than you would make temping like this.'

Kate scribbled mindlessly on her notebook as she thought about Finn's offer. She had never been a big career girl, and had fallen into secretarial work simply because she couldn't think of anything else to do.

Phoebe and Bella were much more serious about their work, but deep down Kate was still nursing the childhood fantasy of living in a cottage in the country with a kitchen where she could make jam and bottle things, roses round the door and a big garden with room for lots of animals and children. Being a housekeeper might not be quite what she'd had in mind, but she was sure she'd be happy pottering around a house all day.

The more she thought about it, the more appealing the idea became. The money would be useful for a start, and a guaranteed job was better than hanging around waiting for the agency to get back to her.

Besides, she liked Alex and she liked Derek. The fact that she would be spending more time with Finn himself was just incidental, and had absolutely nothing to do with the flutter of anticipation that was stirring deep inside her.

She moistened her lips, striving to sound businesslike. 'Would it be a live-in post?'

'Preferably,' said Finn.

'I'd have to check with Bella,' said Kate, looking doubtful. 'It would mean she would be the only one in the house.'

'I'd cover the cost of your rent if you wanted to be sure of keeping your room,' he said unexpectedly, and she glanced at him in surprise.

'The rent's not such a problem since Phoebe married Gib,' she said frankly. 'There's nothing like a lovely, rich husband to stop you worrying about mortgages! Bella and I just pay a token rent now and look after the house for her. No, I was thinking about the cat.'

'The cat?' repeated Finn as if he didn't want to believe what he was hearing.

'I'd have to ask Bella to look after him, and he's bitten

her ankles so many times she might not be that keen! Unless I could bring him with me?' Kate looked at Finn hopefully but he wasn't having any of it.

'No,' he said firmly. 'The dog is enough trouble. I'm sure Bella would feed the cat for you. It's not as if it would be for ever. Stella usually spends a couple of weeks with us, then travels around the country visiting her old friends for ten days or so, before coming back for the last few days before she flies back to Canada, so I don't anticipate needing you for longer than a month or so.'

Well, that told her. Lucky she hadn't done anything silly like falling in love with him, wasn't it?

Kate chewed the end of her pen. There was no point in feeling hurt that Finn wanted a definite time limit to the time she would be spending with him. He was just being practical, and she should be the same.

Did she really want to be a housekeeper?

If nothing else, it would be a change, she told herself. It might be fun. It would be money. It wasn't for ever, as Finn had been so keen to point out.

It would mean that she didn't have to say goodbye to him at the end of today.

'All right,' she said, suddenly making up her mind.

'You'll do it?' Finn sounded almost as surprised as she felt.

'Yes.' She would have to clear the cat feeding with Bella, who would grumble like mad, but she would agree in the end. In the meantime, it was up to Kate to make it very clear that she was going to be as businesslike as Finn.

'When do you want me?' she asked briskly, only to hear the double meaning in her words too late. 'To start,' she added, colour creeping into her cheeks.

So much for sounding businesslike.

Fortunately, Finn didn't appear to have noticed. 'Perhaps

we can discuss the details over dinner?' he said stiltedly. 'Are you free tonight?'

'Yes,' said Kate, ruthlessly sacrificing the opportunity to meet lots of Will's single friends at a party. She would ring Bella and explain that she couldn't make it. Making chit-chat with a lot of corporate types at a noisy party couldn't compare to dinner with Finn, even if it was only to talk about her duties as housekeeper.

'Good.' Finn seemed rather at a loss. 'Could you book a restaurant?'

'Did you have somewhere in mind?' she asked, trying not to sound put out. It wasn't exactly a romantic date if you had to book your own restaurant, was it? Perhaps she should just order a pizza to be delivered and be done with it.

'You choose,' said Finn indifferently, turning away to the window.

Serve him right if she booked a table at the Dorchester, thought Kate, getting to her feet once more. Finn was still staring abstractedly at the rain, so it looked as if her inter-view was over.

'Book somewhere nice,' he said as she reached the door. 'There's something I want to ask you.'

'Something he wants to ask you?' Bella repeated when Kate recounted the conversation that evening. 'He didn't say what?'

'It'll be something to do with being housekeeper, I suppose.'

'Come on, Kate!' Bella rolled her eyes dismissively. 'You don't invite a girl like you out to dinner to talk about how many hours you're going to spend vacuuming!' She paused. 'Maybe he's going to make a pass?'

'I don't think that's very likely,' said Kate, unwilling to admit to Bella that she had already wondered about this possibility and been unable to imagine Finn doing anything of the kind. 'He's had plenty of opportunity to do that without wasting money on a meal.'

'Ah, but you've been working for him up to now,' Bella pointed out. 'He sounds the sort of strait-laced type who doesn't approve of office affairs, but he might have been nurturing a secret passion for you for weeks, and now that he's got a window of opportunity this weekend when you're technically unemployed he's decided to go for it!'

Kate pooh-poohed the idea, of course, but it didn't stop her stomach churning with nerves as she got ready that evening. She had booked the Italian restaurant round the corner, not that she thought that she would be able to eat anything. Bella told her she should have gone for somewhere more expensive, but Kate didn't want Finn to think that she was expecting anything special. Best just to treat it as a business meeting, she had decided.

Which made it difficult to decide what to wear. He had seen all her work clothes and, even though it clearly wasn't a proper date, Kate couldn't help wanting him to see that she could look nice when she tried. At length she settled on a short, flirty little dress with a beaded cardigan and her favourite shoes. They weren't very suitable for walking through a dank March night, but she didn't have anything else that would go.

'You look great,' said Bella when Kate went downstairs. 'Not at all like a housekeeper.'

Kate immediately lost her nerve. Perhaps it *was* a bit inappropriate. 'Do you think I should change?'

'Into what?' Bella was appalled at the very idea. 'A demure grey dress with a white collar and a load of keys hanging from your waist? Of course don't change! You look fabulous as you are. Finn won't be able to keep his hands off you!'

For once Bella was quite wrong. Finn didn't seem to be having any trouble at all keeping his hands to himself, Kate reflected dismally as they struggled to make stilted conversation on the way to the restaurant. He had certainly noted her change of image, and he had looked a bit taken aback, but all he had said was that she looked 'different'. As compliments went, it was hardly overwhelming.

Finn obviously wasn't over-impressed by the restaurant either. Tough, thought Kate. He should have organised somewhere himself. He ought to count himself lucky that she hadn't taken up Bella's suggestion of booking a table at Claridge's.

'Is this it?' he said, looking around him at the red and white checked tablecloths, the faded posters on the wall and the candles stuck into Chianti bottles. The last word in style in the Sixties.

'I'm a cheap date,' said Kate defiantly, and then, when he lifted an eyebrow, lost her nerve. 'Not that this is a date, of course,' she added hastily.

Unfortunately the waiters hadn't got that particular message and kept fussing around them, promising them a secluded table and showering Kate with embarrassing compliments while a muscle in Finn's gritted jaw began to twitch. She wished they would all shut up. Any minute now a posse of violinists would pop up to serenade them, and there would be some pseudo-gipsy insisting that Finn bought her a rose at an exorbitant price.

'She is very beautiful, no?' The head waiter demanded, determined to foster what he thought was a budding romance.

Finn looked across at Kate, who was cringing, sinking further and further down into her seat. She looked so uncomfortable that his own rigid expression relaxed into something that was almost, but not quite, a smile.

'Yes,' he said. 'Very. Now, could we have a menu, please?'

Kate's cheeks burned. 'I'm sorry,' she said when the

waiter had departed, still wreathed in smiles. 'They're not usually like this here.'

'Perhaps you don't usually look as beautiful as you do tonight,' said Finn, picking up the wine list.

Kate opened her mouth and closed it again, but before she could think of anything to say two waiters descended on them again and they were caught up in the kerfuffle of being offered menus and bread and having water poured, while her pulse boomed in her ears and her heart lurched around her chest.

Finn had said she was beautiful.

She risked a glance across at him. His head was bent over the wine list, and his expression was hard to read. From where she sat, he looked as if he was absorbed in the relative merits of Valpolicella and Lambrusco. The fierce, dark brows were drawn slightly together, and his eyes were shielded, so that all Kate could see was the strong nose and the line of his mouth.

Her entrails twisted at the sight, and she looked quickly away. She must have misheard. Nobody, not even Finn, could say something like that and then calmly turn his attention to what they were going to drink. He couldn't tell her that she was beautiful and then carry on as if nothing had happened, could he?

Could he?

Maybe he hadn't meant it. Maybe he had just said it to shut the waiter up. Kate's hands shook as she pretended to study her own menu, but the words danced in front of her eyes and she couldn't concentrate. *Did* he think that she was beautiful? Was Bella right after all?

At last they had ordered, the wine had been tasted and poured, and the last hovering waiter had backed off to leave them alone. Having longed for them to go away, Kate now wished they would come back. They might be annoying but at least they would break the uncomfortable silence that had fallen.

She fiddled with her fork. Finn seemed to have forgotten that he wanted to say something to her. Why had he bothered to ask her out if he didn't want to talk to her? 'When would you like me to start as housekeeper?' she asked eventually, unable to bear it any longer.

Finn had been tearing a piece of bread apart, but he looked up at that, as if relieved that she had started the conversational ball rolling. 'Whenever you can manage it,' he said. 'As soon as possible as far as Alex and I are concerned. It would give you a chance to get settled in before Stella arrives.'

'I could move this weekend if you wanted,' Kate offered.

'Good. In that case, we'll come and pick you up on Sunday,' said Finn, but he seemed abstracted, as if there was something else on his mind.

'When is your sister arriving?'

'Two weeks on Tuesday. We'll need to make a bit of a fuss of her when she arrives,' he added.

'That's all right, I'm good at fuss,' said Kate, feeling a bit more cheerful. 'I'll make everything special for her. Flowers in her room, fresh towels, luxury soap, a nice welcoming meal…we'll lay on the works for her!'

Finn raised his brows slightly. 'You sound like you've done this kind of thing before?'

'We always had lots of guests at home when I was growing up,' she told him. 'I love having people to stay too.'

'I'm afraid I'm a bit out of the way of it,' said Finn, turning his fork absently between his fingers. 'I haven't done any proper entertaining since Isabel died. Stella's the only person we've had to stay for any length of time.'

Their starters arrived just then. Kate waited until the plates had been deposited with a flourish in front of them.

'Is that what you wanted to talk to me about?'

Finn had picked up his knife and fork, but at that he laid them down again. 'Partly,' he said. 'At least...well, no, not really,' he finished abruptly.

'What is it?' asked Kate, puzzled.

'I don't quite know how you're going to take this...' Finn trailed off and she looked at him curiously. She had never seen him this nervous before.

'I won't know until you tell me,' she pointed out.

'No.' Finn drank some wine and set his glass down carefully. 'It's just that Stella rang the other day. You remember I told you that she was very keen to introduce me to women she thinks would make suitable stepmothers for Alex?'

'Yes,' Kate encouraged him when he seemed likely to stop again.

'Alex spoke to her first. Stella was telling her all about some friend of a friend of hers who she thought it would be nice for me to meet and why didn't she invite her to dinner one night, and I gather Alex didn't like the sound of her at all. So she told Stella that she didn't need to bother finding a stepmother for her any more because I'd met someone and was going to get married.'

'Oh, dear...'

'Exactly.' A mirthless smile twisted Finn's mouth. 'Of course, Stella then insisted on talking to me. I could have told her that Alex was joking, but they have quite an uneasy relationship as it is, and I didn't want Stella coming over and going on about how spoilt and difficult she was, which would just make Alex defensive. It was bad enough last time.'

Finn sighed. 'Anyway, the upshot was that I played along. I remembered what Alex had suggested that day we all went to Richmond Park, and I suppose I thought—well, why not? It would shut Stella up at least, although not initially. She demanded details of course, wanted to know the name of my fiancée, how we had met and so on.

There was an odd feeling in the pit of Kate's stomach. 'What did you tell her?'

Finn looked her straight in the eye. 'I told her it was you,' he said.

CHAPTER SEVEN

SHE should have been expecting it, but somehow she wasn't. Kate wrenched her eyes away from Finn's and looked down at her plate, appalled at the sudden realisation of how much she wished that he had meant what he said to his sister, that he loved her and wanted to marry her.

She felt very strange. It was as if all the oxygen had been sucked out of the air, leaving her light-headed and faintly dizzy, so that it took her a little while to realise what Finn was saying.

'I wanted to ask you if you would pretend that it was true.'

Pretend. Kate made herself focus on the one word that made all the difference. This wasn't her wishes coming miraculously true at all, it was Finn making it clear that he wasn't talking about anything real.

'I know it's not fair on you, and that it's a lot to ask, but it would mean a lot to Alex. And to me,' he added after a moment. 'Of course, it would just be a pretence,' he hastened to explain when Kate said nothing but just sat staring dumbly at him. 'I wouldn't expect you to...to think of it as anything other than a job.'

'A job?' Kate latched onto the word as if it was the only one she had understood. Her heart was thudding so loudly that it was hard to hear, and she was afraid she might miss something important.

'I wouldn't ask you to do something like that for free,' said Finn. 'I'd make it worth your while financially. We could agree your salary as housekeeper with a bonus on top of that at the end for...everything else.'

113

He spoke very formally, making it clear that as far as he was concerned it would be a purely business transaction, and somehow Kate managed to pull herself together.

'What exactly would you want me to do?' she asked, amazed at the calmness of her voice.

'To be around when Stella is with us. To make her believe that you and I...'

'Are in love?' Kate finished for him bravely when he hesitated.

Finn let out a breath. 'Yes.'

'I used to be good at drama,' she said after a moment. 'I always wanted a starring role but only ever got bit parts, so perhaps I could look on this as my chance to get back into acting.'

'You mean you will consider it?' he said as if he could hardly believe that she was serious.

'Why not?' Kate had herself under control now.

The one thing she mustn't do was let Finn guess that she had fallen in love with him. He would be appalled if he knew, and he certainly wouldn't ask her to pretend to be his fiancée. Convincing him that she was treating the whole thing lightly would at least let her be near him, Kate told herself. It might not be for long, but it could be her only chance.

'It will be much more fun than temping, anyway,' she told him brightly. 'It sounds like easy money to me!'

'You might not think so when you meet my sister,' said Finn with a wry look. 'She has very sharp eyes and she isn't a fool. She'll be watching us very carefully.' He paused delicately. 'If we're going to convince her that we really are engaged, we might have to give the impression that we're more intimate than we really are.'

Treat it lightly, Kate reminded herself. 'You mean we might have to kiss occasionally?'

'That kind of thing, yes.' Finn seemed a little nonplussed by her casual attitude. 'How would you feel about that?'

How would she feel? Kate let herself imagine being able to reach across the table and take his hand. She imagined putting her arms around him and leaning into his solidity, daring to touch her lips to his throat. She thought about being held by him and how that stern mouth would feel against hers, and desire knotted sharply inside her, driving the breath from her lungs.

'I think I could manage.' She meant to say it casually, but her voice came out treacherously husky and she had to clear her throat and start again. 'It would just be part of the job. It wouldn't mean anything.'

'Right,' said Finn, sounding oddly wary, and Kate was suddenly terrified in case he had glimpsed how badly she wanted him.

'I'll close my eyes and think of the bonus,' she tried to joke.

'Yes, I think I've got the point that you won't be taking it seriously.' There was a distinct edge to Finn's voice now, and Kate eyed him uncertainly.

What had she said? She'd have thought he would have been glad that she wasn't going to go all soppy on him! Kate sighed inwardly, torn between exasperation at the withdrawn look on his face and the longing to reach for him and tell him that all she wanted was to hold him and kiss him and be with him for ever, and you couldn't get more serious than that.

'How does Alex feel about all of this?' she asked instead.

Finn's rigid expression relaxed slightly. 'She's very pleased with herself, taking credit for the whole idea. I told her I was going to ask you if you'd play along tonight, so she'll be cock-a-hoop when she hears that you've agreed.' He glanced across the table at Kate. 'Alex doesn't take to many people, but she likes you.'

'I like her too.'

There was a pause while the obvious question—And what about you? Do *you* like me?—seemed to shimmer in the air between them.

Kate swallowed the words. She wasn't going to ask Finn that. Her eyes fell on her starter, forgotten and growing cold in front of her. She wasn't hungry—love seemed to have destroyed her appetite—but she picked up her fork and began to eat while the silence stretched uncomfortably.

'What have you told Stella about me?' she asked with a kind of desperation at last.

'Just your name and that we met when you came to work with me.' Finn didn't seem to be enjoying his meal any more than she was. 'I thought it would be easiest if I stuck to the truth as far as possible.'

'I bet she wanted to know more than that,' said Kate. 'If my brother told me that he was getting married, I would demand to know every last detail!'

A faint smile of acknowledgment lifted the corners of his mouth. 'She did ask what you were like,' he admitted.

'What did you tell her?'

Finn looked at Kate with an unreadable expression. 'That you were warm and funny and kind, and that Alex liked you. Which is true.'

What was true? That Alex liked her, or that he thought that she was warm and funny?

Kind. Warm. There was nothing wrong with being either, but it was hardly sweep-you-off-your-feet stuff, was it? Kate pushed her mushrooms glumly around her plate. She wanted him to have described her to Stella in rather more lover-like terms. Beautiful. Desirable. Irresistible. How come none of those words had popped into his head when he thought about her?

She knew why.

Because Finn didn't think she was beautiful or desirable, and he could resist her quite easily.

Because he didn't love her.

She was just going to have to live with that.

Kate laid down her fork, unable to face any more. 'Didn't Stella want to know what had made you change your mind about getting married?'

'I said that she would understand when she met you,' said Finn.

Their eyes met across the candle in the middle of the table, and something leapt in the air between them, something that jarred Kate's heart and was gone before she could tell what it was.

She moistened her lips. 'What would you have done if I'd said no?'

'I'm not sure,' he admitted. 'I was relying on your kindness. I suppose I could always have pretended that you'd left me for someone else just before she arrived.'

'I wouldn't do anything like that!' Kate protested involuntarily, and that keen grey glance flickered to her face and then away before she could read his expression again.

'No, maybe you wouldn't,' he agreed.

'You could always have invented some family crisis,' she offered helpfully.

'It would take more than a family crisis to stop Stella,' said Finn. 'She'd track you down somehow!'

'Anyway, I didn't say no,' Kate pointed out.

'No.' Finn abandoned his own plate. 'We'll have to think of some reason to end our supposed engagement after Stella leaves though, or she'll be booking her ticket back to the wedding. As it is, we'll be lucky if we get away with not getting married while she's here! Oh, don't worry,' he added, misinterpreting Kate's flinch. 'It won't go that far!'

'Good.' Kate managed a weak smile. 'We don't want that, do we?'

'No,' Finn agreed, his voice empty of expression. 'We don't want that.'

'Are you sure this is a good idea, Kate?' Bella and Phoebe, sitting across the table from her like an interviewing panel, looked at her in concern.

'Earning money is always a good idea, isn't it?' said Kate defiantly.

'There are easier ways to earn it than pretending to be in love with your boss!'

'Oh, I don't know…'

Kate didn't want to tell them that the problem was going to be a whole lot more complicated than that. She was going to have to pretend to be in love with Finn while pretending not to be. No point in explaining that to them, though. Bella would only say 'I told you so.'

'It'll be better than temping in some dreary office,' she told them instead, 'and Finn's going to give me a huge bonus for the engagement thing which will mean I can clear my credit card bill. I might even have some left to save up for a holiday. Besides, I like Alex and it solves the problem of what to do about Derek during the day.'

'Oh, well, that's all right then!' said Bella sarcastically. 'As long as the *dog* is sorted out…!'

'Look, it will be fine! I don't know why you're both making such a fuss. It's just a job.'

'Just a job where you have to sleep with your boss!'

'I'll have my own room.'

Phoebe looked dubious. 'His sister's not going to believe you're going to get married if you're not even sleeping together.'

'Well…we can say it doesn't seem appropriate with Alex in the house,' said Kate a little defensively.

Bella pretended to shake her head and look disorientated.

'Sorry, I seem to have stepped into a time warp! What year are we living in?'

Kate ignored her. 'OK, so we'll share a room when his sister is there. It's not a big deal.'

'We just don't want you to get hurt,' Phoebe tried to placate her, hearing the edge in Kate's voice.

'I'm not going to do anything silly,' said Kate grittily. It was too late now, anyway, although she had no intention of confessing *that*!

'Finn's still in love with Isabel, I know that. Even if he wasn't still obsessed by her, he's completely different from me. He's much older, his experience is different, his life is different.'

All true, and it didn't make the slightest difference to loving him.

Kate faced her friends squarely, marvelling that they couldn't see how different *she* felt now. Couldn't they tell that falling in love with Finn had turned her life upside down, consuming her to the point where she was prepared to risk the certainty of being hurt just to be with him?

'There's no point in me getting involved with him or his daughter or his dog,' she told them, knowing that was true too but unable to do anything about it. 'But it's not like I've got anything else lined up that I can do instead,' she pointed out. 'It's that or hang around waiting for the agency to get in touch. Frankly, I'd rather be paid generously for living in a comfortable house for a few weeks!'

Phoebe was unconvinced. 'It's very easy to get carried away in situations like that,' she said. 'And I should know!'

'Yes, you're the last person who should be advising Kate against a mock engagement,' said Bella with a grin. 'Look where it got you and Gib!'

Phoebe smiled, but her eyes were serious as she glanced across at Kate. 'Finn's not like Gib,' she said. 'I just think you should be careful, that's all.'

Too late, thought Kate. All she could do now was make the best of the time she had.

'This is your room.' Alex opened the door and showed Kate inside proudly. 'I made it look nice for you.'

Kate looked around her, touched. 'It all looks lovely,' she said. There was even a little vase of flowers on the chest of drawers. 'Did you do it all yourself?'

'Dad made your bed,' Alex admitted, 'but I did everything else.'

Kate looked at the bed and imagined Finn making it, smoothing his hand over the sheet where she would lie. Shaken by a gust of longing, she cleared her throat. 'That was nice of him, but I could have made it myself.'

'I don't think he minded,' said Alex casually. 'Do you want to see my room?'

Maybe that would be safer.

Kate admired Alex's room and was suitably appreciative of the fact that it had been specially tidied for the occasion. A pinboard by her bed was covered in photographs, of Alex and her mother and of Finn. Most of them showed him with Isabel, smiling and relaxed with the sun in his eyes, and Kate felt hollow inside to realise that she had never seen him look happy like that.

Might never see him looking happy.

'That's my mum,' said Alex, following Kate's gaze. 'She was beautiful, wasn't she?'

'Yes,' said Kate. 'She was. Do you remember her at all?'

'Not really, but Dad tells me about her and he kept some of her things for me. Look.' Alex dived under her bed for a box which she pulled out and opened reverently.

Kate sat on the bed and took the things Alex handed her. A lipstick, used. A bottle of perfume, half full. A soft silk scarf. A book of medieval poetry. A diary full of scribbled notes. A pair of earrings. A baby's footprint.

'That was mine,' said Alex.

There was a hard lump in Kate's throat as she thought about Finn carefully choosing the things that would give her the sense of what her mother had been like long after she had gone. It must have broken his heart all over again.

'This was her engagement ring,' Alex said, opening a little jewellery box and pointing at one of the rings. 'Dad says she left it to me, so I can wear it later if I want to. Those blue stones are called sapphires. Dad bought that ring because they reminded him of Mum's eyes.'

'It's a lovely ring,' said Kate, perilously close to tears. Her heart ached for Finn, but she didn't want to break down and weep in front of Alex.

She looked up from the box instead only to find Finn watching her gravely from the doorway. For a long, long moment, they looked at each other, Kate's brown eyes, shimmering with tears, before Alex noticed her father and jumped up.

'I'm showing Kate Mum's box,' she said.

'So I see.' Finn's smile looked strained, but all he said was that he had made some tea if they wanted to come downstairs.

Kate felt awful, as if she had been caught nosing around in his private memories but when she tried to apologise while Alex was carefully putting the box back under her bed, he brushed it aside.

'I'm glad she wanted to talk about Isabel,' he said, handing Kate a mug of tea. 'I don't think she's ever shown anyone that box before. She's always kept her feelings to herself, and it's difficult to get her to talk about what's worrying her sometimes. If you can get her to talk to you, I'd be very grateful. She's already much chattier than she used to be.'

As if to prove his point, Alex came clattering down the stairs with Derek and burst into the kitchen. 'Dad, I've just thought of something when I was putting Mum's ring away. Kate should have a ring too if she's going to be your fiancée, shouldn't she?'

'Oh, no…no, there's no need for that,' said Kate hastily. She held up her hand to show the rings she was wearing. 'I could use one of these.'

Finn took her hand as if it were a parcel, and he and Alex inspected her meagre display of rings. Neither of them was impressed.

'I don't think any of them are likely to convince Stella,' said Finn, looking down his nose. 'Let me have that one,' he said, pointing to the one on her third finger.

Kate's hand was burning where he had touched her as she tugged off the ring. 'What for?' she asked.

'It'll give me your size. I'll get you a proper ring.'

'Really, I don't think it's necessary—' she began, but he interrupted her.

'You don't know my sister. She'd smell a rat if you were wearing a cheap little ring like that. Why are you looking like that?' he demanded, his voice sharpening at the involuntary change in Kate's expression.

'Seb gave me that ring.' The fact that Finn had instantly recognised it as cheap made Kate realise at last just how little Seb had valued her. She had treasured the ring, so certain that the fact that he had given her one at all meant that he cared, but all along it had been worthless, just like Seb.

Finn frowned. 'I won't lose it.'

'It doesn't matter. I don't think I want to wear it again.' Kate summoned a bright smile and got to her feet. 'I'd better start thinking about supper.'

Finn was all for getting a take-away, but Kate was determined to show him that she hadn't forgotten why she was there. 'I may as well start earning my salary,' she said. There wasn't a lot in the fridge, but she found enough to make a sauce for some pasta. It seemed very ordinary fare to her but Finn and Alex carried on as if she had produced something worthy of a Michelin star.

'I think you've been having too many take-aways,' said Kate. 'That's all going to change!'

By half past eight, Alex was wilting. 'Time for bed, young lady,' said Finn. 'You've got school tomorrow.'

Ensuring that she had cleaned her teeth, kissing her goodnight and dealing firmly with her last-ditch attempts to delay the moment of lights out took some time, and then there was the washing up and tidying to do, but after that Finn and Kate had no excuse not to realise that they were alone with the dog.

By tacit agreement, they stayed in the bright, safe light of the kitchen rather than retreat to the comfort and intimate shadows of the sitting room. Kate sat on the other side of the kitchen table from Finn, where there was no danger of brushing against him by mistake.

Now all she had to do was chat brightly to break the yawning silence, but she couldn't think of a single thing to say. All she could think about was Finn sitting on the other side of the table, about his mouth and his hands and how nice it would be to be able to get up and go round to sit on his lap, to put her arms around his neck and kiss the tiredness from his face.

In the end it was Finn who spoke first. 'I hope you're all right with this,' he said, lifting his eyes to fix Kate with that disturbingly acute grey gaze. 'I mean...with the situation.'

'Of course,' said Kate brightly, as if she hadn't given the fact that they were alone together with only the dog as chaperon a moment's thought.

Finn looked around the kitchen as if trying to see it through her eyes. 'A job like this isn't much fun for a girl like you.'

'That rather depends on what kind of girl you think I am,' she said.

He considered the matter seriously. 'I suppose I think of you as someone who likes to have a good time,' he said eventually. 'You seem to have lots of friends, and you're always out. I can't help feeling that you might find it a bit dull stuck in the house all day.'

'It'll be a lot more fun that being stuck in an office,' said Kate. 'I've always liked pottering around the house. I'm not the tidiest person in the world—as you know!' she added seeing the sardonic lift of Finn's brows. 'But I love cooking and sewing and gardening and if I've got a dog to walk and Alex to chat to when she gets home from school…well, I think I'm going to have a lovely time. In fact, I don't know why I didn't think about being a house-keeper before,' she finished.

'You know, you're not a bad PA when you concentrate,' said Finn carefully. 'I'm sure you could have a more in-teresting career than housekeeping if you applied yourself.'

Kate turned her glass between her fingers on the table. 'I don't really want to,' she said frankly. 'The trouble is that I haven't got any ambition.'

'What, none?'

'Only for very ordinary things,' she said. 'It seems a bit shameful to admit it, but all I've ever really wanted was to find someone special. To have children and a house I could make a home. That's not asking too much, is it?'

Finn's expression was unreadable. 'No.'

'Phoebe and Bella think it would be boring, but I'd be so happy keeping chickens and making jam and helping out at the school fête.' Kate sighed a little. 'That's partly why I was so broken up about Seb. I'd made myself believe that he was the one, and that I could have that dream with him.

'I was stupid, of course,' she went on, keeping her eyes

on her glass, not looking at Finn. 'Seb wouldn't be seen dead at a school fête and he doesn't care where his eggs come from. It made it worse when I had to accept that. It's like giving up on a dream of what my life might be like as well as giving up on him.'

'Dreams are hard things to let go of,' said Finn quietly.

Kate knew he was thinking of his dead wife, and her throat tightened. 'Is that what you had with Isabel? The dream?'

He lifted his shoulders slightly. 'It feels like a dream now,' he told her. 'I'm sure it can't have been that perfect and that we must have argued sometimes, but I don't remember that. I just remember how special it was to be with her.'

'You're lucky to have had that.' Kate stopped, hearing her words too late. 'I'm sorry,' she said. 'That was tactless of me. You probably don't feel very lucky.'

'I know what you mean,' said Finn with a faint smile. 'And in a lot of ways I was lucky. A lot of people never find what Isabel and I had. Sometimes I can't believe I found love like that once, and the statistics are against me finding it a second time. It's just not going to happen.'

His mouth twisted. 'That's when I miss Isabel most,' he told Kate. 'When I remember how completely happy I was with her and know that I'm never going to have that again.'

That night Kate lay in bed and stared up at the dark ceiling, thinking about the expression in Finn's eyes. It was terrible to feel envious of someone who was dead, but she couldn't stop thinking about Isabel and how much Finn had loved her.

'It's not going to happen a second time,' he had said, and she would have to accept that, too. It was no use dreaming that she might become his second chance at happiness. The statistics were against it, weren't they?

Kate's heart cracked and she squeezed her eyes shut.

What was wrong with her? Why did she keep falling in love with men who couldn't, or wouldn't, ever love her back?

This job had offered her the chance to be with him and she had jumped at it, but now Kate wondered if it had been such a good idea. It wasn't as if she hadn't always known that falling in love with Finn was hopeless. It might have been better to have said goodbye and walked away while she still could.

But it was too late for that now. She was just going to have to get on with it, Kate told herself. If she couldn't make Finn happy, she could at least try to make him comfortable for a while, and if pretending to be his fiancée would make his life easier during his sister's visit, then she would do that too.

It felt odd not to be going into the office to be with Finn the next day, but having made her decision, Kate was quite as happy as she had said she would be pottering around the house. She took Alex to school and, by the time she had walked the dog, cleaned the house, inspected the cupboards and done the shopping, and walked the dog again, it was time to pick Alex up.

When Finn came home that evening, the two of them were in the kitchen. Kate was in the middle of making supper and Alex was sitting at the kitchen table doing her homework.

Finn bent to kiss his daughter, and then looked at Kate, who had the dizzy feeling that the obvious thing for him to do next was to walk across and kiss her too. She turned firmly back to her sauce.

'How was your day?' she asked, grimacing at the corniness of it. Any minute now she would be offering to bring him his pipe and slippers!

'Fine.' There was a faint frown between Finn's brows as

if he was remembering something that hadn't been fine at all. 'Busy.'

'How was Alison?' Kate made herself ask.

'She was…fine.'

Fine was obviously the key word for the day. Finn wrenched at his tie to loosen it.

'You didn't miss me then?' she said, making a joke out of it.

'Funnily enough, I did.'

Kate's heart stumbled, and without thinking she turned to face him. 'Really?' she said, still clutching her wooden spoon.

'Really,' said Finn.

His eyes seemed to reach right inside her and squeeze her heart until Kate's breathing got into a muddle and she forgot whether she was supposed to be breathing in or breathing out.

He had missed her. He wasn't just saying it, he had really missed her! OK, it wasn't a fraction of what he still felt for Isabel but, as Kate stared back at him, unable to tear her eyes away from that piercing grey gaze, she told herself that it was enough.

There was a long, long pause. Kate could feel the air shortening even as silence lengthened, and when the phone rang jarringly she actually jumped and dropped the wooden spoon.

Her hands were unsteady as she washed it under the tap.

Alex had pounced on phone. 'Oh, hello, Aunt Stella,' she said, and for the next few minutes dutifully answered questions about school. 'Yes, he's here,' she said after a while, and then, ultra-casual, 'He's just talking to Kate.'

She beamed at Finn as she held the phone out to him. He took it, visibly bracing himself. Stirring her sauce intently, Kate could hear only one side of the conversation, which seemed to consist of a lot of talking on Stella's part and brief replies on his.

'No, you can't talk to her,' she heard him say eventually. 'I don't want you interrogating her over the phone… You can meet her when you come… No, we're not planning on getting married while you're here. There's no rush. Kate's living here now and we're all perfectly happy as we are.'

Shaking his head, Finn put down the phone. 'My sister…!' He turned to Kate who was still concentrating fiercely on her sauce. 'Well, it looks as if we're committed now,' he said. 'I hope you don't want to change your mind?'

'No.' Kate took the saucepan off the heat and turned off the element. 'I won't change my mind.'

'Good.' Finn walked over to where she was standing by the cooker. 'Give me your hand. No, not that one,' he said as he pulled a box out of his jacket pocket. 'The other one.'

Kate had to steel herself against the shiver of response that shuddered through her as he took her left hand and turned it over, spreading it so that he could slide a ring onto her third finger.

'What do you think?'

If she hadn't known better, Kate could have sworn that he was nervous about her answer. She looked down at her hand. He seemed to have forgotten that he was still holding it and she was excruciatingly conscious of the warmth of his fingers.

She made herself focus on the ring. It was an antique, a cluster of pearls around a topaz on warm old gold. 'It's beautiful,' she said with difficulty.

Alex was less impressed. She peered round her father, studying the ring critically. 'It ought to be diamonds, Dad,' she said severely.

'Diamonds wouldn't be right for Kate.' Finn seemed to

remember that he was still holding Kate's hand and let it go abruptly. 'They're too cold.'

Kate bit her lip as she twisted the ring on her finger. 'It must have been terribly expensive,' she said worriedly.

'It will be worth it if it shuts Stella up,' said Finn, stepping back.

There was a pause. 'Do you really like it?' he asked as if the words had been forced out of him

'I love it,' she said honestly.

'I could get you a diamond ring if you'd rather.'

'I don't want diamonds,' said Kate. She risked a glance at him, and the light in her eyes turned them almost exactly the colour of the topaz. 'This is perfect.'

CHAPTER EIGHT

ALEX refused to be convinced. 'I still think it should be a diamond ring,' she said stubbornly. 'If Aunt Stella sees that old thing she might think you don't love Kate.'

Kate looked down at her beautiful ring. *That old thing?*

Finn was regarding his daughter with some exasperation. 'We'll just have to make her believe that I do anyway.'

'How?'

'Well...I'll tell her that I do.'

'I don't think that will be enough for Aunt Stella,' said Alex, making a face. 'You know what she's like.'

'I'm sure we'll think of something to convince her,' said Finn, and tried to change the subject by suggesting that she laid the table for supper.

Alex was not to be so easily diverted. 'I think you might have to kiss Kate,' she said as she set out the knives and forks.

'Possibly,' he said repressively.

Kate busied herself draining potatoes and avoided looking at either of them.

'Have you ever kissed her?' Alex asked her father with interest.

There was a frozen pause. 'I don't think that's any of your business, Alex,' he said in a curt voice.

It didn't seem to have much effect on Alex. 'I only thought you might need to practise if you haven't,' she said, all injured innocence.

'Well, we're not going to practise now,' Finn said with a something of a snap. 'We're going to have supper instead, and then *you* are going to bed!'

Only Alex seemed unaware of the air of constraint in the kitchen. She chattered on and Kate smiled mechanically and thought about kissing Finn. She wouldn't mind if it was just a practice. It would still be a kiss.

Please, please let him kiss me, she prayed.

She cleared up in the kitchen automatically while Finn was saying goodnight to Alex. She mustn't seem too keen. If he suggested taking Alex up on her idea, she would pretend to think about it and then agree casually.

Only Finn didn't suggest it. He made no reference to Stella's visit or Alex's conversation or anything at all that might give Kate an opening. He just helped her tidy up, moving efficiently and expressionlessly around the kitchen without once coming anywhere near her.

Frustrated, Kate wondered if she dared raise the subject herself. She didn't think she would have the nerve at first but, as the silence lengthened uncomfortably, she changed her mind. Dammit, they were both supposed to be grown-ups here! Why *shouldn't* she say something? It was exactly the kind of thing she ought to be able to discuss if she was treating this purely as a job.

Folding a tea towel and picking up some plates, Kate took the plunge. 'I've been thinking about what Alex said.'

'Which particular thing?' Finn asked. He was putting glasses back in the cupboard and sounding abstracted, as if he was thinking about something else entirely. 'I can't believe I used to worry that she was too quiet,' he added. 'She never shuts up now.'

Kate eyed his back with some resentment. He obviously wasn't going to make it easy for her!

'We were talking about your sister's visit,' she prompted him, and Finn turned, grey eyes suddenly alert.

'Ah.'

'Alex suggested that it might be an idea to practise a kiss

before Stella arrives,' said Kate, amazed at how calm she sounded.

'And what do you think?' asked Finn.

To her outrage, there was an undercurrent of something that might have been amusement, or possibly surprise. Whatever it was, it was enough to make Kate put up her chin and clutch the plates she was carrying defensively to her chest.

'I think we should,' she said coldly. 'There's no point in this elaborate charade if we're going to look as if we've never touched each other before. If your sister is as shrewd as you say she is, she'll see that we're uncomfortable together and it won't take her long to guess that we're not really engaged at all.'

'I suppose you're right,' Finn admitted grudgingly.

Kate's lips tightened. That's it, make it sound like kissing her would be a tiresome chore he'd really rather get out of!

'It's not going to be easy for either of us,' she said sharply, annoyed with him and even more annoyed with herself for wanting him even when he was making her cross. 'I just think it would be a lot less embarrassing if we don't have to kiss for the first time in front of an interested audience.'

Finn put the last glass away and closed the cupboard door. 'So you want me to kiss you?'

Yes.

'I don't *want* you to kiss me,' lied Kate with a frosty look. 'I'm merely suggesting that it might be sensible if we practised kissing each other in advance so it's not too awkward when we have to convince your sister.'

'OK,' said Finn. 'Shall we do it now?'

'Now?' faltered Kate. Having won her point, she was unprepared for him to follow it up quite so quickly.

'We might as well get it over with.'

Charming! But she was the one trying to convince him

that it was just a job as far as she was concerned, Kate acknowledged reluctantly. She could hardly turn round now and demand a romantic setting or a more intimate moment.

She swallowed. 'All right.'

Finn came over and took the plates from her nerveless hands. He put them on the table and turned back to where Kate stood, her pulse booming thunderously in her ears and her knees treacherously weak.

'Shall we do it then?' he asked, unsmiling.

Her throat was so dry that Kate couldn't speak. She nodded dumbly instead, and Finn took her by the waist to draw her slightly closer. Trying to anticipate and make it easier for him, Kate tilted up her face as he bent his head, but they ended up bumping noses and he released her awkwardly.

'It's just as well we're practising,' she said huskily, trying to laugh but not really succeeding.

'Just as well,' Finn agreed. 'Shall we try again?'

'OK.'

This time, he put his hands on her arms and slid them slowly to her shoulders as he looked down into her eyes almost thoughtfully. Locked into that cool, grey gaze, Kate stood mouse-still while he cupped her face between his warm hands. She was quivering with anticipation, and there was a fluttery feeling of excitement beneath her skin that jolted as Finn bent his head towards hers once more.

It was a better kiss this time. Much better. So much better, in fact, that Kate felt the floor drop away beneath her feet as his mouth touched hers. She put her hands out to steady herself against him, and he kissed her again and then things got a bit confused.

Afterwards, Kate wasn't sure how it had happened, but one moment she was standing there being controlled—relatively, anyway—and the next her arms were sliding round his waist, and she was melting into him, holding him, kissing him back.

Finn's fingers had drifted from her cheeks and were tangled in her hair. Kate had always thought of his mouth as being cool and stern, even hard, but it didn't feel like that now. It was warm and persuasive against hers, and it felt so right that she stopped thinking at all and gave herself up to the heady pleasure of kissing and being kissed while the tiny tremor of excitement inside her grew stronger and stronger, feeding on the touch of his lips and the taste of his mouth and the feel of his hard, solid body against hers, until it overwhelmed that gentle, reassuring rightness and spun Kate out of control.

She clung to Finn, half thrilled, half terrified by the intensity of it, not knowing how to break the kiss, not wanting to, but afraid that unless she did there would be no way she could keep him from knowing how she really felt.

Perhaps Finn sensed her confusion, or perhaps he too was alarmed by how quickly the brief practise kiss had taken on a life of its own, swamping their sensible intentions and sweeping them into uncharted territory, for he hesitated and then, with difficulty, lifted his head.

There was a long, long moment when they just stared shakily at each other, and then he seemed to realise that his fingers were still entwined in her soft, brown curls, and he pulled his hands abruptly away.

Kate was left reeling. It was all she could do to stay upright. She was dizzy and disorientated, and her heart was pumping with something close to terror at how badly she wanted to throw herself back into Finn's arms and beg him to kiss her again.

Finn was looking aghast, and he stepped back as if afraid that she would do just that.

'Well…' he said, and then hesitated, evidently not knowing what else to say.

'That...that was better,' Kate managed unsteadily. The appalled expression on Finn's face was enough to bring her crashing back to earth. So much for dreams when all it took was a single kiss to make the scales fall from his eyes and persuade him that he might be able to love her after all.

All she could do now, Kate decided, was try and treat it lightly and whatever she did, not let him guess how much kissing him had meant to her. She wasn't sure she could pretend to have hated it as much as he obviously had, but she could at least reassure him that she wasn't going to make a big deal out of it.

'Yes,' said Finn, sounding almost as dazed as she felt. 'I suppose it was.'

'And at least we know we can do it now.'

'Yes.'

An agonising pause. What should she do now? Kate wondered wildly. Reassure him that it wouldn't happen again? Ignore the whole thing? Or finish putting the plates away?

In the end it was Finn who broke the silence. 'I've got a few letters to write,' he said as if he had never kissed her, never had his fingers entwined in her hair. 'I'll be in my study if you need me.'

Kate watched him go, churning with frustration and still dizzy with desire. Perhaps she should go along in a few minutes and knock on his study door and tell him that she needed him to take her upstairs and make love to her all night and promise to let her stay with him for ever.

She wouldn't, of course. She wasn't supposed to need him for anything more intimate than the need to service the boiler, or to sort out a muddle with her housekeeping money.

Drearily, Kate picked up the plates once more. Thinking about that look on Finn's face after he had kissed her made her wince. The kiss had been a mistake.

It hadn't felt like a mistake, though. Not to her.

But Finn clearly wished it had never happened. She should never have suggested it, Kate realised. They had just got to the stage where they could talk to each other without too much constraint, and now the kiss had changed everything. Finn had retreated to his study, and there was no point in hoping that he would emerge ready to discuss what had happened. Kate was prepared to bet that he had never read any of those magazine articles which insisted on the importance of communication and talking things through in a successful relationship.

Not that they *had* a relationship, she reminded herself with a sigh. She had a job, and Finn had a potential embarrassment, but that wasn't much of a basis on which to build a life together, was it?

It didn't stop her waiting tensely for Finn to make at least some reference to the fact that they had kissed. It had been pretty shattering, after all, and judging from his expression when he let her go, for him as well as for her.

But Finn never so much as mentioned it. He carried on exactly as before, having apparently wiped the whole experience from his mind. Kate wished, not without some resentment, that she could do the same, but the memory of that devastating kiss was like a constant strumming just beneath her skin, leaving her edgy and unable to settle.

The days weren't too bad, and there were times when she was walking Derek or laughing with Alex that Kate even managed to persuade herself that she was well on the way to forgetting it quite as effectively as Finn. And then he would come back from work and walk into the kitchen looking solid and austere, and she would remember the kiss in such vivid detail that he might as well have bent her over the kitchen table and kissed her all over again.

Although *that* clearly wasn't going to happen. Finn was polite but guarded, and he was very careful to keep his distance. Even a brush of the fingers was clearly out. Swinging wildly between resentment and frustration, Kate grew increasingly tetchy with him until even Finn was driven to comment.

'What's the matter with you at the moment?'

'Nothing.'

'Please don't make me guess,' he said with an exasperated sigh. 'I've had a difficult day and I'm not in the mood for playing games. You might as well just tell me what's wrong.'

Oh, yes, she could just see herself doing that! Well, Finn, she could say, the thing is that I'm desperately in love with you and finding it all a bit frustrating. I know you'd rather pick up slugs, but do you think you could just take me to bed anyway and make me feel better?

Kate was half tempted to say it just to provoke Finn into a reaction other than his habitual range from expressionless to irritable but, as she strongly suspected that it would turn out to be one of unadulterated horror, she thought she would spare herself the humiliation. She took out her feelings on the potatoes instead, mashing them with a vengeance.

'There's nothing wrong,' she said. 'What could be wrong? I'm just doing my job.'

Finn wrenched off his tie and tossed it onto the back of a chair. 'Your job doesn't involve you carrying on like an aggrieved wife!'

'No,' Kate agreed, banging the potato masher onto the side of the saucepan with unnecessary force. 'It involves looking after you, your daughter, your house and your dog. I don't have time to behave like a wife, let alone an aggrieved one!'

He sighed irritably. 'If you want some time off, Kate, why don't you just tell me?'

'Look, I'm just in a bad mood, all right?' she snapped.

If he pushed her any further she jolly well *would* tell him what was bothering her, and then he'd be sorry! 'There doesn't have to be a reason, does there? Or is there a clause in my contract which says I have to be Mary Poppins the whole time?'

'If this is just a bad mood, perhaps you'd better have the night off anyway,' said Finn.

'It's a bit late for that now,' Kate pointed out crossly. 'Besides, I'm going out tomorrow night.'

'Oh? Who with?' he demanded, sounding oddly disgruntled for a man who only a moment ago had been practically pushing her out of the door.

'With you,' said Kate. 'We're having drinks with your neighbour.'

The dark brows drew together ominously. 'Which neighbour?' he asked with foreboding.

'Laura. She's been away for a few weeks and thought it would be nice to catch up on all your news.'

Laura had been a very glamorous divorcee, and Kate had identified a distinctly predatory gleam in her eyes when she had rung the bell earlier that evening and asked for Finn. She hadn't been at all pleased to see Kate instead of Rosa, and even less happy when Kate made sure she could see the engagement ring on her finger.

Finn was still scowling. 'I hope you said I was busy.'

'No, I said we'd love to come.'

'We?'

'Yes, *we*, you and me! I realise that you've wiped it from your mind, but we are supposed to be engaged!'

'Pretending to be engaged!'

Kate flushed. 'That's what I meant.'

'And it's only when Stella's here,' Finn went on crossly. 'There's no need to rope the neighbours into this particular fantasy!'

'I wasn't roping anyone in,' she protested. 'This woman

came to the door, clearly planning an intimate tête-à-tête with you while I had this whacking great ring on my finger. Of course she noticed it straight away, that's what women do.' No need to tell Finn that she had made quite sure that Laura had seen it and was forced to comment on it. 'What was I supposed to do? Pretend I didn't exist?'

'You could have said you were engaged to someone else.'

'Oh, well, excuse me while I just go and shoot myself,' said Kate sarcastically. 'I am just so useless at telepathy and knowing who I'm allowed to tell and who I'm not! What's the big problem with Laura knowing anyway?' she added as a sudden suspicion crossed her mind.

Finn was pouring himself a large whisky. 'The problem is that I've been avoiding that woman ever since she moved in next door and discovered that I was a widower. I've managed to fob her off so far by saying that I'm not ready for another relationship.'

'So? Tell her that you changed your mind when you met me.'

Dream on, Kate!

'Great! So when you go, I'll have to tell her that our "engagement" is off, and then she'll think there's no reason for me not to think about another relationship,' grumbled Finn.

'You'll just have to learn to say no rather than hiding behind the fact that you're a widower,' said Kate robustly. 'I wouldn't have thought *you* would find that too hard,' she added with a slight edge. 'Off-putting seems to be your speciality!'

He paused with his glass halfway to his lips. 'What do you mean by that?'

'Well, you're not exactly approachable, are you?' she said, putting on oven gloves. 'This Laura must be a brave woman or very thick-skinned if she's been after you all that time. The rest of us wouldn't dare—we're all terrified of you!'

'I can't say I've ever noticed you being very terrified,' said Finn with an acid look.

'I just put a good face on it,' said Kate. 'I told you I was good at acting'

'You must be even better than I thought,' he said dryly, and for some reason the kitchen flared suddenly with the memory of the kiss they had shared. It burned in the air between them, bright and dangerous and so vivid that Kate could practically see herself clinging to him, practically feel his lips, and his hands in her hair.

Jerking her eyes away, she bent to take the casserole out of the oven, glad of the excuse to hide her hot face. 'Maybe I am,' she said, not quite as steadily as she would have liked.

By the time she straightened and had taken off the lid to stir, Finn was sitting at the table, staring broodingly down into his whisky.

'You didn't really say we would go round for drinks tomorrow, did you?'

'Yes, I did.' Kate had herself back under control. 'I didn't see any reason not to,' she said, sniffing appreciatively at the casserole. 'Once Laura discovered that she couldn't have you to herself, she started talking about inviting other people as well. It might be fun.'

Finn grunted. 'Making polite chit-chat over a lukewarm drink doesn't sound like much fun to me!'

'Oh, come on, you might meet someone interesting.'

'And what about Alex?' he said as if she hadn't spoken.

Kate rolled her eyes as she turned from the cooker. 'We're only going next door for an hour or so. Alex could probably come with us, or I'll ask Bella or Phoebe to come over. I'm sure they wouldn't mind. Anyway, I've accepted for you, so you'll have to go now,' she said putting an end to the argument. She started to untie her apron. 'See if you can get home a bit earlier tomorrow evening—we're invited for half past six.'

'You look nice.' Bella was playing cards with Alex at the kitchen table when Kate came downstairs the next evening wearing a full skirt with a tight waist and a laced top. 'Very Nell Gwynn! All the men will be panting to buy oranges from you!'

Kate tugged fretfully at her neckline. 'You don't think this is a bit low?'

'No, if you've got it, flaunt it!' said Bella cheerfully.

'I wish I'd brought more clothes with me. Laura looked awfully sophisticated.'

'I think you look beautiful,' said Alex loyally. 'Don't you, Dad?'

Kate spun round. She hadn't heard Finn come into the kitchen behind her, and her heart jerked at the sight of him, tall and austere in a dark suit.

He looked at Kate. 'She looks fine,' he said.

'Oh, Mr McBride, please stop!' said Kate, hiding her disappointment behind a pretence at being overcome. 'You'll turn my head with all these compliments!'

Finn sighed. 'You look absolutely beautiful... stunning...glamorous... What else am I supposed to say?'

'Thin,' prompted Kate.

'Sexy,' Bella suggested.

His eyes rested on Kate's cleavage. 'And sexy,' he said.

There was a tiny pause. Finn checked his watch. 'If you've quite finished fishing for compliments, we'd better go,' he said brusquely. 'The sooner we get there, the sooner we can leave.'

'Quite the party animal, isn't he?' said Bella.

Kate took him by the arm to turn him towards the door.

'Stop grumbling, it'll be fine,' she said. 'Just think of it as a dry run for when Stella comes—and you might at least *try* to look as if you're happy to be with me!'

As she had suspected, Laura had abandoned the idea of intimate drinks alone with Finn since Kate had thrust a spoke in her wheel, and a number of other neighbours had been invited along as well. The women were all wearing discreetly elegant numbers and Kate knew from the moment Laura opened the door that the laced top had been a mistake. Next to the others, she looked garish and flamboyant and more than a little tarty.

Her outfit seemed to go down very well with their husbands, though. Since it was too late to go for a sophisticated image, Kate opted for being fun instead, and Finn grew more and more boot-faced at the gales of laughter coming from the group around her.

'You're back early,' said Bella when they returned. 'We weren't expecting you back for ages. How did it go?'

'Excellent,' Finn bit out. 'Kate managed to ruin my reputation and break up several of my neighbour's marriages in a few short minutes!'

'I don't know what you're talking about,' said Kate crossly, still flushed and more than a little annoyed at being dragged away from the party on the flimsiest of excuses. She had been quite enjoying herself.

'Oh, yes, you do!' snarled Finn. 'You made a complete exhibition of yourself! Laura won't be at all surprised to hear our "engagement" is off after the way you were carrying on,' he said furiously. 'You were practically in Tom Anderson's lap!'

'I was not! Not that you would have been able to notice even if I had been,' she retorted. 'You spent the entire time pinned in the corner by Laura and you weren't exactly struggling to get free and circulate. Your body language is very revealing you know.'

'Not as revealing as that top,' Finn snapped back.

'Now, now, children, play nicely,' said Bella. 'I think you'd better work on how to look as if you're engaged before Stella arrives,' she told them. 'You see, generally when people get engaged it's because they love each other and want to spend the rest of their lives together, and not because they fight at parties. That usually comes *after* they get married!' she explained kindly.

'We're certainly going to have to do something different when Stella gets here,' said Finn. 'She's never going to believe we're a couple if Kate carries on the way she did this evening!'

'That shouldn't be a problem,' Kate informed him loftily. 'I was just excited at being appreciated for a change, and I know that's not going to happen when I'm with you!'

'Perhaps you need to give Stella a bit more evidence,' Bella put in diplomatically. 'I was talking to Phoebe while you were out, and we thought it would be a good idea to have a sort of engagement party for you while Stella's here. It's the sort of thing we would do if you were really engaged, and as you're a friend of Gib's, Finn, and Kate's a friend of Phoebe's, it would be natural for them to have a dinner for you and close friends—that's me and Josh and partners.'

She turned her blue gaze on Finn. 'We'll invite your sister along, of course. I'm sure if she saw your friends treating you as an engaged couple she'd be quite convinced, no matter how much you and Kate seemed to argue.'

'It's possible,' said Finn grudgingly, still in a bad mood with Kate. 'But there's no need for you to go to any trouble. This whole business is getting out of control as it is, without you and Phoebe getting involved as well.'

'Don't worry about us,' said Bella. 'Any excuse for a party! What do you think, Kate?'

Kate suspected, like Finn, that things could easily get out

of control, but he had been so irritating this evening that she didn't feel like supporting him now. 'I think it's a wonderful idea,' she said firmly. 'I'll give Phoebe a ring tomorrow and we'll sort out a date.'

Stella was due to arrive the following Tuesday. Kate spent the day before spring-cleaning the house from top to bottom. She put flowers in the guest room and set out soap and towels before shutting the door so that Derek couldn't roll on the bed. This was a new trick of his that worked better, from a canine point of view at least, the wetter and muddier he was. It hadn't gone down at all well with Finn when Derek had tried it on his bed.

She had planned a special welcome dinner for Stella, too, and was making individual rich chocolate mousses when Finn came down from saying goodnight to Alex the night before she was due to arrive.

'Is everything under control?'

'I think so,' said Kate. After that disastrous evening at Laura's, they had both recovered their equilibrium and were being polite to each other with only the occasional sharp aside. 'I've just got to finish these now. Her room is ready for her, and I'll put some champagne in the fridge tomorrow.'

Finn raised his brows. 'Champagne?'

'It's a celebration,' she pointed out with an edge of exasperation. 'You haven't seen your sister for a while, and we're getting married—at least as far as she's concerned. Of course we've got to have champagne!'

'If you say so.' Finn dipped his finger into the chocolate mixture, just managing to whip it out of the bowl before Kate swiped it.

'There's no point in going through with the whole pretence unless we're going to do it properly,' she said.

'No, you're right.' He licked his finger, ignoring her frown. 'This chocolate stuff is good.'

Carefully, Kate poured the chocolate mixture into individual ramekins. She waited until she had divided the last of it before asking Finn the question that was most on her mind. 'Do you think we'll be able to carry it off?'

'If we don't lose our nerve. Stella's very astute, though, so we can't afford to relax while she's here. She'll pick up instantly on anything odd. In fact—'

'What?' asked Kate when he stopped abruptly.

Finn didn't answer immediately. He paced around the table, his hands in his pockets and his shoulders hunched, debating whether to continue or not.

'I'm not sure how to ask you this, Kate,' he said at last, 'but I wonder how you would feel about sleeping with me while Stella is here.' He saw Kate's head jerk up from the bowl she was scraping and corrected himself hurriedly. 'I don't mean *sleep* with me, of course,' he said. 'I just mean…share a room.'

Of course. He wouldn't want to sleep with her, would he? Kate put down the bowl.

'I think Stella would think it a bit strange if we didn't,' Finn went on.

It's not a big deal. Wasn't that what she had said to Bella? She was the girl who wasn't going to take the situation seriously. The actress who wasn't bothered by silly little things like kisses or jumping into bed with her boss. She couldn't change her image now.

Kate started gathering up whisks and spoons and bowls to wash. 'Sure,' she said.

Finn looked at her, taken aback by her ready agreement. 'You will?'

'I was just saying that we might as well do the thing properly,' she pointed out reasonably. 'I don't mind sharing with you while your sister is around. I know you wouldn't…' She trailed off, embarrassed when it came to the crunch. 'That we wouldn't…you know…'

'I know,' he said dryly.

'We might as well start tonight, don't you think?' Kate suggested, determined to recover her confidence and carry the situation off with style. 'Then we'll look more natural when she gets here tomorrow morning.'

Of course, it was all very well being brisk and practical in the kitchen, but it was a different matter when the moment came. At least she had a nightdress with her. Kate got undressed in her own room and put it on, smoothing the silky material over her hips. She couldn't believe that she was actually going to walk along to Finn's bedroom and get into bed beside him! Her whole body was pumping and twitching with nerves.

Not a big deal, right?

Right.

Wrapping a dressing gown tightly around her, Kate took a deep breath and opened her door.

Finn was waiting for her, looking ill at ease in a crumpled pair of pyjamas. Kate guessed that he didn't normally wear them and had dug them out of a drawer to preserve the decencies.

'I'll take a pillow and sleep on the floor,' he said when she hesitated in the doorway.

'That defeats the purpose of the exercise, doesn't it?' Kate was amazed at how cool she sounded. 'What if Stella came in and saw that you were sleeping down there? It looks like a big bed,' she went on, still without a tremor, and she even managed a sort of laugh. 'I trust you to keep your hands off me!'

A wary expression had descended on Finn's face. He was probably baffled by her transformation from messy, muddled sentimentality to brisk practicality.

'Which side do you normally sleep?' said Kate, taking matters into her own hands.

'Over here.' He pointed, and she walked round the bed

to the other side and pulled back the duvet. Taking off her dressing gown, she draped it over a chair and got into bed. If Finn was waiting for her to make a fuss about the situation, he would have a long wait. Bella would be proud of her. She was cool.

After another puzzled glance, Finn switched off the main light. Kate pretended to be making herself comfortable as the bed creaked and dipped when he got in the other side and clicked off the bedside lamp.

'Well…goodnight,' he said.

'Goodnight.'

There, that was easy, thought Kate, trying not to think about the fact that Finn was lying bare inches away, or about how easy it would be to roll against him in the night. He flexed his shoulders to make himself comfortable and she caught her breath, wondering if it might just be the prelude to him moving closer…but no. He settled and lay still, and after a while there was only the steady sound of him breathing quietly in the dark.

Very, very gradually, Kate let herself relax. When it was obvious that Finn had fallen asleep, she congratulated herself on her cool. Really, there was nothing to it. Everything would be fine.

CHAPTER NINE

IT WAS still dark when Kate drifted out of sleep to find herself lying on her side with an arm over her. A hard, male arm holding her against the hard, male body behind her.

Finn. He must have rolled over in his sleep, she realised, blinking dreamily. She could feel his breath, deep and slow, just stirring her hair and that was enough to wake every nerve in her body, and set each one tingling, alert with wicked anticipation. 'No going back to sleep now!' they seemed to scoff at Kate's attempts to close her mind to his closeness. 'It's too late for that.'

It was much too late. Even with her eyes squeezed shut, Kate was aware of every millimetre of her own body, burning where it touched his. It felt so good to be held by him. She wished she could turn and nuzzle in to him, to wake him with soft kisses, and her eyes snapped open as her entrails liquefied at the thought.

She *could* turn.

She could kiss him.

She could pretend that she was sleeping too.

Once the idea was in her head, she couldn't dislodge it. It would be silly, and it might be very embarrassing, the sensible part of Kate's mind pointed out. She was supposed to be keeping her distance and impressing him with her cool. Snuggling up against him and running her hands over his body while she kissed her way to his mouth wouldn't do that.

But it would feel so good.

She could always stop, Kate reasoned to herself. She

didn't have to go that far. She didn't even need to wake him. She just wanted a glimpse of what it would be like if she belonged here in his arms, if Finn knew exactly who he was holding against him and would smile at the feel of her lips on his skin.

That wasn't asking too much, was it?

Kate stirred experimentally, but Finn just kept breathing into her hair. He must be sound asleep, she thought with a spurt of resentment. How could he be sleeping when she was awake and churning with desire? Couldn't he feel how much she wanted him?

Well, she could lie here all night or she could see what would happen if she turned over. She might as well accept that she wasn't going to go back to sleep either way.

Taking a deep breath, she sighed as if she were dreaming and rolled towards Finn, who promptly rolled away in his turn to lie on his back, the arm that had been around her now outflung across the pillow.

Typical. Kate eyed his slumbering form with frustration. Even in sleep he seemed determined to resist her. Well, they would see about *that*!

She shifted across the sheet, warm from his body, until she could snuggle into the solid strength of him. Finn was much taller than her standing up, but lying down Kate just fitted him nicely. She was very comfortable pressed into his side. She could put an arm over his chest to keep him close and rest her face against his throat, breathing in the scent of his skin, and all without him waking.

Stop now, Kate told herself sternly. Comfort wasn't everything, but it was enough for now.

Only it wasn't. Of course it wasn't.

Without making a conscious decision, Kate touched her lips to Finn's throat, and then again, and again, until she was working her way up and along his jaw. Her hand seemed to have acquired a will of its own, too, sliding under the pyjama jacket and around his lean waist.

She was playing with fire, and she knew it, but she couldn't help herself and she didn't care. Her kisses drifted back down to his collar, and she was just unfastening the top button when all at once Finn's breathing stilled.

She had woken him. Slowly, Kate lifted her head until she could look down into his face and see the gleam of his eyes in the darkness. She couldn't pretend that she was asleep now. With one part of her mind she registered that she might regret this moment in the morning, but now…oh, now was not the time for regrets.

Finn lay motionless beneath her, blinking away sleep. Kate could see him trying to adjust to wakefulness, and she braced herself for the moment when he realised who she was and what she was doing and jackknifed away from her in horror. But he just stared up at her for a long, long time before the arm behind her head came round so that his fingers could slide into her hair, and pull her head down towards him with exquisite, dreamlike slowness.

When their lips met at last, the dreaminess shattered and Kate sank into Finn and they kissed hungrily, again and again, as if to make up for all the waiting. Finn's other hand was sliding insistently over her satin nightdress, searching for the hem, and when he found it, it slipped beneath, rucking up the slithery material as he explored her thigh, the back of her knee, the curve of her hip.

The feel of his hand on her bare skin made Kate gasp, and fumble for the buttons of his pyjama jacket, but her fingers were so clumsy that in the end Finn simply pulled it over his head before rolling her beneath him abruptly. With a sigh of release, Kate wound her arms around his neck, pulling him closer, luxuriating in the feel of his bare back under her hands.

She was terrified that Finn would wake properly and realise what he was doing. She didn't care about the morning, didn't think about what they would do and say to explain this away. For now all Kate wanted was to abandon herself completely, to the touch of his hands, to the feel of his mouth as it drifted tantalisingly over her, to the hard demand of his body.

To the clutching pleasure and the slow, irresistible burn of excitement that left them gasping and powerless while a timeless rhythm swept them both up, up, up, too high, beyond thought, beyond feeling, to the very edge until Kate fell abruptly, tumbling into a heart-stopping intensity of sensation.

When she came to, Finn was lying heavily on top of her, breathing raggedly. She was having trouble working her lungs herself. They seemed to have forgotten how to function by themselves, and it took a conscious effort to draw each tiny, shuddering breath.

After a while, Finn moved away from her, muttering something that Alex would have had no trouble in identifying as a rude word.

Oh, yes! Kate wanted to say. Yes, indeed! But she thought she had better not.

He lay on his back beside her, trying to bring his breathing under control. 'I'm sorry,' he said at last. 'I didn't mean that to happen.'

'It was my fault.' Kate made a half-hearted effort to force some contrition into her voice. She knew she ought to feel guilty, but it was as if all those nerve endings that had been twitching and fretting uncomfortably for the past few weeks were now stretching and smirking with satisfaction. Her body didn't feel guilty at all. It felt very, very good. Better than it ever had before, in fact.

'I forgot where I was.' Which wasn't strictly true, but she was feeling too pleased with herself to worry about little details. 'I suppose I got a bit carried away.'

'I think we both did,' said Finn dryly.

Kate shifted onto her side so that she could look at him properly. 'Are you really sorry?' she made herself ask.

He turned his head on the pillow. 'No,' he said honestly after a moment. 'No, and I can't say that I didn't know what I was doing either, but it was very irresponsible. I wasn't planning on this happening. What if you got pregnant?'

'I won't do that. I'm still on the Pill.'

She still felt amazing, relaxed and replete. Even her toes were tingling with remembered pleasure. It wasn't a feeling she wanted to give up, not yet anyway. Given half a chance, she knew that Finn would say that it should never happen again. Kate wasn't sure that she could bear that.

'Look,' she said persuasively, 'we haven't hurt anybody else tonight. I think we both needed a bit of comfort, and we took it. What's wrong with that?'

She would have to be careful not to alarm Finn by seeming too keen. 'It doesn't mean anything to either of us,' she told him, 'but that's no reason why we shouldn't have some fun. It's not as if we're talking about for ever. I'm only here for a few weeks, and since we're going to be sharing a room, don't you think we should make the most of it? Unless you'd rather not,' she finished lamely, unnerved by the way Finn was watching her in silence.

'I daresay I could resign myself to it,' he said.

It took a few moments for Kate to realise that he was teasing. Dizzy with relief, she smiled at him. 'It would only be a temporary thing,' she tried to reassure him. 'Just while your sister is here.'

'Of course,' said Finn expressionlessly.

'No big deal.'

'No.'

'Neither of us is going to get involved.'

'Right.'

Silence. Kate studied Finn a little uneasily, not sure what to make of his curt replies. Was he regretting his decision already? In the darkness, his face was even harder to read than usual.

The main thing was that he hadn't repulsed her, she reasoned. There would be more nights like this. She couldn't ask for more than that. It was greedy to want him to love her as well, to want her for ever.

For now, Kate decided, she would do what she had said she would do, and make the most of what she had. She looked at Finn through the darkness and thought about his lips against her skin and the feel of his body beneath her hands, and the breath dried in her throat. For now, that was enough.

'Anyway, I'm sorry if I woke you,' she said, and then shivered with pleasure as Finn reached out and pulled her unresisting towards him.

'How sorry?' he asked.

She smiled as he kissed her. 'I'll show you,' she said.

The crunch of tyres on the gravel drive sent Derek into a frenzy of barking, and Kate paused in front of the hall mirror, running her fingers through her hair in a vain attempt to smooth her wild curls. She was surprisingly nervous about meeting Stella. Finn and Alex had gone to pick her up from the airport, and now this would be the moment of truth.

In the cool light of morning, Finn had made no reference to the night before. He had behaved so exactly as normal, grumbling about the state of the kitchen and refusing to allow Alex to meet her aunt in combat trousers and scruffy trainers, that Kate might have wondered if it had just been a wonderful dream if her body wasn't still pulsing with remembered pleasure.

Reeling, replete and short of sleep, she could hardly

string two words together, and her conversation at breakfast had been completely incoherent, at least judging by the funny looks Alex had given her. It was just lucky that Finn had to do the driving and not her.

Now she had to face the terrifyingly astute and perceptive Stella. Still, thought Kate with one last glance at her reflection as she headed for the door, there shouldn't be any problem convincing Stella that *she* was in love. She had that dazed, dopey look down pat.

On first sight, Stella had little in common with her brother. Several years older than Finn, she was plump and elegant, with beautifully cut grey hair, but she had the same shrewd grey eyes.

Waiting to greet her on the doorstep, Kate found herself enveloped in a warm hug. 'I cannot *tell* you how glad I am that Finn has found someone at last!' said Stella. She held Kate at arms' length and examined her face. 'Finn didn't tell me how pretty you were.'

Didn't he think she was pretty? Kate wondered with a pang. What *had* he told Stella, exactly? That she was nice-enough looking, but could never compare to the exquisite Isabel?

Finn was lifting an enormous suitcase out of the car. 'She's not pretty,' he said to his sister, whose jaw dropped, and even Kate was taken aback. She wasn't that bad, was she?

She stuck on a smile. Luckily, some people hadn't forgotten that they were supposed to be engaged! 'Thanks!' she said, finding no trouble at all in acting the part of aggrieved fiancée right then. 'You know, there's such a thing as being *too* honest!'

He set the suitcase on the gravel. 'I don't think you are pretty,' he said. 'Pretty's not enough for you.' He glanced at his sister, who was looking indignant on Kate's behalf.

'She's beautiful, not pretty,' he said, 'and I didn't tell you because I thought you'd be able to see it for yourself.'

There was a moment of stunned silence. Kate's face was hot and she stood feeling foolish and unsure what to do with herself. Finn had sounded so convincing that for a second or two there she had even wondered if he meant it. He was a better actor than she had thought.

Stella recovered first. 'Isn't that typical of Finn?' she said, linking arms with Kate. 'He gets you really cross and then says something like that which makes it impossible to stay furious the way you want to, so he always gets the last word!'

Alex was desperate to introduce her aunt to Derek, who was scratching behind the door to be let out to join the excitement, but the meeting was not a huge success. Stella was unimpressed.

'What kind of dog is *that*?'

'A very badly behaved one,' said Finn.

Alex leapt to Derek's defence. 'He's not!' she said hotly. 'He's very intelligent and perfectly trained, isn't he, Kate?'

'Well, maybe not *perfectly*,' Kate amended, thinking of the hours she had spent chasing Derek to try and get him on the lead, not to mention the chewed shoes and the stolen meat and the bed-rolling game.

Stella eyed Derek askance. She didn't actually say that he was the ugliest dog that she had ever seen, but she might as well have done. 'Where on earth did you find him?'

'It's Kate's fault,' said Finn. 'She fell into a pile of rubbish and came up with the dog, who has single-pawedly managed to disrupt my home and my office and is now costing me a fortune in vet bills and dog food!'

'Oh, Dad...!' said Alex reproachfully, and he smiled as he put an arm around her and hugged her.

Stella's eyes narrowed speculatively as she studied first

her brother and her niece, and then Kate. 'It looks like things have changed around here,' she said.

Apparently it wasn't just her brother who had changed. She frowned in a way that reminded Kate of Finn as she looked around the kitchen. 'I can't quite put my finger on it, but the whole house seems different,' she said. 'It's much warmer and more inviting somehow.'

Kate tried to see the room through a stranger's eyes. Already the kitchen seemed utterly familiar to her, although it wasn't quite as pristine as when she had first seen it, it had to be admitted. 'I think Finn would tell you it's much messier,' she said ruefully.

'I certainly would,' he said, getting mugs out of the cupboard. 'We can blame Kate for the difference in the house too.'

'Well, I think it's a great improvement,' said Stella as Kate plunged the cafetière.

Finn put the mugs on the table. 'So do I,' he said.

Kate's breath clogged in her throat. 'I'll remember that the next time you complain about my mess,' she managed, not knowing what to do except make a joke out of it, as the alternative was to throw her arms around him and beg him to say that he meant it. 'Alex, you're my witness!'

Stella was obviously dying for a chance to get Kate on her own, so she waved aside Finn's offer to show her to her room. 'You come with me, Kate,' she said.

Upstairs, she looked around the guest bedroom with pleasure. 'It all looks perfectly lovely,' she said, sniffing one of the scented soaps that Kate had put out for her. 'You're spoiling me—thank you!'

Kate shifted uncomfortably. 'I know Finn appreciates you coming all this way,' she said. 'He's told me how much you've done for him since Isabel died.'

'Oh, that was a terrible time,' sighed Stella, sinking down onto the bed. 'I did what I could, but Finn isn't easy to help. He keeps things to himself too much. Well, you must know how stubborn he is! It broke my heart to see him struggle on his own all these years. Sometimes it seemed as if he wouldn't ever let himself be happy again.'

'He loved Isabel very much.' Kate made herself say Isabel's name. It was as well to remember that last night didn't change anything, and that whatever Finn might say in front of his sister, her place in his life was only ever going to be temporary.

'I know he did,' said Stella, 'but he had Alex to think of as well as himself. I've been telling him for years that she needed a mother figure, and look at the difference in her now! I've never seen her so animated. She's come out of herself completely, and Finn says it's all thanks to you.'

She smiled at Kate. 'What he doesn't realise, of course, being a man, is that the real difference is in *him*. For years it's been like he was holed up behind a brick wall, refusing to let anyone close, but you've got under his guard. You must have done if you got him to give a home to that funny little dog! Finn doesn't even like dogs.'

'I think he likes Derek more than he admits,' said Kate loyally.

'That just proves my point!' said Stella getting to her feet. 'I haven't seen him look this happy and relaxed for years, and it's all because of you.' There were tears in her eyes as she embraced Kate. 'Finn won't say it, of course— you know what he's like!—but I can tell by the way he looks at you how much he loves you.'

So much for Stella and her famously astute perception!

Kate knew that Finn's sister was wrong. He didn't love her, but he *was* more relaxed, she could see that. Whether he was happy or not, she didn't ask. After Stella's arrival they were rarely alone together except for when they closed the bedroom door at night and they didn't talk then. They had said everything there was to be said that first night.

For both of them, the days that followed were a time out of time. Kate had to keep reminding herself that this was just a brief fling. It was about now and not for ever. They were being grown-up about the whole thing, and not taking it seriously at all. She was in thrall to the long, sweet nights they spent together, and refused to spoil them by thinking about the future or reminding Finn of reality. There would be time enough for that when Stella went home to Canada.

That was what Kate told herself, but it didn't stop her falling deeper and deeper in love with him. Sometimes she would look at him being perfectly ordinary like driving or putting on his glasses to read the paper, or just sitting and listening to his sister and daughter, and the air would evaporate from her lungs, while her heart clutched with the need to go over and touch him, to press her lips to his skin, and wind her arms around his neck and whisper a plea for him to take her upstairs, *now*.

Stella was a demanding guest, but Kate liked her much more than she had expected to. She was forthright and brisk at times, and she could be very tactless with Alex, but she clearly adored Finn, and she entered into whatever was going on with boundless enthusiasm. When Kate broached the idea of going to an engagement party at Phoebe's, Stella was thrilled.

'That sounds like a wonderful idea!' she said. 'If you hadn't been so obviously in love, I might be wondering if you two were actually going to get married,' she said that night over supper. 'You don't seem to be making any plans. Have you even picked a date for the wedding?'

Finn glanced at Kate. 'There isn't any rush.'

'There isn't any reason to wait, either,' Stella pointed out tartly. 'You're both old enough to know your own minds, neither of you has any other commitments and you're even living together. What's wrong with going ahead and getting married?'

'That's between Kate and I,' said Finn, gritting his teeth at his sister's interference.

'Of course, but you might think about other people, too.' Stella wasn't ready to give up yet. 'If you give us enough warning, Geoff and the kids can come over with me. I'm sure Kate's parents will want to know when the wedding is going to be too.'

'They're away at the moment,' said Kate, seizing on the excuse. 'That's one of the reasons we're waiting. I haven't told them about Finn yet.'

'Well, I don't see the need for all this secrecy,' grumbled Stella. 'Thank goodness these friends of yours are prepared to get into the right spirit and have a bit of a celebration! If it was left to you two it might never happen.'

'Stella, will you please stop trying to organise our lives? Kate and I are perfectly happy.'

'If you're not going to think about yourselves, you might at least think about Alex.'

'Alex is perfectly happy with the way things are, too,' said Finn tensely. 'Aren't you, Alex?'

'Ye-es,' Alex agreed cautiously. 'But it would be better if you and Kate did get married,' she added, taking Finn and Kate aback. 'Then I'd know Kate would stay for ever and look after Derek.'

Stella shot her brother a triumphant look. 'Your daughter's got more sense than you,' she told him. 'I might not make that dog my priority, but in every other way she's got it right. You'll lose Kate if you're not careful, and you don't want that, do you?'

Finn looked across the table at Kate, who was looking acutely uncomfortable. She was wearing one of those vibrantly coloured tops of hers and her hair tumbled as messily as ever to her shoulders. Her cheeks were flushed, and the brown eyes which met his for a fleeting moment were bright and clear.

'No,' he agreed softly, 'I don't want that.'

'Hey!' Kate thought it was time to lighten the atmosphere. 'I'm not going anywhere. This is a very nice house and Derek is a very nice dog, and I suppose you two aren't bad either,' she added, winking at Alex. 'Why wouldn't I stay for ever?'

To her surprise, Alex came to stand by her side 'Do you promise?' she said intensely.

What could she say? Kate put an arm around her to hug her close. 'I promise,' she said, and wished that it could be true.

'It's going to be a posh-frock affair,' Phoebe told Kate on the phone the next day. 'Make sure you all come dressed up to the nines.'

'Bella said it was just supper.'

'No, we've decided to have a proper dinner party since you and Finn met at dinner here.'

Kate held the phone away from her ear and stared at it in a puzzled manner. 'We met at work, Phoebe!'

'You met here for the first time socially,' said Phoebe firmly. 'And we want to make it a proper celebration for you.'

'Phoebe,' said Kate carefully, lowering her voice in case Stella came into the kitchen. 'You do know that Finn and I aren't really engaged, don't you? The party is just a bit of icing on the cake to convince his sister.'

'Of course I remember,' said Phoebe with such dignity that Kate was pretty sure that she and Bella had got carried away with their planning and forgotten little details like the fact that she and Finn weren't actually going to get married at all. 'But that's no reason not to do things in style,' she added, making a swift recovery.

'Well, don't get carried away!'

Phoebe pretended to sound hurt. 'Would I?'

'Bella would,' said Kate. 'Keep her under control, Phoebs. Stella seems to have accepted our supposed engagement so far, but she's not an idiot and she's bound to get suspicious if you go over-the-top with this dinner.'

'Relax,' said Phoebe soothingly. 'It'll be fun!'

Kate wasn't so sure. She loved her friends dearly, but she was ridiculously nervous about the night ahead as she and Finn got ready to go out that evening. It was hard enough keeping up the pretence in front of Stella without the interested gaze of all her closest friends on her. They would be watching her and Finn together and, knowing Phoebe and Bella, it wouldn't take them any time to see how she really felt about him. Kate just hoped they wouldn't give her away.

'I wish we weren't going out,' she sighed as she searched for her favourite earrings on top of the chest of drawers.

In the mirror above, she could see Finn shrugging himself into a shirt. The casual intimacy of getting dressed in the same room still gave Kate a tiny thrill each time.

'I know,' he said as he began fastening buttons. 'I'd rather stay in myself, but Stella is raring to meet everyone else.' He sighed. 'She's probably hoping to recruit some allies in her campaign for an early wedding.'

'It's all getting a bit complicated, isn't it?' said Kate, thinking of the promise she had made to Alex. She shouldn't have made a promise she couldn't keep, she thought guiltily.

'It's my fault,' said Finn. He tucked his shirt into his trousers. 'I should have known that my sister wouldn't stop at satisfying herself that you really existed. She won't be happy until she has the details of table settings and flowers and which hymns we have chosen!' He reached for a tie and looped it round his neck. 'I tell you, sometimes I wish we had never started this pretence!'

'Do you?' asked Kate.

Finn's hand stilled at his tie and his eyes met hers in the mirror. 'No,' he said.

His cool grey gaze locked with her warm brown one in the mirror, and for Kate it was as if the world stopped turning. Without taking his eyes from hers, Finn finished his tie and walked over slowly to put his hands on her shoulders.

'I can't imagine what we did without you,' he said as if coming into the middle of a conversation. 'Whenever Stella has been over before the visits have been a bit tense, but it's gone really well this time, and it's all due to you. Stella thinks you're wonderful.'

He paused, his hands warm and strong on her shoulders, and Kate let herself lean back against him just because she could and it felt so good.

'I've never thanked you properly for everything you've done,' Finn said soberly. 'And I don't just mean the pretence. The house looks great, you produce endless good meals, and then there's Alex…she's happy.'

'And you?' Kate nerved herself to ask.

Finn turned her slowly between his hands until she was facing him and he could look down into her face. 'I'm happy, too,' he said, and bent his head to kiss her.

Kate put her arms around his waist and leant blissfully into him. It wasn't a long kiss, but it was very sweet, and it was the first time he had kissed her when it wasn't dark and there wasn't anyone to convince. This kiss was just between the two of them. Neither of them could pretend now that it was only for show.

'Hey, you guys!' Stella was banging on the door, startling them apart. 'Hurry up, the taxi's here!'

When Finn released her, Kate could barely stand. Adrift in a wash of sensation, she felt oddly insubstantial, as if it was another person entirely who shimmered as she walked down the stairs, got into a taxi, and gave the driver directions to Phoebe's house dropping off Alex with Finn's neighbour first.

'Kate, you look absolutely fabulous!' said Gib, jaw dropping in surprise as he opened the door, and the others were just as complimentary.

'Look at her, she's glowing!'

'It must be love!'

Kate hardly heard any of it. She was finding it hard to concentrate on anything except the thought of going home with Finn, saying goodnight to Stella, and closing the bedroom door, when Finn would kiss her again and peel the dress from her shoulders and pull her down onto the wide bed…

'Kate, Kate, wake up!' Bella was waving a hand in front of her face, startling Kate out of her dreams.

'What?'

'We're about to open a bottle of champagne for you. You might at least make an effort to look as if you're on the same planet as the rest of us!'

Blinking, Kate looked around her. Stella was nose to nose with Phoebe and Josh, and the others were encouraging Gib as he eased the cork out of the champagne bottle. Finn was there, too, but slightly apart, smiling austerely, and Kate felt herself melting inside as someone put a glass of champagne into her hand.

'OK,' said Gib, when the champagne had been poured and everyone had a glass. 'I'd like to propose a toast to Finn and Kate. Unlikely as it seemed at first, they seem to go together perfectly, and I think we all want to wish them every happiness, because they both deserve it more than anyone else I can think of.'

'To Finn and Kate!' the others chorused. 'Hear, hear!'

Kate looked at Finn, wondering what they were supposed to do now. He didn't seem particularly perturbed, it had to be said. His grey eyes were alight, and he was smiling, and she couldn't help smiling back.

Oblivious to everyone else, he came over to put his arm around her, and pulled her into his side. 'Thank you,' he said simply. 'We're very grateful to all of you,' he said, glancing around, and then he looked down into Kate's face. Her brown eyes were shining. 'Aren't we, Kate?'

'Yes,' she breathed, not knowing what he said, but understanding that he wanted her to agree with him. 'Oh, yes.' But she wasn't thinking about being grateful, she was just thinking about how much she loved him and how she couldn't wait for his arm to tighten around her and his mouth to come down on hers.

When it did, she gave herself up to the sweetness without a thought for their audience, and when Finn finally released her, it was bizarre to hear a splatter of applause.

'I think that answers all our questions,' said Gib dryly.

'Except when is the wedding?' Stella put in, spotting her chance.

'Yes, good point.' Phoebe and Bella chimed in as Finn released Kate reluctantly. 'When is it?'

Finn didn't take his eyes from Kate's. 'Soon,' he said.

CHAPTER TEN

PHOEBE and Bella had obviously spent days planning and preparing dinner, and had put so much effort into decorating the table and bullying everyone into dressing up that Kate felt desperately guilty that it wasn't for real. They couldn't have made more fuss if she and Finn really had been engaged—in fact, Kate was beginning to suspect that her friends didn't quite believe that the whole thing was a pretence.

Bella's boyfriend, Will, was there, and Josh had brought along a new girlfriend, and together with Phoebe and Gib and Stella, who was on fine form, they made a lively party. Finn and Kate weren't required to contribute much, which was just as well.

Part of Kate wished that she could enjoy it all more, but she was having trouble concentrating on the conversation. All she could think about was going home with Finn and closing the bedroom door and shutting out the rest of the world. She made an effort to laugh and smile at the right points, but with Finn sitting beside her it was hard to focus. She wanted to put her hand on his thigh, to kiss his throat, to make him stand up and drag her away from the chatter and the laughter and the pretending.

'So, that's it then,' said Phoebe, when Kate pulled herself together sufficiently to help carry the plates through to the kitchen after the main course.

'What do you mean?'

'You're in love with Finn, aren't you?'

Kate set the plates carefully on the draining board. 'Why do you say that?'

'It's obvious. I don't think you've even registered that there's anyone else in the room!'

'Sorry,' Kate muttered. 'I really do appreciate all the trouble you and Bella have gone to but…'

'But Finn is the only person in there who seems real?' Phoebe smiled. 'I know.'

'OK, so I am a bit in love with him,' said Kate with a shade of defiance.

'A bit?'

Kate gave in. 'A lot.'

'What about Finn? I mean, I can see he's making an effort to join in, but there's something about the way he's making a point of not looking at you that's a dead give-away. I reckon he's pretty smitten too.'

'I don't think so,' she said sadly. 'He's just a good actor. I haven't told him how I feel, and I'm not going to. We're having a nice time at the moment, but I know it's not going to last. As soon as Stella leaves, I'll get a new job and that will be that. It's just a temporary thing.'

Phoebe looked at Kate in concern. 'Is that going to be enough for you?'

Kate looked bleakly back at her friend. 'It's going to have to be,' she said.

But the conversation with Phoebe had had its effect. It was true that Phoebe knew her better than most, but if her feelings for Finn were that obvious, she would have to be careful.

It would be awful if Finn guessed that she was in love with him. Kate cringed inwardly at the thought. It would make the situation unbearably awkward for them both. The last thing she wanted was to put him in the position of having to explain to her that he wouldn't—couldn't—ever love anyone the same way as he had loved Isabel. It wasn't as if she hadn't known all along that she could never compare to his dead wife.

Kate decided that it would be easier for Finn if she tried to keep more of a distance, but it was hard not to respond when he reached for her in the dark, or to pretend that she wasn't pleased to see him when he walked through the door. She just couldn't do cool and reserved, no matter how hard she tried.

It was even harder when Stella went off to visit various friends. She was away nearly a week, and Kate was alarmed to discover how easy and comfortable it felt with just the three of them—plus the dog, of course—in the house. It was like being a proper family. Sometimes Kate had to make herself remember that she was only a temporary member of it, and that she wouldn't always be able to chatter with Alex or hum as she pottered around the kitchen or climb into bed next to Finn.

Stella's departure should have meant that they could drop the fiction that Kate was more than a housekeeper, but Alex continued to treat her in exactly the same way, and when Finn and Kate discussed the matter in bed the night before she left, they decided that it was hardly worth reverting to the previous sleeping arrangements while she was away.

'You know what Stella's like,' said Finn. 'I wouldn't put it past her to turn up again without warning just to have another nag about fixing a wedding date.'

'We might as well stay as we are, then,' said Kate, trying to sound offhand, as if she didn't really care one way or the other.

'Might as well,' Finn agreed in an equally indifferent voice, but then he rolled Kate beneath him and she felt him smiling as he kissed her throat, and her heart swelled with relief and happiness.

Better to make the most of the time she had left, she decided. Plenty of time to be cool when Stella had gone back to Canada and there was no more reason to share Finn's life, no excuse to turn to him in the night and wind her arms around his neck and kiss him back. She would store up memories instead, and squirrel them away to comfort her in the bleak future that stretched ahead when her job here was over.

Stella's absence meant that Finn took the opportunity to go back to work, and with Alex at school, and the days brightening, Kate decided to spring-clean the house again. She was being paid to be a housekeeper, she reminded herself, so she might as well keep house.

She started at the top, blitzing the bathroom and all the bedrooms. Inspired, she pulled out the beds, vacuumed into the corners, dusted and polished and tidied away the clutter that irritated Finn so much.

When it came to his room, Kate was quite embarrassed at the state she had reduced it to. Each side of the bed reflected their different personalities. On her side, the table could hardly be seen beneath a mass of moisturisers, tissues, pens, nail polishes, emery-boards, books, magazines, bits of jewellery and cotton wool, buttons, torn price tags, receipts...ah, there was that comb! She had been looking for it for ages.

Good God, where had all this stuff *come* from? It was as if her things were breeding and taking over Finn's room. They had yet to make a break for his side of the bed, but it could only be a matter of time.

Kate swept everything away and gave the table a good dust before heading round to Finn's side. Tidying *his* table wasn't going to take long. Apart from the businesslike lamp and electronic alarm clock, all that marred its pristine state was a small pile of coins that he had emptied out of his pocket last night.

Hardly a mess, then, but Kate was determined to tidy them away as a point of principle. Unsure what to do with them, she opened the little drawer under the table and was about to tip the coins in when she stopped. A framed photograph was lying face down in the drawer.

Slowly, Kate lifted it out, knowing what she would see when she turned it over. Isabel.

Of course Finn would have had a photograph of her by his bed, where she would be the first thing he saw when he woke, and the last before he slept. Kate's heart cracked at the thought of how much he still loved and missed his wife.

Holding the photograph in her hands, she sank down onto the edge of the bed. He must have put it away when they had first discussed sharing a room, unable to bear the thought of seeing Isabel's face when another woman was where she ought to be. The contrast would have been too much to take.

Kate looked down at Finn's wife. She had been so beautiful with those great, dark eyes and that sweet smile. How could Finn ever think about putting anyone in her place?

Biting her lip, she leant forward to slip the frame back into the drawer and saw a letter on the floor. She must have pulled it out inadvertently when she took out the photograph. She picked it up, not wanting to read it, but unable to avoid a glimpse of the words 'love always and for ever' written in Finn's black, decisive scrawl.

Always and for ever.

Kate stood up, put the letter back underneath the picture and closed the drawer.

Time to get real. Finn was never going to love her the way she loved him. It was no use hoping and pretending and burying her head in the sand. Oh, of course she had told herself that she knew that Finn still loved Isabel, but she hadn't really *believed* it until now. Finn didn't say things he didn't mean. He *would* always love Isabel. He would love her for ever.

Kate was quiet that evening, but when Finn asked her

what the matter was she smiled and shook her head. 'Nothing. I'm a bit tired that's all.'

And when they went to bed, she clung to him, unable to imagine how she was going to be able to bear saying goodbye, but knowing that she was going to have to find a way.

Stella came back from what she called her 'tour of England' three days later, and immediately noticed the change in Kate. 'What's wrong?' she demanded bluntly the moment the two of them were alone. 'Have you two had a fight?'

'Of course not,' said Kate.

'I know Finn can be difficult,' said Stella, clearly not believing a word, 'but you're so good for him, and Alex is so happy now, too,' she went on. 'I couldn't bear it if it didn't work out between you and Finn.'

Stella was just going to have to bear it, the way she was, Kate thought sadly.

'Really, Stella, everything's fine,' she lied.

They all went to the airport to see Stella off. Kate was sorry to see her go, and not just because her departure meant that there was no excuse to stay with Finn and Alex any longer. Finn's sister could be abrasive at times, but her heart was in the right place, and Kate liked her warmth and her enthusiasm and her no-nonsense approach.

Even so, she was surprised at how emotional Stella got when it came to say goodbye. She hugged Kate tightly and thanked her for everything she had done, and then she turned to her brother.

'You keep hold of Kate,' she told him as she kissed him. 'She's just what you need.'

Alex was the last to be hugged. 'Make sure your father doesn't do anything stupid,' said Stella.

'Promise you'll let me know as soon as you've decided a date for the wedding,' were her parting words before she went through passport control.

'I don't know how I'm going to tell her that there's not going to be any wedding,' sighed Finn as they headed back to the car with that sinking sense of anticlimax that comes with a goodbye. 'She's never going to forgive me.'

'Maybe you won't have to tell her,' said Alex, scuffing along beside him.

'What do you mean?'

'You could go ahead and get married.'

Finn stopped in mid-stride. 'Alex, the only reason Kate and I have gone through all this is because you said you didn't want a stepmother.'

'I wouldn't mind Kate,' said Alex.

There was a moment of appalled silence while the three of them stood as if marooned in the middle of the busy terminal. Kate didn't dare look at Finn, but she could feel the tension in him. She was going to have to do something to defuse the situation before he exploded.

'I think you'd soon get bored of me,' she told Alex in an effort to pass it off lightly. She even managed a feeble smile.

Alex's mouth set in a stubborn line. 'No, I wouldn't.'

'I'd be very strict. It would be bed at eight o'clock every night, and no television during the week. You wouldn't like that, would you?'

'No,' Alex admitted, 'but it would be better than you going.'

'All right, Alex, that's enough,' said Finn in a curt voice. 'Kate's done us a favour, but she's got her own life to live now.'

'But—'

'I don't want to hear any more about it,' he said with an air of finality and strode out through the doors towards the car park leaving Alex and Kate to trail silently behind him.

It was a tense drive home. Finn shut himself in his study as soon as they got back, telling Kate that he was going to do some work and didn't want to be disturbed. Alex sulked in her bedroom with Derek.

Kate wasn't sure what to do. Carry on as normal, she supposed. Whatever normal was now.

At least she could spare Finn an awkward conversation, she decided, and quietly moved all her things out of his room and back into her own before he had to ask her to do it. She made up her old bed and changed Finn's sheets. Now they could pretend that nothing had ever happened.

Finn didn't notice until later that night when he had said goodnight to a still sullen Alex. He came downstairs to find Kate wiping down the cooker and trying not to think about what she was going to do next.

'You've moved your things,' he said abruptly.

'Yes, I…I thought it would be easier that way.'

'Easier?' Finn repeated as if he didn't understand the word.

'We agreed that we would only sleep together until Stella left,' Kate made herself say.

'I know we did, but—' Finn stopped, thinking better of what he had been about to say. 'Yes, you're right of course,' he said stiffly instead. 'There's no reason to carry on now that she's gone.'

'No,' she said bleakly.

There was an uncomfortable silence while the air between them churned with things left unsaid.

'It was just a temporary thing,' said Kate to reassure him that she understood and wasn't going to make a fuss.

'Yes.'

Another agonising pause.

Kate wrung out the cloth she had been using to wipe the hob and fixed on a bright smile. 'I'd better think about what I'm going to do next,' she said, setting about the draining board. Anything other than look at Finn and having to resist the impulse to throw herself into his arms and beg him to let her stay.

'Do you know what you want to do?'

Stay with you and Alex. 'No,' said Kate instead, 'but I'm sure I'll find something. I can always go back to temping.'

Finn took a turn about the kitchen. 'I don't suppose you would consider staying on, would you?' he asked suddenly, as if the words had been forced out of him against his will.

Kate's heart lurched into her throat and she had to swallow hard before she could speak. 'I thought you were going to try and manage without a housekeeper?'

'That was the idea—it was what Alex wanted—but it's going to be difficult. Rosa's definitely not coming back and…well, the truth is that I've been thinking about what Stella said,' he went on in a rush. 'Alex does need a woman here and she likes you. She's just been begging me to ask you to stay.'

He stopped. 'Would you think about it?'

Kate twisted the cloth between her hands. She wanted to stay, but would she be able to bear just being a housekeeper now?

'I don't know,' she said hesitantly. 'I don't think I could be a housekeeper for ever.'

'I was thinking more about you being a wife,' said Finn.

Kate's head jerked up to stare at him incredulously. 'A *wife*?'

'I don't seem to be putting this very well.' Finn raked a hand through his hair with a sigh. 'I'm trying to ask if you'll marry me.'

Kate opened her mouth and then closed it again. 'But… *Why*?' she managed at last.

'It seems sensible,' he said. 'It would solve the problem of finding someone to look after that dog for a start!'

'Oh, well, that seems like a good enough reason!'

'Seriously,' he said, 'Alex likes you. She's never been prepared to even consider the idea of having a stepmother before, but you...you're different. I think she'd be happy if you were here as a housekeeper, but she'd feel much more secure knowing that you would always be there for her.'

Kate looked at him, her brown eyes very clear. 'How would *you* feel?'

'I'd be happy, too,' said Finn, meeting her gaze. 'We've got on well these last few weeks, haven't we?'

Kate thought about the long, sweet nights, about waking to his lips on her shoulder, about being able to turn in the dark and run her hands over his lean, hard body. 'Yes,' she agreed huskily. 'Yes, we have.'

'It would mean you wouldn't have to go back to temping. Of course you could get a job if that's what you wanted to do, but you've always said that you're not that interested in a career, and you're much better at making a home than at being a secretary.'

Finn seemed determined to outline all the advantages for her, as if she couldn't work them out for herself. 'It might not be very romantic,' he told Kate, 'but there are worse reasons for getting married than comfort and security.'

True, thought Kate, but she had always imagined getting married for the best reasons. She had managed to crumple the dishcloth into a tight ball, and she bit her lip as she went back to wiping around the sink.

'What about Isabel?' she asked.

Finn hesitated. 'I think she would understand. She would want what was best for Alex, and that's what I want too.'

So he wasn't even going to pretend that he was marrying her for love, thought Kate, mindlessly wiping. Perhaps it was better that way. She wouldn't have believed him if he'd tried to convince her that he wanted her for more than practical reasons.

It was funny, she thought wistfully. You could dream and dream about something but somehow when it came true it was never quite as you had imagined it.

Be careful what you wish for, she reminded herself with a wry inward smile, or you just might get it. Only a few minutes ago, she had longed for Finn to ask her to marry him, and now he had. What was the point now in wishing that she could have his heart as well? She had known all along that it would always belong to Isabel.

Folding the cloth, she laid it carefully on the draining board. 'Can I think about it?' she asked Finn, amazed at her own calm.

'Of course.' Finn was a bit disconcerted by her self-possession as well. Not surprising, given how eagerly she had always responded to him. He must have thought that she would jump at the chance, Kate thought. 'I don't want to push you into something you don't feel comfortable with,' he said.

Kate looked at him. The only thing that would make her comfortable right then would be for him to put his arms around her, and tell her that he wanted her to stay, not for his daughter, not for his dog, but for him.

But you could only have so many dreams come true in a day, couldn't you?

She smiled at him a little remotely. 'I think I'll go to bed,' she said. 'It's been a long day.'

Finn watched her as she went to the door. 'Kate,' he said abruptly, and she turned.

'Yes?'

'I...' Whatever it was, he changed his mind. 'Nothing,' he said.

'*Marry* him?' Bella stared across the table at Kate. The three of them were sitting in their favourite bar where Kate had called them to an urgent case conference the following evening. 'You're not seriously considering it, are you, Kate? *Are* you?' she added suspiciously before slumping back in her chair and shaking her head. 'You are!'

'Well, I've been thinking about it,' said Kate with a shade of defiance. All night and all day, in fact. She hadn't been able to think about anything else since Finn's proposal.

'I know it's not the kind of marriage we all dream about, but we can't all have the perfect romance like Phoebe. I bet I wouldn't be the first woman to compromise on the starry-eyed stuff,' she said defensively. 'There might be other things that would make up for all that.'

'Like what?'

'Respect…liking…giving a little girl love and security…'

'You wouldn't be marrying Alex—or the dog, before you drag him into it,' Phoebe pointed out astringently. 'Of course marriage is about compromise, but not about something so important and especially not for a born romantic like you. I think you'd need to know that Finn loved you to be happy.'

'You've changed your tune, haven't you?' said Kate, cross with her friends for filling her mind with doubts again just when she thought she had made up her mind. 'You were the one trying to set me up with Finn in the first place.'

'We thought you'd be good together, and you would, but not unless Finn really is over Isabel. Of course he won't forget her, but he needs to move on. He needs to want you for yourself, not just as a glorified housekeeper.' Phoebe leant forward seriously. 'You can't go through life believing that you'll always be second-best as far as he's concerned.'

It would be better than going through life without him, thought Kate. She had lain awake long into the night, missing Finn beside her and envisaging the days and weeks and months and *years* ahead when he wouldn't be there. If she married him, she would at least have him physically. They might have children, and that would bring them closer. She might never have what Isabel had, but she would have *something*. That would be better than nothing, surely?

'You deserve the best, Kate,' said Phoebe. 'Second-best isn't good enough for you.'

'I think it might be,' said Kate.

Phoebe and Bella did their best to caution her against making a terrible mistake, but the more Kate thought about it, the more marrying Finn seemed the right decision. Their marriage might not be perfect, but at least this way she would be able to see him and touch him. Alex would be there, too. They could be a family.

And what, after all, was her alternative? Bella might say that she would meet someone else, but Kate didn't want anyone else. She only wanted Finn. The thought of life without him, with nothing to do except miss him, was too awful to contemplate.

Finn was waiting up for her when she got home. 'I've been thinking about what you said last night,' Kate said baldly as she watched him fill the kettle and set it to boil for tea.

He turned, grey eyes suddenly alert. 'About marrying me?'

'Yes.'

'And?'

'And…' Kate opened her mouth to tell him that she would marry him when she suddenly realised that she couldn't do it, and she stopped. She couldn't live with him and not tell him that she loved him. It had been hard enough up to now. Could she really spend years not being completely honest about how she felt?

'I was going to say yes,' she told him honestly, 'but I've

just realised that it wouldn't be fair on either of us.' Slowly she drew the ring he had bought her off her finger and laid it on the table.

'I thought I could go with all the sensible reasons,' she said. 'I told myself that they were good enough reasons to get married without love, but I think now that they won't be. We nearly made a terrible mistake, Finn,' she said, meeting his eyes squarely. 'I think it's better if I go.'

Finn looked bleaker than Kate had ever seen him, but he didn't try to persuade her. 'Alex will be disappointed,' was all he said.

Alex was more than disappointed. Devastated would have been a better description of her reaction when Kate told her that she was leaving. 'But you said you would stay for ever!' she wailed. 'You promised!'

Finn's face was drawn. 'She had to say that while Stella was here, but you knew the situation all along. You knew Kate was just pretending.'

'She shouldn't have said it if she didn't mean it!' Alex burst into tears, and rushed out of the room.

Kate was close to tears herself by that stage. 'Shall I go after her and try and explain?'

'No, leave her,' said Finn wearily. 'She'll come round.' He pinched the bridge of his nose between his finger and thumb. 'I just hope she doesn't make the new house-keeper's life hell. She's more than capable of it.'

In fact, when the agency sent along a new girl a couple of days later, Alex went out of her way to be nice to her, and punished Kate by ignoring her completely. Megan was an Australian on a working holiday. She was friendly and competent, with a very pretty, open face. Kate tried to be pleased that she was going to fit in so well, but her heart cracked with misery and jealousy as she packed her case.

Finn had said that he would drive her back to Tooting. He asked Alex if she wanted to come, but she shook her

head in an offhand way and said that she would rather stay
with Megan. At the last minute, though, she rushed out to
the car as Kate was about to get in and threw her arms
around Kate's waist to hug her tightly.

'Goodbye,' she said in a cracked little voice, and then,
without looking at Kate directly, she ran inside again.

Kate's throat was so tight that she could hardly speak,
and the tears rolled down her cheeks as she got into the
car. She wiped them away with the back of her hand.

'She will miss you, you know,' said Finn apologetically.
'She's just upset.'

'I know. I'll miss her too.'

'Perhaps you could come and see us sometime,' he suggested. 'You could check that we're looking after that dog
properly.'

At the moment the prospect felt as if it would be too
much to bear. 'Perhaps,' she said.

It was all Kate could do not to howl as they drove away
from the house. She felt as if a great weight was crushing
her. Why, why, why had she chosen to leave? She should
have stayed and then there would be no nice, pretty,
friendly Megan for Finn to go home to, to get to know, to
make part of his life.

Heartsick, Kate let Finn drive her back to her old life.
He carried her case into the house from the car, and upstairs
to her bedroom, while Kate lingered reluctantly in the hall.
She had always liked this house, but with Bella out it felt
cold and lonely. Like her life was going to be from now
on.

She was dreading the moment when she would have to
say goodbye to Finn, but trying to keep her composure was
such agony that she almost wished he would go. 'Thank
you,' she said as he came down the stairs. Her voice was
hard and tight, the only way she could speak without
crying.

Finn seemed very close to her in the narrow hallway. Kate edged towards the front door.

'I should go,' he said, but he didn't move. For once he seemed at a loss to know what to do next.

'Yes,' said Kate. 'Alex will be waiting for you.'

He squeezed past her to turn to her on the doorstep. Kate gazed at him hungrily, as if storing up the memory of his stern face, and that mouth…she might never see him again, she thought in panic.

'Thank you for everything, Kate,' Finn said stiffly, and as if on an impulse leant forward to kiss her on the cheek.

It was only the briefest of touches, the mere grazing of cheeks, but Kate closed her eyes with longing. Instinctively, her hands lifted to his chest to cling to his shirt. 'Goodbye,' she whispered as she kissed his cheek in return.

They looked at each other for a long, desperate moment, and then her hands fell. Finn turned without another word and walked along the pavement to his car. He opened the door and, with one last look back at Kate, he got in and drove away, leaving her desolate and alone in the doorway.

One thing about misery, it made for a great diet. The weight fell off Kate as she struggled through the next few days, but she was too unhappy to appreciate the way her clothes had started to hang off her. She had signed on with an agency, but there were no jobs as yet, which was a pity. Money wasn't a problem after the generous cheque Finn had given her, but not working left her with too much time to think.

Too much time to remember.

Too much time to ache with longing for Finn and the life she had thrown away.

'You've done the right thing,' Bella tried to reassure her. 'I know it's hard, but it's better for Finn to deal with his feelings for Isabel first. He needs closure on that.'

'Closure? What does that mean?'

'It means he has to decide himself that it's time to accept her death and move on. Once he's done that, he can think about his feelings for you.'

'I don't think he has any,' said Kate drearily.

'In that case, it's just as well you didn't marry him, isn't it?'

Kate knew that Bella was right. All the reasons why marrying Finn would have been a bad idea circled endlessly in her brain, but none of them stopped her wishing that she was back in the house in Wimbledon, with Finn coming back from work, wrenching at his tie as he came into the kitchen. Alex would be sitting at the table doing her homework, and Derek would have picked the most inconvenient spot to lie as usual, so that she tripped over him whenever she moved.

The image of them all was so vivid, and her need to be there so acute that Kate pillowed her head in her arms and wept all over again. At the other end of the table, the cat stared contemptuously at her. It had already learnt to distrust the sound of crying which usually meant that the humans would be too preoccupied to think about feeding him.

Kate hadn't thought that it was possible to cry this much. She kept waiting to run out of tears, but after five days there was still no sign of them drying up. Her eyes were permanently red and puffy, and whenever she caught sight of her reflection she recoiled at how awful she looked. No wonder no one would give her a job! What was the point of being thin like this if the rest of you looked so frightful?

Bella put an arm around Kate's shoulders. 'Oh, Kate...' she sighed. 'What are we going to do with you?'

'I don't know,' wept Kate. 'I don't know what to do with myself either!'

'I've asked Phoebe to come round,' said Bella. 'You know how good she is in a crisis. Ah! That'll be her now,' she added as the doorbell went. 'I'll go and let her in. She's bound to be able to sort you out.'

Kate didn't even bother to lift her head. She loved Phoebe dearly, but there was nothing her friend could do about her raw, sore heart. Only Finn could make that better.

'Kate?'

That wasn't Phoebe. Kate stilled, her head still buried in her arms and her hair spilling out over the table where the cat toyed with a few strands in a bored way. It had sounded like Finn's voice. She must be imagining things.

'Kate!' A definite note of exasperation had crept into the voice, the faintly irritable edge that could only belong to Finn.

Very, very slowly Kate lifted her head. Finn was standing there, watching her with hard, anxious grey eyes. She stared at him, hardly able to believe that he was real, that he was *there*.

It was definitely him. Nobody else had that austere face or that mouth that made her melt just thinking about what it could do to her. But he didn't look quite the way he had done whenever she had fantasised about seeing him again. In her imagination, the sight of her had started a smile in his eyes which would slowly illuminate his face as he held out his arms to her.

This was real life, not a fantasy. She could tell by the fact that he wasn't smiling and his expression was one of puzzled irritation.

'Didn't you hear me?' Not *my darling*, or *I can't live without you*.

'Yes, but I didn't think it could be you,' said Kate obscurely.

The faint frown between his brows deepened. 'Are you all right?'

Kate knuckled the tears away from under her eyes. Why did he have to turn up now, when she was looking at her worst? The spurt of resentment was invigorating. After all her dreaming and longing to see him again, he was finally here refusing to follow the script!

'Do I look all right?' she asked tartly.

'You look terrible.'

'Sorry, but I've never mastered the art of blubbing gracefully.' Kate sniffed and blew her nose on a tissue.

It was strange. Part of her was really quite cross with Finn for catching her unawares and being so obtuse about the state she was in, but the rest of her was unashamedly joyful just to see him again. It was as if all her senses had suddenly woken up from a leaden sleep and started carrying on like cheerleaders, high-kicking and shaking pompoms about with sheer exhilaration.

Finn pulled out the chair beside her and sat down. 'What are you crying about?'

'What do you think?' asked Kate almost rudely.

'Is it Seb?'

'*Seb*?' It was so long since she'd given Seb a second thought that it took Kate a moment to work out who he was talking about. 'No, of course not.' She scrubbed a tissue under her eyes. 'Why would I be crying about Seb?'

'You told me that you loved him once,' said Finn. 'I thought that maybe when you said that you couldn't marry me without love you were thinking about him. I was afraid you might be hoping to get back together with him, and that it hadn't worked out.'

It was so far from the truth that Kate made a hiccupping sound between a sob and a laugh. She shook her head. 'No, I wasn't crying about Seb.'

'Then why?'

Kate didn't answer. 'What are you doing here, Finn?' she asked instead.

'I wanted to see you,' he said simply.

Blowing her nose again, she drew a jagged breath. 'Don't tell me Megan hasn't worked out. She seemed so suitable.'

'She's fine, but she's a bit bored with us,' said Finn. 'I think she would like to move on to somewhere more exciting.'

'She's bored with you?' echoed Kate, finding it hard to imagine.

'None of us is much company at the moment,' he told her. 'We're all miserable.' He paused. 'We all miss you.'

Kate stopped in the middle of wiping the tell-tale evidence of tears from her cheeks. 'You do?'

'Alex cries herself to sleep at night, the dog is pining, and as for me...' Finn shook his head. 'I miss you more than either of them,' he said.

Kate's heart began to thud. 'Really?' she asked huskily.

'Really.' He turned in his chair to face her. 'Do you remember when Stella left, she told Alex to make sure that I didn't do anything stupid? Well, I did something stupid. I didn't tell you how I really felt about you.'

'Why not?' said Kate, hardly daring to breathe.

'I was afraid you would think that I was too old and intense for you. You always seemed like so much fun. I couldn't believe that you would really be interested in someone like me. I kept remembering what you'd told me about Seb, and even if you hadn't wanted him again, it was obvious that a younger man like that—or that financial analyst of yours!—was going to be much more your type.

'I couldn't bear the thought of you leaving, though, so I tried to persuade you to stay by making it seem more like a job. And that really was stupid, as my dear sister explained to me at length,' he finished acidly.

'Stella knows about us not really being engaged?'

'She does now. Alex rang her and told her that I had been stupid just as she had warned. The next thing I knew I had my sister on the phone, demanding the full story and

wanting to know why I had thrown away my best chance
of happiness in years. I said that I had asked you to marry
me and that you had refused, but it didn't take her long to
prise the whole truth out of me. She couldn't believe what
a mess I'd made of it. ''For an intelligent man,'' she said,
''you sure are stupid!''''

Kate gave a watery smile. She could practically hear
Stella saying it.

'She told me that I should come back and tell you everything I'd left out before,' Finn said. 'So here I am.'

He looked down at his hands, and then straight into
Kate's eyes, which were still red and swollen with tears,
but shining now with hope. 'Can I tell you now, or would
it make you uncomfortable?'

Kate swallowed the lump in her throat. 'No, I'd like to
hear it.'

'I didn't tell you how much I love you,' he said. 'I didn't
tell you how empty the house would feel without you. How
empty my *life* would be without you.'

Taking her hands in both of his own, he held them
tightly. 'I can manage the school run. I can walk the dog,
and sort out the cooking and the cleaning. I can manage all
of that, but I can't manage without you. And I want to do
more than just manage. I want to be able to wake up and
find you beside me. I want to come home and find you
there.' He paused. 'I didn't tell you how much I need you,
Kate,' he said in a low voice.

The cat chose this moment to yawn widely and stand up,
presenting its bottom to their faces, and then sitting with a
glare of affront when it failed to provoke the usual reaction.

There was a glow starting deep inside Kate, spreading
out to every pore. Her fingers were curling around his.
'What about Isabel?' she asked as she had asked before.

'I loved Isabel,' he said quietly. 'Nothing can change
that, but I don't feel as if part of my life is missing any

more. I never expected to fall in love again,' he told Kate. 'I thought I'd had my chance at love, and that I'd never get another chance at that kind of happiness, and then you came along and turned my life upside down. You made me happy again.'

His fingers tightened around hers. 'You're not a replacement for Isabel,' he said. 'I never wanted anyone to be that. You're *you*, and it's you I need.'

The grey eyes were warm and serious as they looked into Kate's. 'If I had said all that to you when I asked you to marry me, would your answer have been different?'

'Yes,' said Kate.

'So if I asked you again now…?'

Her eyes shimmered with tears. 'I'll say yes,' she promised.

Then there was no more talking and Finn had pulled her into his lap and was kissing her so hungrily that Kate thought that she would pass out with happiness.

They might have stayed like that for hours if not interrupted by the cat, who was tired of being ignored and took a swipe at Finn's arm.

Jerking it back, Finn inspected the scratch. 'What did he do that for?'

'He's just looking for attention,' said Kate consolingly. 'He didn't mean to hurt you.'

'Well, he'll have to learn that I've got more important things to attend to at the moment,' said Finn, gathering Kate back into his arms, only to pause as a thought occurred to him. 'I hope he's not coming with you?' he asked in a voice of foreboding.

'I'm afraid so,' said Kate. 'I can't ask Bella to look after him. He won't be any trouble.'

Finn looked down at the scratch on his arm. 'I suppose the house is going to be taken over entirely by waifs and strays now,' he pretended to grumble, but he was smiling as he kissed his way along her jaw.

'Will you mind?' she asked, winding her arms around his neck.

'Not if you're there.'

Kate turned her head to meet his lips for a long sweet kiss. 'At least Stella will be happy now,' she sighed happily when they broke apart at last and she rested her head on his shoulder.

'Oh, no, she won't! You wait,' said Finn. 'We'll just get the wedding over, and she'll be nagging us about Alex needing a brother or sister.'

Kate laughed and kissed him again. 'I don't mind seeing what we can do about that,' she said.

'Anything to shut my sister up?'

'Anything,' said Kate.

MILLS & BOON
Romance

On sale 6th July 2007

Get ready for some summer romance from gorgeous Greece to the crystal clear waters of Cape Cod, the swirling mists of Irish Valentia and the silent majesty of the Outback...

THE FORBIDDEN BROTHER *by Barbara McMahon*

Laura is in a dilemma when she falls in love with her ex-fiancé's twin brother! Is it him she loves, or the mirror-image of a man she was once engaged to?

THE LAZARIDIS MARRIAGE *by Rebecca Winters*

This award-winning author brings you a brooding Greek billionaire you won't forget in a hurry as he battles with his attraction to international it-girl Tracey.

BRIDE OF THE EMERALD ISLE *by Trish Wylie*

Meet cynical Garrett who's about to encounter the woman who will open his heart again...and give him hope for the future.

HER OUTBACK KNIGHT *by Melissa James*

Take an Outback road trip with Danni and Jim as they begin a quest for the truth which might just turn this journey into one of the heart...

MILLS & BOON

Blaze

On sale 6th July 2007

CLOSER...
by Jo Leigh

Soldier Boone Ferguson is going to train Christie Pratchett
to protect herself...and to become his lover. Together, they're
going to risk it all, on the street – and in the bedroom.

BOYS OF SUMMER 3-in-1
by Leto/Raye/Kelly

Baseball. The crack of the bat, the roar of the crowd...and the
view of mouthwatering men in tight uniforms! A sport in
which the men are men...and the woman are drooling.

MIDNIGHT MADNESS
by Karen Kendall

When Governor Jack Hammersmith requests hairstylist
Marly Fine's services, she tells herself it's just a cut. So what if he's
irresistible? She's immune to any man's charm...isn't she?

NO REGRETS
by Cindi Myers

A near-death experience has given Lexie Foster a new appreciation
of life. She compiles a list of things not to be put off any longer.
The first thing on her list? An affair with Nick Delaney,
her gorgeous new boss.

0607/39

There's the life you planned and there's what comes next...

Lucky
by Jennifer Greene

Kasey Crandall was happily married with a beautiful baby – life was perfect. But things change. She knew something was wrong with her baby. Kasey had to get her child help...even if it meant going against her husband's wishes. Even if it meant turning to another man. Because sometimes you have to make your own luck.

Riggs Park
by Ellyn Bache

Marilyn, Barbara, Steve, Penny and Wish grew up together, their futures stretching before them. But things don't always turn out as expected. Riggs Park had secrets and Penny was one of them. As Barbara sets out to uncover the truth, she must decide if finding it breaks her heart – or sets them all free.

Because every life has more than one chapter...

On sale 15th June 2007

Available at WHSmith, Tesco, ASDA, and all good bookshops
www.millsandboon.co.uk

MILLS & BOON